Praise for
Gone Without a Trace

"Mary Torjussen spins a clever, fast-paced tale with a twist so sharp it will give readers whiplash."

—Tami Hoag, #1 *New York Times* bestselling author of *The Bitter Season*

"*Gone Without a Trace* has one of the most interesting narrators I've ever come across. Suspenseful and subtle, this novel plays with all of your expectations. Not to be missed!"

—Shari Lapena, *New York Times* bestselling author of *The Couple Next Door*

"A tightly-written thriller with a genuinely shocking twist. Mary Torjussen is an assured storyteller who weaves a compelling web of secrets, lies and obsession."

—Anne Corlett, author of *The Space Between the Stars*

"Grabbed me right away with its mind-blowing and heartbreaking premise, and I couldn't read fast enough as the book revealed a series of twisting and even jaw-dropping surprises. This thriller thrills, but it's grounded by complicated, complex and sometimes deeply flawed characters I couldn't stop thinking about. An absorbing, shocking thriller!"

—David Bell, bestselling author of *Since She Went Away*

"With characters who feel real to the bone and a voice that chills through and through, *Gone Without a Trace* had me hooked from the very first line. Torjussen delivers an absolutely thrilling novel with an ending as shocking and satisfying as any I've read. This is a novel you won't want to miss!"

—Diane Les Becquets, national bestselling author of *Breaking Wild*

"Gripping suspense with a chilling twist. Mary Torjussen kept me turning the pages to the very last."

—Meg Gardiner, Edgar Award–winning author of *Phantom Instinct*

Gone
Without
a Trace

Mary Torjussen

BERKLEY · *New York*

BERKLEY
An imprint of Penguin Random House LLC
375 Hudson Street, New York, New York 10014

Copyright © 2017 by Mary Torjussen
Readers Guide copyright © 2017 by Penguin Random House LLC
Penguin Random House supports copyright. Copyright fuels creativity,
encourages diverse voices, promotes free speech, and creates a vibrant culture.
Thank you for buying an authorized edition of this book and for complying
with copyright laws by not reproducing, scanning, or distributing any part
of it in any form without permission. You are supporting writers and allowing
Penguin Random House to continue to publish books for every reader.

BERKLEY is a registered trademark and the B colophon is a trademark of
Penguin Random House LLC.

Library of Congress Cataloging-in-Publication Data
Names: Torjussen, Mary, author.
Title: Gone without a trace / Mary Torjussen.
Description: First edition. | New York, NY : Berkley, 2017.
Identifiers: LCCN 2016034658 (print) | LCCN 2016046453 (ebook) | ISBN
9780399585012 (paperback) | ISBN 9780399585029 (ebook)
Subjects: LCSH: Missing persons—Fiction. | Man-woman relationships—Fiction.
| Triangles (Interpersonal relations)—Fiction. | Family secrets—Fiction.
| Violence—Psychological aspects—Fiction. | Psychological fiction. |
BISAC: FICTION / Suspense. | GSAFD: Suspense fiction.
Classification: LCC PR6120.O75 G66 2017 (print) | LCC PR6120.O75 (ebook) |
DDC 823/.92—dc23
LC record available at https://lccn.loc.gov/2016034658

First Edition: April 2017

Printed in the United States of America
1 3 5 7 9 10 8 6 4 2

Cover photograph by Karina Vegas / Arcangel Images
Cover design by Colleen Reinhart
Book design by Tiffany Estreicher

This is a work of fiction. Names, characters, places, and incidents either are
the product of the author's imagination or are used fictitiously, and
any resemblance to actual persons, living or dead, business establishments,
events, or locales is entirely coincidental.

For Rosie and Louis

And for my mother and in memory of my father

With love

Acknowledgments

I'd like to thank my wonderful agent, Kate Burke from Diane Banks Associates, who had faith in me from the start. Your support and guidance has made all of this possible.

Thank you, too, to my fantastic editors, Emily Griffin and her team at Headline and Danielle Perez and her team at Berkley, for helping me create a better book. Your editorial comments and advice have been invaluable.

My online writing friends have made the whole experience of writing this book such fun. They've tirelessly read my drafts and been supportive and tactful about changes I should make. Special thanks go to Fiona Collins and Sam Gough in particular—I couldn't have done it without your daily emails! Thanks, too, to the rest of the Mumsnet Creative Writing group. If any readers are wondering where they can find supportive writing friends, come along and meet new friends on the forum.

Thank you to my friends Richard Hill, Lorna Wood, and Chris Finnigan, who've put up with me talking about this book over the last year and given me so much encouragement.

And thank you to my brother, Martin, whose writing has inspired me. His is a name to watch for.

Gone Without a Trace

Chapter
One

I WAS SINGING as I walked up the path to my house that day. Actually singing. I feel sick at the thought of that now.

I'd been on a training course in Oxford, leaving Liverpool as the sun rose at six, returning at sunset. I work as a senior manager for a large firm of accountants, and when I got to the reception of our head office and signed myself in, I scanned the list of attendees from other branches and recognized several names, though they weren't people I'd met. I'd read about them in our company's newsletters and knew they were highflyers, and for the first time I realized that must have been what the company thought of me, too.

My skin had prickled with excitement at the thought, but I'd tried not to let my feelings show, relaxing my face into that calm mask I'd practiced so assiduously over the years. When I went into the conference room, I saw the others standing around chatting as though they were old friends. They looked polished and professional, as though they were used to this sort of event, and I was glad I'd spent a fortune on my clothes and hair and nails. One of the other women had the same Hobbs suit as mine, though luckily in a different color; another gave a covetous look at the chocolate Mulberry bag my boyfriend, Matt, had bought me for Christmas. I took a deep breath; I looked like one of them. I smiled at the nearest person, asked which branch she worked for and that was it, I was part of the group and soon my nerves were forgotten.

In the afternoon we were set a task to complete in a team and at the end I was chosen to present our findings to the whole group. I was terrified and spent the break time in a corner feverishly memorizing my speech while the others sat around chatting, but it seemed to go well. Once I'd made the presentation I could relax and was able to answer everyone's questions in full, anticipating follow-up questions, too. Out of the corner of my eye I noticed Alex Hughes, one of our partners, nodding as I spoke, and at one point he made a note about something I'd said. When everyone was packing up to leave, he took me to one side.

"Hannah, I have to say you performed very well there," he said. "We've been looking at your work for a while now and have been absolutely delighted with your progress."

"Thank you."

Just then Oliver Sutton, the firm's managing partner, came to join us. "Well done, Hannah. You were excellent today. When Colin Jamison leaves in September I think you'll be on track for promotion to director. Wouldn't that make you the youngest in your branch?"

I don't know what I replied. I was so surprised to hear him say that; it was like one of my dreams had come to life. Of course I knew exactly when each director had been promoted; I'd pored over their bios on the company's website. I'm thirty-two and I knew the youngest had been appointed at thirty-three. That had helped give a certain edge to my work lately.

The organizer of the event came up to speak to them then, and they smiled and shook hands with me before turning to her. I walked as calmly as I could to the cloakrooms and locked myself into a cubicle where I nearly screamed with pleasure. This was what I'd been working toward for years, since leaving university and starting with the firm as an assistant. I've never worked as hard as I have this last year or two, and now it looked as though it was going to pay off. When I came out of the cubicle I saw in the mirror that my face was pink, as though I'd been out in the sun all day. I took out my makeup bag and tried to repair the damage, but my cheeks still glowed with pride.

Everything was going to be all right.

I reached into my bag for my phone to send a message to Matt, but then the Human Resources director came into the cloakrooms and smiled at me, so I smiled back and nodded at her and took out my hairbrush instead to smooth my hair. I didn't want her to think I was excited about anything, to suspect that maybe I thought I didn't deserve promotion.

There was also no way I wanted to hang around while she was in the loo, so I went back to the conference room to say good-bye to the others. I decided I'd tell Matt face-to-face and couldn't wait to see his excitement. He knew how much I wanted this. Of course it was too early to celebrate—I hadn't actually been promoted yet, after all—but I was sure that Oliver Sutton wouldn't have said that lightly. Each time I thought of his words, I felt a swell of pride.

And then in the car before I set off I thought of my dad and how delighted he would be. I knew he'd hear about it from my boss, George, as they played golf together, but I wanted to be the first to tell him. I sent him a text:

Dad, I'm at a training day and the managing partner says they're considering promoting me to director in a few months! xx

Within seconds I got a reply:

That's my girl! Well done!

I flushed with pleasure. My father has his own business and he's always said that the one thing he wants is for me to be successful.

As far as my career was concerned, he was my biggest supporter, though it could be stressful if he thought I wasn't promoted quickly enough. Another text beeped through:

I'll put a treat in your account—have a celebration!

I sighed. That wasn't the point of telling him. I typed back quickly:

It's OK, Dad, no need to do that. Just wanted to tell you how I got on. Tell Mum, will you? xx

Another message beeped:

Nonsense! Money's always good.

Yes, money's nice but a phone call would be better, I thought, then I shook some sense into myself and started the car.

IT WAS A two-hundred-mile drive home and I did it without a break. I live on the Wirral peninsula in the northwest of England, just across the River Mersey from Liverpool. Despite the evening traffic, it was an easy drive with motorways all the way and it seemed as though the journey passed in a flash. I was so excited I couldn't stop myself wriggling on my seat as I practiced what I would tell Matt and how I would say it. I wanted to stay calm and to just mention it casually when he asked me how my day had gone, but I knew I'd just burst out with it as soon as I saw him. When I reached Ellesmere Port, about fifteen miles from home, I saw the Sainsbury's sign shining brightly in the distance and at the last minute I indicated to take the exit. This was a night for champagne. In the shop I picked up a bottle of Moët, then hesitated and picked up another. One isn't enough when you have news like that, and besides, it was Friday; no work the next day.

Back on the motorway I pictured Matt's reaction as I told him the news. It wasn't as though I'd have to exaggerate. Just repeating what Alex Hughes and Oliver Sutton had said would be enough.

Matt worked as an architect and had done well for himself; he'd understand how important it was for my career. And financially, too, I'd be level with him if I was promoted. I thought of the salary scale for directors and felt a shiver of excitement—maybe I'd earn more than Matt soon!

I stroked my soft leather bag. "There'll be more of you soon, sweetheart," I said. "You'll have to learn to share."

It wasn't just the money, though. I'd take a pay cut to have that kind of status.

I opened the windows and let the warm breeze run through my hair. The sun was setting and the sky ahead was filled with brilliant red and gold streaks. My iPod was on shuffle and I sang song after song at the top of my lungs. When Elbow played "One Day Like This," I pressed Repeat over and over until I reached my home. By the time I arrived, I was almost in a state of fever and my throat was throbbing and sore.

The streetlights on my road popped on to celebrate my arrival. My heart pounded with the excitement of the day and the fervor of the music. The champagne bottles clinked in their bag and I pulled them out so that I could present Matt with them in a *ta-da!* kind of moment.

I parked on the driveway and jumped out. The house was in darkness. I looked at my watch. It was 7:20 p.m. Matt had told me last night that he'd be late, but I'd thought he'd be back by now.

Still. There'd be time to put the bottles in the freezer and get them really chilled. I put them back in the bag, picked up my handbag and opened the front door.

I reached inside for the hall light, clicked it on and stopped still. The hair on the back of my neck stood up.

Was someone in our house?

Chapter Two

FOR THE LAST four years I've had pictures on the hallway walls that Matt brought with him when he moved in. They're huge photos of jazz musicians in heavy black frames. Ella Fitzgerald usually faced the front door, her eyes half-closed in a shy, ecstatic smile. Now there was nothing but the smooth cream paint we'd used when we painted the hallway last summer.

I dropped my coat and bags on the polished oak floor and on automatic pilot stooped to steady the bottles as they tilted to the ground. I stepped forward and stared again. There was nothing on the wall. I turned and looked at the wall alongside the staircase. Charlie Parker was usually there, bathed in a golden light and facing Miles Davis. It had always looked as though they were playing together. Both were gone.

I looked around in disbelief. Had we been burgled? But why had they taken the pictures? The walnut cabinet I'd bought from Heal's was worth a lot and that was still there. On it, alongside the landline and a lamp, sat the silver and enamel Tiffany bowl that my parents had bought me when I graduated. Surely a burglar would have taken that?

I put my hand on the door to the living room, then hesitated. *What if someone's still here? What if they've only just got here?* Quietly I took my handbag and backed out of the front door. On the path, safely away from the house, I took out my phone, uncertain whether to call the police or to wait for Matt. I stared at the house. Apart from the hallway, it was in darkness. The house attached to mine was dark, too; Sheila and Ray, our neighbors, had told me they'd be away until Sunday. The house on the other side had sold a month or two ago and its owners had long gone. A new couple would be moving in soon, but it didn't look as though anyone was there yet; the rooms were empty and there were no curtains at the windows. Opposite us was the wide entrance to another road; the houses there were bigger, set well back with high hedges to stop them from having to view the rest of the estate.

There didn't seem to be any movement in our house. Slowly I walked across the lawn to the living room window and looked through into the darkened room.

At first I thought the television had gone. That would definitely be burglars. Then I froze. The television *had* gone; that was true. Matt had bought a massive flat-screen when he moved in. It had surround sound and a huge fancy black glass table, and to be honest, it took up half the room. All of it had gone.

Now in its place was the old coffee table I'd had for years, which I'd brought with me from my parents' house when I left home. On it was my old television, a great big useless thing that used to shine blue and flicker if there was a storm. It had been in the spare room all this time, waiting until we had the energy to chuck it out. I'd hardly noticed it in all the time it had been up there.

My face was so close to the living room window that I could see the mist of my breath on it.

A car braked sharply in the distance and I jumped and turned, thinking it was Matt. I don't know why I thought that.

My skin suddenly felt very cold, though the evening was warm and still. I took a deep breath and pulled my jacket tightly around me. I went back into the house, shutting the door quietly. In the living room, I put the overhead light on, then quickly went to the window to draw the curtains, even though it was still light outside. I didn't want an audience. I stood with my back to the window and looked at the room. Above the mantelpiece was a huge silver mirror and I could see my face, pale and shocked, reflected in it. I moved away so that I didn't have to look at myself.

On either side of the fireplace, white-painted shelves filled the alcoves. Our DVDs and books and CDs had been on them. On the big lower shelves Matt had kept his vinyl, hundreds of albums, all in alphabetical order by band, the more obscure the better. I remembered the day he moved in, how I'd taken dozens of my books from the shelves and put them in boxes in the spare room so he'd have space for his records.

Those books were now back there, looking as though they'd never been away. Most of the DVDs and CDs had gone. All of the vinyl was gone.

I turned to the other corner. His record player was no longer there; neither was his iPod dock. My old stereo was back; his had gone. Gone, too, were the headphones he'd bought when I'd complained I couldn't watch television because of his music.

I felt as though my legs were about to give way. I sat down on the sofa and looked at the room. My stomach was clenched so tightly I almost doubled over.

What's happened?

I didn't dare go into the rest of the house.

I TOOK MY mobile from my bag. I knew I shouldn't call Matt—what was the point? He'd sent me the clearest message he could. At that moment, though, I had no pride. I wanted to talk to him, to ask him what was happening. I knew, though. I knew exactly what had happened. What he'd done.

There were no missed calls, no new messages, no new emails. Suddenly furious—he might at least have had the decency to let me know—I clicked on Recent Calls and scrolled down to find his name so that I could call him. I frowned. I knew I'd called him a few nights ago. I'd been in the car, just about to leave work; my friend Katie had sent a message saying that she and her boyfriend, James, might come round and I'd phoned Matt to check we had some drinks in. There was no record of that call on my phone. I scrolled down further. Months of calls flashed by. None of them was to him or from him.

I closed my eyes for a second and tried to take a deep breath, but I couldn't. I felt as though I was going to faint and had to put my head down on my knees. After a few minutes, I looked back at the screen, clicked on Contacts and typed M for Matt, but nothing came up. Panicking, I typed S for his surname, Stone. His name wasn't there.

My fingers were suddenly hot and damp, slipping on the screen as I scrolled down the list of text conversations. Again, there were none to him and none from him, though we had sent a few each week. We tended to do that rather than call lately. There were still messages to friends and to my parents and to Sam at work, but nothing to Matt. I'd bought that phone at Christmas with my bonus. I sent him a message then, though he was only in the kitchen, asking him to bring a bottle of prosecco into the living room. I could hear him laugh when he read the message and he brought it in with some more chocolate mousse. I was lying comatose; the agreement had been that I'd cook Christmas lunch for his mother and us, but wouldn't have to do anything else for the rest of the day.

I double-checked now and looked at my texts to Katie. It took a while to scroll through them, as we sent several a week—several a day at times—but eventually I found the first one, wishing her a happy Christmas and telling her that Matt had bought me a Mulberry bag. She'd acted amazed, but I knew he'd asked her advice on it. I don't know how she'd kept it a secret.

My mind whirled. *What had happened to Matt's texts and calls?*

I switched the phone off and on again, hoping that might do something. There were text messages from Katie, sent yesterday afternoon, asking me about my trip to Oxford today. She'd phoned me just before the training started this morning, too, to wish me luck, knowing how much the day meant to me. I'd spent a few minutes talking to her in the car park before I had to go in. There were texts to and from Sam, my friend at work, and Lucy, my assistant, as well as some from my mum and a few from my dad, including those exchanged in Oxford just hours ago. There were also messages from Fran and Jenny, old friends who I run with sometimes, and some from university friends that I still saw occasionally. There wasn't anything from Matt at all.

Of course I knew what was going to happen when I opened my emails. No new messages, but that wasn't a surprise. I tried to think of the last time Matt had emailed me; usually he'd text. Back when we first met we'd email several times a day; we both used to have our private emails open on our computers while we were working, so we could chat to each other throughout the day. You'd think that would have made us less productive but the opposite happened and we found we were firing on all cylinders, working fast and furious and making great decisions. We were so fired up we both got promotions and it was only when Matt's company started logging network accounts after some idiot was found to be looking at porn all day that we had to stop. My heart sank now as I looked at the folders; the one with all his emails in it was missing. I opened a new message and entered "Matt" into the address bar. Nothing came up, not even his email address.

I could hear myself breathing, short, shallow breaths. There was the beginning of a red mist around my eyes and I could feel myself starting to hyperventilate.

I had no way of contacting him.

Chapter
Three

FOR A WHILE I couldn't move. I sat on the edge of the sofa, holding my stomach as though I was in labor. My mind raced and my palms were tingling. When the lights of a car came to our end of the street and shone through a gap in the curtains, I jumped up and before I knew it I was flat against the wall next to the window, pulling the curtains slightly to one side.

If it was Matt, I wanted to be ready for him.

Someone had come to the empty house next door. Car doors opened and slammed; I heard a man say something and a woman laugh in response. I looked through the gap in the curtains and saw a young couple standing at the boot of their car. I watched unnoticed as they unloaded suitcases and boxes and took them into the house. They must have just left them in the hall, as within a minute they were back in their car and driving off down the road. My new neighbors, I assumed. I looked at my watch. It was after eight o'clock. It seemed an odd time to move in, but then I remembered my other neighbor, Sheila, saying that it was a local couple who had bought the house; maybe they were moving their things themselves.

I gathered up my courage and made my way through to the kitchen. I pushed the door open and pressed the light switch. When the light blazed on, I saw a flash of the room and closed my eyes.

He'd done the same thing here.

Gone was the maroon Rothko print, which had glowed above the oak fireplace. Gone, too, was the white metal candelabra that Matt had brought with him and lit on the night he'd moved in. I remembered him blowing out the candles before taking my hand and leading me upstairs to our bedroom. He'd smiled at me, that easy grin that had always made me smile back, and pulled me toward him in the darkened room, whispering in my ear, "Let's go to bed." My heart had melted and I'd hugged him, right where I was standing now.

I shuddered.

The back of the house was one room, with a large marble island dividing the kitchen and dining areas. French doors led out onto the patio and large windows sat on either side, with potted plants and photos on their deep sills. Of course, the photos of Matt had vanished. There were still photos of Katie and me with our arms around each other at parties and one of us that I loved where we were wearing Santa hats and holding hands, aged five. There was one of my mum and dad that I'd taken on their wedding anniversary and another of them with me at my graduation, their faces full of pride and relief. Photos of my friends from university, shiny faced and bright eyed in bars and clubs, were still there and one of me finishing my first half marathon, holding hands with Jenny and Fran as we crossed the finish line, but all the photos of Matt had gone. It was impossible now to see where they'd been.

I sat at the island with my head in my hands and looked out at the room. A square glass vase of purple tulips sat on the dining table, just where I'd put it a few days before. I'd stopped at Tesco for some milk and had seen them by the entrance, their tight buds and dewy leaves a reminder that summer was on its way. The room was clean and tidy, just as it usually was, but it seemed tarnished now, somehow, like a nightclub in daylight.

There were fewer glasses on the cabinet shelves by the door. When Matt had moved in he'd brought with him some heavy crystal wine-glasses his grandmother had given him and placed them in the cabinet. I hadn't liked them, had thought they were old-fashioned and doubted they were nice even when they were in fashion, so their disappearance now was no great loss. My Vera Wang glasses were still there, lined up and ready to party. Ready to party in an empty room.

My stomach rumbled and I went over to the fridge, though I couldn't face eating. The contents of the fridge seemed the same as they'd been at six that morning, when I'd left for Oxford. A super-market delivery had arrived last night, ready for the weekend ahead, and everything was still there. There was twice as much as I'd need now. I'd ordered the food while I was at work and Matt had un-packed it with me, without a word to suggest he wouldn't be there to eat it. I slammed the fridge door shut and stood with my back to it, breathing heavily, my eyes squeezed tight. When my breathing slowed I opened my eyes and saw the gaps on the magnetic strip above the hob where he'd lovingly placed his Sabatier knives. Below was a space where his French press had stood.

I steeled myself and opened the cupboards.

His packets of coffee beans were gone, the grinder, too. If I leaned forward I could smell the faint aroma of coffee and won-dered how long it would last. That was one thing he couldn't erase. I slammed the cabinet door shut. My head throbbed as I opened the lower cupboard and saw the space where his juicer usually stood. In another cupboard I saw his mugs had gone, the huge, ugly ones with logos. He'd carried them with him from university to bedsit and on to his London house and then to our home—*my* home—and I wished he'd left them so that I could smash them now.

I opened the fridge again and checked the compartments in the door this time. The bottle of ketchup that I never touched—gone. His jar of Marmite—gone. No great loss, as I disliked both of them, but why take them? I checked the kitchen bin and they weren't there. All my bottles and jars had been redistributed along the shelves, so it looked as though nothing was missing.

I pulled a chilled bottle of white wine from the fridge and one of my glasses from the cabinet and sat back at the island. I poured a full glass and drank it down, almost in one gulp, then poured another. I kept looking at my phone to check that his number had actually gone. My mind whirred. He'd been fine the night before; in fact, he'd been in a great mood. I'd got up early that morning to shower and get ready for my trip to Oxford. I'd left at dawn, terrified of getting caught up in the morning traffic. I'd panicked the whole journey in case I was late.

I'd leaned over before I left and kissed him softly on his cheek. His eyes were closed and his breathing steady. His face had been warm and still against my mouth. He was asleep, or at least I'd thought he was. Maybe he was awake, waiting for me to go? Maybe his eyes had snapped open the moment he heard my car drive off and he'd jumped up to start packing.

I started to cry then, at the thought of that. We'd been together for four years—how could he just walk out without an explanation? And to put all my things back in their old places; it was as though he'd never been here!

I drank most of the next glass down, too, and that made me cry again. I loved Matt. I'd always loved him, right from the start. He knew how much he meant to me; I'd told him so many times. We spent all our time together and the thought of being without him made my stomach gallop with panic. I reached out for my phone, wanting to talk to someone, but put it down again. I was filled with shame at being left, humiliated at the way he'd gone. How could I tell anyone what he'd done?

I took the bottle and my glass upstairs with me. I needed oblivion tonight and this was the quickest way there.

When I got to my bedroom door I knew what to expect, but still, the sight of the quilt cover, fresh and clean, upset me again. I'd changed the bed linen the Sunday before and just by chance had put on the burgundy cover he'd brought with him when he moved in. That was gone now; the quilt cover and pillowcases on our bed were embroidered white cotton, mine from long before I'd met him.

I steeled myself and opened his wardrobe doors. Of course it was empty. Wire hangers hung on the rail and there wasn't even the faintest smell of his cologne. There didn't seem much point in checking the drawers, but I did anyway. I opened each one and they were as empty as the day I bought them.

I took off my clothes and dropped them in the empty laundry basket in the bathroom, found my oldest and softest cotton pajamas and put them on, all the while avoiding my reflection in the mirror over my chest of drawers. I was too mortified to see my own face.

In bed as the night grew dark, with just the light from the landing coming through to the room, I poured glass after glass of wine and drank it without tasting it. I reached into the bottom drawer of my bedside dresser and found my headphones. They were the kind that canceled noise, just what I needed tonight, when I didn't want to hear anything, not even my own thoughts. In the darkness of the room, I could feel my head buzzing and my cheeks tightening as the alcohol entered my bloodstream. I took the pillow from Matt's side of the bed and curled into it. It smelled clean and fresh; there was no trace of him there. Tears ran down my face and no matter how many times I dried it, within seconds it was drenched again. When I thought of him packing up everything and leaving me without a word, without a hint that he was going, I felt like a fist was clenching my heart, squeezing it tight. I could hardly breathe.

Where was he?

Chapter
Four

I WOKE IN the night, my mouth foul and my eyes sore from crying. Clutched tightly in my hand was the stem of my glass, and the side of the bed that Matt usually slept on was damp and stained from the wine that had spilled. The air was full of the familiar smell of stale alcohol; as I breathed in the fumes my stomach churned and I had to make a mad dash to the bathroom.

Although I should have expected it and braced myself, I felt a jolt at the sight of my toothbrush alone in the holder. I kept my eyes firmly on the basin as I brushed my teeth and cleansed my face, deliberately avoiding the gaps where his shaving things would be, the empty hook where his dressing gown had hung, the space where his shampoo and shower gel usually stood in the shower cubicle. I felt different, somehow, as though everything had changed. As though I had changed. My head was full and my eyes swollen from crying, but it was more than that. All my muscles ached and my chest was sore and tight. I felt as though I was ill, as though I had the flu.

I stood at the top of the stairs, about to go down to fetch a glass of water, but stopped as I saw the gaps where the photos had been in the hallway. Unable to face going downstairs and confronting it all again, I turned back to my bed.

IT WAS HOURS before I could speak to Katie. She was the only person I could trust with this. We'd known each other since we were five and had sat next to each other at school. We'd stuck together through so much since then. I knew she wouldn't judge me or ask me what I'd done wrong. She knew Matt well, too; she knew this was the last thing I would have expected. I knew it was early for her to be awake at the weekend, but still I sent her a text:

I need to talk to you. Are you up yet?

While I waited for a reply I checked Facebook. My stomach fell when I thought Matt had blocked me, but as I searched for his name and saw he wasn't there, I realized he must have deactivated his account. Why would he do that? I looked for the messages we'd exchanged, but the entire conversation had gone. How had that happened? And my folders of photos of us had vanished, too! Quickly I checked Twitter, Instagram and LinkedIn. I couldn't find him on those sites, either.

Katie must have had a really late night because it was over an hour before she replied. I lay there drumming my fingers on the bed, thinking so hard about where he might be that by the time she answered my head was pounding.

Just going round to my mum's. Call you later?

I couldn't help it. At the thought of coping with this on my own I started to cry again.

Please, Katie. Matt has left me. Can you come round?

There was a long pause. I imagined her face, stunned at the news; we'd been together for four years, after all. At last she replied:

He's gone? OK, give me half an hour.

I lay curled up in the darkened room, unable to find the energy to even draw back the curtains. Even though I'd brushed my teeth, I could still taste the wine from the night before at the back of my throat, smell it in the quilt and pillows. It smelled disgusting, like I'd lost control of myself. I couldn't bear Katie to see me like that.

By the time she arrived, I'd showered and changed the bedding. The windows were open and the curtains drawn back, but despite brushing my teeth again, my mouth was still nasty.

"What's happened?" she said as soon as I opened the door.

Instantly my eyes filled with tears and I brushed them away. "I came home from work last night and he'd gone, taking everything with him."

"Everything?"

I nodded. "It must have taken him hours."

"Oh, Hannah," she said and put her arms around me. I clung to her for a minute. I could smell her warm, sweet perfume, feel the slick of her lip gloss against my cheek as she kissed me. "Come on, tell me all about it."

We sat in the kitchen with the French doors open and the fresh spring air wafting in. I made us some tea, but I felt sick at the thought of eating anything. I sat facing the glossy white kitchen units and from here everything looked normal, as though he had never left. Katie stared around the room, as if she might see something I had missed.

"What's upstairs like?" she asked.

I winced. "Same as here. He's taken all his stuff."

"Have you phoned him?" she asked, gently. "Do you want me to speak to him?"

I swallowed hard. "I can't," I said. "I don't have his number."

"Why not?"

"He's wiped it all," I said. "Everything's gone. Emails, texts, everything."

She came over and put her arms around me. "Oh, you poor

thing," she said, and the tears came then. Soon I was sobbing. She held on to me and stroked my hair. "It's okay. You'll be okay."

In all the years we'd known each other, she'd hardly ever seen me cry. I tried to pull myself together, embarrassed. "I know. It's just the shock."

"Don't you remember his number?"

I shook my head. "He's had the same one for as long as I've known him. Once it was on my phone, I didn't need to remember it."

"I'm the same," she said. "I can't remember any numbers nowadays. I don't even notice them. Hold on, I think James has got it."

She took out her phone and called her boyfriend. A minute later she had it. "Hide your number," she said. "He might not answer if he thinks it's you."

I was about to make a sharp retort but I knew she was right. I swallowed my pride and dialed.

"This number is no longer available," said the automated voice.

My face was hot with shame. "Looks like he's changed it."

"I'll try it from my phone," Katie said. She dialed and put the phone on loudspeaker. We heard the message again and she ended the call.

"There was really no sign beforehand that he was going to leave?"

I shook my head. "Thinking back, he did ask me a couple of times last week when I'd be back from Oxford. I'm such an idiot. I thought he was looking forward to me coming home."

My face smarted as I remembered what I'd said to him then. "You keep asking that! Don't worry, I won't be late!" All the time he must have been wondering how long he had.

She seemed at a loss as to what to say. "And you weren't having rows? He wasn't staying out late?"

"Nothing unusual." Again, I could feel the sting of tears behind my eyes. "I thought everything was fine."

"And . . ." she hesitated, "in bed . . . How was it?"

I rubbed my eyes. Slicks of wet mascara smeared my hands and I took some kitchen roll from the counter to dry my face. "It was great." I swallowed. "It was always great."

She was quiet for a long time, then she took my hand. "He's a bastard," she said. "A real bastard."

"I know."

She stood to wash her mug in the sink. "Where do you think he's gone to? Any ideas?"

Suddenly I wanted to be alone. "Leave that, Katie. No, I've no idea where he is and I don't care, either."

DESPITE THAT, ONCE she'd gone, I went back up to bed and spent hours on Google, trying to find the numbers of his friends, his colleagues, his family. I knew I wouldn't be able to rest until I'd found him.

Matt worked as an architect for a large local firm and their offices were always closed at the weekend, though occasionally on Saturdays he'd drive off to see a project he was working on. I couldn't call him there until Monday. Of course, his work number was no longer on my phone. I couldn't remember the last time I'd called him on it, but I knew I hadn't deleted it. He'd done that for me.

In the early days of dating Matt, I'd called him each lunchtime from my car and he'd answer his mobile in a very formal voice, saying, "Oh, good afternoon, Ms. Monroe. Just a moment, let me take this call outside where it's quieter." Then he'd take the phone to his car and we'd spend our lunch hour talking in low, urgent voices about what we'd done the night before and what we wanted to do that night. Those phone calls had naturally become fewer and shorter once we started to live together and we tended to text, as it was quicker, but even so, we'd had several phone conversations over the last few months.

Everywhere I looked, I saw the loss of him. I hadn't realized how much stuff he'd had, how our house—*my* house, I had to keep reminding myself—had become crammed with his possessions. I lay on the bed with my eyes closed, but when I opened them all I could see was that yet another thing was missing. His clock. His radio. Everything he owned.

All I felt was humiliation. My cheeks burned, not with the injustice of him leaving, though that smarted, too, but with the shame of knowing that he'd felt the only way to get away was to run like a thief, albeit in broad daylight. I burrowed under the quilt, my mind racing with questions I wanted to ask and things I wanted to say, but knew I couldn't. Not now.

I lay there as the day passed, gaining solace from the dark. Now I couldn't see that he was gone. If I stayed like that, my eyes fixed on the dwindling light around my bedroom blinds, I could pretend he was still there, behind me, saying nothing, just lying with me, almost touching me.

Chapter
Five

BY THE TIME I got to work on Monday, I was a wreck. The weekend had passed by quietly and after Katie had gone I saw nobody. The friends I went running with, Fran and Jenny, had sent texts asking whether I wanted to meet up early on Sunday morning, but I just didn't have the energy and I couldn't face telling them about Matt, so I replied that I couldn't make it and that I'd be in touch. My mum had sent a couple of texts to ask whether Matt and I fancied coming round for lunch on Sunday, but I just replied, *Sorry, busy*, and she took the hint and left me alone.

I didn't want to see anyone, yet I didn't want to be alone. The atmosphere in the house was full of self-recrimination and fury; at first the television and radio stopped me hearing the voices in my head, but then I panicked and switched them off. I needed to hear those voices in case they said something I ought to know.

When the alarm clock woke me on Monday at seven, I found I was lying in exactly the same position I'd been in at seven the previous night, my shoulders hunched and the skin on my face dry and creased, my pillow damp from tears I'd shed in my sleep.

It took all I had to go into work that day, but after the meeting in Oxford on Friday, I couldn't let myself down. After a lukewarm shower I dressed carefully and used my handbag mirror to apply makeup, making sure I focused on one feature at a time, unable to look myself in the eye.

I was halfway to work when I remembered I hadn't checked the bins in the back garden. It wasn't as though they were even being collected that day, but I found myself doing an illegal U-turn, accompanied by the blare of horns from exasperated drivers, and hurtling back home. I hurried out of the car, forcing myself to nod to Ray, who was peering out of the window next door, and went through the back gate into the garden.

I lifted the lids expectantly.

I don't know what I thought I would find. Just a solitary bag of rubbish sat in the green bin; I remembered emptying the kitchen bin on Thursday night and nothing had been put in there since. I checked the other bins, even the garden bin, but there was nothing different, nothing added to them. I looked at my watch and panicked. If I didn't hurry, I'd be late.

As soon as I arrived at work, I left a note for my assistant, Lucy, to tell her I had a headache and didn't want to be disturbed if possible. In the safety of my own office I picked up the phone to call Matt's workplace.

The woman on reception sounded bored. "Good morning, John Denning Associates, Amanda speaking. How can I help you?"

I swallowed hard. When I spoke, my voice sounded strange, as though it hadn't been used for days. Which it hadn't, I suppose. "Hi, can you put me through to Matthew Stone, please?"

"Hold the line," she said and disappeared for a few minutes. When she returned, she said, "There's no Matthew Stone working here."

"Try Matt," I said. "I'm not sure which he uses at work, Matthew or Matt."

I could hear the click of a mouse, then she spoke again. "I'm afraid there's nobody with that name working here."

I faltered. "Are you sure? He's one of the architects."

"I'm sorry," she said. "I'm new here, so I don't know many people, but his name's not in the database."

Through the glass of my office door I saw Lucy arrive and pick up the note. She smiled sympathetically at me and moved her hand to offer me a drink, but I shook my head and stared at my computer screen until she sat down at her own desk, facing away from me.

All morning I pretended to work. I shuffled papers about, I looked at documents on the screen, I read my emails in a daze, but I couldn't focus and a moment later I couldn't remember anything I'd read. Thoughts were whirling around my head. Where was he? Why hadn't he told me? Why had he deleted everything? They turned incessantly in my mind but I just couldn't come up with an answer.

Eventually, after racking my brain trying to remember the guy's surname, I phoned Matt's boss.

"I'm sorry," he said, sounding distracted. "Matt left us a week ago."

My heart hammered in my chest and I thought for a moment I'd faint. I thought of him leaving the house every morning, dressed for work, arriving home every night, chatting about his day.

"So he's not working there now?"

"No. David Walker's taken over his projects for the time being. Are you a client? Is there a problem?"

"No." I swallowed hard. "No problem at all. Can you tell me where he's gone to?"

"Sorry, we can't pass that information on."

I put the phone down and stared blankly at the computer screen. I'd read in the newspapers about people keeping up the pretense of working and I'd always thought they must be having a breakdown. And maybe if that was all Matt had done, I'd think the same thing. Yet when I remembered the way he had removed every last trace of himself from our house, I knew that wasn't what had happened here. He wasn't the one having a breakdown. He'd left that for me.

Chapter
Six

I COULDN'T KEEP Matt's disappearance from Sam, of course. He
and I were colleagues and had started work as assistants at around the
same time, fresh from university. We worked in different departments,
with our offices on either side of a large open-plan office. We didn't
tend to see each other often at the weekends, though sometimes Matt
and I would invite him and his girlfriend, Grace, to our house for bar-
beques in the summer, and we'd been to their house for a few parties
over the years. We were good friends at work, though; we had each
other's backs if we were struggling. I've always been able to trust him.

He sent me an email mid-morning, saying:

> You look like you need a break. Canteen?

I looked out of my office window. He was watching me. I waved
and he stood up and put on his jacket.

"Are you all right?" he asked, once we were sitting in the canteen.
He put a tray down on the table and passed me a mug of tea and a
glass of water. "You look pale. What's wrong? Hangover?"

I grimaced. "Not exactly, though I did have too much to drink over the weekend." I took the tea gratefully and looked up at him, unable to decide whether to confide in him. I hate people knowing about my private life, but I knew Sam wasn't the type to gossip. "This is strictly between us. Promise?"

He nodded. "Of course."

"It's Matt. He's left me. I don't know where he is."

He looked shocked and said nothing for a few minutes. I don't know what he'd been expecting, but it didn't seem to be this.

"Wow," he said, eventually. "That's a surprise. What happened? Had you had an argument?"

I took some painkillers from my bag and drank half of the water. "No, that's the thing. We hadn't argued for ages. When I got back from Oxford on Friday night I found he'd gone." I wasn't about to mention the forensic nature of his disappearance, the fact that not one thing of his remained in the house.

"What about his friends? Have you asked them where he is?"

"His friends were mainly guys from work," I said. "We'd go out for meals with them and their partners sometimes, but I don't have any of their numbers. When we went out together we usually saw Katie and James. If I was away with work, Matt might go to the pub and see people there he knew from years back, but I'm not going to go down there and ask them where he is."

"He's not on Facebook or Twitter?"

"He was," I said. I could hear my voice tremble and I quickly drank some more water. "Facebook, Twitter, Instagram, LinkedIn. The lot. He's deleted his accounts."

He took his phone out. "Remind me what his surname is?"

"Stone."

He was silent for a few minutes, tapping his screen. Every now and then he grimaced and tapped again.

"I thought he might have blocked you," he said, "but there's no sign of him anywhere." He put his phone back in his pocket and drank his coffee. "Could you phone him at work?"

"He's left his job, too."

"What? I thought he liked it there."

I said nothing. He had; he'd loved his job. He was an easygoing man and people warmed to him. He was happy at work. Mind you, I'd thought he was happy at home, too.

"And you've no idea where he's gone?"

"No, I don't," I admitted.

"He doesn't know anyone who's a bit dodgy, does he? He isn't running away from anything?"

I laughed. "Matt?"

"I know he doesn't seem the type, but it happens. He's not in debt, is he?"

"I doubt it. I went to get some money from the cashpoint for him a couple of weeks ago and he had a few thousand in his current account. He's got savings, too, but surely his current account would be empty if he was in debt?"

"I suppose so. And he hasn't seen anything? Witnessed a crime, or anything like that?"

I stared at him. "Are you thinking he's in a witness protection program?" I laughed again. "You think they're protecting Matt so that he can give evidence in court? And he didn't mention it to me?"

He looked a bit sheepish. "Well, I'm not saying it's happened. I was just thinking of all the possibilities."

"Oh, come on," I said. "There's no way he wouldn't have said something at the time. But . . . do you think I should call the police?"

"Not unless you believe something's happened to him." He must have seen I was upset, because he said gently, "It sounds as though he's just left you, Hannah. There's nothing the police can do. Did he take anything belonging to you?"

I shook my head. "No, just his own stuff."

"Well then, I wouldn't bother," he said. "He's probably gone to his mum's. That's where they all go to, the one place they're always welcome."

"He wouldn't go there."

Luckily he didn't ask me how I knew, because I wasn't sure at all. He'd left home at eighteen, though, and was nearly twice that age now. Would he really have gone to his mother's?

"But on a brighter note," I said, forcing a smile into my voice, "I might be made a director soon!"

His face broke into a huge smile. "Oh, fantastic! I knew you'd get there before me!"

"Let's see what happens, eh? Nothing's definite."

"So tell me all about it," he said. "What did they say?"

We spent the next ten minutes dissecting the conversation I'd had in Oxford, but the fact remained that I'd give up the chance of promotion in a heartbeat to have Matt back home, and I could tell from the sympathetic looks that Sam was giving me that he knew it, too.

LATER THAT AFTERNOON when I was sitting staring out of the window, clearly doing nothing at all, Sam came into my office.

"Hannah," he said, "do you and Matt have a joint mortgage?"

I stared at him. "What? Why do you want to know?"

"Because if you do, how are you going to sort that out when you don't know where he is?"

I shook my head. "No, the house is mine. We kept our finances separate."

When I met Matt I'd been living in my house for years, so I just kept it in my name and he gave me some money each month for the bills. My dad had paid the deposit; it had been a blatant bribe to encourage me to pass all my exams at the first attempt and qualify as an accountant—in his mind a *proper* job. Some days I knew how lucky

I was; on other days, when my job was stressful, I'd daydream about the life I could have lived if I'd been able to make that decision myself.

"Matt does have a house in London that he rents out, though," I added. "He bought it and did it up just before he came back here to work. I met him when he was living there, remember? I used to go down to London every weekend to see him." My voice faltered as I remembered the journeys down there on a Friday straight from work, clutching my overnight bag and wearing new underwear and stockings, knowing they'd be ripped off within five minutes of us being alone. Those weekends had been perfect, like little honeymoons. After only a few months, Matt had started looking for jobs in Liverpool. "I thought we'd get married one day and sell both places and buy something new between us. We talked about it a lot."

I stopped then, realizing I couldn't remember when we'd last discussed it. He'd looked up prices of houses on his street a few months ago, just before Christmas, and when I'd suggested he sell up he said he'd be mad to do that now, that prices were starting to rise and if he left it awhile longer he might get enough to pay off his mortgage. I hadn't questioned it, hadn't even thought he might have an ulterior motive for not selling yet. No matter how much I thought about that conversation now, he hadn't seemed any different when he'd said that; he hadn't looked like he was plotting anything or planning to run away.

"You don't think he's moved back down to London if he's already got a house there?"

"No," I said. "The tenants have it for another year. They only signed the renewal a month ago."

But still, once Sam had gone back to his office and I was left with my thoughts, I called the landline number Matt had had in London all those years ago, that I had called each night when I was in bed. I hadn't thought of that number from the day he left until now, but found I could remember it easily, remember the rhythm of the numbers as I tapped them out and the excitement I'd felt each time I'd called. When the tenant answered with her distinctive Brooklyn accent, her baby crying for attention in the background, I quietly put the receiver down.

I was right. He wasn't there.

Chapter
Seven

IT WAS PRETTY depressing going back into my house that night. I stayed at work as long as possible, but when there were only the cleaners and me left, I saw one giving me a pitying look and I glared at her. She had no idea of the stress I was under! It was nearly breaking me having to do my job *and* think about where I should look for Matt. She turned away quickly, her face scarlet, but that was it; I couldn't stay there with her looking at me like that. I pushed my chair back and picked up my coat. I'd carry on with this at home.

As I parked in my driveway I saw the curtains in Sheila and Ray's living room twitch, as though they'd been clocking what time I got home. Normally I would wave to let them know I'd seen them, but that night I just didn't have the energy and kept my eyes averted.

I let myself into the house feeling like a burglar. The heating was off and though it was the end of April, there was a chill in the air. When Matt was there and home before me, I'd come home to noise and light. Music would be playing in one room, the television in another, and I'd hear the radio playing in the en suite bathroom even when we were both downstairs.

He would always come into the hall when he heard me arrive

home and kiss me. We'd sit in the kitchen and chat about our day, then maybe watch a film or listen to music or go out for a drink with Katie and James. The house seemed dark and gloomy when I was alone in it. I went from room to room switching on lamps and the television, but no matter what I did, it felt like nobody was there. As though I was nothing on my own.

I lit the gas fire in the living room and sat on the sofa with a throw around me, trying to warm up. After a moment, *Coronation Street* came on and I had a sudden dreadful feeling of déjà vu. Before Matt had moved in I'd been single for a couple of years and I would sit there in just that position, a blanket around me, curled up at one end of the sofa, blindly watching television and wishing, wishing I had a different life. A better life.

When we first met it was like a light had gone on in my life, changing everything from sepia to full-blown color.

And the absence of worry alone was enough to make me love him. When I'd lived on my own, if something broke, I wouldn't know what to do and I'd spend evenings agonizing about whether I should repair it myself—usually an impossible task for me—or pay for someone to do it for me. But who? And how much would they charge? And how would I find them? How would I know I could trust them? I'd sit there worrying and fretting and biting my nails and I'd wish and hope and pray for someone to come along to help me, to love me, to make everything all right.

Then he came along and shone a light on me. Now that he'd gone again, it was darker than ever.

I WENT TO bed early that night, lying curled away from his side of the bed, with just the light of my Kindle falling on the space between the quilt and the sheet. If I held it carefully and lay very still, I could imagine nothing had changed.

I was so used to him being there. He'd moved in within months of us meeting. We'd met on holiday in Corfu; we'd each gone with a crowd of people and spotted each other as we waited for a late, rowdy, drunken flight over there. He'd been standing in the airport lounge with his friends, his face strained and tired. He'd looked like he really needed a holiday. His friends were an exuberant bunch, determined to make the most of their time away together. It was clear he was trying to join in but had other things on his mind.

I suppose I was staring at him, though I always denied it. After a while I noticed him giving me those half glances which are so exhilarating when you realize someone you're attracted to is pretending not to look at you. On the plane, by chance, he sat across the aisle from me and as soon as he went to the bathroom, my friend jumped into his seat to chat to his friend, and when Matt came back, he sat by me. Within minutes we'd both casually mentioned we were single, then discovered we were staying at the same hotel. I was supposed to be sharing a room with my friend and couldn't believe my luck when I realized he had a room to himself. Of course, I didn't know why, then.

We were together from that moment.

Matt was working in London when I met him and I was working at the same place I am now. We'd spend every night talking on the phone and then on Fridays I'd get the train down to see him. I was crazy about him, just crazy about him, and I thought he felt the same. He hadn't told me he loved me yet, but I knew it was coming, knew he felt it. I'd shouted it out one night when we were in bed and though we'd collapsed into laughter I knew he felt the same way. He held me close then and I whispered in his ear, "I was only joking," and he laughed again, then kissed me. Neither of us mentioned it for a while, but there was always an extra frisson between us from then on. I liked the fact that he was cautious; I felt the fact that he was holding back a little made things more serious. On my way home from London, I'd rest my head against the window and close my eyes and let myself think of the day he'd tell me he loved me.

Of course, when he did tell me, I wasn't expecting it at all. It was a Friday night and we'd agreed we'd have a weekend apart. I'd found it hard work going away so regularly; I had to do all the shopping and cleaning in the week and my house was starting to show signs of neglect. Matt had to do some work for a meeting on Monday morning, so our plan was to meet up the following Friday in London.

I was so tired that night I was almost glad I hadn't gone away. After we'd finished chatting on the phone, I lay stretched out diagonally on my bed, sending him little text messages and laughing at his replies. I fell asleep holding my phone.

The next thing I knew, the doorbell was ringing. I woke up with a start and looked over at the clock. It was nearly four o'clock and outside it was still dark. I glanced out of the window but couldn't see anything. I put on my dressing gown and went downstairs. I wondered if it was Sheila from next door. Maybe one of them was ill?

I opened the door and Matt was standing there.

"Well?" he demanded. "Do you?"

I looked at him, confused. "What are you doing here?"

"Do you?" he said again. "Just tell me!"

"What are you talking about? Do I what?"

"Do you love me?" He looked absolutely exhausted but his eyes were bright and intense. "Do you love me, Hannah?"

I swallowed. "Of course I do," I said. "Of *course* I do."

"Oh, thank God for that." He started to laugh. "I thought for a minute I was going to have to drive all the way back."

I put my arms around him and kissed him, there on the doorstep.

"Do you?" I asked. "Do you love me?"

"I told you often enough," he said.

"No you didn't!" I said, but when we went up to my bedroom about thirty seconds later, I picked up my phone and found his messages.

I love you, Hannah.

I do. I'm not joking now. I love you so much.

I've been waiting ages to tell you I love you. I love you. I love you.

Then the messages started to deteriorate.

Hannah? Do you love me?

I've made an idiot of myself, haven't I?

I don't care, I love you anyway.

Hannah? Are you ignoring me? Please don't do that.

And so on and so on. He lay on the bed with his head in the pillow as I read the messages out one by one, laughing so much I was almost in tears.

Then I lay down beside him and pulled him to me and showed him just how much I loved him.

I ROLLED OVER in bed, my face wet and my head thumping as I thought of those early days. I missed him now, missed him in bed with me, talking to me. I missed him reaching over to stroke my hair, missed pressing my face against the palm of his hand, his thumb touching my mouth just before he kissed me. He *did* love me. How could he have left me without a word?

I picked up my phone from the bedside table. I wanted to see a photo of him, something to remind me of the good times. I wanted to see him, to see whether there was something there, a look in the eye that should have warned me he was unhappy. Warned me he'd leave.

I groaned as I realized what had happened. Clearly it wasn't going to be as easy as that.

The photos section had had the same treatment as the emails and texts. There wasn't one picture of Matt on my phone. I had everything organized into albums and the one called "Us" that held all my photos of Matt and me together had been deleted, just as the one called "Matt" had been. Frantically I looked in the other albums, scrolled through image after image, but not one of them contained even a shadow of him.

Next to my Kindle was my iPad. The same thing had happened there. Every photo of Matt had been deleted.

Down in the chilly living room I pulled my laptop from its case. I'd always backed everything up, but again the folders had been raided, their contents gone. There were photos of Katie, of my friends from university, of me. There were no photos that Matt had taken of us, nothing of our holidays, of days out or parties. Not one image of a Christmas or a birthday he'd spent with me. My history had been lost. Wiped. It was as though the last four years hadn't existed.

And he'd done it. He'd taken them from me.

I sat back, prickles of embarrassment stinging my face. Why had he done that? I could understand him removing everything that belonged to him, but why take my memories, too? All my photos of him had gone, all my texts. Not one email remained. There wasn't a T-shirt of his I could sleep in, there wasn't even a mug I could hold. How long would it be before I couldn't picture his face or remember what he'd said to me?

Suddenly I wondered whether he'd gone through his own phone and laptop and erased all his photos of *me*. Would I soon be just a dim and distant memory to him? My stomach burned at the thought of him doing that, destroying me. I tried to picture the expression on his face as he deleted image after image of the last four years of his life. Of the woman he'd said he loved. If he'd appeared in front of me at that moment, I have no idea what I would have done.

All I could think about was him talking to me and knowing, *knowing* what he was going to do. I didn't want to remember him like that. If he'd died, I would have been able to remember the good times, the times we'd laughed together, been on holiday, sat companionably on the sofa, our bodies casually touching, chatting about our day. I couldn't bear to think of those times now—and if

I did, the memories had an overlay—a tinge that just ruined them, that made me think, "Was he planning it then? Was it on his mind?"

When we went for an Indian meal the week before he left, did he know he'd never return to that restaurant? When he lay in bed beside me that last night, was he relieved he'd soon be gone? When he felt me kiss his cheek the morning he left, what was he thinking?

That was the moment I died for him, wasn't it? One last kiss and I was gone. I just hadn't known it.

And then I remembered where I could find a photograph. A few years ago, just before I met him, he'd been invited back to his old university in London to talk to students about working as an architect. He'd spent a day there looking at the projects they were working on and giving the students advice on applying for jobs. He'd really enjoyed it, he'd said, meeting these earlier versions of himself and talking about how he'd spent the years between their age and his.

I logged on to the university's website and searched. I'd only seen the photo once before and it didn't have his name tagged, as he was there with a crowd of industry experts, so when I'd searched for him on Google, it hadn't shown up. There was a huge chance it wasn't there anymore; it must have been five years old by now. I pored over the site, holding my breath, flicking from page to page, trying to remember where I'd seen it.

And then there it was. A group of students stood looking at some architectural plans and Matt stood next to them, pointing something out. He was smiling, a broad, happy smile, and a couple of people were looking at him and laughing.

I copied the photo into Paint and cropped it so that only Matt remained. I enlarged it and printed a copy, then lay in bed, holding it. He looked just as he had when we first met, and I knew I still loved him and that I was going to do whatever it took to find him again.

Chapter
Eight

THAT WEEK WAS very quiet. Katie was away in Scotland; she worked in pharmaceutical sales and she'd been talking about this conference a lot for the last couple of months. She'd moved into pharmaceuticals from another sales job and was desperate to make her mark. I knew she would, too. Once she set her mind to something, she always achieved it. I really missed her, though. I was used to her always being free to chat, but that week, although she rang me a few times, she couldn't talk for long.

"They're waiting for me in the hotel restaurant," she told me when I called her on Wednesday at lunchtime. "I'll have to go in a minute, sorry."

"But don't you get any time off?" I asked, hating the whine in my voice. "I'm going crazy here, Katie. I can't concentrate at work and when I go home the house is empty and everything feels off. There's no one else to talk to. Please . . ." I could hear myself begging now and winced with shame. "Please, Katie. Don't you have any time at all?"

"I'm sorry." I could hear guilt and stress in her voice. "Why don't you phone Fran? She'll go out for a drink with you. She always wants to go out. Or Jenny?"

"I don't want to tell them that Matt's gone," I muttered.

"Well, don't tell them! Have a night out and don't talk about him."

I was silent. I knew that was impossible.

She sighed. "I can't see us finishing until really late tonight. After midnight. It's expected that we stay. You know what it's like. That's when you really get to know people. And you don't want to get yourself all upset then. You wouldn't sleep, you know that."

She was right. She and I both knew that once I started talking to her, I'd cry and spend hours complaining, making myself feel awful. I knew, too, that there was a lot of pressure on her on this trip; she needed to sleep well so that she was fighting fit in the daytime. She'd told me it would be meetings all day and networking all night. James had said, "I hope you'll have time to phone me," and she'd laughed and replied, "If you fancy a call at six in the morning, then of course!" I'd tried telling her not to get so excited—it was only a conference—but she'd snapped, "It's okay for you, Hannah, you make a lot more money than I do and you go to things like this all the time. This is my chance and I'm going to take it."

I didn't bother mentioning her company car or her health insurance or her annual bonus, which was easily double my own. She had seen my pay slip one month and it had clearly played on her mind ever since. "It's okay," I said now. "Don't worry about it."

"Have you told your mum and dad that he's gone?"

"No," I said. "I feel bad enough as it is. They'd just blame me and I'd feel even worse."

"Don't be daft," she said. "They're lovely." There was nothing to say to that. "What could they blame you for anyway?"

I thought about it. "Not being able to keep him, I suppose. My dad's never forgiven us for not being married." I don't know who he blamed most for that, Matt or me. Though if we had been married,

I'd be divorcing him now and my dad wouldn't like that, either. He's an older father and very traditional. He wouldn't speak to Matt at all when he first moved in and warned me to make sure he wasn't on the house deeds unless we married, as though Matt was out to cheat me in every possible way. I was glad of that advice now, in hindsight.

I started to cry then, sitting in my office, surrounded by windows into the main office, tears dripping down onto my computer keyboard. I sat hunched over my phone, my elbows on the desk, and I knew that if Lucy saw me like that, she'd be in with tea and sympathy within a minute of my putting the phone down and five minutes later everyone in the office would know about it.

"Oh, Hannah," said Katie, her voice softer now. "Don't cry. I know it's been a horrible shock for you, but you're better off trying to accept that he's gone."

I pulled out a bunch of tissues to dry my eyes. "It hasn't even been a week yet!"

"Yes, I know, but it's obvious things weren't good, isn't it? If he felt the need to leave, just like that, then he wasn't happy. I'm sorry, but surely you must have known something was up."

Humiliation burned through me. "Why should I? He said he loved me. He said he'd always love me."

"And you believed him?"

"Of course I believed him! Why wouldn't I?"

"The thing is, everyone says that in a relationship. And not all of them last."

I was silent.

"Anyway," she went on, "why don't you come round on Sunday night? We can have a curry and a few drinks."

"What about James?"

Katie's boyfriend had always been a bit of a barrier between us. She and I met James when we were seventeen and studying to go to university. Both of us had liked him but then I'd bumped into him when I was on my own one day and he'd asked me to go out with him. We were inseparable for a few months in the summer before we left school. After we broke up, I went off to Australia on a gap year and on to university in a different city to his. We didn't see each other for years.

Matt and I were in bed in his house in London when Katie called to tell me she'd bumped into James the previous night in a club in Liverpool. I knew something was up from the moment she spoke. Her voice sounded different—she was excited and happy, but there was something else there, too. It was only later that I realized she was nervous. I was distracted, though, by Matt. He lay on his side and looked at me as I chatted to Katie and every now and then he'd lean over and kiss my bare shoulder. I couldn't concentrate. I didn't *want* to concentrate. Katie was babbling about how she and James had had so much to talk about. She'd asked him whether he ever thought about that year he and I spent together when we were young and he'd said, "Never." That probably floored her, and I pictured her trying to regain momentum.

He hadn't mentioned my name, she said, hadn't asked what I was doing or where I lived. She was pleased about that, I could tell, but really, I didn't care right then. I just wanted to get off the phone and turn back to Matt, to continue what we'd started hours before. She told me James had asked her to go out to dinner with him that night. Was it all right with me?

I assured her she could do whatever she wanted and good luck, too. She ended the call in a state of high excitement and I didn't give it another thought until a week later, when I realized I hadn't heard from her and discovered that James had virtually moved in with her.

He and I, though, were happier now when we weren't hanging out together. I didn't mind her seeing him—why would I?—but it was a bit awkward sometimes, especially if Matt wasn't around.

"Oh, he'll be fine," she said carelessly. "I've just told him what happened; you'll be able to talk to him about it, too."

"You didn't tell him last Saturday when you came over to see me?"

There was a pause. "Hannah, you hate me talking to James about private things. I didn't think you'd want him to know."

And yet, just a few days later, she'd told him anyway. I'd always hated the idea of them discussing me, but up until now it was just the subject of our teenage relationship I'd been worried about. But now, the thought of them talking about Matt, about why he'd left me, made me cringe. I shook myself. Katie had been away and too busy over the last few days. She wouldn't have had time to talk to James about anything, let alone me.

We agreed that I'd go to her house at seven on Sunday evening. If I'd refused, I knew I wouldn't have seen her at all.

INSTEAD OF DRIVING the few miles from Liverpool back to my house, I stopped at the city center and walked around the deserted streets, feeling pretty dejected. I couldn't stand the thought of returning to an empty house. I went into Waterstones and bought a book, then sat on a sofa there with a drink and a sandwich until eight o'clock, when the shop shut. I would have stayed all night if they'd been open.

Back home I went straight upstairs and into my bedroom, keeping my eyes averted from all those signs that he'd gone. I turned on the lamp on my side of the bed and went into the bathroom to shower. I dried my hair and put on my pajamas. The house seemed so quiet. In bed I lay on my side, away from where he'd lie, and thought about him leaving me.

When he'd got his job at John Denning Associates and moved in with me, I was so full of hope for our future. It had been years since

I'd met someone I liked as much. As soon as he moved his things in, the house was different, full of life. He'd laughed at my old television and had immediately gone shopping for a new one, saying he'd leave his in London for his tenants. I remembered us unpacking it and taking the box to the recycling center afterward. We'd had to stamp on the cardboard in the back garden to break it up so that it would fit into the car and we misjudged the size of the pieces, so they knocked our heads all the way there. We were giddy with laughter by the time we arrived, and I think the men working there thought we were drunk. The new television was huge and black and silver, and that first night we watched film after film and I kept saying in an old lady's voice, "It's just like being at the movies!" and he laughed and laughed.

I rolled over in bed and looked at his pillow, smooth and untouched. I reached out and laid my hand on it, and thought of him lying there talking to me. What would he say if he were here now? Would he tell me why he'd gone or would he close his eyes, his mouth tight and angry, and say nothing, the way he did so many times when we argued?

I didn't let myself think of the bad times. I just wanted to remember him when he was happy and funny and caring for me. Loving me.

And then the doorbell rang.

I looked at the clock on my bedside table. Ten o'clock. For a second I wondered who'd be calling at this time of night, and then I realized.

Of course, it's Matt! He's come back! I knew he would!

I raced downstairs to the front door. I'd bolted it when I came home, never dreaming he'd be back tonight.

"Matt?" I called. "Hold on!"

My fingers shook with excitement as I pulled the bolt back. I turned the handle and pulled the door wide open.

James was standing on the doorstep.

———

"James," I said uncertainly. "What are you doing here?" I was suddenly aware that I was standing there in only my short pajamas and moved to hide behind the door. "Is everything all right?"

He nodded. "Can I come in?"

"Yes. Yes, of course. Go into the kitchen. I won't be a minute."

I ran upstairs and threw on a dressing gown, wondering why he was here. When I got back to the kitchen he was roaming the room, pulling out drawers and opening cupboards. I knew now why he'd come.

"Sorry," he said, when he noticed me watching him as he opened the cupboard where I kept the vacuum cleaner.

"You won't find him in there," I said.

"What happened? Katie said he's left you."

My face burned with humiliation. I nodded.

"You didn't guess something was up?"

"Not you, too!" I said, my voice tight with stress. "I've had all that from Katie."

"Well, it's not the sort of thing I'd expect Matt to do." He opened the door to the utility room and looked inside.

"He's not in there, either!" I said sharply.

He looked behind the door—as if Matt at six feet tall could be hiding behind it—and said, "I'm just checking."

"There's no need to, thanks," I said. "Do you think I haven't done that?"

He shrugged. "It's natural to want to look around."

"You can see for yourself that he's taken everything with him."

He walked out into the hall and looked at the walls where the jazz photos had been. "It's odd, though, isn't it?"

"Of course it is," I snapped. "But it would be even odder if he was hiding in the utility room."

He said nothing, just opened the living room door and glanced inside.

"Do you think you're going to see something I didn't see?" I asked.

"I just thought that if something had happened to him . . ."

"Like what?"

He shook his head. "I was worried, that's all."

"Me, too," I said, then remembered who I was talking to. There was no way I was going to show him I was upset. "For a split second. But once I realized he'd taken every single thing with him, I stopped worrying. It's hard to worry about someone who strips your house of all their possessions and disappears without any warning. Pointless, really."

He stared at me and I met his eyes, forcing myself not to waver. "I suppose so," he said. "I wonder why he didn't say anything to me."

"Or to me! Anyway, I need to go to bed. He's not here. You'll have to take my word for that."

"Okay," he said. "If you need anything, you know where I am." He paused on the doorstep. "Are you going to tell Katie I was here?"

I thought of Katie's reaction if she heard he'd come here late at night, when I was half-dressed and she was away from home. Even though it had been many years since James and I were together, I knew she would struggle with that. We never mentioned that period in our lives; I knew she liked to tell herself she was always meant to be with James. If she heard he'd been here, I was worried her jealousy would burn inside her and she'd find a way to make me suffer as much as him.

"No," I said. "James, I'm really tired and I want to sleep. I won't say a word to Katie as long as you go now."

I stood at the front door and watched his car as it drove away down the road. It wasn't the first secret I'd kept from Katie, of course. You can't tell anyone everything. I was uneasy about this, though. There'd been something there in James, an anger I hadn't seen for a long time, not since we were young.

Chapter
Nine

BY THE FOLLOWING Saturday I'd spent eight nights on my own and I didn't like it one bit. The nights were long and lonely without the familiar warmth of Matt beside me. There were things I'd noticed now that he'd gone that hadn't registered before. Whenever I woke when he was here, there was the background sound of his breathing. I used to be able to lie there and regulate my own breathing by emulating his and within minutes I'd be asleep again. Now when I woke it was deathly quiet. I'd strain my ears to hear anything, just anything, to show I wasn't the only person alive. The rattle of the gate would make me jump and think of strangers trying to break into my house. I'd lie there, terrified, with my phone clutched in my hand, ready to dial the police, until, minutes later, I'd realize that there was no one there and it was just the wind banging the gate against the concrete post. By then my heart would be racing and my mouth dry and I'd have to go downstairs and get a glass of water just to calm myself down.

In the mornings before Matt left I'd always smell coffee just as I woke. I'd lie there breathing in the smell and I'd open my eyes slowly and see him at the basin in the en suite, shaving, his T-shirt off, whistling along to the radio if he was happy, or staring deep into the mirror if he had something on his mind. The room would be warm and I'd know he'd already put the coffee on, squeezed some oranges and cut the bread ready for toasting. It was a little routine he had, he said, from when he was a boy, when he did those jobs for his mum for pocket money.

Now when I awoke I could smell nothing as civilized as coffee and orange juice. If I'd had a drink the night before, the air in the bedroom would be sweet and sickly. I'd lie there until the last minute, then leap out of bed and shower in a hurry. I hadn't had the radio on since I heard "One Day Like This" playing when I was in the shower; I'd nearly broken my leg trying to turn it off. I tended to avoid the kitchen altogether in the mornings, keeping energy bars at work for breakfast and relying on Lucy to bring me cups of tea.

That Saturday morning I got up late. With nothing to fill my day I was at a loss. I spent a couple of hours cleaning, but the fact was I'd made very little imprint on the house in the last week. It was clearly Matt who'd turned the place into a mess, week after week. The living room was untouched; the last time I'd been in there was on Monday when I'd come downstairs in the middle of the night to find every photo of Matt had gone.

At lunchtime my mum phoned me. As soon as I saw her name on the caller ID I rejected the call. I couldn't face talking to her right now. Although she and Matt hadn't met often, she'd loved him. She thought he was the best thing that had ever happened to me and told me repeatedly that I should do whatever it took to hang on to him.

"Kindness is everything," she'd said.

We both knew what she meant. If she'd heard what had happened, she'd blame me; I knew that.

There was no need to tell her he'd gone, anyway; I knew it was crazy, but I still hoped he'd come back, his tail between his legs.

I could picture it now, him sitting at the kitchen table, embarrassed and apologetic, smiling at me, telling me he'd been a fool, that he'd had a midlife crisis, that he'd missed me. In my daydreams he'd give me a box of our photos and tell me his car was full of all his things. All he wanted was to move back in and please, please would I forgive him? He'd tell me I was right to believe him when he'd said he'd always love me.

Those daydreams were easiest in bed, with my eyes shut and the warmth of the quilt wrapped around me like a lover's embrace. When I came downstairs in the cold light of day, it was harder to reconcile the man who'd sworn his undying love for me with the man who'd removed every last trace of himself from my life.

THE PREVIOUS NIGHT I'd spent hours phoning hotels, asking whether Matt was staying there. At the end of the night I sent Katie a text:

I've called every hotel in Merseyside. He's not staying at any of them.

A few minutes later she replied:

He won't be anywhere near here by now. You need to stop obsessing. He could be anywhere in the world. Time to accept he's gone. xx

My stomach flared and I fired another text:

Thanks for your support.

She replied immediately:

I'm sorry. It's just that the best revenge would be to not give a damn. I know it's hard but the less you think about him the easier it'll get. Watch a film or read a book and try to keep your mind off him. xxx

She'd always been a great believer in tough love, at least when it came to giving others advice. I wasn't sure I'd ever get to the point where I didn't care about Matt, but I did as I was told and turned on the television, but then all I could think was that he'd packed up his own television and taken it away from me. I jabbed the Off button on the remote control and picked up my Kindle, forcing myself to read.

Later on I sent Katie another text. There was something on my mind, something I'd started to worry about, though I couldn't think I was right. I didn't know how I'd cope if I was. Panic lodged in my throat every time I thought of it.

Do you think he's left me for another woman?

She replied ten minutes later, by which time I'd worked myself up into a near frenzy at the thought of him with someone else. I imagined his arms around another woman, his breath hot against her face, telling her he loved her, that he'd always love her. The thought made me feel ill.

Was there any sign that he was involved with someone? x

I thought about it, my eyes prickling in the dark, cold room.

No.

Her reply came quicker this time:

Try not to worry. It's late and you need to sleep. We'll talk about it on Sunday. xx

I typed, *OK, see you then. x*, but I lay awake for hours that night, thinking of Matt during his last few days at home. He'd seemed exactly the same. There wasn't one moment when I'd suspected someone else was involved. He wasn't secretive with his phone; in fact, he rarely used it when he was home and left it lying around, as though he didn't mind if I looked at it or not. I hadn't looked at it for ages, hadn't felt the need to. I could kick myself for that now. He hadn't seemed happier than usual or more excited. He hadn't appeared to be planning something like this. Planning to leave me. Planning to erase himself from my life.

Chapter
Ten

I WOKE EARLY on Sunday morning, thoughts about where he might be swirling around my mind. I was confusing places I intended to check with places I'd already checked. When I'd called the hotels, I'd phoned a couple of them twice by mistake, and believe me, there's nothing polite about a receptionist when you ask the same question twice in five minutes. I knew I needed to be better organized. I wouldn't get anywhere with this if I wasn't working to some kind of plan.

I made a trip to the supermarket to stock up on essentials, pausing at the stationery counter on my way to the checkout. This was the sort of thing I needed to help me keep track of things. I picked up a notebook, a couple of blocks of Post-it notes and some colored marker pens and hurried home to make a start.

Back at my house, I opened the boot of the car to take the bags out. When I heard a quiet cough behind me, I nearly jumped out of my skin. My head banged on the opened boot door.

"Careful!" said my neighbor Sheila. "Do you want a hand?"

Swearing under my breath, I stepped away from the car.

"Hi, Sheila. No, I'm fine, thanks. I've only got a few bags."

"Shall I get Matt to help you?" she asked.

I looked toward the house so quickly I cricked my neck. "Matt? Is he here?"

"I don't know," she said. "Isn't he home?"

My stomach unclenched and I could breathe again. "Oh," I said, "no, he's out at the moment. He won't be back for a while."

She nodded, accepting his absence as she would have done any other day of the year.

"You're sure you can manage?"

I looked past her at the front door. She'd been into our house many, many times, and as soon as she saw the missing photographs in the hall she'd know something was wrong. The last thing I wanted was to have to listen to her advice.

"It's okay," I said. "Thanks anyway." I noticed her suitcase then, waiting by the boot of her car. "Are you going somewhere?"

"Just up to the Lake District for a couple of nights," she said. "The weather's so beautiful now, we thought we'd make the most of it."

"Lucky you," I said automatically. I needed to get into the house. To get organized.

In the kitchen I unpacked the bags, then sat at the island with the Post-it notes and the notebook. I pulled a note off the block and wrote:

John Denning Associates
Reception: Amanda didn't know him—he's not in the
    computer system
Manager: Bill Harvey—said he left a week ago

I sat back and stared at the note. What had he been doing that last week before he left? How had he spent his days? He'd seemed just the same as usual, though now that I thought about it, I couldn't remember the last time I'd heard him singing in the mornings. I'd just assumed he was busy at work, as I was. He hadn't seemed in a particular rush to get out of the house, but nor had he tried to make sure I left before him. I wondered whether he'd driven around the block and only come back when he knew I'd gone. I remembered a couple of mornings that week he'd phoned me on my landline at work to ask me what I wanted to do that night, something he'd only rarely done before. It dawned on me now that he might have been checking that I was in the office, though at the time I'd thought he was just being nice. My stomach lurched at the idea of him at home the day he left, packing like a madman, virtually wiping his fingerprints off the house before leaving it.

And then I thought about his key. For a moment the thought that he'd kept it filled me with hope. I found myself thinking, *I knew he didn't mean it! I knew he'd come back!* But then I leapt up to check and there it was on the hook next to the back door, nestled against the spare car keys and the keys to the garage and the shed. I remembered taking it from that hook the first night he moved in. He'd kissed my neck as I looped the key to my home onto his key ring, then told me he loved me.

Now it was back there as though it had only ever been a temporary arrangement. As though he'd always intended to leave.

Chapter
Eleven

I ALWAYS FEEL Sundays have a kind of atmosphere about them, a drab, miserable reminder that work is about to start again. That Sunday was no different. Apart from going to Katie's house in the evening, I had nothing at all to do. The fridge was full of food, the house was clean and the sky was gray, threatening rain. Usually we would sit with the Sunday papers at the kitchen table, but I didn't want to do that alone. All I could do was carry on with my job of finding Matt.

Once I'd made all the notes I could think of on the Post-it notes, I sat at the island and lay them in front of me. On one side were the places I'd called. One reason for writing them down was so that I didn't call them again, but it also helped to still my mind, made me think I was getting somewhere. Once it was all written down, I felt I could cope. So the notes lay in front of me like a game of solitaire and I moved them into columns and across into rows whenever I wanted to jog my memory.

After an hour or two of that, though, I'd had enough. I just wanted to get out of the house, away from the emptiness. I set off in the car, not knowing where I was going, and drove around aimlessly through the small towns of the Wirral. After a while I realized that Matt's mother's house was only a few miles further up the road.

I wasn't a huge fan of his mother, Olivia, and from the way she reacted when I first met her, I suspected I wasn't her first choice of girlfriend for her son. So every Sunday Matt would go off to see her in Heswall and I'd stay at home and paint my nails or go for a run. Sometimes he'd be a bit subdued when he got home, as though there'd been rows or recriminations, but he always denied anything like that had happened. He would, though, I suppose.

He often asked why I didn't go to see my own parents. I think he felt I was just waiting for him to come home, that he'd had to rush his visit. That wasn't my idea of fun, though. I saw them often enough for my liking and although I knew my mum would have appreciated more frequent visits, she wasn't going to get them. There was something about being with my parents that made me revert to childhood, and that wasn't a place I willingly revisited.

I looked at the clock on the dashboard. Two o'clock. The time Matt went to see his mum varied, but my heart suddenly raced at the thought that he could be there now. I put my foot on the accelerator and let the road have it.

THE FIRST TIME I met Olivia was when Matt was working in London and visiting me for the weekend. We went along for lunch at her house on a Saturday, dragging ourselves out of bed to be on time, then finding the shower such a distraction we were late. Really late.

I remembered she'd frowned when she first saw me. My hair was damp and my cheeks were rosy. I'd had to put my makeup on in the car, we were so rushed. With that one glance I knew I didn't live up to her expectations and I felt it like a kick in the stomach. Immediately I asked for the bathroom and tidied myself up, but by then the damage had been done. She was polite enough, offering us lunch and a glass of wine, chatting to us about her plans for the weekend, but she seemed guarded, as though she was holding back.

We used to see her every few weeks, whenever Matt was back from London. He'd always stay with me and we'd go to see her. She'd invite us to lunch and we'd chat, but she wasn't likely to become my best friend. I tried with her, I really did. I didn't have much of a relationship with my own mum, but I really made an effort with Olivia. I'd buy her gifts and invite her to spas and so on, but she rarely accepted, saying she was so busy at work and just wanted to relax at the weekend. What the hell did she think spas were for? I tried not to talk about her with Matt, but sometimes I had to and nowadays we tried not to mention her. He'd go off to see her and I'd be polite when he returned, nothing more. It's the same with a lot of in-law relationships, I suppose.

Now I approached her house carefully. She lived on quite a wide road, with enough room for cars to park on each side and still allow traffic to pass easily. I stopped a few doors away on the other side of the road and sat quietly watching her house for a while. Matt's car was nowhere to be seen and his mum's driveway was empty.

Although the day was gray and overcast, there were children playing out in the street. A young girl glanced into my car as she ran past and I tensed, not wanting her to go to her parents and tell them there was an odd woman sitting outside. I pulled out my phone and pretended to be looking at something on there.

When I looked up again I noticed something strange and stared so hard I thought my eyes would pop. Through the driveway of Matt's mother's home, I could see the top of something blue; it looked like a trampoline, one of those huge kids' ones that's surrounded by a tall net to stop them bouncing off.

I sat back in my seat and thought for a second. Matt was an only child, like me. His mum was in her early sixties and divorced. He'd not said anything about her meeting someone else, never mind someone with young children or grandchildren. She wouldn't have been able to put up a trampoline that size without help from him and he hadn't mentioned it at all.

I started the car and drove slowly up the road. As I passed the house I glanced out of the window and saw that, yes, I was right. There was a huge blue trampoline in the back garden, next to the garage.

I drove for a mile or two, then stopped the car to think. Nothing made sense. Why would Olivia have a trampoline in her garden? I had a mad moment where I thought of her bouncing on it after one gin too many. She was always at Weight Watchers; maybe they had recommended it?

Slowly I turned the car around and drove back the way I'd come. I approached from another direction this time, so that my car was on Olivia's side of the road, her house at my passenger window. I didn't care who was looking at me; I slowed right down as I passed and saw again the huge blue frame. Then I noticed that the curtains in the front room had changed and on the wall next to the front door was a silver plaque with the house number on it. That was new, too. I continued further down the road, then did a U-turn and sat facing the house, though several yards away. There was no sign of life.

I got out of the car and walked toward the house. The children in the street stopped as one to watch and I could feel their eyes boring into my back as I turned into the driveway.

At once I could see that someone else was living there. On my way to the front door, I looked through the living room window. There was a huge television in prime position on the wall above the fireplace, facing a big white leather corner sofa. A low black glass coffee table had a display of flowers made of silver and crystal, and a life-sized portrait of a young girl sat in pride of place on the wall facing the window. It was as unlike Olivia's conservatively decorated living room as it was possible to be.

I knocked at the door. As I expected, there was no answer, and I turned to go back to my car. A little boy was watching me with interest and, as I passed him, I said, "Hello."

He stared back.

"Does Mrs. Stone still live in this house?" I asked. Stupid question, really, but I didn't know what else to say.

He looked bemused.

"Who lives in this house, sweetheart?" I asked.

He stared again and banged his stick against the steps.

I sighed. I was about to go and ask another child when a woman came running up.

"What do you want?" she asked.

"I was just asking your son whether Mrs. Stone still lives there," I said in a conversational manner.

"Why do you want to know?"

I stared at her. "I'm a relative," I said eventually, when I realized eyeballing her wasn't going to bring about an answer. "I was passing and thought I'd call in, but it looks as though she's moved."

"She has. She doesn't live here anymore," said the woman, gripping her son's hand as though I might abscond with him. "Hasn't been here for ages."

"Oh, okay," I said, about to ask whether she knew where Olivia had moved to, but she walked off, clutching her son to her.

I walked slowly back to the car. *Ages* . . . How long was that? She'd come to our house for Christmas lunch just a few months before and there had certainly been no mention of her moving then. I knew she'd lived in the house for years and that she liked the area. She had lots of friends round there, but I hadn't a clue what their names were or where they lived.

It startled me a little to realize that the last time I'd been to her house was two Christmases ago. Matt and I had taken her out for a meal when it was his birthday or hers, but apart from those occasions and Christmas Day, I hadn't seen her. I'd considered myself lucky to get out of the weekly visits but, thinking about it now, after the first couple of weeks Matt hadn't put up a protest. I frowned. If I'd seen her more often, I might have known about her moving house, but then surely he should have mentioned it? I felt a sudden flash of anger. Why hadn't he told me she'd gone? I felt a fool for thinking he was always honest with me. I'd been busy with work and I'd taken my eye off the ball at home, clearly.

Now it was May and the woman in the street had said she'd moved ages ago—did she mean more than five months ago? I turned to ask her but saw she was already back in her house, her child with her. I saw a shadow fall across the window of her front room and knew I shouldn't go and talk to any more children.

I sat in the car and thought about the last time I'd seen her, on Christmas Day last year. She'd seemed okay with me; she obviously would have preferred to have had lunch at her own house—wherever *that* was—but she was polite, praising the food and giving us a couple bottles of champagne as a gift.

Then I remembered Zoopla, the property listing service. They'd have a record of the sale of the house. Some days you just had to love the Internet.

I pulled my phone from my bag and searched for her address on the website. I could hardly believe my eyes. Her house had sold on November 30 last year. Of course there was nothing to say where she'd gone to and no way I could find that out, but it meant that she'd been to my house on Christmas Day and had sat there for more than six hours without mentioning she had moved. And Matt had picked her up that morning and taken her back that afternoon, so clearly he'd known about it, too. He'd known for months and hadn't said a word. Where had he taken her? Had they talked about me on their way home? The thought of the effort I'd made for those two liars that day made me seethe.

I remembered then that Matt's mum had my mobile number. She'd sent me a text later on Christmas night, thanking us for lunch. "Thank you so much for inviting me," she'd said. "We'll do Christmas at my house next year!" I'd guessed there was a subtext there, but had thought it was along the lines of "I'll show you how to make a proper Christmas lunch." How was I supposed to know that it was "Oh and by the way, my invitation only extends to Matt. As for you, I've moved home and you will never know where I live"?

Of course her number was no longer on my phone and the message, too, had disappeared. She was lucky there, I thought, because I might have called her and told her a few home truths.

I sent Katie a text:

I've just found out Matt's mum has moved house. Why didn't he tell me?

I sat there for several minutes before she replied. I had the feeling she wasn't taking this as seriously as I was.

How do you know that? Has he been in touch?

I replied: *No, no word still. I've just been there. Spoke to a neighbor.*

Within a couple of minutes my phone beeped: *That's weird! Tell me all about it tonight. 7 pm OK? xx*

Chapter
Twelve

KATIE OPENED THE door and gave me a hug. She was looking great in a new dress, her hair curled and makeup on. My heart sank. Whenever we bought new clothes, we'd put them on to show each other before wearing them to work or on a night out. Sometimes a sidelong look from Katie would have me rushing to exchange something, but then at other times she'd pick up her iPad within minutes of seeing me and buy the same outfit for herself. That night I hadn't even thought of making an effort and flushed as she gave me a swift sympathetic glance. She hugged me again then and I couldn't help it; my body yielded to her embrace.

"You poor thing," she said. It didn't make me feel any better.

"How was the conference?" I asked. I wasn't particularly interested but I guessed she'd want to talk about it, to show me how well she was doing at work. We'd always been the same, judging our own success in comparison with the achievements of the other. I had no time for that tonight, though.

"I'm not allowed to talk about it," she said in a small voice. "I phoned my mum on my way home and she said I could get it out of my system telling her but that if I went on about it to James, he'd leave me."

"That bad, eh?"

"Thank God for her mum," said James, coming into the hallway and taking my jacket. "Taking it for the team like that. Katie did try to tell me about it on the phone in the week but I couldn't understand a word."

Katie laughed. She was used to people not knowing what she was talking about when she spoke about her job. "To be honest," she said, "I was boring myself."

We sat in their living room, music playing softly in the background and a cluster of cream church candles flickering in the fireplace. They were new and I remembered the last time Katie had been to my house when Matt was there, I'd bought similar candles and filled my fireplace with them. She'd loved them and now, of course, she had them in her home. The room was warm and inviting, everything that my own house wasn't right now. It was spotless, too.

When Katie went to the kitchen to get some drinks, I expected James to say something about coming round to my house the other night, but instead he glanced at the open doorway where we could hear Katie putting bowls and glasses onto a tray, and told me that he'd come home from work on Friday to find her mum and dad packing their steam mop into the car. They'd given the place a spring-cleaning, they'd said.

"Don't you mind them coming into your house like that?"

He shrugged. "I'd have had to clean it at the weekend," he said. "It's saved me the time and they seem to like doing it."

"But to come in without telling you?"

"They're not going to do any damage, are they?" he said. "Besides, they filled the fridge up, too. Why would I object to that?"

I shook my head. "I couldn't stand it, someone coming into my house without my knowing. It would scare me."

"Scare you?" said Katie, returning with the tray. "Your own parents?"

James flashed a glance at me. "It doesn't bother me," he said. "If they want to do it, they can."

"I love having my mum and dad around," said Katie. "They can help as much as they like, as far as I'm concerned."

She snuggled into the corner of the sofa, the lamplight haloing her blond hair, and gave James a little pleading look. He rolled his eyes and poured us all some wine. She licked her lips and just for a second she looked like the cat that'd got the cream. I'd seen that look regularly since I'd known her. It wasn't just that Katie was spoiled, although she was; it was that she was adored. Her parents had longed for a child, and when they were forty, after twenty years together, they finally had Katie. From that moment she was treated like a little goddess and they worshipped at her altar. When she moved away from home it was as though her parents were bereaved, but then they gathered themselves together and focused on her new life, making friends with her friends, bringing her food, washing and ironing her clothes and returning them before she even realized they'd gone. They acted as though she was still a little girl and she loved it, basked in it.

She was sorry for anyone whose family didn't treat their children like demigods, but other than that she didn't give it a second thought. James's family lived up in Scotland now and I think a huge part of her was glad she didn't have to dilute her time with her own family. She went up there with him, with good grace, a couple of times a year, but I knew she wasn't impressed by the way they happily said good-bye at the end of a visit. Her own parents would have been distraught at the thought of not seeing her for months, and anything less than tears and promises, fifty pounds from their pension pushed into her handbag and texts as soon as they left the driveway looked to Katie as though a parent didn't care.

As for me, she couldn't understand how I lived in the same town as my parents but rarely saw them. I've never been able to talk to her about that. She just wouldn't get it. Even when we were little, I used to prefer to go to her house. I'd walk into their kitchen and instantly relax. But then Katie loved coming to visit me, too. Our place was different when she was there, and while she played and chatted to my parents, the tension that was the track of my life just disappeared. She had a sunny expression that my mother loved and she was always laughing. It cheered me up just to see her and I think my parents felt the same. I closed my eyes for a second. The last thing I needed was to think about them now.

I reached over to take the glass of wine from James and noticed his guitar leaning against his armchair. "Been playing much?"

He nodded. "A bit."

"Whenever I'm not here," said Katie. "I bet you played every day last week, didn't you?"

He laughed. "More than I do most days."

"He prefers playing when I'm not here," said Katie.

"Because she sings along?"

He grinned at me then. "I can't bear it."

In that moment I was taken back to that summer when we were seventeen; I'd go round to James's house after college and we'd lie at either end of his single bed while he played the guitar and I would think I had the perfect boyfriend. Those months were the happiest of my life. One day Katie came with me, and when he began to play, we were both startled as she started to sing along. Her voice was awful, really high and reedy, and James and I had looked at each other and laughed until we'd cried.

"What?" she kept saying. "What are you laughing at?"

Now Katie and I sat curled up at either end of the sofa, our feet almost touching, and James sprawled in the armchair by the fireplace. In the candlelight it was almost as though no time had passed.

"So," said James, "he's gone, has he?"

In a flash I came back to the present, just in time to see Katie fire him a glance. This time I was the outsider. I was so tempted to turn the tables and remind him that we'd discussed this when he called round to mine the other night, but I knew that would be the end of the evening for all of us.

"You wouldn't know he'd been there," I said and drank some wine. I don't think they realized how difficult it was for me to talk about it.

"And he deleted his phone number?" asked James.

"And his texts and emails," said Katie.

I glared at her.

"Wasn't his number on the call history?"

I shook my head. "The calls to and from him were deleted, too."

James frowned. "But there must have been loads of calls over the years. Nobody else's were deleted?"

"It doesn't look like it. When I got my new phone at Christmas I changed providers and it kept all my contacts, but the call history and text history weren't saved. Obviously my emails were there, but the rest had gone." I shrugged. "It didn't bother me. Why would I want to keep old texts and records of people I rang years ago?"

"And you hadn't backed it up?"

"Only the photos. But he deleted the backups, too."

"Well, it doesn't matter anyway," he said. "It looks as though he isn't using that phone anymore." He poured us another glass of wine. "Did he leave his key behind?"

I nodded. "It was on the hook in the kitchen."

"And," added Katie helpfully, "her old television and books were put back where they'd been before he moved in."

"What?"

"The room looked just as it did before he moved in, didn't it, Hannah?"

I flushed. James had barely glanced into the living room when he called round and hadn't seemed to notice the change. It had been clear he was only looking for Matt. I'd had no intention of letting him know what Matt had done. Okay, if he already knew about it from Katie, that was fine, but I wasn't going to be the one to tell him. Even though our relationship had ended a long time ago, he was an ex and I didn't want to look small in front of him.

"Katie told me he'd taken all his things," said James. He avoided my eyes. "I didn't realize he'd put your stuff back."

"Yep," said Katie. "Even the bedding. It was amazing, the job he did on it."

"Yes," I said. "It was fantastic."

She shut up a little at that.

"So," said James carefully, as though he sensed danger ahead. "You went to see his mum, did you?"

"I didn't intend to go there; I was just driving nearby and thought I'd call in and talk to her." Suddenly I was hot with anger. "Do you know something? That woman spent Christmas Day in my house and didn't say a word about moving!"

"It probably wasn't deliberate," said James. "Maybe she only decided to put it on the market in the New Year and it sold quickly."

"No." I shook my head. "I looked it up on Zoopla. She sold the house on November 30, so she left there a month before she came to us on Christmas Day."

There was silence in the room.

"I didn't realize you could find that out," said Katie.

"It's on Zoopla as soon as the sale's been registered," said James. "Nothing's private anymore."

"I wonder where she's gone to," said Katie. "Is there any way of finding that out?"

"Electoral register?" asked James.

"I don't know." I made a mental note to check.

"I doubt if she's on there," said Katie. "Remember when we moved in here, we clicked a box to say we didn't want our details made public? The council sells on your name and address and you get a load of junk mail otherwise. Wouldn't she have done that?"

"She might not have registered online," said James. "But what good will it do you if you find out where she's gone, anyway? It's not as though you want to speak to her, is it? You didn't have much of a relationship with her, did you?"

"I was civil enough," I snapped. "But you're right, I don't want to see her. I just don't see it as a coincidence, her moving house and him moving out within a few months of each other."

"They're not going to be living together, though, are they?" said Katie. "I know he got on all right with her, but he wouldn't want to move in with her, would he?"

"No," I admitted. "Sometimes she drove him mad. He often came home in a bad mood after seeing her, particularly in the last few months."

"See?" said James. "There's one advantage to living on your own. You don't have to put up with his moods."

I couldn't think of anything polite to say to this and then the curries were delivered and the subject changed.

LATER IN THE evening we sat listening to music, watching the way the shadows in the room danced as the candles flickered. I know I was a bit drunk and I could tell from the way Katie was slurring her words that she was on her way, too. James hadn't drunk as much as us and was flicking through Facebook on his phone and giving us a running commentary. I was still fuming about Matt.

"I wish I knew where he was," I said for the twentieth time that night.

"Are you sure you were getting along all right?" asked Katie. I could hear that note of patience in her voice and it really irritated me.

"Yes," I said. "Nothing was different, that's the thing. We'd been getting on really well. It had been ages since we even argued." I thought of our lives together the last few months. I'd been happy; work had been going well and Matt and I were getting along. There was no reason for him to go like that. Not then.

Katie stood up and started to take the plates out of the room.

When the sound of water running in the kitchen could be heard, James said suddenly, "You hadn't been having arguments then?"

I flushed. "No, we hadn't." I probably said it a bit louder than I meant to.

"Only . . . for him to go off like that . . . Why would he do that if he was happy?"

I felt like my skin was burning from head to toe now. "Well, how do I know? He didn't exactly stop to explain himself, did he?"

"I know you're not going to like this," said James, "but I bet there's another woman involved."

Of course I'd already wondered about that, but when he suggested it, I was instantly livid. "You would say that!"

"What do you mean?"

"Because that's all people think of when someone disappears like this, that they've run off with someone else! How do you think it makes me feel, knowing people think that?"

He shrugged and went back to his phone.

"Which people?" asked Katie, coming back into the room. "Who've you told?"

I shook my head, unwilling to repeat what James had said. "I've only told Sam," I said. "And he couldn't believe it, either."

"He doesn't really know Matt very well, though, does he?" asked Katie. "Besides, Sam wouldn't believe anyone would want to leave you."

They both laughed. It was a long-standing joke with them that Sam had a crush on me.

"You still haven't told your mum and dad?"

I shook my head, my mouth tight.

"Did anyone see him leave?" asked James. "What about your neighbors? Do you think one of them helped him?"

"Sheila and Ray were at their daughter's in Devon," I said. "There's a new family on the other side who moved in that day. Looks like a couple in their twenties with a little boy."

Just then I heard a text message alert. I picked up my bag and searched through it for my phone.

Katie was halfway out of the room but came back to say, "I didn't know anyone had moved in yet. Did they see anything?"

"No idea. I haven't spoken to them. I don't know what time they got there, either. I saw them bring some of their things at about eight o'clock that night but they might have been there all day, for all I know."

"Are you going to ask them?" James was standing now, stretching and yawning, a clear hint that it was time for me to go.

"I don't know," I said slowly. "I haven't even met them yet. It might seem odd just asking them that."

"I wouldn't," said Katie. "They might think you're a bit strange."

"Oh, thanks!"

"You know what I mean. You've got to live next door to them. You don't want their first impression of you to be that your boyfriend's disappeared, do you?"

I know there's a problem that victims can be tainted by the crime committed against them, but I didn't think I'd be in that position, where I couldn't even speak to my neighbors about my own boyfriend going missing without them thinking I was odd.

"I suppose not," I said. "I won't say anything to them."

I'd walked the couple of miles to their house and booked a taxi for the return journey in advance, knowing I'd have a few drinks and wouldn't want to walk home. The taxi sounded its horn then, and James went to fetch my jacket. I opened my phone and glanced down at the message on the screen. When I saw what it said, I nearly jumped out of my skin.

"What's the matter?" said Katie. "Who is it?"

"I don't know," I said. "I don't recognize the number."

She came to stand next to me and turned my hand so that she could see the message.

It said: *I'm home.*

"What?" she said. "Is that Matt?"

"I don't know." I looked at the phone again. "I don't know who it's from."

James came around and looked over my shoulder at the message. "It's just someone messing about," he said. "It's not Matt, is it?" He checked his own phone and held the screen next to mine. "See? They're different numbers."

I hesitated, confused, then everything became clear. "He's changed his number, remember?" I said. I gave Katie a huge hug, nearly lifting her off her feet. "He's back! Katie, he's come back!"

Chapter
Thirteen

THE TAXI RIDE from Katie's house to mine seemed to take ages. On the way I replied to Matt, sending message after message, full of hope and promises:

Back in a minute xxx

Matt, wait for me, home soon xxx

Wait! Won't be long! xxxxxxxxxxx

When we arrived, I flung some money at the driver, who sped off, leaving me standing on the path. I hesitated for a moment. The front of the house was dark. How had he got in without a key? Then reason left me. I flung open the front door and switched on the hall light.

"Matt!" I called. "Matt, I'm home!"

I raced through the hall and into the kitchen. It was in darkness. I flicked the switch and the room flooded with light. There was no one there.

I ran up the stairs, taking them two at a time, and threw open the bedroom door. Again the room was dark and the quilt on the bed was smooth and straight, just as it had been when I'd left the house. I turned to the en suite—it was empty.

I sat on the bed, breathing heavily. My phone was still in my hand and I looked at the message again.

I'm home.

My heart was pounding and my face was covered in a sheen of sweat.

Why had he sent that message if he wasn't here?

I went slowly back downstairs. I opened the living room door, but of course he wasn't there. I knew it was stupid but I checked the cupboard under the stairs and the utility room and then I went to make sure he hadn't locked himself out in the garden. Back inside, I ran up to the spare room and the family bathroom, in case I'd missed something. When I came back downstairs again I was hot with embarrassment.

My phone beeped and I leaped up, thinking it was Matt again, but it was a message from Katie:

Hannah, is he there?

I stared down at the phone. I knew James and Katie would be talking about me. It beeped again:

Has he come back?

I couldn't face that all night so I sent a quick message:

No, it must have been a mistake. He's not here. Night x

For hours I lay in bed, sending text after text to that number, telling Matt that I loved him, that I wanted him to come home to me.

He didn't reply.

Chapter
Fourteen

IT WAS NO surprise when I woke early the next morning to find I had to run to the bathroom just in time to be sick. Hovering over the toilet bowl, I tried to think how much I'd drunk the night before, but just the thought of white wine made me feel even worse.

Later, in the kitchen, I sat in the cool morning light with a glass of water, staring at the garden, trying not to move my head. My head was pounding, partly from the hangover but mainly with all the thoughts slamming round it. I knew I would have to eat before going to work. I looked awful, and if I went into the office smelling of wine I'd likely lose my job.

I showered and dressed, thinking of the day ahead. I had a meeting at a client's office first thing. Lucy would be coming with me to observe; I had to pick her up at the office at 9 a.m. We'd organized the paperwork on Friday, making sure everything was ready and we were both primed for the meeting. I used to love going to visit clients, enjoying the chance to get out of the office for a few hours, but right now all I wanted was to sit at my desk with the blinds pulled down and call Matt's number to ask him why he'd said he was home when he clearly wasn't.

Downstairs, as I put bread into the toaster, I spotted the little pile of Post-it notes on the island. I looked through them again, then sat down to update them.

Olivia moved house on November 30, I wrote.

I searched online for the electoral register and found I'd have to go to the town hall or a main library to view it. Then I grimaced as I read, "Your name and address will be included in the open register unless you ask for them to be removed." I had no doubt Olivia would have made that request but I still made a note to remind myself to call at the library on my way home from work. It had to be worth a try.

On another note I jotted down the phone number that had sent me the message. I'd googled the number the night before but couldn't find it anywhere.

I sat at the island trying to eat some toast, hoping it would ease my queasy stomach, and looking through the pile of notes. I laid them out again in a different formation, but there just wasn't much there. I needed more information than this, otherwise I'd never find out where he was.

With a start I realized I'd been sitting there too long and I'd have to rush. I sent Lucy a text reminding her to be in reception at nine, then quickly put on my makeup. I couldn't afford to turn up looking like I didn't care.

THE MEETING WENT well, I thought, though I noticed Lucy glancing at me occasionally, and I didn't know what was wrong. That worried me; I'd always prided myself on picking up cues but that day I couldn't understand her at all. Later, as we drove back to the office, I confronted her.

"In the meeting, I noticed you staring at me. Was something wrong?"

She jumped a little and blushed. "No, no, there was nothing wrong."

"So why did you keep staring? It was embarrassing." I drove on, gripping the steering wheel. "If you've got something to say, just say it!"

"It's just . . . sometimes you seemed to drift off. As though you'd forgotten what we were talking about. I wondered whether you were all right."

I stared at her. "What? I didn't do that!"

"I just thought you ought to know," she said quietly. "It was only sometimes." She started to backtrack. "Not often."

We drove on in silence. I was sure I hadn't been doing that! I'd paid really close attention to everything that was said. Did it look like I was thinking about something else? I felt cold at the thought. If it looked like I wasn't concentrating, word would get round in no time.

Back at the office I stopped by to see Sam, troubled about what Lucy had said.

"Sam, when we're in meetings, do you sometimes think I'm not paying attention?"

He flushed. "I think you're fine, Hannah. Just a bit distracted, perhaps, nothing else. I don't think anyone else has noticed."

I left his room, determined to work hard. To focus. Within ten minutes I'd googled Matt's number again and sent him four texts.

I CALLED AT the supermarket on my way home that day, having decided to cook something that night. I needed to look after myself. I hadn't eaten properly since Matt left, and after Lucy's comments I knew I needed to get a grip on myself. So I bought chicken and vegetables and when I got home I started to prepare a stir-fry. I was about to chop an onion when I saw the notes on the kitchen island. I turned off the heat under the wok and picked them up.

As though they were a pack of cards, I laid them out on the marble surface and tried to think what I'd missed. Nothing new came to mind. I'd just arranged them into a different order when I glanced over at the dining table.

I blinked.

The square glass vase was still there, full of tulips. This morning the flowers had been blowsy and full blown, their petals about to drop. I'd left them there, thinking I'd throw them away later.

Now the flowers were fresh, their petals dewy in their tight purple buds, their leaves standing to attention.

MY HEAD POUNDED. Was I going mad? I *knew* the flowers had been nearly dead this morning. I hadn't even dared touch them; I'd been in a rush, then, and thought I'd get rid of them when I got home. Lately I'd had too much on my mind to change the water in the vase; by this morning it had been murky and fronds had come away from the stems and were floating in the stagnant water, the petals drooping so they almost touched the table.

So if the flowers were dying this morning and fresh this evening, someone must have replaced them. And it wasn't me. I shook my head. I *knew* it wasn't me. I'd been at work all day! I was sure I hadn't bought any from the supermarket. I opened my purse to find the receipt and swore as I realized I'd thrown it in the bin as I left the shop.

I tried to remember whether I'd even seen tulips in the shop. I couldn't. I was still thinking of the text I'd had the night before; it had been on my mind all day. And yes, purple tulips were my favorite, and yes, I would have replaced them with the same flowers if I'd been able to, but I hadn't. I *hadn't*. I knew my memory had been bad lately, but surely I'd remember that?

I looked in the kitchen bin. There was no plastic wrapping, no empty sachet of flower food in there. All that was there were the remains of the pizza I'd had delivered on Saturday night. I unlocked the kitchen door and checked the bins outside. The recycling bin only contained the pizza box and newspapers that I'd thrown in there on Sunday morning; the other bin had been emptied on Friday and had nothing in it at all.

The garden bin was empty, too. There were no dying tulips anywhere.

I touched the outside of the vase. It was dry. I lifted it and checked the base and the Moroccan tile I'd used to protect the table from damp. Those were both dry, too. There were no drops of water on the table or on the floor. I'd only been in the house for half an hour or so. Surely if I'd filled the vase with water it would be wet?

I went over to the sink. I hadn't used it since early morning and it was dry, too. I sniffed it to see whether stagnant water had been put down the drain, but couldn't smell anything.

My head started to throb. The flowers had been dying; I knew they had!

Then I saw the kitchen roll, hanging from its holder. On Saturday night I'd put the pizza box on the island and it had knocked my glass of wine. I'd grabbed the kitchen roll but the one on the holder only had one sheet left. I'd put a new roll on and ripped off the top sheet to mop up the wine. I knew I hadn't used it since, but looking at it now, I could see more sheets had been torn off.

I took the roll off the holder and put it onto the island. There were new rolls in the cupboard under the sink and I took one out of its plastic wrapper and laid it next to the one from the holder, end to end. The new one was much bigger. Slowly I unwound the new kitchen roll, wrapping the paper around my hand until the two rolls were the same size. I looked down at the paper in my hand. That would be enough to wipe the sink, the table, the vase and the floor, if need be.

I sat down at the island and looked at the two rolls, the paper, the vase of new tulips. I was so confused.

Had Matt been in my house today? Had he bought me flowers? Why would he do that?

And if he hadn't done it, who had?

Chapter
Fifteen

On Friday, Katie sent a message when I was at work:

Hi Hannah, fancy meeting up tonight? James is going to the gym so it'll just be us. x

We had a bit of a routine, Katie and I, where we'd meet up every now and then and go to see a film and have a meal, but when I suggested a film this time, she wasn't up for it.

Just dinner and drinks? Seems ages since we talked on our own. x

We agreed to meet at an Italian restaurant near her house at 8 p.m. I went home first and showered and changed. I knew I should make an effort, but I almost cried when I looked at myself in the mirror. My skin was dry and flaky and there were shadows under my eyes that made me look like I had jet lag. I knew it wouldn't go unnoticed.

When I arrived at the restaurant, I found Katie already there, sitting with a bottle of prosecco and a bowl of olives. She was looking at her phone and smiling; it made me laugh as I remembered one time I'd caught her beaming at her phone and found she was using the camera on it to check her makeup. She looked up as I came toward her, gave me a huge smile and put her phone in her bag.

"You look terrible," she said, almost before I'd sat down. "Are you having trouble sleeping?"

That took the smile off my face. "Well, yes," I said. "Does that surprise you?"

She gave me a concerned look. "You'll be fine soon," she said and poured me a glass of wine. "Now, what shall we have? I'm starving."

We ordered our food and sat chatting while we waited for the starters to arrive. She talked about her job and the recent conference, and another in Toronto she was booked in for later in the year. She made me tell her again about Oxford and the comments the managing partner had made, though really my heart wasn't in it.

When she started to pour me a second glass of wine, I stopped her. "No, thanks, I'm driving. I'll have some water."

"Water? On a Friday night?"

"I haven't been feeling well," I said. "I don't really want a drink." I worried about losing control if I drank too much; driving was a way of not letting my guard down in public.

She looked at me sympathetically, then poured herself another glass. "It will get better, you know," she said. "You'll get over it, don't worry. It happens to all of us."

I raised my eyebrows. Katie would have a fit if someone dumped her, never mind if he moved out without telling her. She'd cried for weeks when she brutally finished with her last boyfriend, but had a miraculous recovery when she bumped into James and they started seeing each other.

I didn't mention the flowers until our main course arrived. I let her start her tortellini, then said casually, "Katie, something really strange has happened."

She put her fork down immediately. "What? What is it?"

"Do you remember when you were in my house the other day? The day after Matt left?"

She frowned. "Something happened then?"

"Do you remember the flowers on the table?"

She stared at me. "The tulips? Purple tulips in the square glass vase?"

I knew she'd remember them; she loved to look at what I had in my house. I always expected to see the same thing at her place a week later. I was the same. I'd already ordered the dress she'd been wearing the other night.

"Do you remember anything about them? Whether they were buds or in full bloom, anything like that?"

She closed her eyes and thought for a moment. "They weren't buds," she said confidently. "They weren't fully blown, either. They were lovely, I remember that. Really fresh. I bought some just like them the next day. They made me think of summer."

"Me, too," I said. "So how long would you think they'd last after that?"

She picked up her fork and popped another tortellini into her mouth. "I don't know. A few days? A week maybe? It depends if you put any of that stuff in the water."

She knew I would have. I was always careful with things like that.

We ate in silence for a few moments, then she said, "Why? Didn't they last long?"

"Yes, they did," I said. "On Monday before I went to work I was looking at them. They were just about to collapse. You know when the petals are just starting to fall off? And I remember thinking, 'They need to be thrown out,' but I was in a rush so I thought I'd do it later."

"Right," she said. She sounded bored now and I wondered whether I normally talked about such mundane things.

"So I went to work and got back at about six. And the flowers had changed."

Now she was interested. "What?"

"They'd changed," I said. "There were new flowers in the vase."

She put her fork down. "What are you on about?"

"When I left the house in the morning, the flowers needed to be thrown out. When I came back, hours later, there were new flowers there. They were buds. Purple buds."

"But still tulips?"

"Yes, of course they were still tulips!" I said impatiently. "But they'd changed. Don't you see?"

"Well, no, I don't," she said. "Are you saying your tulips had regenerated?"

I nodded.

She tilted her head and looked at me with a sympathetic gaze. "Or maybe, just *maybe*, you'd bought new ones and forgotten? Which is more likely, Hannah?"

I tried to ignore that whisper of doubt that told me she was right. I'd been to the supermarket just an hour before I noticed the flowers. No, I couldn't let myself think that I'd bought them and put them in the vase without remembering. I took another sip of water. "Or maybe," I said, "someone put new flowers there."

She stared. "Who'd do that?"

I looked at her meaningfully.

"What? Matt? Don't be daft."

"Who else could it be?"

"But Matt left his keys behind! You told us that on Sunday."

I faltered. "Maybe he kept a copy."

She raised her eyebrows. "Do you really think he intended to come back?"

"He sent a text *telling* me he was back!"

"That wasn't him!"

She spoke so loudly that quite a few people around us turned to stare. I flushed and rooted in my handbag.

"Look!" I whispered, passing her my phone. "Read the message! It says, 'I'm home.'"

She took the phone from me and stared down at the screen. "But James told you that wasn't Matt's number. You saw his number on James's phone, remember? It didn't match this one. It could be anyone, Hannah. It could be a wrong number or anything."

I knew it wasn't, but there wasn't a lot of point in saying anything. We ate our dinner in silence and it was only when we were given the dessert menu that we started to talk again, this time studiously avoiding the subject of Matt.

THE RESTAURANT WAS only around the corner from her house, so Katie didn't need a lift. I'd parked down a side road and she walked there with me. Just before we reached my car, she said, "Oy, Hannah."

"What?"

She pointed to a dismal display of flowers in a large concrete bowl on the pavement. "Take some of those home and liven them up a bit, will you?"

She laughed and waved good-bye as I got into the car. I was scowling at her and thinking about the flowers, thinking I must be mad, that they *couldn't* have changed, as I put my key in the ignition and switched on the engine. I put my lights on and reversed a little, so that I could pull out onto the road.

The opening bars of a song started to play. I paused and listened. It was "Stand by Me." I smiled. I loved that song. I glanced down to see which radio station was on, then braked sharply.

The music system showed a CD was playing. I frowned. I didn't play CDs in the car; I either listened to the radio or used Bluetooth to play my iPod. I didn't even have that song on a CD. Matt used to have it on vinyl; we used to play that Ben E. King album a lot when he first moved in.

I ejected the CD. It was a blank one, used for recording at home. Scrawled on it in handwriting I didn't recognize was: *Hannah*.

Chapter
Sixteen

I PLAYED THAT track on a loop that night, sitting on the living room floor with my back against the sofa. In the early days, when Matt first moved in, we played every album of his. We'd sit there in the evening with a bottle of wine and talk about our pasts and what we hoped for our futures. I'd tell him about my day, he'd tell me about his, then he'd kiss me and before we knew it we'd be on the floor and the album would be starting again from the beginning. This song, "Stand by Me," had been an old favorite and I had to close my eyes to stop myself thinking of the nights we'd played it. I couldn't afford to get sentimental; I needed to think.

I had only two sets of car keys. One was in the kitchen, on the hook with Matt's house key. The other was always with me. I kept my house keys on the same key ring and I never left the house without them. As soon as I got home I'd checked that the spare car key was on the hook and it was; nothing had changed.

The problem was that the CD had started as soon as I turned the ignition. On the way to the restaurant I'd been listening to a program on the radio about David Bowie and I'd turned it up, thinking about the school discos Katie and I would go to where "Heroes" would be played and everyone would go wild. The song had ended just as I parked the car.

I'd never known Matt to burn a CD. If he wanted me to listen to something, he'd tell me and I'd download it onto my phone or my iPod. I couldn't even remember the last time he'd been in my car; when we went out together we tended to go in his. Besides, I knew that wasn't the point. The fact was that when I turned my car engine on, it automatically played whatever was playing the last time it was turned off. Same channel or device. And I knew that in the two years I'd had that car, I'd never played a CD.

So who had?

WORK WAS BECOMING increasingly difficult. I still wasn't sleeping well and most nights saw me sitting in the kitchen with a bottle of wine, making notes and trying to figure out where Matt had gone.

I didn't know what had happened to me. Although I'd never exactly been a calm person, now I was constantly agitated. It was as though I was on high alert. I thought about Matt all the time, sometimes about the things I'd liked about him, sometimes about the ways he'd frustrated or annoyed me. It wasn't as though I'd elevated him to sainthood: far from it. The thing that really got to me was that I didn't know where he was. It was as though there was a clue that was just out of reach, something just at the corner of my eye, and if I was fast enough I'd see it and I'd know where to find him.

So I'd sit there with just the glow of the laptop lighting the kitchen and I'd go through my notes, moving them around the marble surface of the island, trying to find that missing link.

Then something would occur to me and I'd be focused again, back onto Google, beavering away, in search of him. When I was active, when I was looking for him, it was almost as though I could forget the shock of his leaving. I became absorbed, forgetting in a way that this was personal. I looked up private detectives and their techniques, and wondered what I might have found on his iPad or his phone if I'd looked at them weeks ago. I hadn't done that for months, though.

The next morning I'd jolt into consciousness, aware of the blinding light coming through the window, knowing if the sun was shining that fiercely then I was late. I'd rush into the bathroom and dress in a hurry, and although I tried to look professional, I knew I was slipping.

Lucy would be waiting for me each day in the office with a cup of tea ready. Up until now she used to greet me eagerly and seemed to love the time we'd spend together in the morning, chatting about what we had to do that day. I would guide her through her work and talk to her about the jobs I had to do, so that she could learn more about the business. Later in the afternoon we'd meet again and go through what we'd both done that day. George Sullivan, my manager, had done the same thing for me and it had really helped me when it was time for me to progress. Lucy was ambitious, I knew that and I liked it. I saw something of my younger self in her. Lately, though, I'd noticed she seemed impatient with me.

She used to be a bit in awe of me, I think. As well as talking to me about work, she'd come to me for advice in her personal life and for help in her studies, and she'd always notice what I was wearing and ask where I'd bought my clothes. Now, though she'd sit opposite me and take notes about what I wanted her to do that day, often she'd be reminding me, rather than the other way around. Sometimes I'd catch sight of an expression on her face and recognize it as a mixture of pity and contempt. Though I'd flush with anger, I'd know it was justified. She used to admire the way I worked and I no longer seemed able to work in that way. She would never have looked at me like that in the past. She wouldn't have had any reason to, though.

ONE MORNING AFTER Matt had been gone for nearly three weeks, Sam came into my office. I hadn't been avoiding him, I just hadn't had time to meet him at break times lately. I saw Lucy glance up as he came into my room and she stayed there, looking at us until I gave her a pointed stare and she blushed and turned away. He closed the door then and I wondered whether she was another one who thought he and I were having a fling. She knew Sam was living with Grace; Lucy had met her at our office parties tons of times and she knew I was with Matt, too. I hadn't told anyone, apart from Sam, about him leaving me, and it really annoyed me that she thought either of us would be unfaithful.

I looked back at Sam. He was pale and nervous.

"What's up?"

"Have you got a minute?"

I glanced at my screen, eager to get back to Google. I'd remembered that I hadn't phoned Matt's barber, Johnny, to ask whether he'd seen him. I knew it was a wild card, but I'd come to the end of the road—I hadn't a clue where he was. We'd bumped into Johnny one time when we were in a restaurant in Liverpool, so I thought maybe he'd seen Matt sometime over the last month.

"What is it?" I knew how I sounded. Impatient. Surly.

"I'm worried about you."

"No need," I said quickly, calling up Google. "There's nothing wrong with me."

"Hannah," he said carefully, "I'm *really* worried about you."

I looked away from the screen at that. "Why?"

He hesitated. "You've changed," he said. "Since you and Matt split up. Has something happened? You were always so . . ."

"So what?" I snapped and he jumped.

"So professional. Smart. I've been worried about you for weeks now."

I glared at him and his voice trailed off.

"I don't think I'm any different at all," I said. "Obviously it upset me when Matt left, but I'm okay. I'm dealing with it. You can't expect me to be back to normal already."

"I don't," he said. "Of course I don't. But you seem so . . . so disturbed by it."

"'Disturbed'?" I hissed, unable to keep up the pretense any longer. "What do you mean, 'disturbed'? Have you any *idea* what I'm going through?"

He flushed. "But you said . . ."

"Get out," I said. "I haven't got time for this."

He turned and left the room, his face scarlet and his eyes averted. Lucy continued to work at her computer, but I noticed her gaze stayed on Sam until he reached his own office and shut the door.

I pulled my keyboard closer and entered "Johnny barber Liverpool" into the search bar; over 800,000 results showed up.

I sighed.

If only people would realize, just for one minute, how hard it was to find him.

Chapter
Seventeen

LATER I CAUGHT sight of myself in the ladies' loos. Prior to Disappearance Day I'd made a point of going to the cloakrooms mid-morning, lunchtime and mid-afternoon to make sure I looked okay. I'd always go just before a meeting, too. I'd keep my straighteners in my handbag and while they were heating up I'd powder my nose, touch up my eyelashes, put some gloss on my lips and spray some perfume around. It meant I could go back to my desk confident and happy that I looked the best I could. That was something I'd learned in my first week at work; we'd had a training session from one of the female directors and I saw her in the cloakrooms later. It took her just a couple of minutes to make herself look great. She saw me looking at her and told me she did it three times a day and it gave her confidence. She warned me that she needed all the help she could get, working in a firm like this where most of the partners and directors were male, and said that a woman who wanted to move up the ranks couldn't afford to let her guard down for a second. She was right.

Today, when I saw myself in the mirror, I realized I *had* let my guard down. It had been down for weeks and it showed. It really, really showed.

My hair was lank and tousled. I blushed, unable to remember whether I'd even brushed it that morning. It would be clear to anyone it hadn't been washed for days. I took my hairbrush out of my bag and tried to tidy it up. My straighteners were at home and had been unused since the day Matt left. I had makeup on, I hadn't sunk so low that I'd come to work without it, but my face was dry and pale. I looked exhausted. Dark shadows lay under my eyes and the skin around them was starting to thin and wrinkle. My lipstick had long gone and I pulled a tube out of my bag and applied it, but somehow it made things worse. I looked ill without it, haggard with it. I scrubbed it off and put some gloss on but that only made the rest of my face look drawn and drained of energy. I dabbed my mouth with tissue so that the gloss was barely a sheen.

I pulled out my perfume and gave my wrists a quick spray. It was a Chanel fragrance, Chance. I'd bought it a few weeks ago, ready for my trip to Oxford. A kind of good luck charm. I looked down at the bottle and frowned. That had worked well, hadn't it? I threw it into the bin and rinsed my wrists until the scent had gone.

As I walked past Sam's office I saw him working, his shoulders hunched and strained. It was obvious he was avoiding looking at me. I paused. I was going to lose his friendship if I wasn't careful. I knocked on his door—a first in all the time I'd known him—and went into his office, shutting the door firmly behind me. The last thing I wanted was for someone to overhear me.

"I'm really sorry I shouted at you," I said. "I shouldn't have done that."

"It's okay," he said, with a relieved smile. "I know you're having a tough time. Is there anything I can do for you?"

"Well, there is, actually."

"Anything. Just say."

"Do you know the name of your barber?"

His eyes nearly popped out of his head. "What?"

"Your barber," I said impatiently. "What's his name?"

"Umm, I think it's Sharik."

"But you know his name. And does he know yours?"

He shook his head. "I don't think so. He calls me 'mate.' He calls us all 'mate.' We don't have to book, so we don't have to give a name. Why?"

I looked down. "No reason."

"Are you going to book a hair appointment?"

"Oh no," I said. I shuddered at the thought of someone touching me. Then I remembered the way I'd looked earlier, the state of my hair. "I'll make one soon. Don't worry about it."

For the next few nights I planned my outfit for work before I went to bed. I made sure my clothes were clean and pressed, my shoes polished and a new pair of tights lay next to my underwear. The alarm was set for 6:30 a.m. so that I'd have time to wash my hair and do my makeup.

I did get up at the right time each morning but it was my stomach that woke me rather than the alarm. I'd be halfway to the bathroom before I was fully conscious and, more often than not, as soon as I was sick, the alarm would beep in unison.

By the end of that week, although my hair was still clean and glossy, I'd lost so much weight that my clothes were baggy on me and I looked as though I hadn't slept for weeks. Which, of course, I hadn't.

I walked past Sam's office and by the time I reached my own desk an email from him was waiting for me.

Meeting room one, now. Bring a file.

Quickly I took a random file from the cabinet and realized I should have been working on it anyway. When I got to the room I saw he'd pulled down the internal blinds and put the "Meeting in Progress" sign on the door.

He closed the door behind me and turned to me, his face full of concern. "Hannah, you look awful."

My instinct was to say something sharp in return, but I held back. I needed his friendship. "I know. I was sick again this morning. That's every day this week. I feel dreadful but I've got a meeting with George at eleven and I've got so much work to do on that account I can't see how I'll manage it all."

He must have known I'd spent too much time messing around trying to find Matt, because I saw a flash of irritation cross his face, but he spoke kindly enough. "Come on," he said. "You've got ninety minutes. I'm not busy at the moment. Let's see if we can sort it out." He touched my shoulder tentatively. "You'll be fine."

My eyes filled with tears at his gesture, but I knew it would be a long time before I'd feel all right.

"Unless . . ." he said. He lowered his voice, though we were the only people in the room. "Oh God, Hannah, I've just thought. You've been sick and you're tired all the time. Are you sure you're not pregnant?"

Chapter
Eighteen

THE REST OF the day passed in a daze. It was impossible to concentrate. I stopped Sam in his tracks, telling him not to be ridiculous, and we focused on the work, with him coaching me through the report I'd written, reminding me to make notes at particular points so that I wouldn't forget what to say. I've never had to have anyone help me like that and I smarted with embarrassment, but the truth was, I couldn't do it alone that day. In the end I had to explain to my manager that I was suffering from headaches and was a bit behind with the work. I don't think it went down too well; George has a low tolerance for illness and prides himself on never having a day off sick. I was like that myself until recently. Sam was the only person at work who knew that Matt had gone and I could tell from the way they looked at me that others were wondering what was up with me, though no one had dared to ask.

After the meeting with George I shut myself away in my office, determined to focus on work. I could see Sam in his office on the other side of the room, see the way he'd glance over at me every few minutes. I felt on show, as though part of me was revealed. And of course all I could think of was pregnancy.

When I first met Matt he'd said he wanted a family, but lately he hadn't mentioned it. I frowned. I'd told him I wanted to be made director at least before I even thought about children. I hadn't been interested in a family, not at that stage in my career. It was always something I assumed I'd want in the future, rather than right now.

I sent Katie a text:

Sam thinks I might be pregnant.

Within ten seconds there was a reply:

What? Do you think you might be? What's Sam got to do with it?

At that moment my office phone rang and I had to deal with a client's inquiry about some work I'd done for them a few months back. In that time, text after text came through. The first one pinged and I hurried to turn off the sound, but I could see the messages flashing up on my screen, fast and furious.

Do you really think you might be pregnant?

Call me! I'm in Edinburgh and can't come round.

What will you do? I thought you were on the pill?

The last one came through just after I'd put down the landline.

I know this is a bit personal, Hannah, but when did you last have sex?

I glared at the screen. Katie really was losing all sense of boundaries. I ignored her texts, knowing it was the fastest way to irritate her. She must have realized she'd gone too far because her next one, a couple of hours later, said:

Sorry. I'm just worried about you. xx

I didn't answer that one, either. After her question, all I could think of was the last time Matt and I had slept together. We'd both come home late one night a few weeks before he disappeared and decided to go out for a meal instead of cooking. Things were going well for both of us; I'd had an appraisal that had been so complimentary I was still pink with pleasure when I met Matt hours later and one of his projects had completed early, which meant he'd got a bonus. We had a few drinks that night and it was suddenly just like the old days, when I'd only see him at weekends.

We'd walked to the restaurant and on our way home we held hands and then, when I tripped over a curbstone, he put his arm around me and turned toward me and kissed me there, on the street. We made it home in record time and within seconds we were on our bed and it was fast and frantic, just like it used to be. Afterward we lay there panting and sweating and I remember laughing and curling up to him, telling him I loved him.

I frowned now, thinking about that. Had he said it to me, too? I remember he'd pulled me toward him and kissed my hair and told me I smelled lovely, but had he told me he loved me? It seemed to me that I'd remember if he hadn't, but then surely I'd remember if he had? We'd got ready for bed quickly and I do remember it wasn't long before he was asleep. I'd lain next to him feeling so relaxed, then snuggled up behind him, put my arm around him and was asleep within minutes.

Had I really got pregnant that night? I felt a surge of panic. I'd have to find him and tell him! I couldn't go through that on my own.

ON MY WAY home from work that night I stopped at a supermarket and wandered through the store, putting shampoo and toothpaste into my basket. I looked at the aisle where the pregnancy tests were. A young mum was there with a toddler in a buggy, her face pale as she compared prices. I walked around until the aisle was empty, then went back and put a couple of tests in my basket. I felt calm and icy, quite detached from what was happening.

When I got home I went upstairs to my bedroom, flung my jacket onto the bed and kicked off my shoes. I put on my pajamas and dressing gown and went into the bathroom, locking the door. I don't know who I thought was going to come in.

I'd taken a pregnancy test before, of course; hasn't almost every woman my age? I hadn't done so for many years, though, and I tried never to think of that time of my life, but as I sat there waiting in the locked bathroom, it was almost as if I was that girl again, panicking and wondering what the hell I should do. Just like last time, I knew before the result appeared what it would say. I did the other test straightaway, hoping it would say something different, but knowing it wouldn't.

It didn't.

I sat holding the tests on the bathroom floor, the tiles cold against my legs. I didn't know what to do. I think I was more desperate then than at any time in the last few weeks. Then I found my phone in my bag and sent Katie a text:

Just taken two tests. I'm pregnant.

Chapter
Nineteen

KATIE CALLED THAT night, but I turned the sound off on my mobile and pulled the landline lead from its socket. I lay on my bed as the evening grew dark and watched as my mobile lit up and Katie's name appeared on the screen again and again. I couldn't talk to her. I didn't know what I would say. There was nothing she could say that could help me now. I needed peace and quiet to think about what I was going to do.

Later, I went down to the kitchen, suddenly starving. I opened the fridge and the cold white light made my eyes tired and sore. A bottle of chilled sauvignon blanc sat in the wine rack. Condensation misted the glass and suddenly I was desperate for the release it would give me. My hand stretched out for it without thinking. I unscrewed the lid, heard the whisper of air as it left the bottle and stopped dead in my tracks.

I had to stop drinking.

Slowly I screwed the lid back on and put the bottle back into the fridge, then closed the door. There was food in the freezer that I could cook, but suddenly everything was too much effort. I took an apple and some biscuits instead and ate them as I sat at the island before going back to bed, my hand on my stomach, my thoughts all over the place.

SAM WAS REALLY kind to me at work. He came into my office first thing and asked whether I was okay. I told him he was right, I was pregnant but I didn't want to talk about it. He nodded and said, "Congratulations. Grace will be very jealous."

"Don't tell anyone here, will you? I need time."

"Of course not," he said. "I wouldn't dream of it."

We sat in silence then; when there's something so huge to discuss it's hard to think of anything else to chat about. When my phone beeped with a text from the garage reminding me my car was booked in for a service that afternoon, he immediately offered to take it in for me at lunchtime. "So you can rest," he said, and when I gave him a sharp glance, he said, "I know you're working hard."

If only I was. My days were spent investigating Matt's disappearance; my job was done in the odd spare moments I had when I was stuck for somewhere else to look.

At 10:30, my office phone rang. It was Katie.

"Hannah?" she said, her voice low and furious. There was an echo on the phone; it sounded as though she was in the ladies' toilets. "What the hell are you doing sending me a text like that, then ignoring my messages and not answering your phone?"

"I'm sorry," I said, making a note in pencil of the phone number of a hotel in Manchester which was opposite a bar Matt and I had been to when we first met. "I had a lot to think about."

"But . . ." I could hear her confusion. "Are you sure you're pregnant? I thought you didn't want children yet."

"You know what they told us in sex ed," I said, searching now for hotels near John Lennon Airport and wondering whether he'd flown somewhere from there. I stopped to make a note to remind myself to check which flights had left Liverpool that day. "No contraceptive is foolproof."

"But now . . ." she said. "Of all the times for it to happen. Why now?" She lowered her voice. "Were you having a lot of sex? Was that it?"

I laughed and realized it was almost the first time since Matt had gone. "That's a bit personal, isn't it?"

"Or did you forget your pill? What happened?"

"I've no idea," I said. "I've been sick the last few mornings and Sam asked whether I might be pregnant. I hadn't thought about it so I took a test."

"And you are?" she said. "Oh, Hannah, what are you going to do?"

"How do you mean?" I said.

She whispered, "Are you going to keep it?"

I flinched.

"How many weeks are you?"

"It's early days," I said. "And Katie . . ."

"What?"

"It's not very nice asking someone if they're keeping the baby when they've just told you they're pregnant. Don't you think congratulations might be in order?"

I heard her take a deep breath, then I ended the call.

I did no work that day. Absolutely nothing. Luckily a meeting which had been scheduled for eleven o'clock was postponed for a few days, so I sat at the computer and found the phone numbers for all the hotels in the Manchester and Chester areas. I then phoned each one—this did have the advantage of making me look busy if anyone was looking through the glass—and asked whether Matt had stayed there recently. He hadn't, or at least they said he hadn't. Or he hadn't used his own name. At that thought my head throbbed. How was I going to find him if he'd used a different name?

AT THE END of the day Sam came in to see me.

"Come on," he said, "I'll give you a lift to the garage."

I stared at him blankly.

"I took your car to be serviced at lunchtime," he reminded me. "You need to pick it up."

"Oh," I said. "Yes, of course." I'd completely forgotten about that. "Thanks for taking it."

On the way out to the car park he said, "I've just remembered I need to take a file home tonight. You wait in the car; I won't be a minute."

He beeped open his car and I sat there waiting while he went back into the building. The interior was clean and shiny and vacuumed; I could see how Sam spent his weekends. I pulled down the visor and winced as I saw my reflection. I took out some makeup and tried to repair the damage, then searched in my bag for a tissue. There weren't any there. I glanced around the car and opened the glove compartment, found a handy pack of tissues and took one. Underneath the pack was a phone. I glanced up at the office building. I could see Sam on the tenth floor, running down the stairs, a folder in his hand. He never used the lift; he said using the stairs meant he didn't have to go to the gym. I don't know what made me do it, but I switched the phone on. A prompt appeared, asking me to enter a four-digit code.

It wasn't that I wanted to read anything on his phone; it was more of an idle challenge to see whether I could guess the code. A timed challenge, if you like, given that he'd be back at any minute. I typed in the day and month of his birthday, but it was rejected, as was the month and year. I entered Grace's birthday but that was rejected, too.

I glanced up at the building again and after a second or two I saw him on the staircase. He was now on the fourth floor. I typed in "1234," thinking he might have left it at the default, but he hadn't.

Adrenaline pumped through me. I've always been competitive, even against myself.

Which number would he choose?

He was on the second floor now. And then I thought of his extension number. I typed in "7872" and the screen changed.

Yes!

The door to the building burst open and Sam came running out. I switched the phone off and put it back in the glove compartment with the packet of tissues on top of it. Looking straight at him, I closed the glove compartment and smiled as he ran toward me.

"I was looking for a tissue in the glove compartment," I said when he got into the car. "How come you've got another phone in there?"

I wasn't about to tell him I'd guessed its passcode.

"What?" He reached over, flicked open the compartment door and looked inside. "Oh, that. It's an old one. I dropped it one day last summer and it just stopped working. I put it there when I bought a new one and keep forgetting to get rid of it." He leaned over again and picked it up, putting it into his pocket. "I'll chuck it away when I get home."

We sat in silence as he drove me to the garage. He was a good driver, concentrating fully on the road ahead. I watched him, this man I'd known for years, since he was a boy, really, fresh from university. I'd never known him to lie before; I'd thought his face was transparent. Now he drove calmly, without a flicker of deceit on his face, though he must have known, just as I did, that the phone was working and the battery was full.

Chapter
Twenty

I ARRIVED HOME that night vowing to actually do some work the next day. I'd had a few emails later on in the afternoon reminding me of reports which were due at the end of the week; I'd never had to be reminded before and blushed as I realized I'd handed a couple of things in late over the last month or so. I thought I'd spend the evening making a list of all the things I had to do over the next few days and try to break the tasks down into their smallest parts so that I'd have a chance of at least doing something. In the hallway I put down my bag and pulled out the notes I'd made, ready to go through them again in the kitchen. Then I stopped.

The hair at the back of my neck prickled.

Something's different.

I called out, "Hello!" and crept forward, pushing open the living room door. I put my head around the door—nothing had changed. There was nowhere anyone could be hiding in there; the sofas were bang up against the walls and it was impossible for anyone to hide under the coffee table. I pulled the door gently to and tiptoed toward the kitchen.

The kitchen door was open, just as I'd left it that morning. A quick glance around showed me that nobody was there. The late evening sun streamed through the French doors and flooded the room, dust motes floating in its rays. I walked further into the room, past the island, and looked out into the garden.

Sheila was sitting at her patio table, making up hanging baskets. I opened the back door and called over to her.

"Sheila, have you been out here long?"

"Yes, for a couple of hours. It's a gorgeous evening, isn't it?"

"Did you hear anything?"

She stood up, her face pink from the sun.

"Hear anything? What do you mean?"

"Here. In my house. Did you hear anything this afternoon? Or just now?"

"I heard you call 'Hello,'" she said. "Sorry, were you talking to me then?"

"No, it's okay. I just thought I heard something."

"Maybe it's Matt. Is he around? I haven't seen his car for a while."

I swallowed. "He's away at the moment. Work."

I could see she was revving up to ask me where he'd gone to and when he'd be back and what he was doing, so I thanked her and went back into the kitchen.

On the step I stopped still.

The kettle was next to the fridge, hidden from view when I'd entered the kitchen from the hall. Now that I was coming in from the garden I could see a thin wisp of steam trailing from its spout.

Slowly I reached out and touched the kettle.

It was warm.

"MATT?" I SHOUTED. "Matt, is that you?" I raced through the hallway and upstairs. "Are you there?"

I burst into every room, shouting his name. I looked everywhere, in ridiculous places, under the bed, in the wardrobes, thinking maybe, just maybe, he was playing a trick on me.

When I'd searched all the rooms I sat on the bed, my heart pounding. He must be here. He *must* be! I stood up more calmly and went to each room again. Nothing had changed from that morning. My toothpaste lay on the basin where I'd left it. The quilt was still pulled back to air the bed. Yesterday's shoes were strewn on the floor and a pound coin that had fallen from my purse the night before sat on the bedside table.

I sat down again, trembling. Then everything came at once: his disappearance, my fruitless searches, having to live on my own. Tears rained down my face. I rubbed my eyes with the back of my hand and black streaks of wet mascara slid across my cheeks. Soon I was sobbing loudly.

All I wanted was for him to have come home as usual, to put the kettle on before having a quick shower, to be sitting there drinking tea at the kitchen table, ready and waiting for me to get back from work.

Then common sense took hold and I thought about the weather, how warm it had been today, how Sheila had looked sunburned from sitting in the garden. The sun had come through the French doors, burning through the glass. The kettle had been caught in its rays. Of course Matt hadn't been here. The sun had warmed the kettle, that was all. I'd check again tomorrow; I knew the same thing would happen then.

I scrubbed my face in the bathroom and went downstairs. The beam of sunlight had moved slightly and the room was cooler now. I touched the kettle again and thought what an idiot I'd been. It was just slightly lukewarm. The kind of temperature you'd expect if a metal object sat in a sunny kitchen all afternoon.

Of course Matt hadn't been here. Why would he come in and boil the kettle, then go again? It didn't make any sense at all.

And then I stopped. The wall behind the kettle was checkered in alternate dark green and white tiles. I frowned and touched a green tile.

It was wet with condensation.

Chapter
Twenty-one

THE NEXT MORNING I woke to more texts from Katie:

Have you told your mum yet?

Does anyone else know?

The last one read:

Is it OK if I tell James?

I scowled at that and switched my phone off. I did love Katie, but she was really getting on my nerves lately. I hated the thought of her gossiping about this with James and I knew, I just knew, she would have already told her mum. I could imagine it now, her mum's eyes full of sympathetic tears as Katie told her in low, confidential tones all about my private life. I'd get back to her soon enough but in the meantime I needed to think about Matt coming to the house the day before.

I lay in bed for another half hour, risking making myself late, then jumped up to get ready. I still had the image in my mind of how I'd looked the other day and knew I couldn't let that happen again. The problem was that although I hadn't been sick again, I felt nauseous and exhausted and weird.

I managed to work that day, though I still hadn't written out a to-do list and worried there was something I'd forgotten. I asked Sam to sit with me after work for an hour to help me with something I needed for a meeting in the morning. He agreed, but I knew he was busy, too, and he'd have to take work home to catch up. I just didn't think I could do it on my own and I hated myself for that. I needed to regain control. My manager, George, had asked me in the corridor whether everything was all right, but I was able to reassure him I was fine.

"Make sure you take a good holiday this summer," he said. "Take that young man of yours somewhere hot—it'll make a new woman of you."

I smiled so hard my face ached. "I will," I said. "Don't worry."

THAT NIGHT KATIE came round. I'd had a feeling she'd turn up, though she hadn't called first to see whether I'd be in. From my living room window I saw her pull into the driveway and sit there for a few minutes, staring into space. My phone beeped then and I grabbed it, hoping it was Matt. It was a message from my dad.

I miss you, too. See you later. xx

I closed my eyes. I knew what that meant. Sure enough, within a couple of seconds the phone vibrated in my hand.

That was meant for your mother. Ignore it.

My stomach clenched tight as a knot. *He's at it again.* The first time I'd realized was when I was thirteen. School had closed at lunchtime at the end of the autumn term, and Katie and I had caught the bus into Liverpool to buy Christmas presents. The city center was packed and we were looking at the clothes in the window of Topshop when I saw my father walking down a narrow street just off the main road. He was talking to a woman and smiling. I remember registering how different he looked.

I told Katie to stay there, that I'd be back in a minute, and I followed him up the street, making sure I kept behind a family so that if he turned around he wouldn't notice me. I saw the woman was linking arms with him. I frowned. Had she hurt herself? Why was she holding on to him?

And then they stopped at a shop window and he looked down at her and she reached up and kissed his mouth. I saw a wedding ring on her finger as she put her hand on his shoulder.

Suddenly everything made sense. I went back to Katie, who'd hardly noticed I'd gone, and listened as she pointed out all the things she liked in the shop window. I tried to join in but I was worried I'd start to cry. I couldn't have told her. I never could talk to her about my family. How would she ever understand?

Now all those feelings came rushing back and for a wild moment I felt like calling my dad to tell him what I thought of him, but I knew what the outcome of that would be. I threw the phone onto the sofa and went out to Katie's car. She jumped when she saw me and climbed out, passing me a Tupperware box from the backseat.

"Sorry, I was daydreaming. My mum's made you a cake. She hopes you're okay."

I stiffened. "Thanks. You shouldn't have worried her."

"Oh, she wasn't worried," she said blithely. "She loves a crisis." She leaned over to hug me. "Fancy eating some dinner with me?"

I flinched from her touch. Since Matt had left, I felt like I'd lost a layer of skin and any human contact made me feel sore and edgy.

She squeezed me tighter, ignoring my resistance, and I breathed in a familiar smell. She was wearing Chanel Chance.

Suddenly she let me go and reached into the backseat for a couple of pizza boxes. I didn't have the heart to tell her I was sick to the back teeth of pizza. She passed them to me and I balanced them on top of the Tupperware box so that she could get the bottles of sparkling water from the footwell.

"Thanks," I said. "I've hardly eaten anything today."

She said nothing and when I looked at her closely I saw that under her makeup her face was pale and her eyes were pink and swollen.

"Everything okay, Katie?"

She nodded. "It's just work," she said. "I hate that place. I can't wait to leave."

It seemed only a month or two ago that she'd sat there bragging about her job, how much they loved her, how much more money she'd be making soon. I knew she was very ambitious; I'd seen it even when she was young. I used to think that if people could get somewhere just on willpower, she'd be right at the top. Knowing that had always been the impetus I'd needed to work even harder. It seemed as though she'd reached a point where she was wondering whether it was all worth it, but I knew she'd find it was in the end. I knew that for me, too, once I'd found Matt I'd be back on track again at work. The thought of promotion didn't fill me with the same excitement as the thought of finding Matt, but for Katie, in a stable relationship with James, her job was everything to her.

Katie was the kind of girl who always played down how hard she was working. For tests in school she'd deny on her mother's life that she'd studied at home while I worked every moment I could, scared to fail, terrified that people would see my true worth. She'd get her results, the same as mine, and say, "I'm so lucky; I didn't do a minute's work on that!" And we'd both know she had, that she'd sat up in her room, working and working, while telling me that she couldn't be bothered, that she'd been watching television or reading *Cosmo*. We also both knew I'd never confront her.

She was loyal, though, the fiercest friend I could have wished for, the one who always had my back. Whenever we had a few drinks and were reminiscing about the old days, we'd talk about Mr. Harper, our teacher when we were ten, who'd taken against me for no apparent reason. Whatever I did, it was wrong. I knew it, he knew it, the whole class knew it. One day I was at his desk and he was telling me off for something or other when Katie asked him if she could be excused. He told her to wait; he was busy. He should have known she wasn't well, as her face was pale and her eyes were bulging, but he made her wait in line until he'd managed to make me cry. That was always his goal; we never knew why. That day, after I was finally reduced to tears, he'd looked up at Katie and said, "What?" as though it wasn't his job to help us. She'd opened her mouth to reply and was sick in his pencil case.

Never had we seen him move so fast. She insisted afterward that it was his punishment for bullying me and now, whenever we were reminiscing, she'd imitate him as he shot out of his chair.

Now she came into the hall and was about to follow me into the kitchen when I remembered the notes I'd left on the island. That morning I'd shuffled them around and spread them out in a kind of grid system. I found this method the easiest to work with at the moment. I knew I couldn't let Katie see it, though. She'd think I was mad. Or pathetic. I didn't know which would be worse.

"Come in here," I said, ushering her into the living room. "Sit down."

I put the pizza and cake on the coffee table and lit the lamps.

"How are you?" she said.

"Oh, okay," I said. "Hold on, I'll just get plates." I flicked the television on and passed her the remote control, then went into the kitchen and snatched up the notes, pushing them into the empty bread bin.

I was just in time. As I busied myself with glasses and plates, Katie brought the pizza into the kitchen. "Let's eat in here," she said. She opened cupboards and drawers. I didn't ask what she was looking for but guessed it was some sign of Matt.

"You won't find anything," I said sharply.

She closed a drawer. "What?"

"Any sign of Matt. There's nothing left of his here, you know. I've checked everywhere."

She looked a little embarrassed. "I know. It's strange, isn't it? It's just as it was years ago. Before he moved in."

I could feel my mouth tighten. I slammed a glass of Perrier in front of her. "Of course it is," I said. "He's moved out."

"Yes, yes, I know. It just seems weird, that's all."

I nodded, but in a way it didn't seem odd anymore. The whole thing seemed like a dream. His living there, I mean. Like a dream, or like he'd died. It was as though it belonged in another place, another realm. Because there was no sign of him, it was as though he hadn't existed, as though I'd made him up.

Yet at night, when I lay in bed, I still automatically left space for him. Before I met him I was single for quite a while and I used to stretch out diagonally, taking up the whole space. From the moment Matt moved in it was as though he and I were made to be in that bed together. Our bodies would entwine, his arm would lie across my shoulder, his face would be buried in my neck. Of course over time we moved apart a little, especially if we'd had an argument, when I'd tell him to sleep on the sofa, but when I woke in the night now, I'd think he was in bed behind me. I could almost feel his breath on my neck, the flutter of his lashes against my skin.

I shook myself. That time was gone. When I found him again, things would be different. I wouldn't let him just sidle back into my bed like that, as though nothing had changed. No way.

KATIE AND I sat at the kitchen island and ate the pizza, though I don't think either of us really wanted to. All I wanted was a deep, hot bath with something mindless on the radio to distract me. My brain ached with the effort of thinking. I'd wake in the night, covered in sweat, my heart banging, convinced that he was back, that he was angry with me. Or it would occur to me that I should phone his gym or our dentist and I'd pad downstairs in the chilly night to make a note, to remind myself of something I'd probably never forget.

"So," she said, when she'd finished eating. "Have you decided?"

I shook my head.

"I can't believe your bad luck," she said. "Getting pregnant just as he left." She thought for a minute. "Do you think that's why he left? Do you think he guessed you were pregnant and left so he wouldn't have to deal with it?"

I turned to stare at her. "Do you really think he'd do that?"

She shrugged. "Some men would."

"But Matt? Really?" My stomach dropped at the thought of him doing that to me. "You think he guessed I was pregnant? I wasn't actually sick until after he'd left."

"Oh, I don't know," she said gloomily. "I'm not a good judge of character."

Me neither, I thought. *He's the last person I would have thought would walk out like that.*

"So," she said, "when do you think the baby was conceived?"

I was startled. "What?"

"I was just wondering," she said. "How far gone are you now?"

"A few weeks," I said. I thought about that last time and worked it out. "Seven or eight weeks."

"So you were still sleeping together right up until he left?"

"Of course we were!"

"I'm sorry." She had the grace to look discomfited. "I was just thinking aloud. I suppose I was assuming that your relationship had gone downhill and that's why he left."

"No," I said. "Everything was fine. We were getting on really well. You didn't notice anything odd about him, did you?"

She shook her head. "I've thought about it a lot since he left and I don't think there was any sign that he'd do something like that." She looked down thoughtfully, then noticed a chip in her nail varnish. She scowled. "I'd better go home and get this sorted."

Glad you've got your priorities right.

As she stood to go, she said, "Hannah, think about it. You can't be a single mum. You'd really hate that. It would be lonely and expensive and . . . it's not what you hoped for, is it? And think of your dad! He'd go crazy!"

At the thought of telling my dad I was pregnant I felt dizzy and sick. "That's why I need to find Matt!"

"But would you want him back just because of a baby? Would you be able to live with him, knowing if it wasn't for the baby, he wouldn't be with you?"

"It wouldn't be like that." I swallowed hard. "I know he loved me. And he wanted children, too."

She hesitated. "When was the last time he told you that?"

I couldn't answer at first. I remembered him lying in bed with me in the early days, stroking my stomach and saying, "Can you imagine having a baby inside you? It would be so weird. Imagine it moving. It would be like something out of a sci-fi film."

"Or a horror movie," I'd said. "Don't worry, I never forget my pill."

"I'm not worried. It would be amazing." He'd leaned over and kissed me. "You'd be a fantastic mother."

That had made me cry, though I hadn't told him why.

We'd had those conversations quite a lot in the early days, but I couldn't think of the last time he'd said it.

"Not for a while," I told Katie. "But he knew I wanted to be promoted first. And I wouldn't have a baby unless I was married, either."

She gave me a pitying look then and I said sharply, "Well, you're not married, either!"

"I know, I know," she said and laughed. "My mum and dad can't afford it yet."

When the rear lights of her car disappeared down the road, I went into the kitchen to clear up. The Tupperware box she had brought was sitting on the counter. I took the lid off and stared at the cake, thinking of the love that had gone into it, the concentration on her mother's face as she swirled the chocolate buttercream. I knew she would be so glad it wasn't Katie who'd been hurt like this. I could feel my face becoming creased with a pain I couldn't express and my stomach clenched so tightly I knew I'd have to run to the bathroom in a minute.

All I could think of was the look of pity on Katie's mother's face. I'd seen it before, many times, though not for years, and the thought of her feeling sorry for me now was too much. I picked up the cake she'd so lovingly made for me and shoved it as hard as I could into the kitchen bin.

Chapter
Twenty-two

BY THE TIME Saturday came around, I felt exhausted. I woke up late and went downstairs for breakfast, but then didn't seem to have the energy to even shower or dress. I lay on the couch and pulled a blanket over me. Outside I could hear Sheila and Ray as they mowed their front lawn and washed their cars, and just their little routine tasks with each other for company made my eyes prickle.

I lay there remembering the old days, the glory days we always called them after hearing that song. I thought of Katie and how I'd met her on the first day of school. She'd asked me one playtime if I'd be her best friend. I hadn't known what a best friend was and was delighted when my mum told me. I used to love going to visit her; even at that age I knew there was a difference between her home and mine. There was a different atmosphere there; it didn't depend on who was around. There was no frantic activity when her father's car drew up outside, no relief when he left the house.

She didn't notice the difference, though, and used to love to come over to play with me. My parents were relatively wealthy and I had more toys than I wanted. She was jealous of that, I knew; her parents had much less money than mine, but everything they had, they gave to her. For her, that never seemed enough, somehow.

As we grew up she took to following my every move, copying my clothes, my hair, my makeup. At times I was flattered, at other times annoyed. Sometimes my dad would treat us both to something and that was when she seemed happiest, beaming up at him and telling him that I was really lucky. He loved that. She came with us on holidays, too, and somehow having her there on those trips to Florida or Marbella or wherever made everything easier for all of us. My mum loved her, too, though she was always watchful, especially on holiday.

And then when we were seventeen, we saw James. James with his tall lanky frame, long tousled hair and dark blue eyes. He carried his guitar everywhere and to me he looked like some kind of suburban rock god. I was smitten from the start—well, we both were, really, but it was me he asked out—and I started to hang out with him all the time. Katie would hang around with both of us, though I knew it was James she really wanted and that made me want him more. Toward the end of the relationship, when it was more intense, we saw a lot less of her and I know she missed seeing him just as much as she missed me.

Throughout our teenage years Katie and I kept scrapbooks. The bands we saw, the boys we went out with and the clothes we bought: we'd stick photographs and tickets and newspaper cuttings in a scrapbook. One for each year. Mine were up in the loft; the last time I'd seen them was when I hit thirty and Katie and I had had a few too many and dragged them downstairs to laugh at. When I put them back in their boxes after Katie left that night, I looked through each one again and noticed that a photo of James had gone, one I'd taken of him as he stood waiting for me in the park, his guitar beside him. Katie and I had been walking toward him and he was smiling at me as I took it. Even when I saw it that night, nearly thirteen years later, it made me smile back. I sent her a text:

Oy, where's my photo?

A couple of minutes later, my phone beeped:

Which photo?

You know damn well which one! I would have got you a copy if you'd asked.

She didn't reply until the next morning when I woke to find a new message:

I've no idea what you're talking about. x

I guessed she was going to try to change history, to pretend to herself that James was really smiling at her that day. He wasn't.

It was only then, when I was thinking about the scrapbooks in the loft, that I remembered I hadn't been up there since Matt left. I hadn't even thought of it. All my things he'd brought downstairs, my television, books and so on, had been in the spare room.

The last time I'd been up there had been just after New Year's when Matt and I were putting away the Christmas decorations. It was always a bit of a struggle because there was no lightbulb, so one of us would have to hold the torch and the other would wrangle the boxes and bags into position. The fact that we had hangovers hadn't helped at all.

I tried to remember what he'd had in the loft. He'd brought tons of stuff with him when he moved in, but most of it was distributed around the house, which was why it looked so bare now. I'd loved my home before he moved in, thinking it was minimalist and cool, but with his things in it, it looked suddenly vibrant and inviting. Welcoming. It was as though a sepia photograph had become full color. Now it just seemed empty and lost, as though it was waiting for someone to come and breathe life into it.

WITHIN MINUTES I'D dressed, got the stepladder out of the shed and dragged it upstairs to the landing. The only access to the loft was via a hatch in the ceiling on the landing outside my bedroom. I steadied the ladder and lifted the hatch door up and to one side. I chucked the torch in, then heaved myself through the opening into the loft space.

I hated being there on my own. There wasn't a proper ceiling, just rafters and thick insulation, and the torch cast shadows everywhere. I gritted my teeth and looked around.

In the far corner were boxes containing stuff from when I was young: school reports that brought back such vivid memories, things I'd made in sewing classes long ago, books I'd loved that I'd been saving for my own children. That thought stopped me in my tracks for a minute, then I put it from my mind.

It was clear Matt had been here to take his belongings. It didn't seem as though he'd left anything behind. There'd been a couple of suitcases and weekend bags and they had gone. A box of old cigarette cards his granddad had collected in the twenties that he kept saying he'd put on eBay; that had disappeared, too. I made a mental note to check eBay; I'd put it on my to-do list when I went downstairs. There was also no sign of the yellow plastic bag containing some of his teenage clothes.

Carefully I walked farther into the loft. Chipboard had been laid on the joists long before I moved into the house but I never felt safe walking on it and I knew it was stupid to be up there when nobody else was around. In the distance I could hear my phone ringing in the living room and realized that if I had an accident I'd be stuck until someone came to the house. Even then I doubted they'd hear me calling for help. The thought scared me. It was Saturday afternoon and nobody would know I was missing until Monday morning, when Sam or Lucy might be worried and call me, though if I didn't answer, they would probably just think I wasn't well. I could be up here for days, without my phone, the battery dying on my torch, unable to call anyone. My stomach twisted at the thought. I needed to get out of there.

I turned toward the opening to the loft. Below, the light streamed in through the landing window, shards of pink and green light from the colored glass there. As I turned to go back down the ladder, I grabbed a rafter for balance and yelped as something scratched my finger.

What was that? I shone the torch on the rafter and gingerly ran my fingers over the sharp edge of a sharp metal nail that was sticking out of it. Something was stuck to it and I pulled it away. It was hair—a few strands of hair. They felt odd. Rough. I held them close to the torch and peered closely at them. They were coated in something dry and were the color of rust.

And then I remembered.

It was Matt's hair. Matt's blood.

Just after New Year's we'd put the Christmas decorations back in the loft. I glanced over to the side and saw them there, large cardboard boxes filled with little glass ornaments and golden bells and fairy lights. It was always a horrible job but this year Matt had tripped just where I was standing. He'd banged his head on the rafter and when I'd shone the torch on him there'd been a patch of blood on his head from the same nail that had scratched me now.

Now I looked down at his hair in my hand. It didn't even feel like his hair; it was matted and dry, no longer dark blond.

I put it in the pocket of my jeans.

It was all I had of him now.

Chapter
Twenty-three

When I finally reached my phone, there was a voicemail message from Katie.

"Hey, Hannah, tried to reach you. I was talking to James about you being pregnant and he says that you need to get a checkup with a doctor. He said his sister had to register with a midwife when she found out she was pregnant and then she was put onto the system and had scans and things. What do you think? Do you want me to come with you?"

I scowled at the message and sent a text instead of calling her back:

This is why I need to find Matt.

My phone beeped. I groaned. *Katie, again.*

But when I looked down at the screen, I saw it was a text from a number I didn't recognize. Not that I would recognize it, anyway; I'd hardly recognize my own, but this one didn't have a name attached to it. It said:

I know where you are.

I STARED AT the phone.

What?

I read it again. It didn't make any sense. I was in my own home! Who had sent it?

Cautiously I went to the living room window and flattened myself against the wall to look outside. The street looked the same as usual. Cars were parked outside houses, children played in the spring sunshine. A delivery driver was knocking at a door across the road. Nobody was looking at my house. There was no van with blacked-out windows, no sniper crouching in the shadows.

I went into the kitchen and checked the number against the text I'd received saying Matt was home. They were different.

I tried to call Katie but her phone rang out.

Agitated, I phoned her home landline and James answered.

"Is Katie there?" I asked.

"I thought she'd gone shopping with you. Isn't she answering her mobile?"

"I tried, but she didn't pick up. Am I supposed to be meeting her? My brain's fried at the moment."

"I might be wrong," he said. "I wasn't really listening. She's probably at her mum's. Any message for her?"

I hesitated. He and I rarely spoke on our own nowadays but I couldn't keep this to myself.

"I've had a text come through on my phone," I said. "I don't know who it's from."

"What, another one? What happened with the text the other night that said 'I'm home'?"

"I've no idea," I said. "It might have been a wrong number." I blocked the memory of how I'd raced around the house like a madwoman, trying desperately to find Matt. "Anyway," I hurried on, "this text today . . . it's just weird."

"Weird?" he said, sounding distracted. "Sorry, I thought that was Katie at the front door. What does it say?"

"It says, 'I know where you are.'"

"What?"

"'I know where you are.'"

"Well, where are you?" he asked and I laughed, feeling lighter. It was ridiculous to get wound up over such a stupid message.

"I'm at home."

"Well, I suppose anyone could guess that, on a Saturday afternoon. What's the number?"

I read it out to him and heard him tapping something on a keyboard. "What are you doing?"

"Just seeing whether the number's anywhere online," he said. "No, nothing's coming up."

I made a mental note to check it myself, later.

"James," I said, unable to keep the thought to myself, "do you think it was from Matt?"

"Matt? It's not his number, is it?"

"No, but his number was dead after he left. He must have got a new phone."

"Or blocked you."

"I tried it from different phones." Including a phone box at Liverpool Lime Street station that I'd gone to one evening, desperate for him to pick up and talk to me.

"And it's not the same number as the one the other night, is it?"

I wished I hadn't told him about this now. "No."

"He wasn't there when you got home, was he?"

I flushed with shame. "No."

"Well, why would he send you that message?"

"I don't know," I admitted. "I've no idea."

"You could always ring the number," he said. "Or do you want me to?"

"No," I said, feeling dejected. "It's okay. It'll just be some nutcase. I'm better off ignoring it." I ended the call, feeling worse than I had before I'd spoken to him.

Within a few minutes my phone rang. It was Katie. "Hi, did you want me?"

"Katie, were we supposed to be meeting today?"

"What?"

"I've just spoken to James and he said he thought we were going shopping."

"Oh," she said and laughed. "No, I'm shopping for his birthday present. I know it's not for another few weeks, but I wanted to look at cameras and I knew it would take me ages to choose one he'd like. I didn't want him with me, so I said I was meeting you."

"I would have gone with you," I said. "I'm just sitting here making myself feel worse."

"I'm sorry, sweetie," she said. "I didn't think you'd be up for it. Anyway, how come you were talking to James?" The subtext was loud and clear; all communication between James and me should go through Katie. I'd been aware of this since she first started seeing him, when she shut her mind to the fact that he and I had been lovers years before. Now she never mentioned the fact that we'd been together and James and I certainly didn't; it was as though it had never happened.

I told her about the message I'd received and she was silent. For a moment I thought the signal had gone, then she said, "But who would send that?"

"I thought it might be Matt," I said, knowing I sounded like a complete loser. "Who else could it be?"

"Matt? Why would he do that?"

"I don't know," I was forced to admit. "That's what I don't understand."

"What time did you get it?"

"Just a few minutes ago."

"That's weird." There was another silence, then she rallied and changed the subject, talking about her job and how mean someone had been to her. I put her on speakerphone so that my hands were free, and while she talked, I picked up my pen and updated my notes.

Two texts now. Different numbers.

Were both from Matt? I couldn't believe he would send me a text saying he knew where I was. It just didn't seem like the sort of thing he'd do. So if he didn't send it, who did?

The flowers, though, were different. My face softened at the thought of him choosing them. He knew I loved having fresh flowers in the house, knew purple tulips were my favorite. And the CD, too. Now that was a gift I'd treasure. Of course I would stand by him. Of *course* I would! He knew that.

THAT NIGHT I lay in bed, unable to sleep. Now all I could think of was the text I'd received that afternoon. Who had sent it? What did they mean, they knew where I was? I was in my own house!

Just before midnight I picked up my phone and stared at the message again. I clicked on the Contact button at the top of the screen, then touched the phone symbol. The screen lit up as the call was put through. It rang and rang, but nobody picked up.

Then I dialed the number of the text which had said "I'm home." I lay on the bed, stiff and tense, and listened to it ringing, but I knew.

I knew that he wouldn't answer. I just didn't know why.

THE NEXT DAY when I woke up I was facing Matt's side of the bed. The sheet was cool and smooth and it was as though he had never slept there. As though he'd never been here at all. I shook my head, then reached under my pillow and took out the photo of him at London University. He looked just as he had when I'd met him on the plane, and my heart yearned for him. I wanted to be close to him again, to put any problems behind us. To start over. I'd known we'd be together as soon as I first saw him and I think he did, too, deep down. We were a couple right from the very beginning.

Not now, though. Now I was more single than I'd ever been and I felt the loss of him constantly. In every room I saw ghosts of the things he'd taken away, at night in bed I felt the absence of his breath against my neck, the gap where his body should have been, lying next to mine.

Chapter
Twenty-four

THE EMAIL FROM HR was waiting for me when I got into the office on Monday morning. I was ten minutes late, having struggled to wake up on time after a night of disturbed sleep. I took off my jacket and turned on the computer, thinking that I'd google those numbers again before I started work.

> Dear Hannah,
>
> Please attend a meeting in my office today at 9:30. George Sullivan will be present.
>
> Best wishes,
> Emma Carter

I put my head in my hands. The door opened and I sat up quickly, trying to look as though nothing had happened. It was Sam.

"Everything okay?" he asked.

There was no point trying to fool him. I needed him on my side.

"Not really. Emma from HR wants to see me with George this morning."

"Oh no," he said. "I assume that's not good news."

I glared at him.

He reddened. "Come on, Hannah," he said. "This is me you're talking to. They're not stupid, you know. They can tell your work's been slipping lately."

I started to tremble. "But a formal meeting?" The only times I'd seen HR were when I'd had a promotion and one lovely day when I was told I'd won an award. The thought of going in there for a disciplinary made me feel sick.

A mug of tea was on my desk waiting for me. I picked it up, sipped it and pulled a face.

"It's cold."

He looked at me steadily. "Lucy put it there at eight o'clock. You said on Friday you'd be in early, as you had a lot to do."

I bristled at the implication that I was late. "I've not been well."

"You can't expect them not to notice. You've sent off one or two things past their deadlines, haven't you?"

He was so nice. So tactful. Both he and I knew how much my work had suffered. I'd never handed in anything late before all this. I'd prided myself on it. "I'll give it to Hannah—she'll do a good job on it *and* it'll be done on time" was something I'd heard George say time and again. God knew what he was going to say today.

"What am I going to do?" I could hear the desperation in my voice.

"Tell them you're pregnant and that you've not been well. Say you think you need a bit of time off and that you'll get a doctor's note. They'll understand."

"I can't," I said. "I can't."

"It's the only thing you can do," he said. "Just tell them the truth."

My face flamed. Not for the first time, I wished I hadn't told him I was pregnant. He just didn't get it and I wasn't about to explain it to him. "I don't know," I muttered. "What time is it?"

He looked at his watch. "Twenty past nine." He stood and picked up his coffee. "I'll come and see you afterward. Good luck."

I SORTED OUT some papers for later that morning and was just about to leave the room when the phone rang. I ran back to my desk to answer it.

"Hello, Hannah Monroe."

There was silence.

I frowned. "Hello? Hannah Monroe here." I could do without this; I really needed to run, but I couldn't just put the phone down in case it was a client. "Hello?"

There was a faint sound. I frowned and listened harder. Were those footsteps? I pressed the receiver so close to my ear it hurt. Yes, they were footsteps. They paused. Then there were more steps. I counted them; there were five steps before another pause. Had Matt called me without realizing it? Was he walking down the road? Then there was silence and I clung to the phone trying desperately to hear. Suddenly something on the other end of the line smashed and I shrieked.

I slammed the receiver down, shaking, then saw the clock on the wall. It was 9:29. I had one minute to get to HR on the seventh floor.

Chapter
Twenty-five

THE MEETING SEEMED to go on forever. When I came out I felt exhausted, as though I'd been put through a wringer. My eyes were sore from crying and I noticed that people averted their gaze as they passed me in the corridor. It seemed like everyone knew where I'd been.

I stopped at the ladies' cloakroom on the way back to my office. It was empty, thank God, and I stood against the basins and closed my eyes. The door opened and Alice, a woman I used to work with ages ago, came in. She gave me a sympathetic smile.

"Oh, you poor thing," she said. "They're not worth the effort, are they?"

I stared at her. "Who?"

She went into a cubicle and locked the door. "Men," she called out. "They're a complete and utter waste of time. Most of them, anyway. Don't get too upset, love. Someone else will come along. Hopefully it'll be someone better."

I stared at my reflection in the mirror. My eyes were red and my makeup was blotchy.

Had someone told her that Matt had left me?

Well, there was only one person that could be. I left the cloak-room and went back to my office as quickly as I could, my head bowed so that I couldn't see people looking at me. As soon as I got there, Lucy jumped up and came into my room with me.

"I'll make you a drink," she said.

"Thanks."

She was back within a few minutes with a mug of tea. "Is every-thing all right, Hannah?"

"I'm not feeling well," I said, avoiding her eyes. I knew damn well she'd seen the email about the meeting, but I wasn't about to confide in her. I could see sympathy in her eyes and I just couldn't stand it. "I'm taking the rest of the day off. Is there anything you need me to go through?"

"No, no, it's fine. I hope you feel better soon."

She left the room and sat down at her desk. I sipped my drink, then stood up and looked around the room. Lucy was on the phone. Most people were working on their computers, others sat in small groups, chatting. Over in his office on the other side of the room, Sam picked up his phone.

Lucy's conversation lasted five minutes or so and during that time I stood at my filing cabinet, shuffling papers around. Eventu-ally I saw her say something, blush and laugh, then put the phone down.

Across the room, Sam put down his phone, too.

Well, that's interesting.

I watched him stand up and look over toward my office. He waved and came through the central section toward me. I noticed he didn't look at Lucy and she appeared to be focusing hard on a spreadsheet.

"Hi," he said. "Are you okay?"

"Not really. I need a word with you. Can you close the door?"

He looked at me warily. "What's up?"

"Have you been telling people that Matt left me?"

He wasn't expecting that. "What?"

"You heard."

"No," he said. "No, of course not! Why, what's happened?"

I shook my head. I wasn't going to tell him anything; he'd go running to Alice and they'd cook up some story between them. "Nothing," I said. "Absolutely nothing."

My room was dark now, though it was early. Outside the sky threatened rain. I felt that if I didn't get out of there soon I'd go crazy.

Sam moved back toward the door. "How did the meeting go?"

I knew he'd hear it anyway. "It was awful. They gave me a verbal warning."

"A warning? That's harsh."

"Not really. I told them that Matt and I were having problems and they said that at my level I shouldn't be bringing personal problems into the workplace." I buried my head in my hands. "They had a great big list of things—times I was late, meetings I'd missed, deadlines I'd completely forgotten about." I looked up at him and grimaced. "I think they're employing someone just to watch me."

I thought then of the text. *I know where you are.* I was getting it at work as well as at home.

"So what's the plan?"

"They've given me the rest of the day off. I think they knew I wouldn't get much done. They told me to come in tomorrow and start from scratch."

"You can do it," he urged. "You know you can. Don't blow this chance." Across the room we could see his manager walking toward Sam's office. "Better go. I've got a meeting with him now."

I gathered my things together, switched off my computer and tidied my desk. I looked at the phone and remembered the call I'd had just before the meeting. I couldn't believe it wasn't meant to scare me.

I phoned the technicians' office and asked to speak to their manager.

"I had an odd call this morning," I said. "Is there any way I can find out who it was from?"

"Sorry. We don't keep a log of incoming calls. Let me know if it carries on and I'll see what I can do."

I thanked him and put the phone down.

Who would make a call like that? And what did they want from me?

Chapter
Twenty-six

I DIDN'T KNOW what to do with myself for the rest of the day. I couldn't face going back to the house so I spent a couple of hours just driving round. I found that if I drove fast, I could forget for a while. I could focus on my driving and block out everything else that was happening.

By lunchtime I found myself in Chester, near to Katie's workplace. I parked on a double yellow line next to the railway station car park and called her.

"Hey, are you free for lunch?"

"What? Today? Aren't you at work?" She knew I didn't normally stop for lunch.

"I've got the afternoon off," I muttered. "I've got to use up my annual leave before the end of the month."

"Lucky you! I'll have to speak to Lauren; I was supposed to be meeting her in ten minutes. She won't mind. Where are you? Where shall I meet you?"

"I'm just around the corner from your place now. I'm at the entrance to the car park at Chester station."

"Okay, I'll see you in five minutes."

When she hung up I twisted the rearview mirror to look at my face. My makeup had come off when I'd cried and my eyes were red, my skin tired and lined. I looked awful. I wouldn't be able to go anywhere nice with her; we'd have to hunt out a backstreet pub and hide away in a corner. I unzipped my handbag and pulled out my makeup bag. I searched through it for my foundation cream, opened the lid and looked up at the mirror again.

I froze.

Isn't that Matt?

In the mirror I could see the back of a man. He was wearing a tan suede jacket that I'd never seen before and was walking through the door to the station.

It's him! I'd know him anywhere.

I leaped out of the car. A traffic warden was working his way along the cars at the end of the road and I looked frantically from him to the entrance to the station. In the end I chased after Matt. I had to. This might be my only chance.

I raced down the road, weaving in and out of passengers with suitcases and trolleys, and hurtled into the station. There were quite a lot of people dotted around, some buying tickets, others standing waiting with coffee in their hands.

I couldn't see him.

I ran onto the nearest platform. There were a few men there, but nobody who looked like Matt. I raced back to the ticket office. From there I could see the stairs going up to the other platforms. I saw a woman push past some people, and as the crowd parted for her I saw a man with dark blond hair wearing a tan jacket walking across the far end of the bridge.

I dashed up the stairs and across the bridge to the other platform, darting around groups of students. As I ran I heard the announcement that the train to Birmingham was about to leave from platform five and there was a sudden surge behind me as passengers panicked and ran toward the waiting train. I ran with them.

On the platform the guard hurried the last lot of passengers onto the train before the doors shut. Opposite, another train stood waiting, its doors still open, its engines idling.

I didn't know where to look first. I ran up and down the platform, looking for Matt on the train that was about to depart, then a whistle blew and the guard waved a flag and the train started to move slowly down the track. I raced alongside it, desperate to catch sight of him. I didn't know what I would say to him; I just wanted to see him, to talk to him.

The train picked up speed and disappeared out of sight. I turned back to the other train. I walked slowly now alongside it, looking in each carriage, hoping it was this one he was on. There were elderly couples, women with shopping bags, teenagers cuddled up together. I couldn't see Matt. I walked up and down the platform but there was no sign of him.

Then my phone rang.

"Hannah?" said Katie. "Where are you? You need to get back to your car before they clamp it."

I LEFT THE station, my eyes full of tears. When the traffic warden spoke sharply, telling me I was parked illegally, I said nothing, tears running down my face. When he handed me a note and told me to pay the fine within the next month, I shoved it into my bag and didn't say a word. Katie drove my car; I could hardly see where we were going. She parked near to the river, then took out her phone and rang her assistant.

"I'm taking a long lunch," she said. "Something's come up. I'll be back in the office by three." She put her phone back in her bag and turned to me. "What was all that about? Where were you?"

"It was Matt," I said. "I saw him." I blurted out what had happened, how I'd seen him in the distance and had run after him. "It was definitely him."

"Hannah," she said patiently. "You do know that wasn't Matt, don't you?"

"It was! I'm sure it was."

"What was he wearing?"

"A suede jacket. A tan suede jacket."

She frowned. "I didn't know he had a suede jacket."

I shook my head. "It must be new. He must have bought himself a new jacket."

She laughed then. "Matt, buying himself clothes? Do me a favor."

Matt wasn't exactly known for being much of a shopper. I'd always bought his clothes; he had things in his wardrobe that he'd worn for years and years and he was quite happy wearing them until they fell apart. Or until I threw them away.

"It must have been someone else," she said. "Someone who looked like Matt. It wasn't him, sweetie."

I shook my head.

"I bet you've seen him in other places, haven't you?"

My face burned. I'd seen him everywhere in the first few days after he left. Literally everywhere. I couldn't walk down the street without thinking I'd caught sight of him. I'd gone into bars and followed people into shops just to see, just to double-check they weren't him.

We sat in silence for a while, watching a boat taking tourists down the River Dee. I could hear their chatter and laughter from where we sat; it seemed years since I'd been so carefree.

"How come you were around here anyway?" she asked. "You said you had a half day's annual leave; were you going shopping in Chester?"

"No." I shifted uncomfortably in my seat. "I've got into trouble at work."

She listened while I told her everything, far more than Sam knew. I told her how disappointed they were in me, how fed up they were, how my actions had caused problems for them with clients, how I was bringing my personal life into work and they didn't like it.

"Didn't you tell them you were pregnant?"

I shook my head. "I didn't want them to get involved in that."

"Oh, Hannah," she said and put her hand on my arm. "Sweetheart. I wondered whether you were thinking of that, too."

"What?"

"I've been thinking about it since you told me you were pregnant. It seems like the best way out."

I glared at her.

"I know, I know," she said. "I *know* it's awful, but it would be a solution to all this. You could nip into a clinic and get it all sorted. Have a holiday afterward, perhaps. I'll come with you! And then when you get back you could have a fresh start. Look at a different house, if you wanted. A new job, even."

Her voice petered out as she saw my reaction.

"I'm sorry," she said meekly. "It's just that I thought it would solve everything."

"Not quite everything," I snapped. "It's nice to know you think a baby's a problem, but getting rid of it wouldn't solve the problem of Matt, would it?"

"Matt isn't the problem." She sighed. "He's gone, Hannah. He's left you. He's made it clear, hasn't he, that he doesn't want to be with you? You have to get over it. I'm sorry, but that's the fact of it."

We drove back to her work in silence, and I felt her giving me worried little glances every now and then. I knew she felt sorry for me; I could feel pity pouring out of her and it tainted me, making me feel dirty and ashamed. Furious, too.

Chapter
Twenty-seven

BY THE TIME I arrived home the sky was overcast; though it was still early, the house was dark and gloomy. I took my jacket off in the hall and slipped off my shoes. I picked up the mail and went into the kitchen, then put some milk in the microwave. I'd make hot chocolate. That's what I wanted, something warm and sweet and comforting.

I made the drink and found some biscuits in the cupboard. I needed energy before I could think about today. My head was pounding and I took a couple of tablets with some water, though I thought I'd gone beyond that kind of help.

At the island I pulled my notes toward me. I peeled them off, one by one, and placed them side by side on the marble. On a new note, I wrote, *Matt at Chester Station—train to Birmingham?*

On my iPad I found a site which showed all the hotels local to Birmingham. There were tons of them. Then I looked up the trains leaving Chester that afternoon. I sighed. I was going to be here all day.

I pulled the mail toward me. There was a gas bill which I ignored and a bank statement for my savings account which I ripped open. Being without Matt's money had certainly made a difference there.

I logged onto my online banking and reduced the amount I was saving each month. I'd been overpaying my mortgage with some of the money Matt gave me for bills and I changed that, too. I had a sudden panic as the reality of having less money set in. A better paid job was out of the question; I was barely hanging on to the one I had.

Another envelope was at the bottom of the pile, with my name and address typed onto a label. It had a stamp, but no postmark. I ripped it open, thinking it would be junk mail, some local company advertising their wares. There was a single sheet of paper inside, folded in half.

On it was typed just one word:

Satisfied?

I STARED DOWN at the paper in my hands.

What?

I started to shake. Who had sent this? What did it mean? Why would anyone send something like that?

I went back to the front door but there was nothing else, no other post. I didn't know what time the postman arrived in the week; I was never at home to see him. He delivered the post at about 11 a.m. on a Saturday, but that didn't mean a thing. I went outside and for the first time ever I was glad to see Ray there.

"Ray, do you know what time the postman comes?" I called across the front garden.

He came bustling over, pleased to be able to help. "Well," he said, "he's normally here by ten o'clock . . ."

I felt like saying, "Thanks!" and slamming the front door, but I had to listen to him tell me what time the guy delivered mail all around the neighborhood, including the shops, and how he was sometimes late and how they—he and Sheila—thought he stopped off somewhere for a coffee in the middle of his round. He said this as though the postman was going up an alleyway to sniff an illegal substance.

When I eventually got rid of him, I came back into the kitchen and sat down with the note on the island in front of me.

This was my proof I wasn't going mad. All the other things, the texts from unknown numbers, the odd phone call at work, the flowers that came back to life, even the CD in the car: all of them could question my state of mind. I knew that as far as my nerves and my memory were concerned I wasn't the same as I normally was. I was quite aware that I was obsessing and probably making things worse for myself. But this . . . this piece of paper proved that it wasn't me. Someone *was* out to get me!

I was almost relieved to receive that message.

My first thought was to call Katie. I was still smarting from her laughing at me when I told her about the tulips. I know it did sound ridiculous—God knows I stared at them for long enough, unable to believe my eyes—but she could at least have come home with me to look at them. I stuck the note and the envelope to the fridge with a magnet shaped like a question mark and called her.

"What, like an anonymous letter?" she said when she heard about the note. "Was it posted or just pushed through the door?"

"I don't know," I said. "It was there with the rest of the mail, so I can't tell. It had a stamp on the envelope, but it didn't have a postmark, so who knows?"

"And that's all it said?" she asked, as though if *she* were there she would have seen more. "Are you sure?"

"Of course I'm sure," I snapped. "I'm looking at it now. Just one word."

She was quiet for a minute, then said, "I don't know what it means. It's like it's saying, 'Are you happy with what you've done?'"

"I know! And all these things keep happening and suddenly I'm to blame!"

"What sort of things? What else has happened?"

For a moment I just couldn't remember what I'd told her already. "Oh, just things," I muttered. I knew I'd have to sit down and make a note of what she knew and what I could tell her and what I mustn't.

"Hmm," she said, clearly not believing me. "You don't still think the flowers came back to life, do you?" She made a skeptical noise then that was so familiar to me I was transported right back to school.

It was as though I was inside my younger self, looking out from those eyes at her trying not to laugh at something we'd seen. Her lips would tremble and I'd feel mine start to move upward and I'd have to put my hand to my mouth to force them back down. I'd avoid her eyes but then I'd hear that little noise that heralded a fit of giggles and I wouldn't be able to stop myself and I'd look at her and just explode with laughter. We got into so much trouble for laughing at inappropriate things.

Today, though, that laughter was aimed at me. A sudden fury swept through me. I was at my lowest ebb and doing everything I could just to survive and she was laughing at me!

Without trusting myself to say another word I clicked the button to end the call. I didn't know what to do with myself, I was so angry.

Then I saw the flowers in the glass vase—the tulips, the new tulips, which were now halfway between life and death. I knew exactly how they felt.

I pulled them from the vase. They dripped water onto one of the notes I'd made about a café he used to frequent at lunchtime—I'd planned to go there to ask whether they'd seen him—and in a flash I saw how pathetic I was.

I snapped the tulips in half and threw them into the bin, but that wasn't enough to quench the fury inside me. I picked up the vase, still full of water, and threw it as hard as I could against the kitchen wall.

Chapter
Twenty-eight

DESPITE COMING DOWNSTAIRS in the middle of the night to sweep up the glass and mop the kitchen floor, I woke early the next morning, far too early to go into work. I'd been counting in my dream, counting and listing the things that had happened to me. I'd thought the first text saying "I'm home" was from Matt; I thought the flowers were, too. The CD was definitely from him, though I couldn't think how he'd got into the car or how he'd known it would be there outside the restaurant. The second text, which said "I know where you are," didn't sound like it was from him, but then I could swear those were his footsteps I could hear when he called my office. The note, though. It just didn't seem like him. He had his own laptop, of course, but he would have had to print out the note and the label. Why would he do that? Why wouldn't he just handwrite it? And why send it anyway? It didn't make sense.

As the numbers of the digital clock changed to 5:30 a.m., I could see the first hint of sunrise through the cream cotton curtains. I lay in bed thinking of the hour ahead: I could lie there and think about

Matt, or I could go back to sleep—very unlikely—and wake up feeling awful at seven, or I could get up and do something.

In the days when Matt still lived in London and we just met at the weekends, Katie and James started to go running down by the river every evening and Katie would always ask me to go with them, though I guessed she only asked because she thought she'd be faster than me. That summer, without telling her, I spent every morning running alone along the river as the sun rose, when I knew she'd be safely in bed. What kept me going was the thought of entering a 10K race on the same day as Katie and beating her, without telling her I'd been practicing.

That day did come to pass and it was one of the best of my life; just the thought of it could bring me out of a deep depression. After that I used to ask her to come running with me, but she was always too busy.

Then Matt moved in with me and any spare time in the early morning was spent on other things.

Now I forced myself to get out of bed and into my running gear. I put my house key and phone in my pocket and set off down the road toward the river. There was no sign of life for the first mile or so, then a police car drove slowly past and I spotted a woman with a dog that was so huge she must have had to walk him for miles.

I put some music on so that I didn't have to think about the day ahead or anything that had happened in the last few weeks. After a while I got into a rhythm and found I could switch off and think about nothing: my favorite state of mind.

Back home after an hour's run, I was tired from the exercise but refreshed, too. Invigorated. I had a quick shower and washed my hair, then took my time straightening it. I wore freshly washed and ironed clothes, too, shutting my mind to the fact that I hadn't always done that over the last few weeks. I sat on the side of the bed and painted a happy look onto my face so that I could convince everyone at work that I was okay, that everything was under control.

I was just finishing off my lipstick when a text came through on my phone. I picked it up, thinking it was Sam, glad to be able to reassure him I was fit for work, that the disciplinary the day before had taught me a lesson, making me determined to focus on my job and not let anyone down. On the screen was a message from yet another unknown number:

Enjoy your run?

I froze.

Then a video appeared on the screen. My mouth was dry as I clicked on it. I could see myself, on the path down by the river. My ponytail was bouncing, my face was determined. I played it right through, then again, trying to work out exactly where I'd been when I was filmed.

I *knew* it.

There had been a moment when I was running in a place where the sand dunes bordered the walkway when I'd felt distinctly uncomfortable. I hadn't been able to work out why. I'd stopped and looked around, but couldn't see anything suspicious. Nobody else was running. An older man was walking his dog further on and a cyclist came past at full speed, startling me. I looked over to the dunes and caught a flicker of something, just a tiny flash of light. I'd thought it was the sun's rays shining on some metal that someone had dropped. A can or something.

The anger from the previous night had gone, or rather I needed Katie at that point more than I hated her. I called to tell her about the video.

"Who would do that?" she asked.

"I don't know." And I didn't. I couldn't see who else it could be but Matt, but what would he be doing down at the river so early in the morning?

"No," she interrupted my thoughts. "It's not going to be Matt. Don't start going down that road, Hannah. Why would he do that? I doubt he's even living around here now."

"But why would anyone else be interested?"

"Phone them back," she said. "Get angry. Ask them what the hell they're doing."

"Okay," I said, fired up now. "I will."

I cut her off and called the number. It rang several times, then just like last time, it was cut off mid-ring. There was no answer-phone message available.

Furious, I sent a text:

Who the hell are you and why are you sending me messages?

I waited half an hour for an answer, almost making myself late for work, then sent a final message:

Matt? Is that you?

There was no reply.

Chapter
Twenty-nine

I SPENT THE day at the office with my head down, working hard. All around me I could see mistakes I'd made over the past few weeks that had had to be corrected for me and emails I hadn't read properly so I hadn't done what was asked for. I was scarlet with shame. I'd always been so proud of my work, so ambitious for my future. It was the one place I'd felt in control.

I'd never seen myself as someone who needed a man to make her life complete. In fact, that was what bugged me about myself now; when Matt was around we would often go days without saying much to each other, particularly if he was working late. Now that he was gone, though, I could feel the physical pull of loneliness. As I closed the door to my house at night, something inside me burned at the thought that I'd be alone until the morning. Of course I could call people but, apart from Katie and Sam, there wasn't anyone I could talk to about what really mattered. And what mattered to me more than my job, more than anything else now, was finding Matt.

SAM WAS NEITHER use nor ornament when I told him about the messages. I had to be so careful what I said to him; I didn't dare mention the flowers. If he had the same reaction as Katie, I'd think I was going mad. I didn't tell him about the almost-silent phone call I'd had the morning of the disciplinary, either, though I'd thought about it myself time and again, wondering who was on the other end of the line and why they didn't speak. We sat in the canteen at work and I showed him the texts and told him about the CD in the car and the note through the door. He was shocked and worried about me, too.

"Who do you think has sent them to you?" he asked. "And a video of you running?" He watched it through from start to end. "You're sure you don't know the number?"

"I've not used it on my phone before," I said. "I've checked. And I don't recognize it. Or any of the others, for that matter."

"Search for it on your laptop and your iPad tonight. And we'll search your work computer, too. You never know, it might show up as a number someone's given you, even if it was a while ago."

"It's giving me the creeps."

"I bet. Do you want me to start running with you?"

I groaned inwardly. That was the last thing I wanted. "It's okay, thanks. I'll vary the times when I go. I can't imagine anyone's going to be hanging around all day and night waiting for me to go for a run."

There was a long pause and then he said, "You think it's Matt, don't you?" I suppose he could tell from my face that he was right. "But why would he do that, Hannah? Think about it. He's gone off and left you"—I winced—"so why would he be following you around?"

I shook my head. "Who knows? Maybe he wants to talk to me."

Sam's eyes were on me and I could feel my face, tight and proud.

"But Hannah," he said, "if he wanted to speak to you, he could. He could just come to the house and see you anytime. Or call you at work." I could see he was struggling to be tactful. "Or he could even call you on your mobile. To chat."

Then I remembered the fright I'd had when I'd found the warm kettle. "Sam, this might sound like a really random question, but how long do you reckon it takes a kettle to cool down?"

He looked startled, as well he might, and I explained what had happened.

"I can see why you're worried," he said, "but it's pretty obvious that if you put a metal object in the sun it'll get warm!"

"Yes, but what about the tiles getting wet? I know the kettle would be warm, but it shouldn't produce condensation unless it's switched on, should it?"

He shook his head. "I think you saw that because you were expecting it. What, you really think someone broke into your house and boiled the kettle?"

I shook my head. "Not *someone*. I think Matt came home from work and put the kettle on. That's what he always did. It was his routine. Kettle on, quick shower, cup of tea, then he'd go to the gym."

He stared at me. "You honestly think it was Matt?"

"Who else could it be?"

"And these messages. You think they're Matt, too?"

"Who else would want to send me a message?"

He shook his head. "You're going to drive yourself mad."

We walked back to the office and I could tell from his sidelong glances that he was thinking I'd drive him mad, too.

That afternoon I sat at my desk and made a list of everything that had happened. The flowers and the kitchen roll. The text saying "I'm home." The CD in my car. The warm kettle, the text saying "I know where you are" and the letter through the post asking whether

I was satisfied. I stopped to think. Oh yes, the phone call at work. Were those Matt's footsteps? Was that call even meant for me? And then the video of me running and its accompanying text—was he really down by the river then? My head started to ache. Why hadn't he said something if he was that close to me? And why didn't he leave fresh flowers before he disappeared if that's what he wanted to do? Why would he say he knew where I was, when it was obvious I'd be at home?

I felt like screaming with frustration. I looked up and saw Lucy at the doorway, looking at me. I quickly turned my notepad over.

"I was just about to make some tea," she said. "Would you like some?"

"No, thanks. Not at the moment."

She hesitated. "Can I do anything for you, Hannah?"

"No, I'm fine." I know I sounded dismissive but she was interrupting my train of thought. She flushed and immediately I felt guilty. "Sorry, Lucy; I'm just in the middle of something."

She smiled and went back to her desk and I turned over the notepad and got back to work.

"Stand by Me." That *had* to be from Matt. He must have been thinking about those nights we'd spent on the sofa together, close enough to feel each other's hearts beating. What a romantic message to send! And he'd set it to start as soon as the car started, to be sure I'd hear it. He must have known I'd guess it was from him.

But then why would he send the note asking whether I was satisfied? With what? That really bugged me. Where the CD had been a loving gesture, that was hostile.

Unless . . . That note had arrived after I'd seen him. My head thumped. Was he asking whether I was satisfied now that I'd seen he was alive and well? But how could he have known I'd be in Chester that day? I hadn't even known myself that I'd be going there. No, that wasn't what that meant, was it?

I rubbed my eyes, exhausted. The texts and the video bothered me more than anything. They seemed designed to upset me. Nobody wants to think they're being spied on, especially by their partner. I just couldn't believe that Matt would do that, though. And I knew that no relationship was perfect. He and I had had the odd problem over the years, just like any other couple, but he'd never been cruel to me.

So if it wasn't Matt, who was it? And why would they want to hurt me?

Chapter
Thirty

LATER THAT AFTERNOON, Sam and I looked online for anything resembling that phone number and searched our company emails, too, just in case it was someone I knew from work. Nothing came up. I gave him the other numbers, too, with a muttered, "You might want to look for these, too." He gave me a sharp look, but I didn't say anything else.

"I know you've already done this," he said when we were at our wits' end, "but I'll call the numbers from my phone and see what happens."

I read out the first number to him and he dialed it on his phone. It rang out several times, then cut off.

"Have you tried calling from the office phone?"

We tried it again and this time it didn't ring at all.

"He's just switched it off!" I said. "He must be at work."

"Or driving."

"Or in a meeting."

"The fact is," he said, "we have no idea who it is who's calling you anyway or where they are. Do you think it's worth going to the police?"

I shook my head. "And say what? It's not as though whoever it is has committed a crime."

"Stalking?"

I could see George approaching my room. "Quick," I whispered and we started to talk about a meeting we were preparing for, so that when he came into the room we looked a picture of innocence.

He gave us a strange look and said, "Hannah, can I have a word?"

Sam hurried out of the room.

"How are you getting along with the Johnstown Company's accounts? I believe their deadline's coming up soon."

I tried to keep my face neutral and calm, but inwardly my heart was racing. I'd forgotten all about it. "Everything's fine. I've almost finished."

"Make sure they get them on time, won't you? Send me a copy, too. I'm off early now to go to the airport; I've got a week off, as you know."

I nodded and wished him a good holiday. I'd forgotten he was going away; usually before he left I'd go into his office to chat about his plans and he'd let me know if there was anything extra he needed me to do while he was away. That hadn't happened this time and I wondered who he'd trusted in my place. Understandably, he looked a lot less happy with me nowadays and I knew I'd have to work hard now to make things all right again.

After he left I went out to Lucy's desk. "Lucy, can you set aside tomorrow to proofread the annual return for the Johnstown Company? Send it off before the end of the day, will you? George needs a copy, too. It's due at the end of next week, but I don't want it to go at the last minute."

She nodded. "Will do."

"Let me know if there's anything you don't understand."

She gave me a look as though it was highly unlikely that would happen and carried on with her work.

I transferred all my calls through to her, switched off my mobile and got down to work. For a time I was fully absorbed; every detail was meticulously checked and I knew I'd done a good job. I sent the accounts through to Lucy, reminding her to send a copy to George; I knew that reminder would irritate her.

It was 8 p.m. by the time I finished and for the first time in ages I felt happy. I'd been so involved in my work that I hadn't thought of Matt for a second, and I think I started to realize then that I was going to be all right.

I was back on track.

ON MY WAY home I decided to treat myself to something nice for dinner. I'd been living off takeaways and snacks since Matt left; I couldn't face cooking our usual meals and sitting down on my own to eat them. I considered various restaurants, rejecting anywhere that he and I had been to together. I didn't want those memories that night.

Sam had told me about a new Thai place that had opened up recently in Liverpool. He'd gone there at the weekend with a group of friends and the food had been great. Normally I don't like eating out alone, and when I got there and saw it was crowded with couples, I panicked and asked the waiter whether I could order a meal to take away instead.

He brought me a glass of sparkling water and I sat in the restaurant's foyer, choosing my meal. I'd go home and watch television, I thought. I wouldn't look at the notes in the kitchen, I wouldn't go online to search for Matt. I'd eat this lovely dinner and I wouldn't give him another thought. I gave the waiter my order and sat reading the local newspaper, trying to switch off.

The meal arrived and as I stood to pay, a woman came out of the ladies' room and walked over to a table at the back of the restaurant. She sat down, said something and laughed. I smiled. It was Helen, a woman who worked for my dad. I'd had a job at his company one summer when I was on holiday from university and she'd been my boss. She was only a few years older than me, so in her twenties then, and I'd really liked her. She'd helped me an awful lot and had given me a great reference when I applied for jobs after graduation.

I said to the waiter, "Just a moment, I've seen someone I know," and took a step into the restaurant. A pillar blocked part of my view. I was just about to wave to attract her attention when I saw who she was with.

I stood stock-still. My dad was sitting opposite her. He was holding her hand and as I stood there, she leaned over and touched his face. They kissed.

My head started to buzz and for a second I thought I was going to faint. I turned back to the waiter. "Sorry, I made a mistake," I said. I had to force myself not to look over toward them and I felt so exposed, knowing they could glance over and see me at any moment. My fingers shook as I opened my purse. I took out some money and didn't wait for the change. I took the bag of food, though I didn't want it now, and hurried from the restaurant.

I ran to my car, my heart thumping in my chest. I didn't know what he would have done if he'd seen me. Bluffed it out, probably. Maybe even invited me to join them. I shuddered at the thought of that, trying to eat while he looked at me, trying to gaslight me into thinking I hadn't seen what I had seen. He would never forget, I knew that. His weakness would become mine, just as it always did.

I drove away from the restaurant and turned down the first side street I saw. I guessed he wouldn't have parked on the main road, not if he was somewhere he shouldn't be. Eventually I saw his car and drew up several yards behind it. I needed to be sure of this. I'd had my suspicions for years, though not of Helen. I'd never thought her capable of that. I closed my eyes for a second as I realized just how long she'd worked for him. It was twelve years since I first met her. Had something been going on the whole time?

It was half an hour before they came out of the restaurant. They must have driven there separately, because they stopped at another car which was next to his. For five minutes they stood on the pavement, chatting, then she put her arms around his neck and he put his around her waist and they kissed. It was a lovely warm night and her arms were bare, his jacket off.

And I don't know why but I pulled out my phone and took shot after shot of them as they stood there, betraying my mother with every kiss.

I WAS ON my way home when the next message came through. I was stuck in traffic for the Kingsway Tunnel, on the inside lane on the curve toward the river. I switched on the radio in time to hear that there had been an incident in the tunnel and it was just starting to clear. There was no alternative route; two solid lanes of traffic were heading toward the tunnel entrance. Everyone looked fed up.

My phone beeped just as the traffic report ended. The message was from yet another number I didn't recognize. It said:

I can see you.

My heart pounded. I dropped the phone on the passenger seat and quickly looked around me. There must have been hundreds of cars queueing, two lanes of traffic going toward Wallasey and two in the other direction. The road was stationary.

All I could see were lorries and cars, none of which I recognized. I sat up high in my seat and tried to look around the lorry in front of me, but it was too wide. I stared in my rearview mirror but there was a family in the car behind me and beyond that I couldn't see. In the neighboring lane there was a bus. I stared at each passenger in turn until a couple of them looked at me as if I was mad.

I felt frantic with nerves. Where the hell was he? I glanced in my wing mirror for motorcyclists, then opened the door and jumped out. I looked up and down the approach road but didn't see any cars I recognized. My heart sank. He'd probably changed his car, just as he'd changed his number. How was I meant to find him if he was in a different car? Then there was a blast from a horn that made me jump and a woman shouted something through her window. With a start I realized the traffic ahead had begun to move and I leapt back into my car and moved along, my eyes all over the place. I don't know how I didn't crash.

I flashed my tag in payment and drove up the slip road toward Wallasey, my nerves jangling. I looked behind me constantly, trying to find a car I recognized.

At home I opened the front door and stopped dead in the middle of the hallway.

What's that?

I could smell Polo. Ralph Lauren. It was the cologne I'd bought Matt for Christmas last year.

Chapter
Thirty-one

I MOVED SLOWLY to the front door and stood there with my back against it. The smell was less noticeable here. I kicked off my shoes and silently, in bare feet, I took a couple of steps forward onto the woolen rug which lay in the center of the polished oak floor. I closed my eyes and took a deep breath. It was still there, the cool citrusy scent of Matt's cologne.

It took me a second to galvanize myself.

"Matt?" I shrieked. "Matt, are you there?"

I raced into the kitchen, took a swift glance around. I half expected to see him, drinking tea and playing some stupid game on his phone.

"Matt! Matt!"

With the energy of a bloodhound I ran into the living room and looked wildly around. He wasn't there; the room looked exactly as I'd left it that morning, I ran upstairs, throwing open doors and shouting his name. In every room I threw myself to the floor to look under the beds, flung open wardrobes to see whether he was hiding behind my clothes. He was nowhere in sight.

I stood on the landing, gasping for breath. My head was swirling. I knew he'd been there. I knew it.

As I took a deep breath in, I realized the smell was fainter upstairs. I went back into the bedroom. I couldn't smell it there. I went into the bathroom. Nothing there either. When I checked the spare room and the other bathroom, there was no smell at all.

I went back downstairs, desperate to find out where he'd been. The living room looked untouched but there was a faint smell of spice in the air that I knew hadn't been there that morning.

In the kitchen the smell was stronger and I knew, I just knew, he'd stood where I was standing, surveying the room. I looked around wildly. What had he been doing in here?

And then I realized.

Before I'd left for work that morning I'd tidied my notes into a pile and put them next to the fridge, just in case Katie called round unexpectedly. The last thing I'd wanted was for her to look through them. Now, they were spread out neatly in the grid pattern I favored myself, lined up with an inch of space between each of them. You could have drawn a line along them and it would have been dead straight. Normally I like that kind of precision.

When Matt had looked at those notes, he would have understood how much he meant to me. He must have seen my lists, how I'd crossed off the gym, hotels, his office, car hire companies. He would have seen how thorough I'd been, checking his mum's address, his barber's and the garage he took his car to for its service.

And he must have seen those numbers written down with their text messages next to them. He'd know they'd be driving me crazy.

Was he the one behind all this? How did he feel when he stood here and saw my notes, my distress? Did he feel guilty? Glad?

For a moment I considered it might not be him, then I shook my head. I could smell him here now. If I'd wondered before, now I knew.

And then I thought of something I'd heard, though I don't

remember where. Whenever a criminal commits a crime, something is left at the scene and something is taken away. It's true of any crime, apparently. And this *was* a crime, a crime against my privacy.

Now I knew that what they were usually referring to were specks of DNA that would be found on tiny bits of skin or maybe one drop of blood or sweat.

But that saying was true here, too. He'd left behind the smell, the lingering citrusy smell that reminded me of him freshly dressed and ready for the day.

What had he taken with him?

I looked around the room. I knew he'd been in here, knew he'd moved the notes. I counted them; they were all there. I couldn't see anything out of place. I went into the living room and up to my bedroom, but nothing was missing. Because I couldn't smell the cologne upstairs, I assumed he hadn't been up there, so I just had a quick look around and came back downstairs.

As soon as I returned to the kitchen, I knew what he'd done.

The note saying "Satisfied?" had gone from the fridge door. The envelope had gone, too. Only the question mark magnet remained.

Suddenly I was dizzy and felt as though I was going to faint. I grabbed hold of a chair and slowly sat down. The note had been my only piece of evidence. The only thing that told me I wasn't going mad.

Someone had taken it.

Chapter
Thirty-two

I HARDLY SLEPT at all that night; I had too much on my mind. I left all the downstairs lights in the house on, just as a warning in case someone tried to get in. I took my notes up to bed for safekeeping and put my phone under my pillow. I knew someone had been in my house. Should I phone the police? I closed my eyes and thought of how that conversation would go. They'd think I was insane to call them just because I'd lost a piece of paper.

And there was nobody I could talk to. Katie had thought I was crazy to think the flowers had been changed, and from then on she hadn't believed anything I said. If I told her I'd stuck a piece of paper on my fridge and now it was gone, she'd laugh at me. Sam thought I was losing it, and besides, I couldn't be sure he wasn't telling Lucy things about me. Were they seeing each other? How had I not noticed that until now? And what about Grace? He still talked about her; he was clearly still living with her. Was he seeing Lucy at the same time? I wanted to trust him, I really did, but that phone call they were both on at the same time . . . was that coincidence?

And then I thought of that spare phone in the glove compartment. Why had he said it wasn't working when it clearly was?

For a second I wondered whether he had sent me any of those texts and my stomach lurched at the thought. Surely he hadn't! Why would he?

I needed someone to talk to, but who?

I couldn't call my mum. She'd worry too much, and besides, she'd want me to come home for a while and that was never going to happen, particularly not now. I had to plan my visits home and my escape afterward; if I spent more than an hour there I'd start to feel anxious. It was always just a matter of time before something was said or assumed. Once I'd left home the summer I was eighteen, I rarely returned and only ever when I had good news. A promotion always went down well, a pay rise, too. News of a headhunter who'd called me could be enough to turn the tide of a conversation.

I rarely took Matt home with me, though my mum really liked him and would have liked to have seen more of him. After a while my dad would remember we weren't married, that Matt was living in my house, and then it would be time to go, to hurry Matt out to the car with a manufactured excuse to him, to my parents and to myself. He knew nothing important of my life before I left home; once I met his mum and saw how she doted on him, I knew I could never tell him. He was the same as Katie; people brought up in happy families find it so hard to understand what it's like to live in a home where you have to think twice before speaking, to move quickly to avoid trouble, to avert your eyes so that you don't take on the responsibility of others.

And how could I talk to my mum without telling her about my dad's infidelity? My head felt like it was gripped in a vise at the thought of telling her that. I think it was the only thing that kept her there, the thought that deep down he loved her and that they'd married for life.

THE NEXT DAY was Saturday and I decided to tackle my neighbors. Ray was outside in the front garden, simultaneously weeding and checking up on what was happening in the street. He took his Neighborhood Watch role very seriously. He was in his early sixties, a retired sales manager, and I tried never to be in a room with him on my own. His lucky wife, Sheila, was indoors, from the sound of the roar of the vacuum cleaner.

They'd been my neighbors since I first bought the house, years ago. They were so eager to meet me when I moved in that I was suspicious at first, wondering whether they were one swinger short of a party, and even the absence of pampas grass in their front garden did nothing to reassure me. When Matt moved in he used to say he was unnerved by the way Sheila kept her lipstick and perfume by the front door, so that when you knocked you could see her shadow move as she got herself ready for visitors. He used to ask me to go with him when he had to go round. I have to admit I made fun of him for it until I spent an hour of my life alone with Ray when Matt had accidentally gone to work with my car keys and I was locked out of the house. He sat too close, right up next to me on the sofa, and I could feel the heat from his thighs against mine. I'd moved until I was at the edge of the sofa and each time he moved, too. I swore I would never go through that again and despite them telling me numerous times that they'd keep a spare key for me, I just knew that one night I'd wake up to find Ray in my house, investigating a fictitious burglary, particularly if he knew Matt wasn't there.

In other ways they were ideal neighbors as they took Neighborhood Watch to a totally new level. Everything Matt and I knew about the people in our street was discovered via Sheila and Ray. We just tried to make sure they told us outdoors, so we could escape if we needed to. I was glad that our houses joined at the hall wall; God knows what they would have told people if they'd heard what was going on in the bedroom.

That afternoon, I knocked at their door, my stomach tied up in knots; I knew I would have to tell them that Matt had gone. I hated to think of anyone feeling sorry for me.

As usual, I saw Sheila's shadow through their frosted glass, saw the shake of her head as she brushed her hair. No lipstick needed for me, clearly.

"Oh, hello, Hannah." She beamed. "Come on in. I'm just about to put the kettle on. Fancy a cuppa?"

I followed her into her interrogation room.

WE SAT IN the kitchen overlooking the garden, a perfect picture of early summer. Flowers crowded the beds, spilling out onto the lush lawn, and plants tumbled out of the hanging baskets she'd hung from hooks on the fence.

"I was going to come round to see you, actually," she said as she put out a plate of moist, sweaty Battenberg cake. My stomach gave a slight heave and I winced, hoping the sickness wasn't going to start again.

"Nothing for me, thanks," I said quickly.

"Dieting?" She smiled. "No need for that! You've gone quite thin."

"No, I just won't eat my lunch if I eat now." *Particularly if I eat that!*

"How's Matt? I haven't seen him around for ages. Ray and I were only saying the other day that he seems to be working away a lot."

"He's left me," I said and despite myself I couldn't help sounding forlorn.

"What?" She sat up in alarm. "Ray! Ray!"

Ray came racing into the room as though he was going to have to rescue her from harm. "What is it?"

"Matt's left Hannah," she said, as though it was the most exciting thing she'd heard for a long time. It probably was. I felt a pulse in my temples throb as I thought of Katie and James, of Sam and Grace, or whoever he was friends with, and now Sheila and Ray enjoying my trauma just as if it was a soap opera. Entertainment. As though it didn't really matter.

"What? When?"

"Oh yes, when did he leave? Sorry"—she turned to Ray—"I forgot to ask."

He tutted and sat down at the table with us. I half expected him to get out a clipboard and wondered for a moment whether they kept notes like I did to monitor the activities of the street. They both looked at me, bright and expectant. *This is better than the telly,* I could see them thinking and the pulse in my temples beat harder.

"A couple of months ago," I said. Actually, it was fifty days ago, but it was easier to round up.

"What?"

They exchanged disbelieving glances. How had this escaped their notice? I could tell they felt manners constrained them from asking why he'd gone, then they threw caution to the wind and Ray urged Sheila on with a gesture I'd seen many, many times before.

"Oh, darling," she crooned, stroking my arm. "That's such bad news. We did like Matt. What happened? Did you have a row?"

Ray blustered, "Nothing wrong with having a row occasionally. We all do it. Not that we ever heard you or anything . . ."

I flushed. I was sure he had heard us sometimes; those walls weren't that thick.

"No," I admitted. "I came home and he'd gone. Taken everything with him."

Their eyes boggled and I could see them both thinking, *How on earth did we miss that?*

"You were away," I said. "Remember when you went to your daughter's in Devon for a long weekend? You went Thursday to Sunday, didn't you? Well, he left on the Friday."

"The sly bastard!" burst out of Ray.

"But . . ." said Sheila, "wasn't that the Friday you went to Oxford? I remember telling our Rebecca about it."

"Yep. I came home and he'd gone."

She clutched her hand to her mouth. "Oh my goodness. You poor thing! If only we'd been here for you."

I shook my head. "It's okay. It's just . . . well, I wanted to ask you . . ."

They leaned forward, eagerly. "What? What is it?"

"Have you seen him around?"

They looked at each other and it was obvious their minds were whirring.

"I don't think I've seen him for months," said Ray. "Not since he helped me change that tire."

"That was before we went away, remember? I don't know . . ." mused Sheila. "I think it was just before we went to Rebecca's, but I can't remember when."

"I think I know when it was." Ray turned to her. "You told me you'd seen him in B and Q."

"Oh yes, that's right," she said. "I had to pick up another pot of paint for the spare room. We'd run out and . . ."

"When was this?" I cut in. "The weekend before he left, do you mean? Do you remember which day? The time?"

"It was Saturday morning," she said promptly. "The Saturday before we went away. It was ten o'clock. Maybe a few minutes before. We'd just done our Tesco shop and we were on our way home. Ray went to Halfords while I nipped in."

"Brake fluid," said Ray.

I stared at him blankly.

"I bought some brake fluid in Halfords," he said as though I was stupid.

I shook my head and thought back to that morning. Matt had gone to Tesco for a newspaper and croissants. He'd been a bit longer than I'd expected, but he'd told me there were crowds of people there. Tesco and B&Q were less than half a mile apart on the same road.

"Could you see what he'd bought?" I asked. I couldn't think of anything we'd needed from B&Q.

"Boxes."

"What?"

"You know those big plastic boxes with lids that you store things in? He had loads of them. Two trolleys full."

I stared at her. I had one of those under my bed with all the house details in it. I'd had it since I was at university and it was the only one in the house.

"That's why I noticed him, you see," she went on. "He was across the other side of the store to me and he had two trolleys. He was trying to push them both, but he was on the phone at the same time, so they kept rolling away. I heard him laughing first, actually, and then looked up and saw him."

"Laughing?"

"Oh yes," she said. "He was on his mobile, chatting to someone. And the trolleys were rolling away and he was laughing."

"And he didn't see you?"

"No. I was at the till and he was walking around. He didn't see me."

I stood up, unable to bear their sympathetic glances any longer. I knew they would want me to go through the nitty-gritty with them, and they looked really disappointed when they realized I was leaving.

"And you haven't seen him since?" I asked. "In the last few days in particular? You haven't seen him come to the house?"

They looked startled.

"No, I haven't seen him at all since then," said Sheila.

"Me neither," said Ray. "Though I'll have a damned good word with him if I do." He puffed his chest out. "Leaving a young woman like that. It's a disgrace!"

"Have you asked the new neighbors?" asked Sheila. "The ones on the other side?"

"No," I said. "I don't know them. I've hardly seen them."

"And you want to give a good impression," said Sheila. "You don't want them to think there's something up with you, do you?"

Smarting with hurt pride, I moved toward the door.

"I'll show you out," said Ray. He walked just that bit too close behind me as I left. I could almost feel his breath on my neck and when he touched the small of my back, I flinched.

I turned the handle on the front door to open it but he put his hand over mine, blocking my path. "Just let me know if you want anything." His voice was low and I knew he didn't want Sheila to hear him. "Anything at all. I'm your man."

I had a horrible feeling he was about to hug me. Quickly I pulled my hand away and opened the door. I glanced back and saw Sheila standing behind him. I don't know how long she'd been there. She was staring at me and I flushed, thinking she'd realized I found him repulsive. As I hurried from their house I just knew they were standing in their doorway looking at me. I hunched my shoulders, bent my head and ran the last few steps.

Back in my own house, I could no longer smell the cologne that Matt wore. I didn't know whether it had dissipated or whether it had been nothing but a figment of my imagination. In my kitchen, knowing that Sheila and Ray were just yards away dissecting this new gossip, I picked up my notes and my pen and began to write.

Chapter
Thirty-three

THAT AFTERNOON I lay on my bed for hours, thinking about the day that Sheila had seen Matt.

He'd woken just before me and I'd heard him in the shower with the radio on low. It seemed ages since he'd stayed in bed on a Saturday morning to see what happened, and that morning was no exception. He came out of the bathroom already dressed—another change—and said he was off to get the newspaper. I asked him to pick up croissants and he was quite happy, in a good mood, really, shouting good-bye as he left the house. I'd stayed in bed a bit longer, then got up and showered, too.

I'd noticed it was a while before he came back but didn't think anything of it. He'd been carrying a bag of food, looking just the same as normal. I closed my eyes and tried to think whether he'd brought anything else into the house, but I knew he hadn't. I'd vacuumed the hallway and living room by the time he returned and there was no room in either place to put anything like those big plastic boxes without my noticing. I'd been in the hallway when he got back, now that I thought about it. He must have expected me to be in the kitchen because he'd started a little as he came through the door, but gave me a smile and said, "Sorry! Have you been waiting long?" before passing me the bag.

I tried to think whether I'd seen inside the boot of his car that weekend but I knew I hadn't. Why would I? The only time I would do that was if we were going on a trip somewhere. He often had stuff in the boot from work: his hi-vis jacket, his helmet and so on that he needed when he went on building sites. We didn't tend to drive each other's cars, though we were both insured to. I assumed that had changed now and made a mental note to write it on my Post-its in the kitchen so that I'd remember to call the insurers.

So on that day we'd had breakfast and read the papers and talked a little about the news and then we'd cleaned the house and he'd taken each of the cars in turn to the car wash in the afternoon and gone to the gym, while I went to get my hair cut and highlighted, ready for the meeting in Oxford the following week. It had been a typical Saturday.

And then it was as though the fog in my head cleared and I thought, *Who was he talking to when he was in the shop?*

I sat up on the bed. Sheila had said he was laughing and chatting on the phone. Now, Matt's one of those guys who, if a friend rang to ask him down to the pub, the conversation would last less than a minute and consist of, "Where? What time? I'll see what she says," and that would be it. He'd be friendly enough, but there was never much laughing involved, nor any chat.

The only time I'd known him to laugh and chat on the phone was when he'd first met me.

I knew then that he'd been talking to a woman. Talking and chatting and laughing with another woman.

Within a week he'd gone.

Then I remembered something. I'd seen him in Chester. Even though I'd only caught sight of his back as he'd walked among the crowd at the station, I was sure it was him.

My heart sank. Ruby was from Chester.

Ruby, the woman who'd apparently broken Matt's heart, the woman he loved before he met me, lived in Chester. I'd just seen Matt there. How could that be a coincidence? How could I not have thought of her the moment I saw him at the station?

I grabbed my iPad and started to search for her.

Ruby Taylor. Even her name made my stomach tighten.

ONE DAY, AFTER I'd been with Matt for a few months, he was home with me for the weekend and we'd called in to see his mum on the Sunday afternoon. She'd asked him to come and help her with something in the garden and I was sitting in the living room, bored rigid, while he helped her. I didn't need to be with him; I was just still at the stage where I couldn't bear to be apart from him. It was a job for two people and it was cold and windy outside, so I wandered around Olivia's house, looking for something to do.

There were some photo albums on her bookcase and I took them out to have a look. Most were photos of Matt as a child. My heart melted as I saw him as a baby, a toddler, starting school and then older, as a teenager. There was one in particular that I loved. He was about five years old and on a swing in a park in winter; he had a little red duffle coat on that matched his rosy cheeks and on his face was an expression of pure happiness. I took it from the album to ask Olivia whether I could get a copy made and carried on looking, past his football training at high school to his graduation photos.

Toward the back of the album there were some loose photos. They were of a girl about my age, maybe a bit younger. She had long dark hair, just as I had, but hers did as it was told and curled gracefully around her head. She was taller than I was, slimmer than I was, more vivid, more alive. There were photos of her on the beach, on the London Eye, skiing. I stared down at them. I had no idea who she was. Matt had mentioned girlfriends before, obviously; we'd told each other a little bit about our past partners when we first met. I didn't know whether she was one of them; I hadn't seen any of their photos.

Olivia came in then, her hair windswept and her cheeks scarlet from the cold.

"Oh, you're looking at the photos!"

I asked whether I could have a copy of the photo of Matt on the swing and she said she'd be happy to get it done herself. She did, too, and I'd had it framed and put it on the windowsill in the living room. Of course he took it with him when he left me.

She stroked the photo. "He was a gorgeous boy," she said.

He waved at us through the window.

"He still is," I said loyally. He was, too, with his dark blond hair and brown eyes. Just one smile from him and I was lost.

"What are those you have there?" She took the loose photos from my hand. "Oh," she said, her voice softening, "Ruby."

"Ruby?"

She smiled. "Yes, Ruby Taylor. She was an old girlfriend of Matt's. She was a beautiful girl."

She was. Everything about her was striking.

"You remind me of her, actually," she said. "It was quite a shock when I saw you."

I looked back at the photograph. Although there was a superficial resemblance, I knew that I looked like a sepia version of the girl there. "I don't recognize her name," I said, forcing myself to sound casual. "Was she someone Matt knew from work?"

"Oh no," she said. "She was from Chester; I think they met in Liverpool on a night out. He went out with her for a few months last summer. He used to come up from London to see her at the weekends. She finished with him the day before he went on holiday. I was really shocked; I thought it was going to last." She looked at me then, smiling guilelessly. "But then of course he met you and he's never been happier!"

She went back outside and carried on working alongside Matt. I stood up, the photos in my hand, and looked out at them in the garden. It was as though a piece had fitted into a jigsaw and now I could see the whole picture clearly. I'd wondered why Matt hadn't been as enthusiastic as his friends when I'd seen him at the airport. They were in high spirits and I'd thought he must be tired, he looked so low. He must have been heartbroken when she dumped him. I looked down at the photo. Anyone would be. And that holiday he and I had talked and laughed and relaxed together and he hadn't said a word about Ruby. He hadn't even hesitated on the plane when I'd asked whether he was single, yet she'd ended the relationship just the day before.

I put the photos back in the album and turned to the last page. One picture was facedown, sticking to the inside cover of the album. Slowly I peeled it off. I thought I knew what it would be.

Matt and Ruby were sitting together on the sofa that I was sitting on at that moment. She was smiling up at him and in her profile shot I could see her little straight nose, her curling eyelashes and lips that were so luscious even I would want to kiss them. Matt was looking down at her and his hand was stroking her hair and his face was just suffused with love.

I closed my eyes.

Olivia must have taken that photo. She must have seen the way he looked at Ruby and now she'd seen the way he looks at me.

It wasn't the same.

I slid that photo into my bag and returned the albums to the shelf. When Matt went back to London the next day I took it into the garden and burned it, before sweeping up the ashes and burying them in the garden rubbish. It was no use. Even now I can remember the way he looked at her, remember the calm confidence on her face that he loved her beyond all others.

And then she dumped him.

My memories of that holiday in Corfu were tarnished then. I'd seen it as serendipity, our meeting like that. Now when I thought of our first glance, our first kiss, I wondered whether he'd felt unfaithful to Ruby or wished I was her.

And I thought that no matter how long you've known someone, you never truly know them.

I NEVER KNEW what had happened to Ruby after she and Matt broke up. I never mentioned her name to him. I couldn't stand to hear him talk about her. They hadn't been living together, though according to Olivia, Matt would spend every weekend at Ruby's home in Chester. It didn't go unnoticed by me that I was the one to travel to see him, while he'd come up here to see Ruby. I loved my weekends away and tried not to let Ruby taint them, but still, week after week I would arrive at Euston exhausted and anxious in case Matt wasn't there. Then I'd see him jockeying for position at the gate and my heart would pound. I'd see his smile, see him push past someone to rush toward me, and I'd feel faint with relief.

So now, looking for Ruby online, I realized I had no idea whether she was still in Chester or what kind of job she was doing. I looked on Facebook first. There were several women there with the same name. I saw a Facebook link to a Ruby Taylor in Chester, but it was set to private and I couldn't see anything, just a photo of some flowers, so I didn't know whether it was her or not. There was another Ruby Taylor on Twitter, but again she had no photo and had only used her account to retweet. It hadn't been used at all for a couple of years. She wasn't on LinkedIn, which surprised me; it seemed the sort of thing that she'd be on, with a really flattering photo and thousands of qualifications.

Katie sent a message while I was looking for Ruby:

Hope you got home OK yesterday. Try to move on, Hannah. It's just not worth getting into a state about him. x

She really had no idea. She must have thought my relationship was very shallow, that I could give up on it just like that. I knew that if it had happened to her, she would have been bedbound, with her mother holding a cold compress to her head while her father went out to teach the guy a lesson. I was just about to text back saying that I thought Matt was with Ruby in Chester, but I managed to stop myself in time. She already thought I was mad without bringing Ruby into it. She knew about Ruby; I'd phoned her as soon as Matt was back on the train to London that weekend, but I hadn't mentioned her in years, probably not since Matt had moved in with me. She'd really think I was losing it if I told her my thoughts now. So I sent a quick text saying I was okay and carried on my search.

And then I found her.

Chapter
Thirty-four

RUBY WAS WORKING as a wedding planner. Immediately I had a vision of her roaming around stately homes with a clipboard, wearing one of those headsets with a microphone, ordering the staff around and enjoying the lustful gaze of the groom. The photos on the website showed her in a variety of hats and suits and little dresses, looking as pleased as punch with herself.

"The devil is in the detail," the blurb on the website stated.

I wouldn't be too sure about that.

The offices for the wedding planners were in the center of Chester, just on the edge of the Roman walls. Matt must have been visiting her, I thought. But he was getting on a train . . . Where was he going? Was he living in Chester now? Was he living with her?

At the thought of Matt living with Ruby, my heart started to race. I leaned back, closed my eyes and did the deep breathing a counselor at university had shown me years ago to help me cope. It had helped me then, though it took many sessions before I could do it alone. It was soothing to have her put her cool hand on mine and count my breaths in and out. I'd focus on her face, soft and concerned, and she'd nod gently and count until I was calm. I was eighteen then and I wished I'd learned those skills so much earlier.

I checked the company's opening times on their website. Tuesday to Saturday, 9 a.m. to 6 p.m. I looked at the clock. It was 4:30. If I was quick, I could be in Chester by 5:15.

Part of me knew it was madness, I'll admit that. Or rather not madness—I wasn't going to label myself as mad just because someone had driven me to distraction—but it was a little over the top. I knew that the last thing I needed to do was to go and confront this woman from the past, but it had suddenly become more important than finding Matt right then. If he was with her, then I'd become just an isolated incident in his life. A blip. An interruption to the proper course of his life. Something he might look back on as he and Ruby celebrated an anniversary. I wondered what he'd think of me years later.

Then I wondered whether I would give up the chase. Would I accept she'd beaten me? I tried to imagine myself admitting defeat.

I couldn't.

Within a couple of minutes I was in my car, driving down the motorway, hands gripping the steering wheel, my vision blurred, my foot heavy on the accelerator. It was just as it was four years ago, when all I could think about was Ruby.

I ARRIVED AT her offices just after five o'clock and parked on a meter. The house was a Georgian terrace, with half a dozen steps up to the front door. A black railing ran along the front of the house, with steps down to a basement. Lamps were lit in the ground floor rooms, casting a soft, warm glow on the apricot walls. A silver sports car was parked in the residents' parking spot, its black soft-top rolled back to reveal leather seats, and I thought that if that was Ruby's car and if she was with Matt now, I'd come back that night with bags of sand and fill it to the brim.

The house looked so much more expensive than I'd imagined. I swallowed hard. I had no idea what I was going to say. Should I pretend I was getting married? But what if they asked for a down payment? I had a vision of myself being forced into handing over my credit card as a deposit on a wedding when I didn't even know where my boyfriend was living.

Then the lamp in one room was extinguished and I panicked. Were they closing now? I jumped out of the car and hurried up the steps. There was a huge brass knocker on the front door and two bells. One was for the wedding planners, the other had no name. I pressed the bell for the planners and waited.

The ornate lamp above the front door came on and then the door opened. A horsey-looking woman appeared, her silk scarf wrapped around her neck a dozen times. She wore an elegant little cashmere suit and more makeup than I had in my bathroom at home.

She smiled at me. "Hello? I'm so sorry, our offices are closed now. Can I help you?" I felt like tapping my watch and reminding her she still had forty-five minutes to go, but she added, "I know we're closing early, but I'm off to see one of our brides. She just can't decide whether to go for a train!"

I gawped at her. A train? Someone was such a bridezilla she couldn't get on a train without help?

The woman beamed at me. "Fiona King," she said and held out her hand.

"Oh." My palms were damp and surreptitiously I rubbed them on my skirt before I shook her hand. There was no way I was telling her my real name. "I'm Katie Dixon."

"I'll give you my card," she said, searching in her bag. "Maybe you could make an appointment? Only I do have to dash."

I just blurted it out. "I want to see Ruby."

"Ruby?"

"Is she here? Can I see her?"

"Oh, gosh, are you a friend of hers? Didn't you know?" I must have looked completely blank. "She got married last week! So quickly, the little minx. We were so cross with her."

She'd *married* him?

"Well, we would have planned her wedding! We would have loved that, she was such a darling. But no, off she went and got married in secret and now she's traveling the world. For a year! So romantic."

"She's gone away for a year?"

"Yes, can you believe it? Not that they're slumming it, of course. I think it'll be mostly boutique hotels and yurts. We are so jealous!"

"But . . ." Frantically I imagined Matt, off traveling for a year. Why hadn't I thought of that? He loved traveling! He loved being abroad, feeling free. "She married Matt?"

"Matt?" The woman climbed into the sports car and turned back to me. "I'm awfully sorry, I don't know anyone called that. Goodness, when was the last time you saw her? She married Jonathan Courtney-Cooper. They'd been together for six months. It's been a positively whirlwind romance!"

I said, "How romantic" and "Do pass on my congratulations when you speak to her" and "Gosh, what a surprise," but all I could think was *Oh, thank God. Thank God.*

Back in my car I caught my reflection in the rearview mirror before I set off. My face was feverishly bright. There was a sheen of sweat on my forehead and my hair stuck to it in strands. My makeup had disappeared, leaving gray marks around my eyes to show where it had been.

So yes, thank God Ruby hadn't gone off with Matt, but thank God, too, she hadn't seen me like this.

Did it mean, then, that Matt *wasn't* with another woman? And if he wasn't, was it him sending me those messages or someone else?

Chapter
Thirty-five

WHEN I GOT back, the house seemed so gloomy and unwelcoming that I couldn't bear the thought of being there alone. I went upstairs and washed my face, then changed into my running gear. I sent Fran a text asking if she wanted to go for a run, but she replied saying she was tired and wasn't up for it. I sighed, guessing she was feeling neglected and this was her way of punishing me. She was right; I just didn't have time for her or Jenny nowadays. At the same time, I was so fed up of doing everything on my own. For a second I considered staying home, but I knew I had to get out, otherwise I'd find myself lying on my bed, thinking poisonous thoughts and driving myself crazy. I thought briefly of the person who'd filmed me running and shrugged my shoulders. If I came across him tonight, I'd be ready for him.

I dragged my hair back into a ponytail and pushed my feet into my trainers and I was off, running down the road, my eyes darting from side to side in case someone was filming me and my heart pumping harder than it should at the thought of Matt with someone else. Of course it wasn't Ruby; I felt stupid at the thought now. But who could it be? I tried to remember the women he worked with. I could recall some names and the odd comment, but he'd never spoken about the women at work much. I'd never had any concerns about him like that. Not really. It made sense, though, that he'd gone off with someone else, and I wanted to see the look on his face when I confronted him.

Then I remembered the phone in Sam's glove compartment—a phone he'd said wasn't working. I knew he was lying. Was Matt the same? If he was seeing someone else, had he bought another phone? For a second I thought of turning around and going to Sheila and Ray's house to ask Sheila what kind of phone Matt was using when she saw him in the shop. I knew that was pointless, but still I had to force myself not to do it.

If Matt had bought a new phone just to talk to another woman, that meant there was a whole new level of deception going on. Where would he keep it? My mind ran wild as I thought of him hiding a phone from me, sliding it out from under the bed when I was in the shower, or parking down the road to call another woman, then coming home to me with a smile on his face and his new phone hidden in the boot of his car.

I felt sick at the thought of him racing out to call her at lunchtime, just as he used to do every day when we first met. Sometimes, lately, I'd called him and his phone had rung out. I'd thought nothing of it, but now I wondered. Was he talking to her then? Was he in his car, his head thrown back with laughter, his eyes soft and loving as he talked to this other woman? Had I called him on his regular phone while he was talking to her and had he looked at the caller ID and said, "Oh, don't worry; it's no one"? Had he gone back to his office and hidden his private phone in his filing cabinet and then called me back and told me he'd been in a meeting?

I ran for miles that night, hardly noticing the distance. It was good to concentrate on my breathing and to get rid of some of the anger inside me. Just as it was getting dark I was running back up the riverside to make my way home when I realized I was near the pub Matt and I used to frequent if we were going out locally. The Boathouse was an old half-timbered place, full of tiny rooms and real ale and locals who'd been going there for years. We'd loved it there and used to be regulars, but lately with work becoming more hectic for both of us there was less time for socializing. We tended to stay in if we wanted a drink; I suppose that's what happens when you hit your thirties. Now I stood outside, wondering whether he'd have the nerve to go somewhere so close to our house. I wondered, too, whether any of the people we'd mixed with there would question the fact that I wasn't with him.

James had asked me whether I'd been in touch with the guys from the pub, to ask whether they'd seen Matt, but I hadn't been able to face it. I didn't think they'd tell me the truth if they did know, and the thought of them discussing us made me cringe. I didn't have their numbers, either; it had always been Matt they'd call, though usually we'd all just drift down there on summer nights after a long walk by the river.

The first week he'd gone, though, I came here a few times. I drove down and parked in a side road where I could watch who was coming and going. I saw his friends there one night and I waited all evening, staring out into the dark, but Matt didn't join them. They all left together at eleven, chatting outside on the pavement before going their separate ways. I had my window open but couldn't hear them clearly, no matter how much I strained. I thought maybe it was time to do that again. Maybe once he'd gone for a few weeks, he'd miss them and start to come down here again. Maybe he'd come down here with someone else.

I thought of them accepting someone new, someone they hadn't met before, a woman they could impress with their old stories that, frankly, I was sick of. I stood outside the pub and thought, *Maybe she's with him now. They might be in there, sitting where I used to sit, having a drink with his friends.*

I could feel the heat rising in my body until my face was flaming.

Maybe she'd become part of the gang! All sitting around having a good time, with nobody even mentioning the fact that I wasn't there. As though I didn't exist.

A couple came toward me, the woman first, dressed up for a Saturday night. I could smell the heady scent of Calvin Klein's Obsession, see the soft wet slick of her lip gloss as she brushed past me. I shrank back, feeling invisible in my running gear, my face makeup-free, sweaty and red.

As they entered the pub I darted behind them, trying to see whether Matt was there. The door closed in my face, but I just had time to see there were only a handful of men at the bar and none of them was Matt. The windows facing the river were frosted on the lower half and for a mad moment I thought of jumping up to check who was in the room, but even I knew how that would appear to anyone inside.

I sat on the bench outside, looking out over the river. The offices and warehouses of the Liverpool docks were lit now, lacing the riverbank like a daisy chain. That skyline was one of my earliest memories and one I'd always love. The sky was dark blue with a thin rim of gold as the sun finally set and a breeze in the air chilled the sweat on my body. I shivered.

I heard a noise at the door of the Boathouse and turned. A couple of men were coming out, shouting their good-byes to someone inside. In the brief instant that the door was open, I saw James walking to the bar.

I froze.

Earlier that day I'd sent Katie a text asking whether they were doing anything tonight. She hadn't replied for a couple of hours, then when she did she said they would be staying in with a box set and a takeaway. It had sounded so much like my life before Matt left that I'd suddenly been furious and had sent a reply, saying *Oh very nice. Have a good night.*

Ten minutes later she sent, *Thanks x*, which had made me even more mad, as I knew she would have clocked my sarcasm.

Remembering that text, I pushed the door open and went into the pub.

James was standing at the bar, chatting to the barman, an older guy who'd worked there for years. As I approached him he turned, startled, then looked back at the barman.

"Thanks. Keep the change." He moved toward me. "Hey, Hannah."

"Are you here with Matt?" I asked.

He seemed amused for some reason and I saw that as confirmation. I looked around wildly. There were four rooms leading off the main bar. I knew that if I didn't move fast, Matt could be out of there without my seeing.

I flashed a glance at the little room behind me. It only seated a dozen or so people and tonight it was half empty. Matt wasn't there.

I backed toward the door and scanned the room to my left. This was bigger, but had just couples in it. I had a quick hard look at the men, but none of them was him.

That left the other side room, which faced the bar, and a large room at the back. I walked swiftly toward the side room, then stopped abruptly. Katie was sitting in there, alone at a table, twisting a strand of hair around her index finger, her eyes on her empty glass.

Chapter
Thirty-six

I FELT JAMES'S arm brush mine and turned to find him beside me.

"Going to join us?" he said.

Katie looked up when she heard his voice, then saw me and jumped. "Oh, hi, Hannah!"

"Fancy seeing you here," I said. "I thought you were staying in. With a box set and a takeaway."

"Yes," she said, not meeting my eyes. "We were going to, weren't we, James? It's such a nice night, though, we thought we'd come out for a walk." There was an awkward pause, then she said, "So, have you been for a run?"

I looked down at my sweaty tank top, Lycra leggings and running shoes which had definitely seen better days and then back at her cool summer dress and high wedge sandals showing off a light tan and pretty little painted toes. She looked how I'd looked until a couple of months ago.

I pulled up a chair and sat down next to her. "Just had to get out of the house."

"Is it safe?"

I frowned. For a minute I thought of the video I'd been sent. "Safe?"

"When you're pregnant, I mean," she said. "Aren't you meant to take it easy?"

"Oh, no, it's fine," I said. "Don't worry. Exercise is recommended."

"Are you on your own?" she asked. "Didn't Fran or Jenny go with you?"

I hadn't even bothered asking Jenny, assuming she felt the same way Fran did. "They didn't feel like it."

"Do they know Matt's gone?"

"No." I was starting to feel as though I was being cross-examined. "I only see them when we go for a run. I haven't told them anything."

"I'll go running with you if you want." From the expression on her face then I think she'd just remembered that 10K race from years ago, when I'd left her standing. "Or James will."

I shook my head. "It's okay. I'll be all right. I'd rather go on my own."

"Fancy a drink?" asked James.

"Diet Coke, thanks. Sorry, I don't have any money with me. I didn't think I'd be needing it."

"Any news?" Katie whispered as soon as he went to the bar. "Have you found out anything more?"

I looked around to see why she was whispering. There were a few other couples in the room, but nobody who looked the slightest bit interested in us.

"My next-door neighbor, Sheila, saw him buying boxes in B and Q the weekend before he left," I said. "I hadn't spoken to her about him until today. They were away when he left, so I assumed they wouldn't know anything."

"Boxes?"

James sat down beside us, putting my drink in front of me. "What's up?"

"Matt was seen buying boxes the week before he left," I said again.

"What kind of boxes?"

"It doesn't matter what kind of boxes!" I snapped. "Plastic boxes. Packing boxes. Something to put his stuff in, I suppose."

He reared back. "Okay, okay!"

"Did he buy anything else?" asked Katie. "How long was she watching him for?"

"She wasn't watching him! They were just both in the shop and she noticed what he was buying."

We sat in silence for a bit. I looked up and saw Katie give James a warning look. I glared at her. The silence continued.

"So, work going well?" asked James. "Hit that promotion yet?"

I looked down again but not before I saw Katie nudge him hard.

"Hannah," she said gently. "What's up? Has something happened? Apart from him buying boxes, that is. Is there something else?"

I nodded miserably. "Two things."

She took a long drink. "What's the first?"

"Have you had more texts?" asked James.

"Yes, but they're the least of my problems. I can't even begin to tell you what's been happening."

"What?" asked Katie. She sounded concerned and I thought, *At last you are taking this seriously!*

"Someone's been coming into my house."

"What?" she said again. "When you're in there?"

"No, thank God," I said. "When I'm at work."

"You've seen them?"

I shook my head. "I know it sounds stupid, but I know someone's been there."

She leaned back and had another sip of her drink. I sensed she was losing interest. "I doubt it, Hannah. Why would anyone do that?"

"Who do you think it is?" asked James. "Who'd do that?"

I stared at him. "Who do you think? It's Matt. He's been coming into my house when I'm not there."

"Matt?" Katie looked dumbfounded. "But why would he do that? He's left you."

"I know he's left me!" I hissed impatiently. "You tell me that every time I see you! But he's coming back. I know it. He's texting me and he's coming to the house."

"But how would he get in?" asked James. "You said he left his key behind."

"He could easily have made a copy." I saw Katie dart a look at James and fury raged in me. "I'm not crazy, you know!"

"Nobody's saying you're crazy," said Katie in a patient voice that made me want to slap her. "Why don't you get a burglar alarm? That's what I'd do."

I stopped in my tracks. I hadn't thought of that. "But what use is that to me if he's coming in when I'm at work? I'd have Ray round all the time if a bell was ringing out."

Katie shuddered. "Ugh, you can't have that."

"You can buy a program that uses your webcam on your laptop," said James. "It picks up any movement in the house. It's activated when there's a sound or a movement. Just leave it switched on and if someone comes into the house when you're not there, it'll record them."

"Really?"

He nodded. "It's not expensive, because you don't have to buy any hardware, just a program. You simply point your webcam in the direction you want to film. Make sure you change your settings so your laptop doesn't automatically time out, though." He took out his phone and showed me the sort of thing he meant on Amazon. "And the beauty of it is that you can watch it while you're out of the house. On your phone or on your computer at work."

I sat quietly for a second, furious with myself for not thinking of this. I remembered seeing a YouTube video of a woman in Florida whose home was burgled. She was at work when it happened and saw the whole thing on her computer.

"Right," I said, getting up. "Thanks for that. I'll go and buy one now."

"Stay here for a bit," said Katie. "Have another drink."

I shook my head. "Are you kidding? He might even be there now. I'm going home to get it sorted."

"Want any help?" asked James.

I thought of the state of the kitchen. The notes were stuck all over the cabinet doors at the moment and I couldn't stand to see their expressions if they saw that. I knew how it would look to anyone who wasn't involved. "No, I'll be okay, thanks."

As I turned to go, Katie said, "Oh, you said there were two things. What was the second?"

"The second?" I said. "The second is that I think Matt had a girlfriend. I think he left home to be with her."

Both of them stared at me. Before they could ask me why I thought that, I smiled, thanked James for the drink and left the pub to run home.

Chapter
Thirty-seven

ONE DAY, A couple of weeks later, a text came through from my mum, asking how I was, and suddenly I wanted to see her, to talk to her. I called her landline and she answered within a couple of seconds.

"It's me," I said. "Hannah."

"Hannah? Oh, hello, sweetheart. It's lovely to hear from you."

I cleared my throat. I never found it easy to talk to her, and now the pity I felt for her because of my dad's affair made it even worse. "Are you free later? I might call round."

"Of course! Do you want to come for dinner? Dad will be home early tonight for a change. We'll be eating at half past six."

I flinched at the thought. Since I'd seen him with Helen in the restaurant I was furious with him, and no matter how much I tried to dampen those feelings they still rose up and made my blood boil. It would be worse if I went when he wasn't there, though, especially after getting the text he'd sent me instead of Helen. If it *was* Helen he was texting. It could have been anyone. He could be seeing a number of women; how would I know? But I knew that if he thought I'd gone home to see my mum and deliberately avoided him, he wouldn't be happy. He might even come round here to talk to me about it. My blood ran cold at the thought of that.

"I'd love to stay for dinner, Mum, but do you mind if I come a bit earlier? I want to chat to you."

I could hear her racking her brains, wondering what was going on.

"Something to celebrate?" she asked coyly.

"No."

"Oh okay, well, I'll be home all afternoon, so come whenever you like, pet."

I ARRIVED AT their house just after three that afternoon. I parked in the driveway and sat for a moment, gearing myself up. I hadn't seen them since February, when Matt and I were invited to my dad's birthday dinner. It was all right, but in a way I found it harder being there with Matt because I had to make sure I didn't show I was getting stressed, otherwise he would have got upset on my behalf. I usually tried to go for a swim or a run after visiting them, but that night it was too late by the time we got home and I was a bit of a wreck afterward.

I've never had that feeling that so many others have going back to their family home. I remember at university that by the end of term my friends would all be looking forward to seeing their families. One of my best friends there, Sarah, said that she never slept anywhere as well as she did in her own bed at home. I remember looking at her and realizing the gulf between us. It was so far from my experience.

Even as a child, I knew the second I entered the house who was there and what was going on. That's why I was so sure Matt had been making those stealthy visits. Sometimes, when I was young, if I wasn't overheard coming into the house, I'd hear enough to make me leave immediately and go to Katie's, or later to James's. Katie's mum used to accept my excuses that I'd forgotten something or that I was allowed to stay out later and would fuss over me, making me a hot drink and something to eat. She'd always phone my mum before I left their house and it was years before I realized the call was to warn her to be prepared for my arrival. She never said a word to me, though, and I know she didn't say anything to Katie, either. There'd always be a hug for me whenever she saw me, and she told me several times that Katie thought of me as her sister. I felt a twinge of guilt as I remembered how I'd rammed her chocolate cake into the bin.

That day when I rang the bell and my mother answered the door, I knew immediately that she was alone and that all was well. For now. She hugged me and I noticed she seemed a bit smaller than usual. We used to be the same height and, okay, I was wearing heels and she was wearing slippers, but I seemed to tower over her. She was only sixty; surely she shouldn't be frail already?

I gave her a bouquet of flowers and a box of chocolates. Before I left the house I'd noticed on my phone that over the last few months she'd made so many missed calls and left messages I hadn't bothered to answer and I knew it was wrong of me. I knew she would have wanted me to turn to her as soon as Matt left, but I'd felt humiliated, ashamed of the way he'd done it. What did it say about me, that he had to leave like that? I couldn't bear to have her look at me with pity in her eyes.

My mum . . . I don't know, I've always seen her as kind of weak. She never really had much of an opinion about anything. Before she said anything, she'd look to my dad for approval, and if he disagreed with her, she wouldn't stand up for herself. It used to drive me crazy when I was growing up, when I was dying for her to speak up for me and for herself. She wasn't a good role model for me, really.

As for my dad, all we had in common was work. I couldn't confide in him. If I tried to it always ended in tears. My tears.

As soon as my mother hugged me, I started to cry. I couldn't help it. The shock and frustration I'd felt, the loneliness since Matt left, all of it came out when she put her arms around me.

She was startled, I could tell. I hadn't been so upset since my teens, when I'd suffered the usual angst that teenagers go through. Even then I tended to cry on my own; I've never liked anyone to see me that way.

"Sit down, sweetheart," she said and put her arm around me, guiding me to the sofa in their living room. The wood-burning stove was lit, despite the warm day, and suddenly it was just what I needed. I'd felt cold for so long. It was just as if the dread I'd felt when I realized Matt had gone had turned into something solid, as though within me was a block of ice that was building day by day. I'd felt it in my stomach first, but now it had moved up to my chest and at times it was as though it was stopping me from breathing.

She made me a mug of hot chocolate and put the biscuit tin in front of me.

"You've got awfully thin," she said. "Are you all right?"

It was clear I wasn't all right; why else would I burst into tears? But she seemed willing to let me bide my time and tell her when I was ready. I dried my face on some tissues and gave her a watery smile.

"Matt's left me," I said and started to cry again. She sat next to me, put my drink on the coffee table and put her arms around me once more. It was so comforting; I don't know why I'd never let her hug me before. Well, not for years. Decades. Since I was very young.

"You'll be fine," she said, and I really wished that was true.

I DRANK MY hot chocolate and told her what had happened, how I'd come home and found he'd gone, taking all my memories of him. She sat quietly and said nothing, just let me tell her all about it.

"Well," she said in the end, "it looks like that's over, anyway."

"But I want to find him!" I wailed. "I want to talk to him!"

"I know you do," she said sympathetically, "but he's made his decision. It's a shame, pet. I really liked him and I know you did, too, but you can't make someone stay with you. If he's not there voluntarily, it doesn't mean anything, does it?"

"I think he wants to come back, though," I said and I told her about getting a text while I was at Katie's, saying he was home.

"And was he?"

I shook my head. "No. I looked everywhere."

She winced at that and I knew she was picturing me running around the house calling his name, just as I had.

"Can I see the message?"

I took my phone out of my bag and showed her.

"So that number . . . is it Matt's?"

"No, not his old number," I admitted. "I told you, he deleted his details from my phone. But James had his number and it's not the same. And I rang his old number and it's out of service. It stands to reason he's got a different one now."

"Have you called *this* number?"

I nodded. "I did, but it just rang out. Nobody answered. And I sent a couple of texts." That was a slight underestimate; I'd been texting all night.

We sat in silence. I wanted to tell her about the flowers, but after seeing Katie's response, I was frightened of the same thing happening again. I still felt like I was going mad when I thought of that.

"Do you know why he left?" she asked then. "Had you been having rows?"

"Well, obviously sometimes we had rows. Everyone does. But I didn't have a clue he was going to leave. The night before he went, everything was fine. He ran me a bath and brought me up a glass of wine." And then the floodgates opened again and I sobbed, "And the next day I got home and he'd gone and taken everything with him."

My mum looked horrified and hugged me again, but this time she said, "I wonder why he did it."

WHEN I WAS calmer, she made me sit and watch a film with her.

"You don't want to be sitting dwelling on that all afternoon," she said. "You need to take your mind off it. You must feel like you're going mad, thinking about it all the time."

I did.

So we sat and watched *Pretty Woman* for the millionth time. She was right, I did need something to take my mind off Matt. This was something we'd often done, Mum and I, sitting and watching television on our own when my dad was out. Then we'd see his car headlights swoop up the drive and we'd leap into action. Long before he was due home we'd have made sure the kitchen was spotless, the living room tidy. Nothing could be out of place. My job would be to plump up the cushions and then disappear. Hers would be to make sure that his dinner, which he was usually late for or didn't want anyway, was ready, hot and fit to eat. As we never knew when he'd be home, it was hard to relax.

That day, on the sofa together, I found myself watching her as she sat absorbed in the film. She'd never been a really strong woman and I knew I'd held that against her in the past. She was pretty enough, but she was thin, and even when her face was in repose she still seemed to look wary. Alert. Mind you, I knew how that felt. I paused the television when she went out to the kitchen to check the leg of lamb that was roasting in there and followed her out to help. As she walked to the oven, I noticed her limping.

I closed my eyes and the familiar panic swept through me.

I'd thought that was over.

I said nothing, of course. I never did.

My dad came home half an hour earlier than he'd said, at six o'clock. Even though I hadn't lived there for years, my body responded to the familiar sound of his key in the front door lock just as it did then. My heartbeat increased and there was the usual buzzing in my ears for a second. He seemed to take a while to come through the hallway and I heard him put his briefcase on the table there. He knew I was there, as my car was in the driveway, but he didn't call out. My mother and I were still. Frozen. He came into the kitchen and stood in the doorway, looking at me.

As soon as I saw him, I knew I was in trouble, and from the way my mum became suddenly flustered, she knew it, too. We seemed to each become hyperaware at the same moment, our senses acutely tuned to the situation. I think my dad was the same, actually.

He gave us no greeting, just said, "I hope dinner's ready."

He was trying to catch Mum out. He'd come home half an hour earlier than he'd told her, expecting to have to wait for his meal.

My mother, however, was used to this sort of manipulation and was one step ahead of him. The look of relief on her face was evident.

"Of course it is, darling," she said.

She poured him a glass of wine and took the lamb out of the oven. She and I carried the dishes to the table while he washed his hands in the downstairs cloakroom. Neither of us looked at each other as we hurried to make sure everything was ready by the time he came out.

"I had an interesting conversation today," he said, as he sat at the table.

My heart sank and I saw my mum give me a worried look.

"I bumped into Katie's mum. Remember Katie, your old friend?"

"Of course I remember her," I said. "I see her a couple of times a week."

My mother was pale now and her eyes pleaded with me to shut up.

"Well, she told me that she believed congratulations were in order."

I put my knife and fork down. I felt more nauseous now than when I was being sick in the mornings.

My voice sounded weak and scratchy. "Congratulations?"

"Yes," he said smoothly. "She said it was a shame about Matt leaving." He fired a look at my mum. "Did you know about that?"

I could have slapped both Katie and her mother. "I've just told Mum," I said quickly. "I came round to tell both of you."

He looked as though he didn't believe that for a minute. "And then she said that it would be hard on you with the baby, but that she knew you'd cope."

The only sound in the room was my dad's knife and fork on his plate as he cut up his meat and popped it into his mouth. I kept my head down, my eyes averted from my mum. Any sign of allegiance would be seen as an open challenge.

"Baby?" said my mum. She looked as though she didn't know whether to laugh or cry. "You're having a baby, Hannah?"

Panic raced through me. If Katie had been there in front of me I don't know what I would have done. I knew I shouldn't have told her I was pregnant! I looked from my mum to my dad. "No," I said. "No, I'm not."

There was a silence so heavy I wanted to scream. I had to carry on talking. That was how it always was. The silence made me talk until I incriminated myself. I put my hands in my lap and clenched them. Hours later there would still be marks from my fingernails in my palms.

"I thought I was," I stuttered. "When he left. I kept being sick and I panicked, thinking I was pregnant. But I'm not. I'm not."

My dad carried on eating, not looking at me, not looking at my mum.

"She must have misunderstood," I said in desperation. "You know what she's like. You know she's a bit daft." I tried to laugh. "You always used to say it, didn't you?"

"Because if you were," he said slowly, "if you were pregnant, then we'd have a problem on our hands, wouldn't we?"

My mum was wringing her hands across the table. She was the only person I'd ever seen actually do that. Her neck was scarlet and her eyes were rimmed with pink.

I could see the fear in her eyes and I said, louder this time, "I'm not pregnant, Dad. Look at me." I stood up and flattened my shirt against my belly. "Do I look pregnant to you?"

My mother started to say, "Well, no, pet . . ." but she was quelled by a glare from my father.

"I remember last time," he said when he'd finished his meal. He pushed his chair away from the table and my mum and I both flinched. "The last time you disgraced us."

I started to shake. I knew he hadn't forgotten that. He hadn't mentioned it in all these years. He hadn't had to. It was always there between us.

He lifted his glass, drank some wine. I saw the grip he had on his glass, saw the way his knuckles were white and his eyes were calm, as they always were just before it happened. His gaze held mine and his voice was soft, a warning in itself. "You lost the baby, then, didn't you?"

That was one way of putting it.

Even though my mum and I were expecting it, as usual his fury came as a shock. He slammed his glass onto the table and we both lurched forward. He shouted, "I will *not* go through that again!"

For a second we were frozen in a hideous tableau, then my mum and I leaped up, desperate to defuse the situation. She grabbed a cloth from the counter and started to mop up the spilled wine. She didn't dare speak, didn't dare utter platitudes, for fear of making things worse. All that was plain on her face; I'd seen it before so many times. I cleared our plates from the table and started to load the dishwasher but she put her hand on my arm and jerked her head toward my car outside.

I didn't need to be told twice; I was desperate to leave. When I spoke, they both had their backs to me, my mum bent over the dishwasher, my dad sitting rigid at the table. "Thank you for the delicious meal, Mum. I have to go now, I have work to do." Work was the one thing my dad understood. "Dad, Matt and I have split up. He moved out when I was at work and I came home to tell you both. Mum knows the details; she can tell you all about it tonight." I started to gabble. "Don't worry about a baby, though. I promised you last time I wouldn't do that unless I was married. Katie's mum must have misunderstood, that's all."

I grabbed my bag and was at the door before either of them could stop me.

"See you soon, pet," said my mum, her face pale and strained as she kissed me good-bye.

"Don't let your mother down now, will you?" said my dad.

I knew exactly what he meant by that.

Chapter
Thirty-eight

As soon as I got home from my parents' house, I went straight to bed, though it wasn't even eight o'clock. I was still shaken by my dad's reaction and too scared to think about what was happening between him and my mum now. I knew it wouldn't be good. He wouldn't believe she'd known nothing about what was going on.

One of the skills I'd gained as a child was to be hypersensitive to atmosphere. Once, when I was at university and out at a pub with my friend Sarah, I'd grabbed her arm and pulled her outside just before a fight broke out. She'd asked me how I knew—there'd been no shouting or arguing—and I could never explain. Well, I could, but I didn't.

And then one night just after I met Matt, I was in Liverpool with him. We were at the Everyman bar and there was a couple having a violent argument. I knew it was staged. Everyone was frightened or trying to calm them down and I said to Matt, "Don't worry, they're putting on an act." Within minutes the manager appeared and threw the pair out, saying they were students on a drama course

who were acting out a piece they'd been set. Matt couldn't understand how I knew; he'd been completely taken in.

I couldn't tell him that I knew what it was like to be scared. I
knew when violence was real; I knew only too well the goose bumps
that would pop up as soon as the threat was there, the clamminess
of the skin, the way your heart rate would accelerate. Those students, they did a good job, but they didn't fool me for a second.

I left the landing light on and undressed in the darkness of my
room. I brushed my teeth and climbed into the cold bed and lay on
my side facing the window, just as I always did when Matt was
there. But for once, I wasn't thinking of Matt. All I could think
about was what my dad had said tonight.

For most parents, a child in the family was a source of joy. I knew
that for my mother it would be, certainly, but for my dad it didn't
work like that. In his world, he was an important man. He had his
own business and employed a few hundred people, but it was more
than that. In his mind, what his family did, how they looked and
what they said, all reflected on him. So when I was doing well at
work, it was as though his own star was in the ascendant. It wasn't
as if he gave me any more time; he rarely answered his phone if I
called and his texts were sporadic, but the aura surrounding him
would be good then. It was important to him that I did well; he took
it as a sign that he himself was doing well. But when I was doing
badly, that was a different thing.

His biggest fear was that either my mother or I would do something to cast him in a bad light. The two of us should have been
collaborators, given that we both saw the nuances that would lead
to our downfall. It was only today that I felt we were in unison, that
we were both aware, both terrified, and for the first time I knew
I would have pushed myself forward to protect her. She'd always
done that for me, and my cheeks burned at how readily I'd called
her weak.

I shuddered to think of how her night would be now, of the questions and the insults she'd have to bear. Now that Katie's mum had told him I was pregnant, he would blame my mum, just as he blamed her all those years ago when I was in my teens.

But that time was different. My boyfriend then hung around. He wanted to marry me, even though we were both so young. And my dad, well, he was having none of it. I was in that clinic before you could say "consent" and within a breathtakingly short time his problem had disappeared.

Nobody had referred to it since. We hadn't had to.

I shouldn't have gone there today. I was weak and had wanted my mother's comfort, but the price was too high.

Furious, though I hardly knew with whom, I sent Katie a text:

Please tell your mother to stop telling people I am pregnant.

I got an immediate reply:

Sorry, she must have overheard me talking to James. I'll tell her to keep it quiet. Hope it hasn't caused a problem. xxx

She hadn't a clue. She really hadn't a clue.

I TRIED TO keep my head down at work, but it was difficult, what with everything that was going on. I felt I'd lost a bit of ground with Katie, and while she still texted every evening to ask how I was and whether I had any news, I knew she just wanted me to say I was going to the doctor to arrange a termination and then going to look for another man.

Until Matt left, I never needed Sam's help at work. Sometimes we'd bounce ideas off each other but usually we worked independently. Lately, though, he'd come over to chat and I'd have to ask him to check my work for me. I found it hard to think straight and he discovered errors that I would never have made before. I'd sit there, hot and tight with embarrassment, while he dismissed my apologies, saying anyone could make a mistake like that, but he'd look concerned and I'd avoid meeting his eyes.

I'd bought the security program for my laptop the other night and I'd been close to tears trying to set it up. I think I was just too stressed to follow the instructions. Katie came round the next evening and tested it for me while I sat outside with my iPad; I could see everything that was going on in the living room, though the picture quality wasn't great. I'd put my laptop on the edge of the sofa, facing the living room door, and from my garden chair I watched her as she went into the room and sat on the sofa. She was laughing as she did so and waving at me, though of course she couldn't see me at all. It worked on my phone, too, but the screen was too small to see much. I'd have to remember to take my iPad everywhere I went. My head ached at the thought of how awkward that would be. I couldn't use it if I went for a run, so that would have to stop.

So the camera was great but the consequence was that I was paranoid that I'd miss something happening at home. I couldn't have my iPad on in the office, obviously, so I worked with a split screen, half showing the work I was doing and half showing the interior of my house. Luckily the back of my monitor faced my office door, so nobody coming into the room could see what I was doing. I knew I was supposed to get alerts if there was any sound or movement, but I just didn't trust the program that much. It wasn't expensive enough for me to think it was really reliable. The only way I'd be convinced that nobody was there was if I could see the evidence in front of me.

I started to make more mistakes because I couldn't take my eyes off the screen. I couldn't think straight. I couldn't focus on figures or emails or reports. I'd always been proud of my ability to focus, to shut out the world while I worked out a solution to a problem, but suddenly that had disappeared. Every time I started to do something, my eyes would flick back to the screen, to check just once more that nothing had changed. It was exhausting. I felt like I was constantly on high alert and could feel my heart racing whenever there was the slightest noise.

I'd had the choice with the program of either recording once there was a sound or movement, or continuously monitoring the room. I knew I'd have to monitor it all the time; I needed to catch him and I needed to be able to see the room myself to know when he was there. I couldn't rely on the device recording him if he made a noise. What if he didn't? What if he crept in and it wasn't picked up?

And of course I couldn't watch the screen while I was traveling to and from work, which meant that if Matt came to the house just after I'd left, I'd miss seeing him. I kept pulling over when I was driving to work to check my iPad to see whether he was there. I knew it was mad. I knew it was too much. If he came to the house, there wasn't much I could do about it. I knew that by the time I'd turned around and driven back home—a journey that took at least half an hour—he'd be long gone, yet I still couldn't resist it. But the stress of watching the screen all the time and worrying and worrying about what I'd missed, even if I went to the loo, was becoming too much. If I was away for ten minutes, I wouldn't know whether something had happened in that time. If I rewound it and watched it for those ten minutes, something might have happened in real time that I would have missed. There seemed no way out of it.

That morning I received an email reminder about a meeting with my manager later in the day. My skin crawled with shame. I would never have had to be reminded before. The fact he felt he had to do that said so much about the way I'd been working. The problem was that I could read something and understand it, but then my eyes would be drawn to my living room on the split screen and instantly I'd forget. This email was one I'd find hard to forget, though. George had said that Alex Hughes would be at the meeting. Alex Hughes, the partner who'd thought so highly of me in Oxford, just a couple of months ago.

My mind flashed back to the conversation we'd had, when he and Oliver Sutton had said how well I'd done and that there were hopes of my becoming a director soon, and my stomach tightened as I thought about what I'd lost.

Just then Sam appeared at the doorway to my office. I beckoned him in and told him to shut the door.

"What's up?" he asked.

"Alex Hughes is going to be at the meeting with George," I said. I started to cry. "He's going to be furious with me!"

Sam came over and put his arm around me just as Linda, George's secretary, knocked and came into the room. She paused for a second, her expression calm and considered, taking everything in. It must have looked like a lovers' tiff with my red eyes and his conciliatory arm around my shoulder. Quickly I moved away from him, but it was too late. She turned politely and pretended to look for a pen on my desk.

"Alex Hughes will be popping in to your meeting at twelve, Hannah," she said, pointedly ignoring Sam. "Make sure you're on time, won't you?"

I nodded, smarting. "Don't worry."

She gave a brisk nod and left the room.

Chapter
Thirty-nine

WHEN I REACHED the meeting room on the top floor, both men were there. Alex Hughes stood up as I entered the room.

"Hello again, Hannah," he said, but his voice wasn't as warm as it had been when I'd talked to him in Oxford. He stood behind the table and it was clear he wasn't going to shake my hand. "How are you?"

I didn't know what to say. Did he want the truth?

I sat down cautiously. "Fine, thanks. How are you?"

"Never better," he said, then he looked down at the papers in front of him and his voice became grave. "Until I saw this."

I tried desperately to decipher his notes but they were upside down and in shadow. I glanced at George, who was studiously avoiding my eyes. It was clear there'd be no support from him today.

Alex passed me a sheet of paper. I tried to read what was on it but I was so scared, the words started to swim before my eyes. I blinked hard and looked back up at him.

"This is a list of the company accounts you were responsible for which had filing deadlines in the last quarter," he said. "Three out of eight were not submitted to Companies House on time."

Panicking, I started to say that I hadn't had enough time and that I was overworked, but he interrupted me. "All of your colleagues have completed theirs. Six months ago you would have finished these with a month to spare."

I flushed, knowing he was right.

He took off his glasses and looked at me. "You know, Hannah, that really is the most fundamental part of our service. All three companies will now receive a penalty, which, if we want to keep their business, we will have to pay. I wouldn't be surprised if they hadn't already decided to go elsewhere. You know that. It was the first thing you learned when you started here, I imagine."

My manager nodded furiously, desperate to distance himself from me. "Indeed it is, Alex."

Alex Hughes looked at him sharply and said, "I take on board what you said about not feeling you had to supervise Hannah and, of course, you've had a holiday recently, but we will have to meet later to discuss your role in this. From now on I want you to monitor deadlines for all your staff. Is that clear?"

George nodded, his face puce.

"Which ones were late?" I asked.

"Let's see." He glanced down at the list. "The Johnstown Company—they still haven't received anything. They will be going elsewhere, I fear."

"I finished that on the day you went on holiday!" I said. "I remember emailing it to Lucy to proofread and send on to them the next day. I told her to copy you in, too. She had plenty of time to do it."

"I spoke to her today," he said. "She said she didn't receive it."

"What?"

"And this one, to Powell's," he said, "was incomplete when you emailed it to them."

"I have never submitted an incomplete document!"

"They say that it only went up to page eight."

"No," I said. "That has to be wrong. I finished it, and anyway, I wouldn't have sent something off half done. I'm always careful."

"It said 'Version 1' in the footer," said George. "How many versions were there?"

My head started to buzz. I was *sure* I'd sent Lucy the final version.

George sounded cold and distant and I knew that he'd checked the final copy—Version 4—but would have to take ultimate responsibility for the early version being sent out. "You *were* always careful," he said, "which is why I felt I could trust you. But lately, Hannah, things . . . well, they seem to have got on top of you and your work has suffered."

"It's not just your work that's suffered, from what I've heard," said Alex and his voice held a thread of steel. "I understand you've been acting in an unprofessional manner. You've already had a verbal warning, but you've made no effort to redeem yourself. You're late to work, you leave early. You've been crying in the office. Only today you were seen with your arms around a colleague."

"What?"

"I appreciate you've had a bad time. I've heard the rumors that you and your partner have broken up."

My head shot up. How had he heard that?

"But there is a basic standard that we expect you to reach. We're a business, Hannah. Our work has to be performed to the highest standard."

Stung, I said, "I gave those documents to Lucy to send off," I said. "Powell's was complete and checked and Johnstown's was emailed to her with plenty of time to proofread it." I looked down at the list. "Which is the other?" I scanned it quickly. "NRS? That was definitely sent to Lucy on time."

The two men looked at each other, a look of resignation on their faces. Clearly they had anticipated this.

"She says she didn't receive that, either. Have you been date-stamping your work? Did you email them to her?"

"Yes!" I said. I couldn't remember what I'd done but I needed to get out of there. The small room was full of tension and I couldn't stand it any longer. If I stayed in there I knew I'd start to cry or scream or worse.

"Give me ten minutes," I said. "I'll prove it to you."

Alex shrugged. "Very well."

I stood up and pushed back my chair. "Thank you. I won't be long."

I raced down the stairs and along the corridor to my room. Lucy wasn't there and I was dead certain that was deliberate. She must have known I'd be after her blood.

My computer had timed out. "Come on! Come *on*!" I said and banged the side of the monitor with my hand. The screen flickered back to life.

I tried to log on but a red mist was swirling around my eyes, and it took three attempts before I could enter the right password.

I opened my emails and searched the Sent box for my messages to Lucy. There seemed to be thousands of them and I couldn't remember the dates now. I scrolled down, then stopped abruptly as I saw something out of the corner of my eye.

What was that?

I sat down heavily. An alert appeared at the bottom right of the screen. "Warning!" it said. "Action detected!"

The right side of my screen showed my living room. What I'd seen then, just a glimpse, was my living room door closing.

But it was shut this morning!

I stared wildly at the screen but nothing else happened. I clicked to replay. It took one second, maybe two, and then I saw it clearly. The door to the living room opened, just two or three inches. If I strained my eyes until they almost bled I could see a faint shadow on the wall. Then it shut again.

I played it again and again. I forgot about the emails to Lucy, about the incomplete accounts. I watched the door of my living room open and shut, open and shut, until I could feel my blood simmering in my veins.

I stood up. I saw the emails then, a reminder of what I should be doing. I shook my head. They could wait.

I fumbled in my bag to check my keys were there, and grabbed my jacket from the coat stand.

I'd had enough of Matt coming into the house, trying to drive me crazy. I needed to get home, to see him, to talk to him. To ask him why he'd left. And why he kept coming back.

Chapter
Forty

WHEN I GOT home there was no sign that anyone had been in the house at all.

I parked around the corner so that I could approach the house without being noticed. On tiptoe I entered through the back door. I wanted to catch him in the act, to catch him off guard.

The kitchen was exactly as I'd left it that morning. The Post-it notes were all over the wall and island as usual, and my skin prickled at the thought of Matt seeing them. Slowly, I turned the door handle and peeped out into the hallway. It was heavy with silence and I knew, I just knew, that nobody was in the house now. Still, I crept toward the living room, giving a quick glance upward at the stairs just in case. I eased the door open and saw that the laptop was still in place on the sofa. I was about to walk into the room but remembered just in time that it would be recording me and sending alerts to my computer at work and I quickly shut the door again. My head started to buzz at the thought of them seeing me at home when I should be in the meeting and I stood with my back to the door and closed my eyes for a second. I was rigid with stress.

Then my eyes snapped open and I looked at the stairs. Slowly and quietly I climbed them, gripping the banister to stop myself shaking.

There was nobody upstairs. The bedroom looked as it had earlier that morning, with shoes all over the floor and dirty clothes lying half off the armchair. I squirmed at the thought of Matt seeing it like this, particularly as I'd nagged him for the last two years to be tidier.

I suppose I'd been hoping I'd have fair warning before he came home, a phone call apologizing, maybe, or an email to my office, asking me to meet him first. I hated to think he'd come into the house while I was out, judge my messiness and look at things that had nothing whatsoever to do with him. I sighed and wondered whether the sound would be picked up by the webcam. I glanced into the bathroom. Towels going back two weeks or more lay crumpled and sodden in the corner of the room. The screen of the shower had long lost its shine and I don't think there was one toiletry bottle that had been reunited with its lid. I closed the door firmly on the mess, checked the spare bedroom and bathroom for evidence of intruders, then went back downstairs.

With a rush of relief I realized my computer at work would have timed out by now, so I went into the living room and sat on the sofa, replaying the webcam film from the moment I left that morning. I sat and watched as the screen filled with early morning sun, then darkened as the sky threatened rain. I tried to fast-forward, but that was too stressful, thinking about what I might miss.

Then I watched it through again. I didn't want to miss a thing.

I heard a beep and my nerves shrieked. My handbag was in the kitchen, my phone inside. I paused the playback and fetched my bag.

When I saw the message was from Sam, I knew it wouldn't be good news.

Hannah, where are you? I've just got out of a meeting and George and Alex are looking for you.

I dropped my phone on the coffee table. They were after me! I trembled at the thought of what I'd done. I wouldn't be forgiven for leaving like that.

I pressed the computer's Off switch hard and bent over, holding my head in my hands. They would think I was mad. My chances of promotion were nil now, that much was inevitable. Tears streamed down my face as I remembered my excitement when I'd come home that day to tell Matt that I was probably going to be made a director. He'd destroyed all that by leaving.

Suddenly I was sick of everything. Sick of Matt, sick of the job and sick of myself.

I paced the room, trying to think what to do. Clearly I couldn't go back to work. It was after 3 p.m. by then and I'd left the office at about 12:30. There was no way I was going to walk blithely back in there, as though nothing had happened. Besides, they might not let me in. I had a brief vision of myself being stopped in reception by security; just the thought filled me with horror. In my first couple of weeks at the company, years ago, I'd seen a man being escorted from the premises by security. His face was gray and damp with sweat. I remember worrying he would have a heart attack. He'd been found fiddling the books, apparently, and was unceremoniously thrown out. It had terrified me, the way other staff turned away from him. A woman who'd worked with him had stood there sobbing and George had whispered that she was the whistle-blower.

I went back to the kitchen and looked at the notes. They were everywhere now, and usually I liked them spread out like that. Walking around the kitchen looking at them helped me think about things, see the links. But now I felt defeated, as though I was losing my grip on everything that had been dear to me. I had no partner, I doubted I would have a job after today and if I didn't, how could I afford the mortgage? I'd overpaid it, so I was covered for a while, but if I was unemployed for long enough I'd have to ask my dad for money and he'd want to know why I needed it. The band which had been tight around my head all day ratcheted up a notch at the thought of telling him I'd been fired.

I opened the fridge and took out a bottle of wine. I needed a drink now. Just one. I went to the cabinet to get a glass and stopped dead. There had been a pair of Vera Wang glasses there; I'd bought them for my first anniversary with Matt. We'd only used them for special occasions and they would always be lined up together at the front of the cabinet.

One of them was missing.

So Matt had come home and taken his glass with him. Was that so he could remember me or so that I couldn't remember him?

Chapter
Forty-one

THE WINE WENT straight back into the fridge. I knew the last thing I should do was drink. I needed to think. The bottle was so seductive, the way it promised release, oblivion, but I knew from experience its darker side. I sat at the island with just a glass of juice instead, but of course it wasn't the same, and thought about the things that had been happening to me. I pulled the notes off the wall where I'd written everything down. The flowers, the texts, the videos. The CD. The phone call, the note through the door, the missing glass. I shuddered.

What did he want? Why did he leave if he wanted to stay in touch like this?

And then I let myself think again of the other alternative. *What if it's not Matt who's coming into the house? Who else could it be?*

At the thought that someone else had been here my heart raced and for a moment or two it was as though I'd forgotten how to breathe. I closed my eyes and focused on my breathing like the counselor had taught me. "It doesn't matter how shallow the breaths," she'd said, her voice calm while I struggled. "Just focus. Come on now, in, two, three, four, and out, two, three, four." It took me as long today as it did then, when I was a student, to get my breathing under control, and by the time I'd done it I was sweating and dizzy.

I put the radio on, just for something to do, for something to override the dark, helpless thoughts that whirled round my mind. It took me a few minutes to focus but eventually I calmed down and shut those thoughts out of my head.

It had to be Matt. That was the only explanation. Who else could it be? But why was he coming here when he knew I'd be at work? Had he forgotten something? Left something behind? Did he just want to remember being here with me?

On the radio a government minister was talking about unemployment. I felt a wave of nausea at the thought of applying for jobs without a reference. I'd worked in the same company since I was twenty-one, fresh from university. I was now thirty-two and would have no other reference unless they wanted one from Topshop, where I'd worked one summer when I was a student.

I opened the fridge again and looked at the bottle of wine, chilled and wet with condensation, and for a moment I nearly took it and drank the lot. Luckily I had enough sense to see the consequences of that and left it there, taking out a bottle of water instead. Just as I reached out to switch the radio off, the minister mentioned that he wanted a huge increase in apprenticeships.

Apprenticeships.

I stopped dead in my tracks, remembering a conversation I'd had with Matt a year or so ago. I turned the radio off and sat with my head in my hands, trying to recall what he'd said. He was telling me about one of his apprentices who was having to apply for jobs and was struggling to get one. Matt's company had told that set of apprentices when they first started that if they worked hard enough and their work was of a high quality, they would have the chance of being taken on permanently, once their apprenticeship was over.

Once that time had elapsed, however, the apprentices were told that unfortunately times had changed for the worse, economically, so they couldn't be kept on. All of them had been really understanding, but then Matt had overheard a couple of the directors laughing about it in the toilets, saying they'd had no intention of keeping them on and it had just been a ploy to get them to work hard. The staff, feeling guilty the apprentices had been lied to, had collected money for a leaving present and the directors had made a show of each putting in twenty pounds to go to ten apprentices.

I thought then of that young man who'd worked for Matt. His name was Andrew Brodie. Matt had written him a great reference; he'd shown it to me and said Andrew had nearly cried when he read it. *Andrew Brodie.*

I looked at my notes. I'd spoken to Matt's manager, I'd spoken to reception and I'd spoken to HR. I hadn't thought of speaking to someone who'd worked for him.

I couldn't believe I'd been so stupid.

In the living room I googled his name. He was there on Facebook, though his account was nailed down so I couldn't see anything at all. He wasn't on Twitter, but there he was on LinkedIn. I wanted to look at his full details, but knew that if I logged in, he might be able to see who was looking at him.

I set up a fake account using the name Lyndsey Harding and searched for Andrew Brodie. There he was, working for another firm of architects in Liverpool.

I could have kicked myself. I'd never thought of phoning other firms to ask whether Matt worked there. I think I'd just assumed by now that he'd be miles away. My heart thudded at the thought that he might still be local, still living nearby. I thought of seeing him when I was shopping or in a wine bar on a Saturday night and I just didn't know what I'd do. Luckily I'd given myself warning now; I would be on constant high alert.

I panicked as I realized I'd run out of Post-its. I looked around for my notebook and couldn't find it, then remembered I'd left it on the passenger seat of my car. Sometimes it was handy having something to jot ideas on when I was at traffic lights. For a moment I didn't know what to do; I knew that if I didn't write Andrew's details down somewhere noticeable, I'd forget them, so I picked up a red marker pen and made a note on one of my white glossy cabinets. It would come off easily once I'd found Matt.

My phone beeped with a message from Lucy:

Hannah, George says you should check your email.

I flinched.

After three attempts to log into my work email, I realized the password wouldn't open the account.

My heart sinking, I opened up my Gmail account. There was an email from Human Resources. It was polite and succinct and absolutely clear.

I had been suspended.

Chapter
Forty-two

I LOOKED FROM the HR email to Andrew Brodie's LinkedIn page. I knew I wouldn't be able to put up a good case at work unless I'd sorted out this thing with Matt. If I could just talk to him again I'd be able to focus on my job and try to regain the ground I'd lost. I tried not to think about how unforgiving the company could be.

Finding Matt had to be my priority.

I picked up the phone and called the company where Andrew worked. In that moment before the phone was answered, I realized that Matt might actually be working with Andrew now and my heart jolted. *I could be speaking to him in a few minutes!* My mouth was dry and I had to swallow hard before I was able to ask the receptionist if I could be put through to Matthew Stone. I was almost relieved when she said that nobody of that name worked there. I asked for Andrew instead, and the call went straight to voicemail. His message said he was out of the office working on a project and that he could be reached on his mobile.

I made a note of the number on the cabinet, drew a big circle around it and stood looking at it. I didn't know how to play this now.

I looked at the clock. It was 4 p.m. I decided to wait until after 6 to call him. I didn't want him to be surrounded by people when I spoke to him.

I was too agitated to do anything for the next hour. I could hear Ray outside, power-washing his garden wall, and I couldn't face him right now, so a run was out of the question. In any case, how could I go out when I had to guard the house? And my sickness had returned with a vengeance since seeing the webcam evidence of the door opening and closing; that visual proof that someone had been in my home had been really shocking. I don't think I could have run more than a hundred yards in the state I was in.

I picked up my tablet and closed down the email from HR. I couldn't stand to read it again. I tried to call Lucy on her mobile; it rang once, then cut off. My mind went wild then. *Had she just rejected my call?*

Then I remembered. Just as Lucy could access my emails, I could access hers. I knew her password; she knew mine. She'd told me hers when she was off sick a few months ago; I'd been able to go into her emails and sort some things out for her.

Using Lucy's password, I logged on to the firm's intranet. I knew it was wrong. I knew it was illegal, but I wasn't going to let that stop me. I wanted to know what she was up to.

It's very strange, looking at someone else's email in-box. It looked familiar because it was similar to my own, of course, but essentially it was completely different.

I searched her in-box for the projects Alex had mentioned. The emails I'd sent her weren't there. I frowned and searched the days around that date, but I couldn't see them. I clicked on the folder with my name on it and they weren't there, either.

I clicked the Recycle Bin icon. It was empty. I frowned. Surely a Recycle Bin would usually have deleted mail in it? Then I saw the Recover Deleted Items button. I clicked it and stared at the emails that appeared. It's funny how I had never noticed that button before but now it looked like it might be the one thing that would save my job.

There, among a lot of other emails, were the ones I was looking for, the very ones I'd told Alex I'd sent. Lucy hadn't even had the sense to permanently delete them.

I opened the email to Powell's that I'd sent her. Adam had said they had an early version. The attachment opened and I looked down at the footer. There was nothing there except the page number. I scrolled down. There were twenty complete pages, exactly as there should have been. Just as I'd told Alex, I *had* sent the full document to Lucy. All she'd had to do was proofread it, check it was complete and forward it on to Powell's from my email address.

Relief flooded through me. I'd known I was right and this proved it.

I remembered now that after she'd proofread it, she hadn't emailed back to confirm it was all right. She'd just popped into my office and said, "Powell's is fine, Hannah. I've sent it on." Had she done that on purpose, so there was no trail? And I wondered at what point she'd decided to send off the first version to make me look incompetent and a fool. I felt a flash of anger as I thought of her accessing my files to find the wrong copy. That had been explained to her on the very first day; as my assistant she could send documents out in my name, but it was imperative that she only sent ones that I'd approved.

I forwarded the relevant emails to Alex, with copies to George. I didn't write a note; I couldn't think of a thing to say, but I included a screenshot of the list of deleted items.

Frustrated, I sat back. Though I was relieved to retrieve those emails, I still had so many questions I wanted to ask Lucy. Why had she done that? Why was she lying about receiving emails and why had she sent out an incomplete document? Was she deliberately trying to discredit me?

Then I thought of the woman I'd seen in the cloakroom. Alice. She'd known about Matt. There was no way she was making a general observation about men there; she'd known that we'd broken up. There was only one person I'd told at work. Sam.

And it seemed Sam had been having cozy conversations with Lucy.

I knew then that Lucy had known about Matt. I think she must have known from the start. There had been those sly looks she'd given me that I'd stupidly ignored. She'd gone from being subservient and apologetic all the time to looking at me as though I was a fool. As though I was making wrong decisions. She was a bright young woman, educated at a top university. I'd known she was after my job one day, but that was all right; I'd felt the same when I was her age. I didn't sabotage my boss's work to get it, though.

I searched for Lucy's emails to Alice. Those, too, had been deleted and I recovered them. There was one from her the day I'd had the verbal warning. I opened the latest and saw the others set out as though in a conversation. Lucy had written:

> I told you not to say anything!

Alice had replied:

> Oops, sorry! I thought everyone knew. Lunch?

And then Lucy had written:

> Sorry, seeing Sam in Costa. And don't go telling her that, either! You're the only one who knows about him and me so shh!

So Sam *was* seeing Lucy. I thought back to the times I'd seen him with Grace. They seemed really happy and he'd always spoken about her affectionately.

I thought of my dad and Helen, and Sam having an affair with Lucy. Now Matt was probably seeing someone, too. My eyes prickled with tears. Who could I trust?

And because Sam was sleeping with Lucy, he'd felt free to tell her about Matt leaving me and she'd taken advantage of my distress by sending out documents that would destroy my reputation. I realized just how out of it I must have been for the last couple of months, to not notice what was going on between them and what she was doing to me.

I considered searching through the rest of Lucy's emails to find further treachery, but the thought was too depressing. I knew she had betrayed me; that was all I needed to know. I couldn't bear the thought that Sam might have been trying to get me fired as well.

The sun had disappeared and the room was gloomy and dim. I switched off my phone in case Sam called. I didn't want to speak to him or to anyone else. Upstairs I ran a bath, just for something to do. I wanted warmth. I wanted comfort. My skin crawled with shame. I should never have trusted Sam. I should never have trusted anyone.

In a sudden fury, I switched my phone back on and sent Sam a text. I would wait to deal with Lucy face-to-face; the last thing I wanted was for her to use a furious text message against me.

I know everything. You bastard.

Seconds later there was a flurry of messages from Sam:

I'm sorry!

I can explain.

I'll come round to yours—I need to talk to you.

I sent him one more:

Just you dare. If you come round here I'll call the police on you. And her.

I turned the phone off again and got into the bath. I couldn't relax, though. I lay in the hot, soft water, breathing in the steam and the scent of Chanel, my mind racing. I wasn't worried about Lucy.

She wasn't a friend. If they let me go back to work I'd insist on a different assistant. It would be her loss. Now that Alex had my original emails to her, she should be out of a job anyway. Sam, though: his deception was different. I knew I'd have to deal with that and I didn't know how I'd do it without breaking down.

And I thought again of the phone in his car. Was it a phone he kept to call Lucy or could he have sent me those anonymous texts? Had he videoed me? Did he have a number of SIM cards that he'd just change every time he wanted to torment me?

I felt like I was going mad. I lowered my head into the bathwater and felt it thrum in my ears.

Suddenly I sat upright, squeezing the water out of my hair as I remembered the last time I'd had a bath. It was the night before I went to Oxford; the night before Matt left me. I'd left the office earlier than usual and worked in the garden for a few hours, making the most of the warm weather. I remembered I'd sent him a text before I left work and asked him to bring home a takeaway for dinner, as I wanted to spend the evening in the garden rather than cooking a meal. Later I was stiff and aching all over and Matt had suggested I have a bath instead of a shower. He'd smiled at me and rubbed my shoulders, saying it would be more relaxing. He'd run it for me, putting in bath oil and getting the water as hot as possible, just how I liked it. He told me about a podcast I'd like and passed me my headphones, resting my iPod on a towel on a stool beside the tub so that it wouldn't get wet. He'd brought up a glass of wine halfway through and I'd soaked in the bath for forty-five minutes, topping up the hot water and listening to the program. I'd thought he was being really kind and I'd reached up and pulled him down to me so that I could kiss him.

When I'd finally climbed out of the bath and put on my pajamas, I'd felt relaxed and sleepy. I lay on my bed and opened up Facebook on my iPad, then Matt came upstairs and asked if I fancied watching a film. I was asleep within minutes of the film starting and then, of course, the next morning I'd had to get up early to drive to Oxford. By then, my iPad was on the bedside table, as usual, and I hadn't given it a second thought.

In that forty-five-minute period while I was in the bath, he must have wiped every trace of himself from my phone. He'd deleted all my photos of him from my laptop and iPad and then, when I was asleep, he had looked through my Facebook and deleted every message we'd exchanged and every photo of him and of us. And he'd done it by making me feel cared for, by making me feel loved.

Chapter
Forty-three

AT SIX ON the dot I was ready to call Andrew Brodie. My hands were shaking so much I could hardly hold the phone and I caved in and drank a glass of wine straight down before I dialed his number. I had a pen ready and a piece of paper with my script written on it; I couldn't trust myself to remember what to say. At the last minute I grabbed another pen, then another, just in case they ran out. I couldn't stand the thought of not being able to write down something important. I took a few deep breaths, wiped my hands on my jeans and keyed in his number, withholding my own.

He picked up on the third ring, sounding flustered and out of breath. I could hear traffic in the background and I quickly clicked Record to make sure I didn't miss anything.

"Hello, is that Andrew Brodie?"

"Yes, yes, it is. Who is it?"

"It's Lyndsey Harding here," I said, reading from my script. "I'm calling on behalf of Reed Recruitment and I wondered if I might have a word in confidence?" I'd chosen a company that already existed; I couldn't take the risk of him googling a fictitious company while we were speaking.

There was a long pause, then he said, "Well, it depends. What's it about?"

"We have a post we're trying to fill," I said. "It's for a trainee architectural technician. We thought you might be interested."

"Wow," he said. "Yes, I would be!"

He sounded so excited that I felt really mean that the job didn't exist.

"I'm not allowed to tell you the name of the firm unless you go to interview, but I can tell you it's a large company and they're offering a good package. It's in Chester, so it's pretty local."

"That would be great," he said. "But . . . have I met you? I don't recognize your name."

"Oh, no," I said. I remembered my training at work, where we were told that if we smiled when we were on the phone we would sound friendlier. My cheeks ached as I beamed as widely as I could. It had been months since I'd used those muscles. "It's my job to find out who's the best in their field and your name was mentioned a while ago. When I heard about this opportunity I thought of you immediately."

He bit.

Of course he did.

"Who mentioned me? Are you allowed to tell me?"

"It was someone from John Denning Associates," I said smoothly. "Matthew Stone, one of the architects there. I believe you were an apprentice with JDA?"

"Oh yes," he said. "Matt was a really good boss. He recommended me?"

"He did," I said. For the first time I didn't need my script. "He said you were the best apprentice he'd had working for him. He told me you were part of the team working on the design of the new Japanese restaurant down on the Liverpool waterfront. Is that right?"

He took five full minutes to tell me I was right about that. I held the phone away from my ear, my excitement mounting.

Just ask him!

"Now that I know you might be interested, I'll have to arrange a time when we can meet," I said. "Damn it, I've left my diary in the office. Are evenings better for you?"

"Yes, anytime after 5 or 5:30 is fine. Sometimes I work late but I can always leave on time if you want to meet."

"Well, I'll give you a call in the morning, if that's all right," I said. "Sorry I can't fix a date right now. I'll call you before nine."

"That's fine."

My stomach tightened. This was the clincher. "I'll give Matthew Stone a call at JDA, too, to thank him."

I was just about ready to explode with excitement. I could feel the pressure mounting in my head and stars appeared on the periphery of my vision.

Andrew didn't let me down.

"Oh, he's not working for them anymore." I held my breath. "I bumped into David Walker the other day. I don't know whether you know him; he's an architect at JDA, too. He said that he'd taken over Matt's projects. Matt's in Manchester now, working for Clarke and Bell."

I breathed out. My whole body relaxed.

"He is?" I was surprised he didn't notice the change in my voice. "I suppose it's a while since I spoke to him." *Well, that was true enough.* "How long has he been there?" I looked over at my notes, scattered on the island and scrawled on the cabinets. "I'll have to update my records."

"Not long," he said. "Only a few weeks, I think."

"Oh, well, I daresay I'll come across him sometime soon. Thanks so much, Andrew. I'll be in touch."

I ended the call.

The chase was almost over.

Chapter
Forty-four

I STOOD IN the kitchen, unable to believe it. I'd done it! I'd found him. I think I felt prouder of myself at that moment than I'd ever felt before.

I fetched my laptop from the living room and sat at the kitchen table with the notes I'd made while I was speaking to Andrew. Google sent me to the company's web page and I scrutinized it closely. A search of the site didn't turn up his name. I downloaded their newsletters but couldn't see any reference to Matt. I frowned. He was a well-respected architect; his joining them should have been a big enough coup for them to bother mentioning it.

My phone rang, startling me. It was Sam. I let it go to voicemail. I'd deal with him later.

I was just looking up the route to Matt's new office when the phone beeped. It was Katie.

Hey Hannah, how're things? Any news? xx

It was her standard text, the one she sent almost daily. This time I actually had something to tell her! Fizzing with excitement, I started to text, *Katie, I think I know where Matt is* when something stopped me. Andrew Brodie might be mistaken. I couldn't bear the pitying looks Katie and James would share if I got all excited for nothing, the way they'd talk about it, saying there must be something up with me for my boyfriend to run off like that. There were always rumors flying around about where people were working; Matt might just have gone for an interview at Clarke and Bell, or perhaps he'd just told someone he'd seen a job advertised there.

I paused for a moment, thinking of him applying for a job without a word to me. The whole process of job hunting took so long: the search, the application, the interview.

I thought back. Had there been a day when he'd been dressed up for an interview? Had I missed something? It was impossible to know; some days he went to work dressed in jeans and a North Face jacket, coming home chilled and muddy, other days he had meetings with clients and would wear a suit. I knew, though, that he'd make a special effort if he was going to an interview. I sat there as the room grew dim and tried to identify days when he'd looked particularly good.

I couldn't. Mornings were a bit of a rush and I always had a lot on my mind, so frankly I never paid him much attention before work. Maybe he'd taken the day off for an interview, then come home straightaway and changed his clothes. He might have spent the afternoon relaxing at home, watching daytime television, then spun me a line about what he'd been up to.

Whichever way he'd done it, though, he'd deliberately misled me. He'd sat with me in the evening and he hadn't said a word about applying for a job, being interviewed for a job or getting a job. Not one word. He'd sat there and smiled and chatted and not even in the course of an argument had he shouted that he had another job, that he'd be leaving.

And at night we'd go up to bed and he'd lie next to me, thinking about getting out. Shame suffused me at the idea of that. I thought of the nights I'd tried to make love to him, nights when I'd lain next to him, thinking he would definitely want me this time. And he did, sometimes, but the humiliation of those occasions when I'd put my arms around him and start to kiss him, only to have him say he was tired, that he'd had a tough day, that he wanted to read instead, made me burn inside, particularly now, knowing that he must have been thinking of someone else.

The phone rang. Sam again. I rejected the call. I felt like I was going crazy with so many things to think about, so when I replied to Katie, I didn't mention Matt at all. I told her another truth instead.

Suspended from work today. I've really messed things up.

Straightaway her reply came:

We're coming round.

I looked at the kitchen in a panic. It was a complete mess. The island was laden with notes about Matt and of course now I'd spread out onto the units and covered the cabinets in red ink. Hopefully that would wash off, but I needed to leave it on until I found Matt anyway; I could always replace the units then if I had to. I couldn't face having to clear it all away before they came round and then put it back in the order I liked it.

Suddenly I felt exhausted, almost too tired to move.

I'll come round to you, I texted. *I feel like getting out. I'll get a taxi.*

Why can't you drive? she replied. *It's not as though you're drinking, is it?*

And then, within a matter of seconds:

Oh Hannah, does this mean you've been to the clinic?

I stared at the phone, furious. Did she have no boundaries at all? I was tempted to back out and stay at home, but I knew she'd call round if I did.

Frustrated, I sent her a message:

I'll drive. Be there in 10 minutes. And no, I haven't been to the clinic and stop asking me about it or that'll be the last you see of me.

Two minutes later my phone beeped:

Sorry! Oh and James says bring round the note you mentioned the other day. Envelope, too. He wants to check something. x

Chapter
Forty-five

I STAYED AT Katie and James's for about an hour but my mind was racing and all I wanted was to be at home.

I sat in the armchair while they faced me on the sofa and fired questions at me as though I was in court. Of course I couldn't drink but they had a bottle of wine between them and I think they'd already had the best part of another bottle before I got there, too. I had one glass of lukewarm Perrier that had long ago gone flat and thought I would remember this if Katie ever got pregnant.

They kept on asking questions about my job. What had I done wrong? Why hadn't I met the deadlines? Did I have proof that I'd sent those documents to Lucy?

When I told them I was locked out of my work email system, there was a sharp intake of breath from Katie. James just sat back, shaking his head.

Then I told them about finding the document I'd sent Lucy to proofread.

"You used her password to log into the intranet and read her emails?" asked James. "You know that's illegal, don't you?"

"I don't care," I said. "I knew I was right. I knew I'd sent her the right documents."

"It doesn't matter whether you care or not," he said. "You've just made things much worse."

I looked at Katie but she wouldn't meet my eyes.

"And the documents were sent to the clients from your email account anyway, weren't they?" he asked.

"Yes, but she sent them."

"Under your name?"

"Yes. She often has to do that."

"Well, how can they prove who sent them?" he said. "Surely there's no way of telling which machine sent the email?"

My eyes filled with tears. "I hadn't thought of that."

"She'll struggle to explain herself," he said, "but you're not exactly covered in glory, either, Hannah."

Katie sighed. "Why don't you just explain that you're pregnant and having a tough time? You could go to the doctor's and tell them everything; they'll give you a note to help you at work."

"I don't want to do that. I don't want to see a doctor until I've decided what to do."

James stood up. "I need to get some work done," he said to Katie. "I'll do it upstairs." He looked at me. "So you're thinking of keeping the baby?"

I flushed. "I don't think so."

He gave me a pointed look, then left the room.

"I'm sorry," I said to Katie. "I'll go home. I'm getting on James's nerves."

"Everyone's getting on James's nerves lately," she said. "Take no notice of him. He's got too much work on and he hates doing it in the evenings. He's had hardly any time off for weeks now."

We heard him going upstairs, then their study door banged shut.

"But he's right," Katie said. "You have to see a doctor. You're supposed to register with one as soon as you find out you're pregnant. I've told you that!"

"Leave it," I said. "I don't want to talk about it."

I sat there sullenly, wishing I'd never told either of them I was pregnant in the first place.

"Okay, but remember Matt's been gone for three months now. Surely you don't think he's coming back to you?"

"Not quite three months," I mumbled. It was only a few days off that and from the way her mouth tightened I think we both knew it.

The door swung open. James was back for his glass of wine. He filled it up and Katie said, "Come on, James. Forget about work for tonight."

"I can't," he said and drank some of his wine.

Her mouth tightened and she turned away from him. "How are you feeling?" she asked me. "What's it like to be pregnant?"

I shook my head, not wanting to talk about it. "I haven't had much time to think about it. Work's been busy . . ." My voice trailed off as I realized how stupid I sounded saying that when I'd just been suspended for not doing anything.

"Have you been sick?" she asked.

"A few times. I feel sick all the time." I shuddered. "It's horrible."

"You're avoiding thinking about it, aren't you?" said James. "The problem won't go away, you know."

While he was speaking I'd realized I could go onto Google Street View and have a look at Matt's office before I actually went there. I was itching to be back at home with my laptop and my notes.

I stood up. "I know. You're right. I'd better get back now."

"Oh, did you bring that note with you?" asked Katie. "You wanted to look at it, didn't you, James?"

"Yeah, I've got a good magnifying glass," he said. "I thought we could have a look at the postmark."

I hesitated. "There wasn't a postmark."

"Oh, that's right, you said that," said Katie. "But I thought it came in the post. Have you got it?"

"No," I said. "Someone's taken it."

"What?" she said.

"Someone's taken it from the house."

I couldn't mistake the look Katie gave James.

"Are you sure you didn't just lose it?" he said.

My face burned. "Of course I'm sure! I stuck it on the fridge and when I got home the other day, it wasn't there."

I saw Katie glance at him again. I knew she thought I'd made it all up.

"Anyway," I said. "Time for me to go." I picked up my bag.

"Don't go," said Katie. "We didn't mean to upset you. Stay a bit longer. Do you want some dinner? My mum brought us round a casserole earlier. Why don't you eat with us?"

"It's okay. Thanks, but I need to be at home. I shouldn't have come out. I feel really awful."

"Do you feel safe in the house, though," asked James, "when you've had all those weird things happen?"

"James!" said Katie. "Stop that. You'll frighten her even more."

I wasn't really listening. All I was thinking was that when I saw Matt again, once I got to talk to him, I would ask him about that, ask him why he'd come into the house and sent me messages. I'd ask him why he hadn't just called me and admitted he wanted to be with me.

I closed my eyes for a second. I was almost within reach.

I'll see him tomorrow.

It was all I could think about.

Chapter
Forty-six

I WOKE AT six. As soon as I turned over and saw the empty space beside me I remembered that this was the day I'd be seeing Matt. I sat up so quickly I felt light-headed and realized I'd had nothing to eat the previous day.

Downstairs in the kitchen while I waited for the bread to toast I decided to plan my day on paper, so I ran out to fetch my notebook from the car. I couldn't risk anyone seeing this.

Manchester was an hour's drive from my house and I knew I'd have to factor in an extra half hour or so to find his office. I wasn't familiar with the area and I didn't want to arrive after he'd gone home. I decided to get there at around 3 p.m., to give myself plenty of time. There was no way Matt would be leaving at that time. He was often late getting home to me.

And then I wondered. Did he really work late most nights? Maybe he was seeing his girlfriend then? I thought of days when I'd waited ages for him to come home. Days when dinner was spoiled, the evening was ruined, when I'd drink too much just to fill the time. He was ambitious; I'd always known it and assumed that's why he was out until all hours. It made me work harder, too, I have to admit that, but it was lonely at home as well. Now I wondered whether he'd been with someone else, someone who'd meant enough for him to do a disappearing act. Well, I'd see what he had to say about that today.

At times I knew there was a chance, just a small one, that there wasn't another woman, but without her, none of it made sense. And it was easier to blame her, too, for taking him away. At night I'd burn with jealousy that he had someone else but by day I knew that if I were to just see him again, just talk to him, he'd remember how much he loved me. And then he'd come back.

I showered and washed my hair but when I came to dry it I just couldn't make it look as good as I'd been able to do in the past. It was lank and drab. I stared into the mirror in despair. There was no way I could meet him looking like this. One glance at me and he'd be glad he'd left.

When my usual salon opened, I booked myself in for a cut, highlights, manicure and pedicure. I needed to look the best I could, be the best I could, to keep him. I sighed heavily. The pressure of keeping a relationship going was tremendous sometimes.

The last time I'd been to the salon was the weekend before I'd gone to Oxford. Unfortunately, the stylist, Zara, remembered that I'd been going there and asked me all about how the day had gone and what had happened since. She asked me about Matt, too, and how he was. Of course I couldn't tell her he'd left, so I had to rack my brains to think of things he'd been doing lately. It made me realize that he hadn't talked about any future projects, the way he used to do, and I wondered when he'd first thought of leaving that job, when he knew there would be no more projects with that company. Zara asked question after question about him and about my job until I felt like I was going to scream.

By the time I left the salon I was a wreck and although my hair was a bit better, all it seemed to do was emphasize the fact that over-all I looked awful. My head was thumping and I thought I wouldn't go back there again.

At home I tried on dress after dress before realizing I was treat-ing it like an interview and trying to impress him. I couldn't give him that power; I couldn't let him see I'd put in so much effort when he was the one at fault. I searched in my wardrobe and found a tur-quoise halter top from last summer that I'd loved. Neither the top nor my white jeans were anything like as tight as when I'd worn them last and I remembered Katie the night before saying, "I thought your boobs would be bigger now you're pregnant!"

My hands shook as I put my makeup on and I had to do my eye-liner three times before I was fit to go out. As I applied some lip gloss, I wondered about the protocol when you saw your old boy-friend after he'd been missing for months. Did you kiss? Shake hands? Shake *him*?

My heart was beating faster and despite my efforts my hands were slick with sweat. All my senses seemed heightened, more vivid, and not for the first time I wondered whether I was going mad.

It was a weird sensation. On the one hand I was like a child the day before Christmas, wanting to jump up and down with excite-ment. I just couldn't wait! On the other, I was terrified. I dreaded seeing the look in his eyes when he saw me standing there.

Chapter
Forty-seven

THE DRIVE TO Manchester was a familiar one; I'd been there tons of times for work, for shopping, for nights out with Matt and with Katie. I was fine as far as the ring road surrounding Manchester, but once I left that, I was in unknown territory.

When I could see from the sat nav that I had less than a mile to go, I pulled over into a tiny car park beside a row of shops and tried to calm myself down. My hands were still damp with sweat; they'd been slipping and sliding on the steering wheel all the way there. I reached into my bag for tissues and dried them but they were clammy again within seconds. I twisted the rearview mirror so that I could see my face and wished I hadn't. My hair was already lank; beads of perspiration dotted my forehead. My makeup looked awful, caked on my skin. I'd been in such a state when I was putting it on that I'd missed bits and I looked like a clown. I felt like crying.

I opened my handbag and took out a little silver mirror. I could only see an inch or two of my face at a time, so it took a while to get it sorted out. I hadn't been eating properly since Matt left and it was pretty obvious my skin was suffering. I thought of Katie saying to me, "I thought your skin was supposed to glow when you're pregnant?" and I wondered how it was that two women could be such good friends but absolutely hate each other at the same time.

I tried as hard as I could but I knew that I wouldn't be looking my best when Matt saw me. But, then, why should I? Would he warm to me more if I looked happy and pretty and carefree or sad and lank and worn out? I had a horrible feeling I knew the answer to that and had to stop myself thinking about it any further. I just had to go along with the hope that if he could see I'd suffered a bit, he'd feel guilt rather than revulsion.

I packed my makeup away and started the car again. I had a broad idea where I was going because I could see the map on the sat nav screen, but of course I needed to be in a good position to watch him. I didn't want to park somewhere he'd see me from inside the building. I also didn't want him to see me as soon as he came out. Suddenly I wasn't sure whether I wanted him to see me at all today.

What was important was that I saw him.

I wanted control. I wanted to decide what to do about approaching him.

His office was in the center of a small shopping complex on the outskirts of Manchester, near the canal. It was a tall, modern building made of glass and concrete and it had a car park just beside it, surrounded by trees and leading onto a small grassy area. The area was mainly small offices and shops, though further down the road there were houses and purpose-built apartments. It was a nice area; I could see how he must have been attracted to it when he came for his interview. He must have thought about it all the way home and then when I was sitting there next to him, too. I wondered what we'd watched on television that night or whether he'd said he'd rather read. I pictured him pretending to be absorbed, one hand on a glass of beer and the other holding the book steady, thinking about his future. Thinking about his past and how much he didn't want that life anymore.

He must have looked over at me that evening, watched me laugh at something on the television and thought, *Enjoy it while you can.* You can't plan to go and not think of the consequences.

At what point did he decide to take my memories away?

I DROVE ALONG the road and past his office block. As the office building was on my left, the passenger side of the car was nearest the sidewalk; this meant that if Matt came out of the office he was less likely to notice me. I went around the block and down the road again and again, trying to see him. A quick look at the car park told me his car wasn't there, but then I didn't know whether he was still driving the same car or had sold it. I'd rung round some local garages weeks before but they hadn't been able to tell me anything. On the last call the owner sounded like he thought I was mad and I had to make up a story about how it was my car and it had been stolen. He'd burst into a diatribe about how he didn't handle stolen goods, then slammed the phone down on me. Later that night I'd looked on Gumtree and Motor Trader and all the other sites I could think of, but I couldn't see it there and by 4 a.m. I'd given up; I was going to work in a few hours and I had to try to sleep.

I found a side road which faced the reception area of his office block and hid there behind a row of other cars. I must have sat there for a good couple of hours, my eyes strained for a glimpse of him. The problem with spying on someone is that you can't relax for a second. You turn to look the other way and your opportunity could be gone. And I didn't know if he'd be coming up behind me or from the side, whether he'd be going into the building or out. I didn't even know for sure that he actually worked there.

At half past five the building started to empty. First out were the young ones in their early twenties, who left with such intense relief in their bodies that I wondered what kind of company Matt had gone to work for. A few minutes later small groups of men and women in suits came out; clearly there wasn't a culture of presenteeism. They stood on the pavement chatting, then dispersed to go to the car park or to wait at the bus stop further up the road.

The car in front of me drove off and I edged forward into a much better position.

I was just about to turn off the engine when I saw him.

Chapter
Forty-eight

As soon as he was outside the building, he pulled his tie off. That simple gesture was so familiar to me that tears immediately welled up in my eyes. He rolled it around his hand a few times, then pushed it into his jacket pocket and undid the top button of his shirt.

I bit my lip so hard I tasted blood.

He glanced right and left. I was right in front of him, just a few cars back. If he'd thought to look, he would have seen me there, hunched down like a criminal. He didn't look, but turned left and started to walk. I leaned forward and saw him pass the car park and continue on down the main road.

Rigid with tension, I slid the car out of the parking space and drove to the end of the side road. By craning my neck I could see that he was still on the other side of the road. I looked in the rearview mirror; luckily there was nobody behind me, though someone had already grabbed my parking spot.

I didn't know what to do. If I drove past him, I risked him seeing the car. I knew he'd immediately recognize it as the same model as mine. I pictured his eyes narrowing as he looked down at the number plate, followed by shock as he realized it actually was my car. Then a glance, fast as lightning, to the driver's seat, to see my hair and my profile as I looked at him in my rearview mirror.

I wasn't ready for that. I wanted him to see me when I decided, not because he'd randomly glanced my way.

A car drove up behind me at the junction and I froze. I didn't want it to sound its horn at my indecision. I didn't want to attract Matt's attention at all.

There was no choice. I indicated right so that I would be driving down the road at the same time as Matt was walking. I'd try to park somewhere behind him and just hope he didn't turn around.

Luckily the traffic was slow once I was on the main road and I was able to creep forward. I spotted him ahead of me in the distance, then saw him disappear into a road a hundred yards ahead of me. I glanced at the sat nav and found the road he'd taken. It led to the canal.

The traffic moved forward and I followed suit. When I reached the road that Matt had turned into, I could see him walking along as though he hadn't a care in the world. His jacket was off now and he held it over one shoulder. He looked like any young man going home at the end of the working day. I made a quick turn into the same road and parked the car at the side of the road some way behind him.

He walked along for a hundred yards or so and I sat back and watched him, holding my breath. I would have known that walk anywhere. He didn't look behind him once, clearly completely unaware he was being watched. He was generally oblivious to people around him, I knew that. In the past we'd go shopping and separate for a while so we could go into different shops, and when I'd finished I'd always look out for him and follow him for a while without him noticing. You couldn't do that to me; I was the kind of person who always looked behind me even if there was nobody around.

And then he walked past a building with black wrought-iron railings and took a left turn at a porter's lodge. I rolled the car further down the road and stopped to look. The gates were wide open. He hadn't stopped at the lodge but had gone straight through. I moved further down again, my hands gripping the steering wheel hard.

The building was one of those Victorian canal warehouses that has been turned into apartments over the last couple of decades. We'd been into a similar one on the Liverpool docks; inside it was all brickwork and arches and high-end furnishings. It had belonged to Katie's friend, who was celebrating her thirtieth birthday and had invited us along. I remembered the conversation we'd had on the way home; Matt had loved the building and talked about it for hours, about how they'd changed the function of it but kept the design to such a high standard. I got fed up with him talking about it and told him if he liked it so much he should go and live in one. It looked like he'd taken my advice. This one, though, was far more run-down than the one we'd been to. "To Let" signs hung like bunting from windows, and a row of dumpsters along the wall were piled high with rubble.

I edged further down the road, not so close that anyone living there would see me, but close enough to get a good view of the place. A couple of minutes later a light came on in one of the windows, three floors up and just above one of the arched entrances. I saw a figure move across the room. A man. Then the light went off, the French doors opened and he stepped out onto the small balcony.

It was Matt.

I slid down low so that he couldn't see me.

He stood out on the balcony and undid the buttons of his shirt, then went back into the apartment, leaving the doors wide open. Filmy curtains concealed the interior. I waited to see whether he'd reappear and after ten minutes he came out again with a mug of something—tea, knowing him—and wearing a T-shirt and jeans. His hair was damp and his feet were bare.

As I looked at him I remembered the day we'd met; we'd run straight down to the beach that first night after the long, hot flight. He'd stood in the water with his arms stretched out in the soft breeze and when he'd turned to me and laughed I could see all the pressures of work disappear.

He looked like that now; younger, tanned and completely relaxed.

He stood there awhile longer with his drink, gazing down toward the canal, then turned back into the apartment and disappeared from sight. There was a brief moment when I felt like running into the building to find him, but I managed to hold back. I stared at the balcony for another ten minutes, but he didn't reappear.

Chapter
Forty-nine

BACK HOME, IN the dark quiet of the night, I thought of Matt in his new place and how he must have looked forward to it, planned it, put a deposit down on it. My ears hummed at the thought of him walking around, agreeing on the price, letting them know the start date of the tenancy, all while I was in complete ignorance. I pictured him coming home to tell me about his day, carefully leaving out the part where he'd arranged to live in a canal-side apartment in Manchester.

My phone rang a few times that evening, when I was already in bed. My mum called first. I couldn't face her questions after my visit home the other day. I knew I should ask how she was, whether she was all right. I should ask her what my dad said after I left. I couldn't tell her I'd tracked Matt down. I knew she would tell me to write to him but not to go there.

All of my life I'd thought my mum didn't understand me. When I saw her the other day I realized she knew me better than I'd thought. Better than I wanted her to. I couldn't let myself think about the look in her eyes as I'd cried. She knew more than she ever told me. That was why I couldn't see her for a while, couldn't bear to look at the expression on her face. I didn't answer the call and let her leave a message. I'd listen to it tomorrow, after I'd talked to Matt.

Then Sam was back in touch, first with a phone call which I left unanswered, then a carefully worded text:

Hannah, I need to speak to you. HR is sending you another email. Can you call me when you've read it?

I'd heard an email pinging into my in-box on my way back from Manchester and had taken a risk by checking it while I was driving, but once I saw it was from HR my brain seemed to freeze and I'd ignored it. I knew I couldn't just delete it, but I couldn't face reading it so I'd shoved my phone back into my bag. If I didn't think about work, if I kept my mind on a thin thread of hope that Matt would come back, then I could cope. I knew that if I started to think about the repercussions of everything that had happened lately, I'd go mad. Once he was back home, I could handle anything.

Now Katie was ringing me every few minutes. She knew me well enough to know that if I didn't take her call, I wouldn't listen to a message, either, so she just played the numbers game, figuring I'd get fed up of her calling. I did, but not enough to speak to her. Then she started with the texts:

Hi Hannah. What have you been doing today?

Hi, just wondered how you are. Have you booked an appointment at the doctor's yet?

Hi, did you call HR to explain about the baby?

On and on she went. I don't think I'd realized up to now quite how persistent she could be. She had some stamina, I'll give her that. I would have got fed up long before she did. I was resolute; I wouldn't answer any of those questions. The next time I'd speak to her would be after I'd seen Matt again.

If any of these people—Katie and James, Sam, my mum—heard that I was going to speak to Matt tomorrow, they'd all say I shouldn't. I knew that. I wasn't stupid. It was nothing to do with them, though. Some things were private. When Matt came home there would be time to tell them how it had happened. I would daydream, sometimes, about how I'd invite people round for the evening and not tell them he was back. I loved to imagine their faces as they saw him right where he should be, back home with me.

I didn't want them to help me get him back; I didn't even want them to know about it. It was between him and me. The two of us. Just as it always had been.

And then the landline rang. I swore. That would be Katie, realizing she had no chance with my mobile but thinking I would be sure to answer the landline. I reached over to the bedside cabinet and looked at the caller ID.

I stopped still. I recognized that number! I'd written it down when James gave it to Katie the day after Matt left. It was in my notes and I still tried it every now and again, just in case.

It was Matt's old number, the one he'd had when he was with me.

My hands were suddenly so slippery and shaky I could hardly pick up the phone.

"Hello?"

There was silence.

"Matt? Is that you?"

Silence again. I pressed the receiver as hard as I could against my ear.

"Are you okay?" I started to cry. "Matt! Say something, will you?"

The call ended then and all I could hear was a dead tone. I lay back in the bed, tears streaming down my face.

I pressed Redial but an automated message stated, "This number is no longer available." I frowned. How had he called me if the number wasn't available?

I took my iPad from the bedside table and started to google, but I didn't have much luck. All I could find out was how to block someone. I didn't want to block him—I wanted to do the opposite!

Then the phone rang again. It was the same number.

"Hello?"

Silence.

"Matt, how are you calling from this number?"

He didn't answer, but this time I heard something, something faint. I could hear breathing.

My skin tingled. I pressed the receiver closer to my ear. Yes, I could definitely hear him breathing.

"Matt? I know you're there. Say something!"

There was no response. I could still hear the breathing, a bit heavier now.

"Stop acting like some pervert who gets a kick out of frightening women!" I yelled. "You called me, so speak to me!"

At the sound of the tone as he ended the call, I shrieked in frustration and threw the phone across the bed.

I tried to sleep after that, but I couldn't stop thinking about seeing him the next day and asking him what the hell he was playing at. It was obvious he wanted to see me; why else would he be calling? Was he missing me? Was he lying in his own bed, wishing he was with me, wishing he'd never left me?

When the phone rang again, I was half asleep and had to blink hard to make sure it was his caller ID.

"Hello?"

Again there was silence, but then I heard something else. Not breathing this time. I could hear music. I strained my ears. What was that? It sounded familiar.

"Matt? What are you playing?"

There was no reply. I could hear the music more clearly now. "You've Lost That Lovin' Feelin'" was playing. For the duration of the song I lay on my bed, imagining him on his bed, too, both of us listening to the same music. It made me think of those days when he was in London and I was in Liverpool and we'd talk on the phone for hours. Sometimes we'd play the same tracks as we talked, shouting "Now!" down the phone so that our music was in sync. Other times we'd put on the same album and just lie in our beds, not talking, just drifting off to sleep to the sound of music and each other's breathing. I loved those nights, loved the intimacy despite the distance. Listening to that song now reminded me so much of those days that tears drenched my face, but I made no sound. It was perfect, really.

The music came to an end and there was silence. I thought he was holding his breath, thought he was about to speak, but then there was a click and the call ended.

I tried to call him back. I called again and again. I just wanted to tell him that I did still love him, I always had. I wanted to tell him I'd see him tomorrow, but the line was dead. No one was there.

Chapter
Fifty

I DIDN'T SLEEP well that night. I dreamed of Matt and, in my dreams, I was angry with him and shouting. I kept waking, gasping for breath and sweating, then falling straight back into the same dream. I woke early and the dreams didn't disappear, the way they normally did, but lingered in my mind so that although I was excited about the day ahead, my head ached with the memory of the arguments we'd had.

I jumped out of bed and into my running gear. I needed to run, to forget my dreams, to plan the day ahead. I put my house key and phone in my pocket and quietly closed the front door behind me. Outside on the pavement I stood still, trying to steady my breathing for the run. The houses nearby were still in darkness. In Sheila and Ray's house the bedroom curtains twitched, then Sheila drew them open and stood staring out into the road.

I gasped with fright as I saw Ray standing at their living room window, beneath their bedroom. He was flattened against the wall by the window and he was looking out. I'd almost missed him there, hiding in the shadows. He was watching me. Uneasy, I glanced back up at the bedroom window. Sheila was still standing there. She saw me looking and I gave a tentative wave. She stared a moment longer, then lifted her hand and disappeared into the room.

I looked back at the living room. Ray had gone.

Unsettled, I ran down the street, guessing they would be watching me. I thought again of the text, "Enjoy your run?" and realized I didn't know Sheila and Ray's mobile numbers, though I'd given them mine ages ago, when Matt and I were going on holiday one time. Had they always watched me like that? I'd thought it was Matt, down by the river, tracking me. I'd thought he'd missed me. The thought that it might be Ray or Sheila, filming my every move, unnerved me. Then I shook myself. Of course it wasn't them. Why would they watch me run by the river?

It was hard to relax, though, when I didn't know whether I was being observed, and by the end of the run I felt like my shoulders were up around my ears. I would book into the salon for a massage soon, I thought. Mind you, once Matt was home, I wouldn't need one; he could just rub my shoulders the way he used to and I'd be able to relax again.

I thought of those early days, when he'd kneel over me on the bed and knead my shoulders and back until I fell asleep. Bliss. Those days would return, I knew. It wouldn't be long before he was home and I'd be back at work and everything would be as it was. Yes, he might have to travel to Manchester to work for a while, but maybe his old company would take him back. You never know; he had a good reputation with them. He might have to wait awhile, but that's the price of being impetuous, isn't it?

Back at home after my run, I had a bit of time to burn. I assumed Matt would be going back to his apartment at about the same time as the evening before, but I wanted to make sure I left in good time.

I looked around and realized how long it had been since I'd tidied the house. Full of pent-up energy, I spent a couple of hours cleaning with a vengeance. If he was coming home with me tonight, I wanted it to be perfect. I polished the floors, vacuumed the rugs, cleaned the windows and washed down the woodwork, all on a high.

I'd left the kitchen until last and when I finally got to it, the rest of the house looked immaculate. I stood in the doorway and my heart sank. My notes had taken over the room. The cabinets were covered in writing and Post-it notes, and the island was covered in a sea of red and black ink, where I'd sat at night, scribbling reminders to myself.

I hadn't really eaten properly since Matt had left and the kitchen bore evidence to that. On the counters lay pizza boxes and takeaway containers amidst piles of dirty plates and glasses. I'd been so busy working out where he was that I'd figured I had time either to eat or to tidy the kitchen and it was obvious that eating had to come first. Anyone would do that. The kitchen did smell stale, though; even I had to acknowledge that. I couldn't remember the last time I'd emptied the bin and next to it were a few over-full bin bags that I'd already tied up. A couple of flies buzzed around the rubbish and I found some fly spray under the sink and spritzed it around the room.

The rest of the house was beautiful. I'd gone to the shops that morning and bought huge candles, the kind with several wicks in them, and bunches of summer flowers. I'd arranged the candles in the hallway, in the living room fireplace, on the coffee table, on the tops of the bookcases. The fragrance of roses and lilies filled the air and the wax polish I'd used made the room smell warm and festive. I couldn't wait for him to see it like this.

I looked at the kitchen, then glanced at my watch. I was cutting it fine now. And in any case, just as the living room and bedroom would remind Matt that I had a lovely home and that he really did belong here, the kitchen would show him just how much I had suffered while he'd been away.

He needed to know that. He needed to *see* it. There was no point hiding it from him. He had to look at those notes, at all the work I'd done, and recognize exactly what he'd put me through. I closed my eyes for a second. I could just picture his face as he saw it.

I shut the kitchen door behind me and went out the front door, diving into my car before Sheila or Ray could see me.

I wore the same clothes I'd worn the day before. They were my lucky clothes now. And I'd lain awake all night in them, too, so that the luck didn't wear off. I couldn't risk that.

Chapter
Fifty-one

I'D ONLY GOT halfway down the road when my phone beeped with a message. I pulled over and dug deep down into my bag to find it. I looked down, hoping it wasn't an email from work. There was no way I would read it. My stomach tightened when I saw a text from my dad.

I bumped into Alex Hughes at a dinner last night. He told me you've been suspended. Do you have any idea how embarrassing that was for me? Yet again you have let me down.

Panic rose in my chest and I thought I was going to choke. In that moment it was as though I was standing in front of him again. Cowering. He wanted to draw me back in line, to show me who exactly was boss. He needed to. How could I have forgotten how he'd been the other night? That should have been my priority, not Matt! Now I was really in for it. I forgot about Matt and called my dad. It went straight to voicemail and I knew he was ignoring me. I tried to speak but I couldn't, or not without crying. I canceled the call and sent him a text. My fingers slipped on the keypad and I had to keep deleting what I'd written and start again.

Dad, I'm really sorry. I need to talk to you. Can you call me? xxxxx

I waited a few minutes, my stomach knotted and tight. I could hear the rasp of my breath and closed my eyes and visualized my counselor, her face so warm and kind. I pictured her mouth moving as she whispered instructions, and I breathed in and out the way she'd shown me. It worked. It nearly always worked. When I opened my eyes, five minutes had passed and there was no reply. If he was going to call he would have done so straightaway. I kept the phone on the passenger seat just in case and started the car again.

I was halfway to Manchester when my phone beeped for a second time. I was going at quite a good speed, as I was trying to get ahead of the lorries that were thundering along. Thinking it was my dad again, I swerved in to park as soon I came to the Sainsbury's, just off the M62. The message was from Matt's phone.

On the screen was a photo of me at the supermarket that morning. My trolley was full of candles, wine and beer, strawberries and brie, and there were a couple of huge bunches of flowers on the baby seat. I was reaching up for a bottle of the Nuits-Saint-Georges that Matt liked; it was on the top shelf and the halter top I was wearing had ridden up around my stomach making me look desperately thin. I looked closely; I didn't think I'd ever been that thin, not even when I had food poisoning in Australia when I was eighteen and lost twenty pounds in a matter of weeks. I twisted the rearview mirror and saw the circles under my eyes and the hollow of my cheekbones.

How many phones did Matt have? I wondered. And why didn't he just approach me in the supermarket? Why bother sending me photos? I tried to remember what time I'd been in the shop; had he told his colleagues he was out on a project?

Just then I caught sight of the time on the dashboard clock and panicked. I drove quickly out of the car park. I thought I'd only been there a minute or so but somehow twenty minutes had passed. I'd have to get a move on.

This time I didn't need the sat nav and found my way to Matt's apartment on autopilot. I drove past the entrance to the apartments and parked on a side road at the back of the block. I walked up toward the building, wondering whether I would bump into Matt and thinking of his reaction if he saw me there. He obviously wanted to see me if he was calling me, but maybe he wanted to make the first move. It was too late for that now. There was still nobody on duty at the porter's lodge and I made a mental note to remind Matt to put in a complaint about that.

When I reached the doors, I realized I couldn't get in without a key-code, so I wandered around the building until I saw a young couple coming out of another entrance and then I just smiled and walked in, saying, "Thanks a lot."

IT TOOK ME a while to find Matt's apartment once I was inside. The building itself was huge, with a small marina in its center. Some of the internal doors needed codes to be entered before they'd open, but others were held open by fire extinguishers, completely breaking the fire regulations. I knew Matt would be annoyed at this but I hoped he'd see it was better for me that way. I weaved my way around the building, up a couple of flights of stairs and along corridors until I knew I'd found it. It was the only one on the corridor that didn't have a name outside, which was as big a hint as he could possibly have given me.

It was 4:15 by the time I got there; later than I'd hoped but I guessed from the silence inside that I'd beaten him to it. I had nothing to do but to stand against the wall, by his door, and wait.

I WAITED TWO hours in that little alcove by his front door and by then I thought maybe he'd gone out for the evening and I'd have to come back later.

But then I heard the ping of the lift and somehow I just knew it would be him. I held my breath as I heard him coming down the corridor, keys jangling. I wondered whether he'd kept the same key ring, just replacing my key with this one.

As he turned into the alcove where I was standing, he caught sight of me and, you won't believe this, but he nearly jumped out of his skin. His face was white and his eyes were popping out of his head. I could see him starting to back away and I leaped over and grabbed his arm.

"Hello, Matt," I said.

Chapter
Fifty-two

I took the keys from him and opened the door. I turned to smile at him and ushered him in ahead of me. I wanted to make sure he got in there, and I knew he knew it.

"After you," I said and slammed the door behind us. There was a glass shelf to one side of the door and I placed his keys there.

Matt stood there, his face pale and his mouth open. I was so tempted to snap it shut.

Adrenaline coursed through my veins, making my head spin, and as I glanced around the room, all I could see were stars bouncing off the light coming through the French doors. I leaned against a sofa and clung onto it in case I fell.

I was in a large living room with functional furniture that looked like it had been rented with the apartment. His jazz photographs were up on the walls—the photographs that belonged in my hallway. His television was on its table, though it looked less impressive here in this huge space than it did in my modern semi. The doors leading off the room were wide open and I could see a large silver refrigerator in one, a glass shower enclosure in another. Still clutching the sofa, I moved across and saw that the third door led to a bedroom.

There was a double bed in there and a wardrobe with a tan suede jacket hanging up. The last room was small—a storage room, really. In it were piles of plastic boxes, the sort you might buy in B&Q if you were leaving your girlfriend without telling her you were going.

Nobody else was in the apartment. I don't know what I was expecting but I was glad of that.

Matt stood stock-still, as though in a trance. I stared at him and he looked away; I could feel his brain whirring, though. I knew he'd be thinking hard.

I walked over to the French doors leading to the little balcony that I'd seen him on the day before. I flung them open and bright sunlight poured into the room. I dropped my handbag on the floor, then turned to him.

"That's better," I said. "So, thanks for your calls. And all the other messages."

He stared at me, then shook his head as though trying to clear it. I saw him swallow before he spoke. "What? Sorry, Hannah, you need to leave now."

"Leave?" I roared and he jumped a mile. "What do you mean, leave?"

I took one step toward him and he took five back. He was up against the wall.

"This is my home," he said, his Adam's apple bobbing in his throat as he swallowed again. "I don't want you here."

"Frankly, Matt," I said, "I don't care what you want. I want to know why you walked out on me like that." I took another step toward him and he shut his eyes for a second. "Why you walked out taking everything with you."

"I only took my own things!" he said.

"Sneaking out like a thief," I said. "Humiliating me. Making me look a fool in front of people. Have you any idea how you made me feel?"

"I'm sorry," he said. "I didn't mean to humiliate you."

"Then why did you go like that?" I shouted. "Why just go and leave me to come home feeling like I was going mad?"

"Hannah," he said quietly, "you know why I left. You know it."

"What?"

He moved away toward the window.

"What are you doing?" I exploded. "I'm talking to you and you're looking out of the window!"

"I'm sorry," he said, and then again, "I'm sorry." He moved back into the room and for a second his profile reminded me of Olivia.

"You're not the only one who left, either, are you?"

He looked blank.

"Your mother."

"Leave my mother out of it," he said with the first real sign of spirit he'd shown since I'd got there.

Instantly I was livid. "Leave her out of it? When she was sitting in our house on Christmas Day and didn't say a word about moving house? What was all that about?" He said nothing and that infuriated me more than anything. "Well?"

He sighed. "She didn't want you to know where she was living."

"Why not?" I screamed. "Why shouldn't I know where she's living?"

"Because she wanted me to leave you and she wanted me to have somewhere to go," he said, so quietly I had to strain to hear him.

"What a bitch!"

He flinched.

"Well, if you were so keen to leave me, why have you been sending me messages and calling me?"

He stared at me. "What?"

"Texting me and phoning me and coming into the house. Did you think I wouldn't know you were there?"

He shook his head. "I haven't . . ."

"Don't lie to me!" I yelled. "You've been coming into my house, touching my things and sending me stupid messages." He looked confused but I saw right through it and screamed, "Are you trying to drive me crazy?"

He jumped back and his shoulder hit the wall. "Hannah, I haven't done anything," he said. "I haven't been home . . . I mean to your house since . . . well, since I left."

"Right," I said. "Did you think I wouldn't recognize that cologne? Do you think I'm stupid?"

"What? What cologne?"

"Ralph Lauren," I said. "Polo. The one I bought you for Christmas."

He shook his head again. "I don't wear it. I haven't worn it since I left."

"Liar!"

My stomach twisted at the thought that he hadn't wanted to wear it to remind him of me. I was about to mention the flowers and the warm kettle but I knew he'd tell me he didn't know what I was talking about. He'd say I was mad. I didn't know whether I *was*. My heart was pounding so hard I thought he'd hear it and I couldn't have that. I took a few deep breaths to try to control myself.

"So why *did* you leave?" I asked again and this time I couldn't help it. There was a pleading note in my voice and it made me so angry.

"I had to go," he said. He spoke gently now and if I hadn't known better I would have thought he still loved me. "You know why I had to go."

I blinked. "I don't. I don't know."

He looked at me as though he wasn't sure whether to believe me. Then he drew himself up, his back straight.

"Hannah, I thought you were going to kill me."

Chapter
Fifty-three

Six months before
January 1

It was New Year's Day and as usual we were having a row. I hated Christmas and this one was no exception. We'd had plenty to eat and drink, that's for sure; my clothes were tighter and I had headaches every morning that lasted until mid-afternoon at times. I could tell I was going to have to start cutting back and that never put me in a good mood. On top of that we were pretty much housebound for several days because the weather had been so bad and that didn't help, either.

That morning we'd got up late, hungover and fed up. The wind was high around the house and the bins in the alleyway had already blown over twice. I kept telling Matt to put them in the back garden, behind the gate, but he wouldn't take any notice at all, saying that if rubbish spilled there we'd have all sorts of problems with rats and foxes.

"It's not as if you're the one cleaning it up anyway," he'd said over his shoulder the second time he went out, and my eyes had narrowed, knowing he was spoiling for a fight. We'd spent the previous night with Katie and James, drinking in the local pubs, then back to theirs at midnight for champagne and bacon sandwiches. James had been a bit off, too, and by then I was completely fed up.

"He'd rather be in bed watching the fireworks," Katie had said, glaring at his back.

It had been one of those nights when you go out determined to have fun but the fun is beyond you. There were crowds of people, all drunk out of their minds, all pushing and shoving and I hated it. The more I had to drink, the worse I felt.

"There's nowhere to sit," I complained in the third pub we went to. Katie and James were at the bar, doing their best to get served.

"You sound like my mum," said Matt, looking me straight in the eye. "She always says that's why she never goes to pubs nowadays."

Instantly I was filled with fury. His mother was over sixty! I was looking good that night, if I said so myself, and I was not going to be compared to her!

"What's that got to do with it?" I snapped. "Your mum's an old woman!"

"She's not that old," he said.

"You'd think it, with all the rubbish she talks." His mum had spent Christmas Day with us and I was still trying to recover from the mind-numbing boredom of that day. "Honestly, I was going to tell you that I think she needs a checkup."

He flushed. "What?"

"A *checkup*," I said more loudly. "There's something wrong with her. She needs to get checked out. I've never spent a more boring day in my life." I glared at him. "You needn't think she's coming next year."

He shook his head. "She wouldn't want to."

"What?"

He said nothing, just looked into the distance. It always annoyed me when he did that and he knew it.

"I said, *what*?"

Then Katie and James were standing behind us.

"It's busy here tonight," said James. "Everything okay?"

"We're fine," I said shortly. "It's just noisy. I couldn't hear what Matt was saying."

Matt looked away. "I wasn't saying anything."

There was an uncomfortable silence for a few minutes, then Katie dragged the conversation around to a funny incident at work and soon she had us laughing at some poor guy who'd been found in the stationery stockroom with his manager and without his trousers.

Back at Katie and James's house we'd played our part, acting as though we were getting on, but I could feel in the air that Matt was after trouble. In the taxi going home he sat staring out of the window, saying as little as he could get away with. I could see the taxi driver looking at us in the mirror and knew what he was thinking.

Next year, I thought, *next year will be different. Too right his mother wouldn't be here. We'd go off to somewhere hot, Jamaica maybe, and have a good time without her.*

I looked at his profile as he stared out of the window, his jaw set and mutinous.

Or maybe I'd go on my own. Maybe I'd meet someone there. I could come back with an all-over tan, looking like I'd been up all night every night having fun, and see what he has to say about that!

I decided not to speak to him when we got into the house. He tried to do the same, but he could never keep up that game and would always ask pathetic questions like, "Shall I lock up?" which he should have known the answer to.

We lay in bed with our backs to each other, neither of us able to relax enough for sleep. Eventually I heard his breathing become slower and felt his body loosen up and then he started to snore.

All the old resentments came flooding back as I lay awake that night. I thought about each one in turn, examining it closely as it revealed his unreasonable behavior. By the time morning came, I was ready for a fight.

Chapter
Fifty-four

January 2

THE NEXT DAY was miserable outside, with black clouds overhead threatening rain anytime I felt like leaving the house. We'd woken up with headaches that neither of us would admit to, and when it came to breakfast I realized we'd run out of bread. There was a bit of an argument about who was going to the shop, but in the end Matt went and made such a martyr of himself that I didn't even want to eat it when he brought it back. Of course that really cheered him up.

We were both back at work the next day and had to take the Christmas decorations down. God forbid we should risk bad luck by leaving them up past January 6. It's always so depressing taking them down that it makes me wonder whether it's even worth putting them up in the first place. I love the anticipation of Christmas, love buying the tree and dressing it and putting fairy lights all over the house, but everything looks so dark and dingy afterward that I go into a gloom that's hard to come out of.

So that afternoon we weren't speaking really and we were trying to take the decorations down separately when we actually needed to be working together. I had to ask him for help when I got stuck with a strand of fairy lights that had wrapped itself around my leg while I was up the stepladder and I could see the sly grin on his face that told me he'd known I'd cave in.

By the time we were ready to go up to the loft I was so fed up. His mum had called him just as we were about to take everything up there and I'd carried box after box upstairs, struggling with the sheer unwieldiness of them. Every time I went past him he mouthed, "Leave it, I'll do it in a minute," and after the third trip I whispered, "Get off the phone, you're meant to be helping me!" I think she must have heard me because he said, "I'll call you tomorrow, Mum," and I knew, I just knew, he would call her from work so I wouldn't be able to hear him and they'd be bitching away like mad, ripping me to shreds.

Finally we opened the hatch door to the loft and flung it back. There was no electricity up there and I really hated going up there first. He knew that but still said, "You go up and put the torch on the floor and I'll pass the boxes up to you."

When I turned to him he did jump a bit, as though he knew he was wrong, but just said, "What? They're heavier than they look!"

I glared at him and scrambled up the steps, fully aware that I'd put on weight over Christmas and fully aware, too, that he'd be watching my ever-increasing bum heave itself into the loft and that image would cheer him up when he was feeling down. So to stop that from happening, I kicked out when I got to the top step and caught him bang on the side of his chin.

The first blow is always easy. A memory. No warning. That was the trick I'd learned.

"What the hell are you doing?" he shouted. He stumbled on the steps and I turned just in time to see the box crash to the ground.

"If you've broken anything in that box . . ." I said, suddenly furious at the thought. "Pass it to me. *Pass* it to me!"

He went back down the ladder, picked up the box and shook it.

"There's nothing to break in there," he said defiantly. "It's just the lights."

I simmered with rage. Just the lights! Just the lights I'd gone out and bought. Just the lights I'd put up when he was working late one night and came home smelling of brandy, having walked from town in the snow without phoning to say he'd be late. You'd think he would have learned something from that.

When he was up in the loft space with me, I said, "Those are my lights. Just be careful with them."

"They're mine, too," he said and I could tell he was using his reasonable voice. It was a voice that always drove me mad, just as it was designed to do.

"No, they are not," I said. "They're mine. I bought them."

"I gave you the money for them, remember?"

I winced as I remembered him coming into the room later that night and giving me fifty pounds toward decorations.

"Do you really think that was enough? Do you really think your paltry contribution makes any difference?"

He flushed. "I'm happy to give you more, Hannah."

"Yeah, right. You're tight, that's your problem." I thought of all the bills I had to pay and the mortgage and the food and the petrol I had to put in to go and buy the lights in the first place and my blood started to boil. "You are so selfish, living here for virtually nothing."

He flinched. "I'm not. I'm happy to give you more money. I give you what you told me to give you."

"Yes, three years ago!" I shouted. "Haven't you heard of inflation? Haven't you heard of the recession? Don't you realize I'm subsidizing you?"

His face was set. "I didn't know you were. I'm sorry. I'll sort it out as soon as we get downstairs. You always said it was plenty, but if it's not, I'll give you whatever you need."

I wouldn't let it rest. I couldn't. "Always watching your money. Always being careful. Paying off your own property in London while you live with me. How does it feel to live off a woman's wages? A woman you won't even marry!"

I pushed him, hard. His head hit the beam and he screamed. His reaction was so extreme it made me even more furious. I flashed the torch at the beam and saw a nail sticking out with his blood and hair on it. How was I meant to know it was there? He was always looking for sympathy, moaning if I so much as glanced at him. He crouched down low and kept touching his head and complaining.

"What did you do that for?" he shouted. "And marry you? Why the hell would I marry you, you lunatic?"

"What, me?" I yelled. "*I'm* the lunatic?" And I kicked him in the small of his back. I kicked him as hard as I could, in fact my foot hurt for days afterward, but he didn't complain again. He just lay there and started to cry like a baby. I stared down at him and all I felt was contempt.

I climbed out of the loft and down the steps. I moved the stepladder away from the hatch, so that when he had to jump ten feet to get down, he'd really have something to cry about.

And then I decided to go out, rain or not, and see a film on my own. I needed something to take my mind off that miserable bastard.

Chapter
Fifty-five

Present day

I STARED AT him.

"You hit me so many times, I thought you were going to lose it completely," he said. His voice was soft, but I noticed his body was taut. Waiting. "I can't live like that."

"Like what?" I whispered.

"Afraid," he said, and as the blood rushed to my head it seemed as though his voice was floating on the air around me. "Constantly afraid."

"I . . ." I faltered. I didn't know what I was going to say. My mouth was as dry as parchment and my eyes itched from staring at him. "I . . . I didn't . . ."

"I know you didn't mean it sometimes," he said, and his voice was kinder than it needed to be, I understood that. "I know it's a problem for you. But I can't cope with it."

It was as though the ground beneath me was marshland, as if I'd disappear into it. I stumbled onto the sofa and put my head in my hands.

"I'm sorry," I said. It wasn't the first time I'd apologized to him;

each time was as miserable and uncomfortable as the last. "I'm really sorry."

He sat down carefully on the sofa opposite me. "I know. I know you are." He didn't say, "You always are," but I knew that was what he meant.

It was a re-creation of a scene we'd played out many, many times.

"Please get help, Hannah," he said and there was no mistaking the tension in his voice. It was always there when we had this conversation. But this time, instead of berating him, instead of this simple request inflaming matters so that I'd explode, asking him what he was talking about, what help was it that he thought I needed, exactly, I really heard what he was saying.

He was right. I did need help.

"You seemed so angry all the time," he said. "So on edge."

And again, I heard him loud and clear. He was right. I did always feel like I was coming to the boil, that I had to be watchful and wary all the time, in case someone overtook me, stabbed me in the back, took something from me that was mine or that I wanted. I could never relax; I was always on guard. I'd been like that since I was a child and I'd never known why.

I think this was the first time that I realized he was right. I'd paid lip service to it in the past, just to get him to shut up and forget what I'd done. If he didn't mention it, then I could put it from my mind, but if he kept on and on talking about why I hurt him and why I had to start arguments, I felt like I was going mad and before too long there'd be another explosion, worse than the last.

Tears pricked the back of my eyes. "You're right," I said, eventually. "I don't know why I'm like that."

"You can get help," he urged. "Beta-blockers or antidepressants or something. There will be something that'll help you."

I thought of my home, how it was no longer a sanctuary. And my job, all but gone now. Images of my kitchen as it had been earlier today flashed through my mind, the rubbish, the overflowing bin, the dishes that hadn't been washed for months. I thought of the paper plates I'd bought to avoid washing up, the cutlery I'd stolen from work when I'd run out of clean stuff, all of it piled up, filthy on the counter. And the mad, mad ravings that were all over the kitchen island and the cabinets.

In that moment of clarity I knew I needed help. I knew I couldn't do it on my own.

"Will you come home, Matt?" I pleaded, suddenly scared of his reply. "Will you come home and help me?"

He looked away from me. "I think it's something you have to go through on your own," he said.

"But I can't." I started to cry. "I can't do it. Everything's messed up. I'm losing my job and if I do, I'll lose the house, too! I'll have nowhere to live."

"I can help you with the mortgage," he said. "I can give you some money to tide you over for a few months. Or even a year or so. Money's not a problem." He looked at me steadily. "But I can't come home, Hannah. I'm sorry, but I can't. This is something you need to do on your own. I bring out the worst in you and I don't want that."

I hadn't wanted to break down in front of him, but suddenly I was sobbing. "You bring out the best in me, too."

His face relaxed for a moment and he smiled at me. "I know. I did at the beginning, didn't I? We were great together. I loved it."

"I did, too."

"But then . . ." he said, and I wished he'd just shut up and let me remember him saying he loved being with me. "But then it changed, didn't it? Everything I did was wrong. I used to think you hated me, even though you told me all the time you loved me. And hurting me like that, time and time again. I can't live like that. I just can't."

He was gaining strength from his words, I could see that. As he sat facing me he was almost the man he'd been when we'd met. Proud and strong, determined and fair. I'd loved him then, and now, looking at him, I knew I still loved him.

"Please?" I said, hating to hear myself beg, to let him see I was weak. "Please? I promise I'll be different. I promise I'll get help. I'll call the doctor first thing and you can come with me and we'll tell her what I'm like."

I'd never gone so far in my promises and I swear I could see indecision on his face, just a sliver of doubt. He hesitated and suddenly I was filled with hope. Wild with exhilaration, I said, "Come on, Matt. Just come home."

And then behind me I heard the sound of a key in the lock. When I turned, it seemed like I was in slow motion and in the long, long time it took for the apartment door to open, I saw Matt blanch.

"Hey, Matt, I got off work early!"

It was Katie, standing in the doorway holding an overnight bag.

Chapter
Fifty-six

"COME IN, KATIE," I said as my blood started to hum in my veins. "Make yourself at home."

She stood frozen, her face aghast.

My head roared as I stared from her to Matt. I could see an imploring expression on his face, one I'd seen so many times. But this time he was looking at Katie, not me. Katie: my best friend.

"Come on in," I said again and my voice sounded harsh and distorted.

She walked in, shutting the door behind her. It seemed she'd got over the shock remarkably quickly. Maybe this sort of confrontation was what she'd wanted. With a deliberately casual air she put her keys next to Matt's on the glass shelf by the apartment door and walked over to him, dropping her handbag and overnight bag on the floor beside her. She stood next to him as protective as a mother.

As she turned to face me, her chin tilted, her eyes steady, I saw that her face held the same expression I'd seen in school when I'd told her I was going out with James; years later, too, when she told me *she* was going out with James now. I saw pride there and determination.

"Hello, Hannah," she said. "I wasn't expecting to see you here."

Her insouciance and the familiar way she stood right next to

Matt, almost touching him, but not quite, but definitely comfortable with the distance between them, made my head throb. I could hear buzzing, feel my skin react to her. My blood pounded round my body, overheating my skin and making me pant. I swallowed hard to try to calm myself, but it was no good.

"I could say the same," I said. I heard a weak tone in my voice and swallowed again. I couldn't let them hear that. "Why are you visiting my boyfriend?"

"He's not your boyfriend, actually," said Katie. "He's not been your boyfriend for months. How long is it exactly, Matt?"

Matt was tense and pale. I could see beads of sweat on his face, see his hands shaking. "It's . . . it's been three months now," he muttered.

"So why are you here?" I asked her.

I don't know why but I was still hoping she'd say that she'd bumped into him a couple of weeks ago, that she was just here for a chat, to try to persuade him to come back to me. I think we could have recovered from that.

"Why do you think?" she said, confident and in control. "Think about it, Hannah. Why do *you* think I'm here?"

I looked from Katie to Matt and back again. His whole body was shaking now and I knew she was having to be strong for him. She edged closer to him until their arms touched. She wore a cherry pink dress with spaghetti straps which showed her summer tan. Her cheeks were flushed with excitement and she looked more beautiful than I'd seen her in years. Her hair, glossy and sleek, framed her face and tumbled down to her cleavage. Beside her, Matt appeared pathetic; he couldn't even stand up straight; it looked like his legs were buckling. His face was wet with sweat and his hair was dark and lank.

"I think," I said, not taking my eyes off Matt, "I think you've been deceiving me." I could see him struggling to speak. He wiped his mouth with his hand, then gave up. "I think you were cheating on me and treating me like a fool."

There was silence in the room.

"And as for you!" I took a step back, then jumped forward and spat in Katie's face.

She shrieked, "What? Ugh!" and wiped her face with her hand, then shuddered and rubbed it on her skirt.

"You bitch," I said in a low voice. "Sending me messages every day, asking me if I had any news. And all the time you were seeing him? You . . ." I was lost for words. "Pretending to be my friend . . ."

"I *was* your friend!"

I stepped over to where she stood and slapped her hard across her face. She didn't see it coming and her head moved fast, whipping to one side. I knew that would hurt like hell tomorrow. She stumbled backward, narrowly avoiding a footstool, and stood behind one of the sofas, as though that would give her sanctuary. I climbed up on top of the sofa and grabbed her hair, pulling it as hard as I could, until she was screaming like a banshee and struggling to get away from me.

Matt stood in the center of the room shouting, "Get off her!"

I turned so fast he jumped and ran behind the sofa to be near Katie. "Why should I? She's been pretending to be my friend, phoning me and texting me, day after day." I pulled her hair so hard she fell facedown on the sofa. "Why did you do that? Why would *anyone* do that?"

She gave a scream and grabbed hold of me. I pulled her hair tighter and she dragged her nails down my arm. I felt my skin break and yanked her hair harder for that.

"I asked her to!" shouted Matt. "I needed to know what you knew. I needed to know whether you'd found me."

I let go of Katie's hair and pushed her off the sofa onto the floor. She landed with a cry.

"And I did," I said in a low voice, so he had to strain to hear me. "I knew I would. You knew I would, too, didn't you?"

He didn't answer, but I could see his hands tremble again.

"You destroyed everything, Matt," I said. "Everything. Not only did you take your things from my house"—he tried to speak but I shot him a glare to stop him—"you destroyed all my photos and all my emails and texts."

He said nothing now, just stood white-faced, staring at me. Katie gave a moan and he started to move toward her but I shouted, "Don't you dare!" and he slammed himself back against the wall.

"Why would you do that?" I asked, moving around the sofa toward him. Strands of Katie's hair were stuck to my hand and I had to rub it on my jeans to loosen them. I could hear her moaning and whining and I was glad, really glad, that I'd hurt her. "Why would you take everything from me?"

He moved further along the wall. His eyes hadn't left mine.

I glanced at Katie, still sitting slumped on the floor, then back at him. "Why would you do that?"

I could see his Adam's apple moving in his throat. He ran his tongue across his lips, then said, "I didn't want you to have anything of mine. Anything to remember me by."

"But you did leave something, didn't you?" I said softly. "Up in the loft."

I saw a flicker in his eyes. There was recognition and . . . was that triumph? My blood started to boil.

"I wondered whether you'd see that," he said. "I should have guessed you would."

"See what?" asked Katie. "What did you leave?"

He said nothing; his eyes met mine, unwavering.

"What?" said Katie again, panic in her voice. "What was it?"

I took a step forward. "Why don't you tell her?"

He straightened his shoulders. "Blood and hair," he said. "My blood and hair. From when she hit me at Christmas."

My voice was almost a whisper. "And why did you leave that?"

"For you to remember," he said. "To remember what you did."

MY ROAR SEEMED to come from nowhere. "Remember what *I* did? When *you* were the one having an affair?"

"He wasn't having an affair then." Katie was standing now, one hand on the back of the sofa and the other rubbing her head. She looked dazed. "I called round that day to see you. You were out and he was there on his own. Hurt."

"Hurt!" I scoffed.

"He had to jump from the loft," she said, her voice harder now. Steadier. "You'd taken the ladder away, knowing he'd struggle to get down without it. He'd hit his head on the nail and then you kicked him in the kidneys. His head was bleeding." There was contempt in her eyes. "What the hell were you doing, treating him like that?"

I faltered for a second but soon rallied. "You have no idea what I've had to put up with, living with him."

"And yet you were so keen to find him." She glared at me. "You're an idiot. You didn't know what you had with Matt. He was so loyal and you just hurt him again and again."

For a moment I was speechless. Loyal? Matt? When he was having an affair with Katie? And then I looked at her, my best friend, and it all fell into place. I realized what I'd missed before, what had been on the periphery of my thoughts.

"You helped him, didn't you? You were there the day he left, helping him take everything from the house."

She gave me a look, hard as you like. "Yes, I was there."

I glared at Matt. "You're pathetic," I said. "You couldn't even do that on your own."

"He didn't have to," she said. "I wanted to help him. Wanted him to get away from you."

I realized something else. "You were with him the week after, weren't you? You weren't at the conference at all."

She raised her eyebrows.

"You told me you were going to that conference in February!" I shouted.

Still she said nothing and I understood then just how long this had been planned. My face burned. I thought of him zealously removing everything of his from the house. Bringing the television downstairs. Making it look as though he'd never been there. As though he hadn't existed.

And then the final piece of the jigsaw fell into place. "You changed the bed linen, didn't you?" How had I not realized? "He wouldn't have thought of that. It was your idea, wasn't it?"

She glanced over at Matt, but said nothing.

"You've always wanted what I had. First James and then Matt. Can't you see a pattern, Katie?"

She flushed. "You were only with James for six months and that was years ago! Fifteen years ago now. Get over it."

Out of the corner of my eye I saw Matt walking toward the windows.

"Where do you think you're going?" I said.

He turned to face me. "It's time for you to leave."

"What?"

Katie slid around the back of the sofa and went to stand beside him. "Yeah. Time's up, Hannah."

I stared from one to the other. I could feel the mist rising and I knew they should be very careful what they said.

"And don't go telling Matt that you're pregnant, either," said Katie.

Automatically I looked down at my stomach, nearly concave now. I'd almost forgotten about that.

"We hadn't had sex for ages before I left," said Matt. His voice trembled and I knew he was showing off for her.

"That's what he's told you?" I asked Katie.

For a moment she looked uncertain and my heart leaped.

"Ask him what happened in March, after we came back from that wine bar. You know, the one in New Brighton? We went to its opening night. You and James were busy, remember?"

Her eyes flashed from me to Matt. His face reddened and I felt triumph course through my veins.

"Ask him what happened when we came home!" I goaded her. "Go on!"

"There's no need," he said. "Katie and I weren't together then. Well, we were friends, but we didn't get together until the day after that."

The day after! He'd gone straight from me to her?

His face was scarlet now and I think he thought he was being brave. "Remember, Katie?"

She nodded and now she was the triumphant one. My body tensed in anticipation.

"That night," he said, "I knew then that it was all wrong. That I had to leave you."

I saw pity on his face. My body flamed and I was desperate to get out of there.

"I'm sorry, Hannah," he said gently. "I'm in love with Katie. I wouldn't sleep with someone else if I was in love with her, would I?"

"So . . ." My voice rose uncontrollably. "So you left me because of her?"

"No." He spoke so quietly I had to strain to hear him. "I left you because you hurt me. I know I can be annoying . . ."

"Stop it!" said Katie. "She shouldn't have hit you no matter what she thought of you."

It was as though she hadn't spoken.

"I couldn't be myself when I was with you, Hannah. Not at the end. I was on tenterhooks the whole time." He stared at me, scared still. "I loved you, Hannah, but it's over. I would have left anyway, but now . . . now I'm with Katie."

My eyes suddenly filled with tears, then Katie said, "And we're going to get married!"

At that my head started to hum and my ears buzzed. I didn't seem to be able to see properly. I looked at Katie and she was a blur. I shook my head to clear it and she must have misunderstood because she said, "Oh yes, we are!"

I shook my head again and looked at her. The haze had gone and I could see her clearly now. Her eyes were bright with malice and she opened that pretty little treacherous mouth again and that was all I could see, those perfect white teeth and her dainty pink tongue with its little silver stud. She'd made me go with her to get it pierced after Christmas. Made me hold her hand. I knew now why she'd had it done.

And she said, "Then we'll have a baby." She glanced down at my stomach. "A real one."

"Do you know what?" I said. "I've had enough of this."

I ran toward her. It seemed as though my whole body was light, as though I weighed almost nothing. I reached her so fast she shrieked and stumbled back onto the balcony. Matt was behind me and tried to grab me, but I pushed him away.

I took a deep breath, clenched my fist and punched Katie hard in the face.

I heard her cheekbone crack. I think we all did.

Her head lashed to the side. Matt screamed her name and leaped toward her but I wasn't looking at him. I wasn't listening to him. My eyes were on her. She straightened up and turned to face me, her mouth open, ready to say something more.

She always wanted to have the last word. It was what my dad used to say about my mum. It drove him mad and the rage that must have filled him then, filled me now.

In that moment, I felt like I *was* him, as though I was looking through his eyes. As though it was his blood that was racing through my veins.

To stop her talking I pushed her. I pushed her in the chest, really hard, and she staggered back against the balcony railing. Again she opened her mouth to speak, and I just couldn't stand to hear what she had to say.

And then I noticed something weird. I couldn't see Matt, though I knew he was there, standing on the balcony next to Katie. He was just a blur. A mist. I couldn't see the net curtains, either, though I could feel them flapping against my arms.

All I could see was Katie.

I pulled her forward by the shoulders until her hot, sweet breath was on my face and then I just threw her as hard as I could against the railing. Her face was pink and her mouth was still trying to shout insults when she clutched at the ironwork for balance. It jerked in her hands and my heart pounded with fear.

And then my vision cleared and I saw the bottom of the railing pulling itself loose from the concrete balcony floor.

As if in slow motion, Katie turned, her face white and her knuckles strained as she gripped the railing. I thought she was turning toward me and frantically I reached out to grab her.

But it was Matt she was turning to. Then the railing jolted and I saw Katie's arm jerk with it.

There was the sound of metal scraping against concrete as the railing came loose and instinctively I jumped back.

Matt shot forward but he was too late. He shouted, "Katie! Katie!" I saw a wild look on her face as she tried to steady herself, but her feet slipped and she fell backward.

Her scream tore through the air, followed by a thud that seemed to rock the apartment block.

And then there was silence.

Oh God, oh my God, what have I done?

Chapter
Fifty-seven

My heart pounded fit to burst. I backed away from the balcony, knocking into a sofa on my way. For a moment all I could see was a red mist; all I could hear was the roar of blood in my veins. I felt myself begin to fall and blindly reached out, grabbing the side of a chair and holding on tightly. Images of Katie as she fell flashed into my mind and I closed my eyes tightly, until I saw only stars.

I looked up and saw Matt staring at me.

"What have you done?" he whispered. His eyes were black, his pupils dilated with shock. "Hannah, what the *hell* have you done?"

I stared at him, frantic now. "What do you mean? She fell! She fell against the balcony and it broke!"

He stared at me as though he didn't know me, then turned and ran toward the door.

"No!" I shouted. "Matt, I just need to . . ." I didn't even know what I was going to say.

He turned as he ran and shouted, "Stay away from me!" and as he turned back again, his foot slid inside the handle of Katie's overnight bag and he fell with a crash. There was a crack as his head hit the corner of the black glass table that held his television.

He lay still.

I tried to run toward him but my legs gave way and I collapsed beside him. I grabbed his shoulders and shouted, "Matt! Matt!" but he didn't move.

I didn't know how to feel for a pulse. I'd never had to do it before. I touched his wrist, but my hand was slippery with sweat and shaking so much I couldn't feel anything. I touched his face, his mouth. He didn't move. When I tried to turn his head toward me I saw the gash on his temple, saw the blood pooling on the floor. I felt like my eyes were going to pop out of my head.

Oh my God, he's dead!

Panic surged through me and I looked around wildly. The French doors stood open, their filmy curtains blowing in the breeze. Even from here it was possible to see that the railings had gone from the balcony. Katie's bag lay wrapped around Matt's ankle, linking him to her.

My handbag was on the floor by the sofa. I threw the strap over my shoulder and fumbled inside to check my keys were there. I needed to get away from there. My hands were shaking so hard I could hardly keep the keys in my hand.

I looked out of the door into the corridor. Nobody was there.

I quietly closed the door behind me and started to make my way down the stairs to the side of the building where my car was parked. My heart was banging hard against my chest wall and beads of perspiration popped up all over me. My blood pressure was so high I could hardly see, but I was hyperalert and I knew nobody was around. The corridors were silent and the staircases empty.

The door swung open into the car park and I was hit by a blast of hot evening air. I tried to walk casually across to the side road where I'd parked, but my balance was so poor I think if anyone had seen me they'd have assumed I was drunk. My hand slipped on the car door handle and I had to use both hands to wrench it open. My head buzzed relentlessly as I dragged my seat belt on.

What should I do? What should I *do*? My boyfriend. My best friend. They'd betrayed me, but how could I just leave them there? I reached into my bag. I had to call for help. I had to! Just as my finger touched the last 9 of the emergency number, I heard the sound of sirens in the distance and I almost lost control of myself. They were coming to get me!

Blindly I turned the ignition and drove out of the side road at the back of the apartment block. I took a couple of turns into a road parallel to the entrance to the apartments and stopped at the end, looking down the hill. A few people were gathered around. Katie's cherry pink dress was splashed on the ground; the broken railings lay alongside her. Two women knelt beside her. A man was pointing up at the gap where the railing had been on Matt's balcony and I knew it would only be minutes before he was found.

I didn't know what to do. Should I go home and act as though I'd never been here? Or should I drive down there and tell them Matt was dead, too? There was no need to ask how Katie was now. Most people had moved back from her but one of the older women who was kneeling next to her looked as though she was praying. Two younger women were crying, their arms around each other.

I felt almost mad with panic.

The car was stiflingly hot and I opened the windows, my fingers fumbling on the buttons. The sirens were closer now and their blare made my heart race. That decided me. I put my foot on the accelerator and took a right turn away from them. I found a way through the side streets and parked the car a couple of miles away, down by the canal. It was deserted; there wasn't a person or a car in sight. It was the sort of place I'd never normally come to on my own but to be honest, I don't think anyone was as much of a danger to me as I was to myself right then.

My heart was still pounding so hard I could hardly focus. I glanced in the rearview mirror and saw my face, white and hollow eyed. Terrified.

I tried to slow my heart rate down. At first I closed my eyes but I was still on high alert and couldn't do that for long. My mind raced as I tried desperately to think what I should do. I stayed there for more than an hour, trying to breathe in and out, slower and slower. I couldn't bear to picture my counselor's face. All that time I'd talked to her about my dad's violence and this was what I'd become.

I just wanted to be at home, in bed. I wanted it to be yesterday, or six months ago. Anything, anything but now.

And then I realized that whatever happened now was inevitable, that it was written. Nothing I did from this point on could make any difference. My life had changed and so it should, too. I'd lost the two people I thought were closest to me; nothing could alter that.

I started the car and drove away slowly. I found the main road for the motorway and pulled into a gap in the traffic.

DRIVING HOME WAS terrible. Shocking. I stayed in the slow lane, though I wanted to rush. I saw Matt and Katie everywhere, in the passengers who overtook me, in people at bus stops. The blond hair of a baby became Katie's, red cars that passed me were Matt's blood. I just wanted to be home but I was frightened of what would happen once I was there.

I shook with anger as I thought of the row with Katie. She was the one person I'd believed I could trust. I had thought of us as sisters and so had she. She had told me this so many times. I could hardly remember a time when she wasn't part of my life. And all the while I was searching for Matt, she'd pumped me for information, relaying it to him each night. She had pretended to be my friend. She'd betrayed me. I couldn't forgive her.

Since I'd gone out with James when we were seventeen, she'd always wanted what I'd had. And of course she wasn't happy until she was going out with James herself. She'd waited years for that! It was as though just because I had something, it had more value in her eyes. And look at her house now; we had the same paintings on the walls, the same shoes in our bedrooms, the same glasses and duvet covers and cushions. Matt and I had laughed about it sometimes, but really the fact was that my best friend had always wanted what I had.

But for her to go after Matt like that . . . It shocked me that she'd been so calculating. She'd betrayed me without flinching. And for him to be involved with her—I could hardly believe it. It was as though I didn't know them. I hadn't thought either of them capable of deception on that scale.

More than two hours after leaving Matt's apartment, I reached the Kingsway Tunnel, which links Liverpool with the Wirral. The traffic was light, so I slid through without a problem. I was just out of the tunnel and on the road leading to my home when my phone rang.

I nearly jumped out of my skin.

For one mad moment I thought it was Katie, making her daily call to ask me whether I had any news. I pulled over to the side of the road and scrabbled in my bag for the phone. The screen lit up with the name of the caller.

James.

I tried to take a deep breath, but I couldn't. I was light-headed, and on the periphery of my vision I could see sparks. The call ended and then immediately the phone rang again. This time I managed to answer it.

Act normal, I thought frantically. *Act normal.*

"Hannah?" shouted James. It sounded as though he was driving. "Hannah, where are you?"

"What?" I looked around wildly and saw the red and blue Tesco logo in the distance. "I'm just going to Tesco."

"Are you driving? You need to park," he said. "I've got some bad news."

My head started to spin. My voice sounded as though it was coming from miles away. "I'm not driving."

"It's about Katie and Matt," he said. His voice was hoarse and I knew he'd been crying.

I tried to swallow the lump in my throat, but it just wouldn't go down. "What about them?"

"I've just had a phone call from Katie's dad," he said.

My stomach plummeted. I'd tried not to think of her mum and dad. I couldn't bring myself to speak.

He cleared his throat. "There's bad news, Hannah. Katie's had an accident. She's fallen off a balcony."

And even then, even after all that I'd done, all I could think was, *Oh thank God, thank God. He didn't say she was pushed.*

"There's something else." I steeled myself. I knew what was coming. "Her dad said she was at Matt's."

My voice was faint. "At Matt's?"

"Not at your house," he said. "At Matt's new place. Apparently he's been living in Manchester."

I couldn't speak.

"Matt's had an accident, too," he said. "I can't believe it. Both of them!"

I had to ask this question even though I knew the answer. "What happened to him?"

"I don't know," he said. "Katie's dad said something about him falling over and banging his head." His voice broke. "I couldn't tell what he was saying some of the time. You can imagine how he was."

I tried to speak, but I couldn't. I thought of Katie's dad crying and felt as though my heart was going to explode.

"I couldn't believe it, either," he said. "Hannah, I think they were having an affair."

I wept then, bitterly ashamed that it was this that finally made me cry.

"I thought Katie was up to something," he said. "We were getting on all right, but there was just something about her. Something had changed."

I couldn't stop the tears. "Hold on," I said. "Just a minute." I reached into my bag and found some tissues.

"I'm so sorry, Hannah," he said. "I'm so sorry."

I sat back, exhausted. I couldn't think of anything to say to him. All I could think about was whether anyone knew I'd been there. "So her mum and dad are at the hospital?"

"Yes," he said. "I'm on my way there now. Matt's mum is going there, too." He hesitated. "She . . . she said she wanted to see him on her own."

I knew what he meant. I wouldn't be welcome. I nodded, my throat tight with tears. "James," I said. "James, are they badly hurt?"

All I wanted was for him to tell me everything was all right.

"The nurse said that Matt was in a coma. I don't know any more than that."

I squeezed my eyes tight. I had to ask. I had to. "And Katie?" My voice was high and strange. It didn't sound like me.

He made a sound then and I knew he was trying not to cry. My stomach lurched.

"I'm really sorry," he said. "Katie didn't make it."

"What?"

"Hannah, she's dead."

Chapter
Fifty-eight

ONCE JAMES HAD ended the call, I put my head on the steering wheel. I didn't know what to do.

At the thought that Katie was dead, I started to shake. What had I done? Why had I bothered trying to find Matt? I should have listened to Katie when she told me to forget him. I should have known she'd have a reason for telling me that.

My hands were clammy and when I rubbed them on my jeans I could feel something on them, tangled around my fingers. I stared down and saw strands of Katie's long blond hair wrapped around my hands. For a second it looked like Matt's hair, when I'd taken it off the nail in the loft.

I shrieked. There was a bottle of water on the passenger seat and I poured some over my hands, shuddering as the hair freed itself. I pulled out more tissues and rubbed my hands again and again until they were clean.

My phone beeped with a message and my head nearly hit the roof of the car. I would have given everything then for it to be Katie. I'd never have another message from either of them. My eyes filled with tears and I brushed them away angrily. They were bastards, both of them, cheating on me like that. I had to keep thinking that; I knew I'd break down otherwise.

My stomach lurched as I saw the message was from my dad.

I've just spoken again to Alex Hughes. I tried to put in a good word for you. He told me he'd heard from one of your colleagues that you are pregnant. He thought I knew. You lied to me. Lied to my face. Does your mother know?

I felt almost blind with panic. I called his number. I had to get through to him. This was nothing to do with my mum. There was no answer. I phoned his secretary who said, "Oh, Hannah, you've literally just missed him. He's just got into his car to go home." She sounded a bit shaken and I guessed she'd borne the brunt of some of his anger.

I knew what I had to do. I had to stop pretending this wasn't happening. It was time for it to end. I speed-dialed my mum's mobile.

In the moment it took for the call to register, I realized she was in the same position that Matt had been in throughout our relationship and the thought was so dreadful that I banged my head against the car window to stop myself thinking it.

"Mum, get out," I blurted as soon as she answered the phone.

"What?"

"He's coming home. He's furious."

There was a silence. I'd never acknowledged their fights, as he called them, before. I felt sick now at the thought of that. I'd never talked to her about him, just as I'd never talked to her about the way I was.

"It'll be okay," she said eventually. "I'll be able to manage him."

I knew what managing him meant. Over the years I'd averted my eyes from many, many bruises that had occurred when she'd managed him. She was limping the last time I saw her because she'd "managed" him. And I was so stressed-out by what had happened with Katie and Matt, I couldn't help it. I screamed, "Why do you put up with it?"

"He's my husband, Hannah," she snapped. "I've told you I'll handle it."

The memory of him kissing Helen, his arms around her, flashed into my mind. Kissing her in the street, without a care in the world. I took a deep breath. "Your husband? Open your eyes, Mum! He's having an affair. I've seen him."

There was a silence, then she said, her voice trembling, "You've seen him?"

So that was her tipping point. He could do whatever he wanted to her and she'd forgive him, but an affair? It reminded me of that old line, "He's a bastard, but he's my bastard." I'd never understood that. I should have, really.

"I've got photos. Mum, you need to get out. He's furious with me and he's blaming you. You need to get out before it's too late." I thought of Katie, on the concrete outside Matt's apartment, of Matt lying in a pool of blood. My voice broke. "Before he kills you."

When she spoke next her voice sounded different. Resolute. "How long do I have?"

"He left the office a couple of minutes ago. So fifteen minutes? Maybe ten, now. Five, even. Don't come to my house. Go to Auntie Chris's." My mother's sister lived in Scotland; Mum hadn't been allowed to see her for years. She had a huge husband, who despised my father.

There was a pause, then Mum said, "Thank you. Thank you, pet."

She cut the call and I threw my phone into my bag and started the car. All I wanted was to get home and go to bed. To be alone.

The rest of the journey home was horrendous. I could hardly see where I was going. Tears streamed down my face and all I kept thinking about was Katie and Matt. I'd lost them both.

Katie, the girl I'd known for most of my life. Funny, beautiful, jealous Katie. I'd thought we'd be friends forever.

And Matt. When I'd seen him walking down the hill yesterday, his jacket swinging behind him, he'd seemed happy and carefree, just as he was when we first met. Yet today, in his apartment, he was a shadow of his former self, and although he looked the same as he'd done for months and months when we were living together, it was like looking at a stranger.

If only I hadn't gone up there today. I could have written to him. I could have seen him at his office after work. Why had I gone to see him on his own? I kept thinking of Katie's expression as she fell and Matt's face, his eyes shut and his temple bleeding. It was all because of me.

By the time I reached my street I was almost hyperventilating with fear and guilt and something else, too. My hands drummed on the steering wheel as I tried to think what it was.

At last I realized. It was loss. My heart ached at the thought of never seeing either of them again.

I turned into my driveway and slammed on the brakes. Through my living room window I could see that a light was on.

Chapter
Fifty-nine

I SAT IN the car and stared at the window. I remembered leaving the house earlier that day, though it seemed like weeks ago now. The whole place was ready for Matt's return. I'd thought we would sit at either end of the sofa in the living room and talk things over like adults. Like adults who wanted to make a go of their relationship. I'd bought flowers to welcome him home, candles to light as the night grew dim, wine to toast his return. I'd hoped for so much that morning, believed it would happen, too. And when I thought of the way he'd hesitated when I'd asked him to come home, my heart tilted. I'd been sure he was about to agree; I could tell he wanted to.

But although everything was ready and waiting for us to return, I was sure no lamps had been lit. Only the soft glow of candlelight had been planned for his homecoming; the sharp yellow glare of the electric bulb wasn't part of my plans for the seduction of Matt.

In my mind I tried to track my movements just before I left the house. To turn on the lamp there I would have had to reach over the end of the sofa and pull a little silver chain which would switch on the bulb.

Try as I might I couldn't retrieve that physical memory.

Slowly I got out of the car and carefully locked it. There were no lights in the neighbors' houses, no cars in their driveways. I went up to the living room window and looked through. Everything was as it had been that afternoon when I'd left the house. Everything except the lamp.

I *must* have put it on.

Mist from my breath fogged the glass and as I thought of all that had happened since the last time I'd done this, I shuddered and let myself into the house.

The hallway was dim and quiet and I knew nobody else was there.

In the living room the lamp glowed brightly and I stared at it for minutes, willing myself to remember switching it on. I couldn't. I turned it off at the socket and shut the door.

I was more exhausted that evening than at any other time in my life. I felt weary with sadness. No matter whether Matt lived or died, I'd lost both him and Katie today, but it seemed I'd actually lost them months before. Slowly I walked into the kitchen.

All I could see were the photos of Katie, standing with her arm around me and smiling at me as though she was my friend. I looked again at the picture of us holding hands aged five and for the first time in my life I wished I'd never met her.

I picked up the photos and put them facedown into a drawer. I had no idea what I would do with them.

The smell of the waste bin was heavy in the air and more flies circled the sink. I opened the back door and heaved the rubbish into the bins outside. I couldn't think why I hadn't done it before. It had seemed too much effort, what with all I'd had to think about. I disinfected the kitchen bin and washed out the sink. Even through the rubber gloves I could feel the slime and crumbs that had built up over the past months. I looked at the filthy crockery toppling in greasy piles on the kitchen units and I saw the madness I'd gone through during those days and nights I'd spent searching for Matt.

I loaded the crockery and cutlery into the dishwasher. Though I crammed in as much as would fit, there were still tons of dirty dishes on the counter and I filled the sink with hot soapy water and scrubbed them all until they were clean. I kept my eyes averted from the mess. Everything reminded me of the time I'd spent looking for Matt, the time when Katie was in touch daily, hourly sometimes, asking for information. I felt betrayed on so many levels.

I was spraying the kitchen counters with bleach when I looked up at the units and saw the extent of my notes. It looked like I was mad. I didn't think I'd ever be able to read them again and, what was more, I didn't want to.

I ripped off all the Post-its and threw them into the bin. I lifted the bottle of bleach and squirted it over the cabinets. The words I'd written in red marker looked as though they were dripping blood and I had to squeeze my eyes shut as I scrubbed and scrubbed at them.

Even though I scoured those cupboards for over an hour, I knew they'd never be the same again. They wouldn't stand up to scrutiny in the early morning light and would always show the marks beneath. I didn't care anymore; it was the least of my problems. I was no longer the same woman who'd spent weeks choosing the units, paying for them out of my savings. I'd stood for hours in the kitchen when the builders had gone, seeing the room as a testament to my success. Now I knew what a failure I was.

When the kitchen was gleaming, I opened the fridge door. My notes hadn't reached as far as here and there had been nothing to clean. On the counter next to it I saw the bottle of Nuits-Saint-Georges I'd bought for Matt and me to share that night and I threw it into the recycling bin. At the back of the fridge was a bottle of white wine. I'd forgotten it was there and breathed a sigh of relief when I found it. I needed this now.

I shut the fridge door. Just where the note saying "Satisfied?" had been were some of my alphabet fridge magnets. Matt and I used to use them to write little messages to each other. Since he'd gone they were crowded in a bunch toward the bottom of the door. Now some of them had been moved and rearranged into a message.

It said "See you soon."

MY MIND SPUN almost out of control. Matt had been here today? I thought of the light that was on in the living room. He'd done that?

I shook my head. It couldn't have been Matt. He'd been at work today, surely? He'd had his suit on when I saw him; he wouldn't be wearing that if he wasn't at work. And if he had been here, surely he would have been happy to see me at his apartment door? In my heart I knew he hadn't wanted to see me; I could picture his face now, though I could hardly bear to. He was shocked when he saw me. Terrified.

I flinched at the thought.

I knew then that all these messages, the calls and the notes through the post, had been nothing to do with Matt. It wasn't his cologne—there probably wasn't any cologne—and the flowers? Well, I must have bought them myself.

I was sick to death with lying to myself about this. It wasn't Matt. It never had been Matt.

So who was it?

I was so tired and so shaky from what had happened today that when I saw the message all I could think was, "Bring it on. I'm ready for you."

I was no longer scared. Katie was dead. Matt might die.

The worst had already happened.

I took the remaining Vera Wang wineglass from the cabinet and out of habit wondered whether Matt had its partner with him in the apartment in Manchester. I couldn't see Katie being too happy about it if he had. He couldn't hide its significance, either, since she'd bought identical glasses for her next anniversary with James and would have recognized it a mile off.

I shook my head. *Matt hadn't got the glass. Matt hadn't been near the house.*

I went upstairs with the wine and the glass and lay on my bed and all I could think was it was exactly the same as the night I'd come home from Oxford to find Matt had gone. I was exhausted; every muscle in my body ached. I propped the pillows against the headboard and the photo of Matt slipped out. I picked it up and looked at it. He was smiling in the photo, but not at me. I hadn't known him then. I wasn't sure I knew him now. I put on my headphones, the ones that blocked out noise. I'd used headphones like that every night when I was young and lived at home, so that I wouldn't hear my dad hitting my mum, wouldn't hear her crying.

I was as bad as he was, really.

Now I sat like he did, night after night, drinking without tasting, like a man on a mission, and as I drank I thought, *I am just like my father.* I couldn't see any way out of this. It was as though he permeated me, just like the letters in a candy stick of rock, so wherever you broke it, there he was. The evil inside me.

Chapter
Sixty

I DRANK AND thought and drank some more, and eventually I must have slept because I woke in the middle of the night, just as I'd done the night Matt left home, with my hand clutched around the stem of the glass and the room reeking of alcohol and sweat and tears. The smell was so familiar but I didn't know why and then I remembered my dad, the smell of him the mornings after he'd hurt my mum. I shuddered and jumped out of bed, throwing my headphones on the floor.

In the bathroom I brushed my teeth, just as I had when Matt had first gone. Just like then, I avoided my face in the mirror, too ashamed of what I'd see.

Back in bed I rang the hospital and said I'd heard that Matt was there and asked how he was. Apparently being an ex-girlfriend doesn't put you on a list of people who need to know, and the nurse I spoke to wouldn't tell me anything. I noticed, though, that her voice didn't change when she spoke to me and when I'd put the phone down I thought that if he'd died, her tone would have softened, maybe just a fraction. It hadn't. She'd sounded busy, impersonal and abrupt.

"You'll have to contact his family for any more information," she'd said.

"I will," I'd replied. "I'll give his mum a call now."

I tried to imagine how that conversation with Olivia would go, if I ever dared to have it. I didn't even know how to get hold of her, but if I did, if I turned up there at the hospital . . . I cringed at what she'd say to me.

I thought of her sitting by his bed, holding his hand. That was where I should be now; that was what I should be doing. There was no way I'd get past her, though, no way she'd allow me into the room, never mind let me sit beside him.

And I knew he would wake up. It was inevitable. He'd hit his head hard, hard enough for me to think he was dead at first, but how many people died from that sort of injury? Whereas Katie . . . I shuddered as an image of her falling flashed into my mind.

I forced myself not to think of that.

If Matt woke up, even for a second, I knew he'd say my name. I knew he'd blame me. He wouldn't say a word about how much he'd upset me or how he'd humiliated me by running off like that with my best friend and dumping me in front of her. He'd say I pushed Katie.

It felt like a metal band was tightening itself around my head. I lay down and tried to do my deep breathing, to shut out all thoughts. This time, counting my breaths didn't work. I couldn't think those words, couldn't obey the instructions, because at that moment in the distance, for a split second only, I thought I heard a siren.

I think that's when I realized that the police were going to get involved. I started to shake. I knew they'd come here. They'd come whether Matt woke up or not. Had Katie told her parents why Matt had left me? I closed my eyes tightly, unable to bear the thought of them judging me. But then I remembered the cake her mum had baked; she wouldn't have done that if she'd known. Matt's mum, Olivia, wouldn't need much encouragement, though. She'd judged me all along. I couldn't bear to think of the conversations she'd had with Matt about our private lives. She had no right to know any of that!

For a wild moment I thought of running away and leaving them to it. I had about fifteen thousand pounds in savings that I could access immediately. I had a passport, a car. I could work anywhere; I knew that. My mind raced as I thought of starting from scratch with a new name. A new identity. I didn't have a clue how to go about doing that.

But then I thought of being caught by the police. Cornered. I imagined seeing a photo of myself on television, with the word "Wanted" above it, and for a moment I couldn't breathe. No one could be anonymous nowadays. My car registration would be tracked wherever I went. There were cameras on every major road. My phone would be easy to trace. I knew I'd be crazy to run away. I'd be caught almost immediately and then they'd never believe anything I had to say.

And that was when I decided I'd call the police myself. I'd tell them what had happened before anyone else could. I'd get my say in first.

I trembled at the thought of that. I didn't think I could do it. I wished I hadn't told my mum to go to Scotland. I knew that if I called her she'd come back down, but by then Matt might have woken up. The police might have come for me by then.

Even so, I needed her. I knew I wouldn't be able to speak to her, so, my hands slippery with sweat, I sent her a message:

Mum, I need your help. Something terrible has happened and Katie has died. Matt is in a coma and if he wakes up he'll say it's my fault. I'm sorry, I'm so sorry.

I sat back, my eyes flooded with tears. I wanted her there, I couldn't wait for her to come back from Scotland. When I didn't get an immediate response I guessed she had turned her phone off. My dad had probably been calling her nonstop since he'd discovered she'd gone.

I didn't know my aunt's number and all I could remember of her address was the town she lived in. I rang Directory Enquiries but the woman answering the call said they didn't have a number for her.

I'll have to do it on my own.

I forced myself out of bed. I needed to pack a bag in case I was kept in for questioning. My knees buckled beneath me at the thought, but I told myself to get a grip. If I didn't pack, someone else would do it for me. I might as well make sure I had the things I wanted in it. And if all went well and they believed me, then I'd take off on holiday somewhere.

So I put a few changes of clothing in, some nightwear, too. And toiletries. I added my Kindle but guessed I wouldn't be able to use it and so put a couple of paperbacks in as well, just in case. I thought of packing a notebook and pen, but knew I wouldn't want anyone to see anything I was prepared to write down.

I was just about to leave the room when I remembered the photo of Matt. I'd had it under my pillow for months now and would sleep with it in my hand. I pulled it out and looked at it again. It was just a color printout rather than a proper photo and the page was creased and torn. Though the image was of poor quality, I could still see his smile and the way he looked completely at ease. He hadn't looked like that yesterday when he saw me.

As I gazed at him I was suddenly filled with fury. If he hadn't run off like that, we wouldn't be in this situation! Katie would be alive, he wouldn't be in hospital and I wouldn't be here, thinking of escape. Why had he done this to me? For a moment I wanted to rip the photo to shreds, to stomp on it. I wanted to never ever see his face again. And then I calmed down enough to know there would be a day when I'd want to look at him once more, would want to remember the good times we'd had together. I didn't know when that day would be, but I knew it would come. Eventually.

I put the photo in my bag. I didn't want to leave it here for anyone to find.

I TOOK MY bag downstairs and left it in the hall. I didn't know what to do, whether to drive to the police station or to call a taxi.

In the kitchen I looked over at the clock on the wall. It was nearly two o'clock and pitch-black outside. The lights from the neighboring houses were out and all was quiet.

Now would be a good time to go and report it, I reasoned. *It'll be quiet there and I'll be able to talk to them without them getting interrupted all the time.* I knew that what I had to say would take some time.

I put the kettle on to make tea. I thought I'd go after I'd drunk it, though to be honest I still wasn't sure whether I'd be setting off for an incognito life in France or going to my mum in Scotland or to the police a mile away. I poured a cup of tea and took it into the living room at the front of the house. I just needed an hour to sit in peace. It might be the last time I'd spend in my house for a while. I didn't know where I was going to; I didn't know what would happen. I didn't know whether anyone would believe me or even whether they should.

There in the living room were the candles I'd bought that morning to celebrate Matt's return. I thought of him in hospital, not far away, but a million miles from me. My heart heavy with longing and regret, I lit them for him now. For him and for Katie.

On the mantelpiece, church candles clustered in groups, magnificent against the huge silver mirror. The hearth held two big cream candles, each with eight wicks, which flickered fiercely as I walked past. The smell of vanilla and roses and lilies filled the air. Tea lights sat in colored glass holders on the coffee table, trembling in the draft. By the time I'd finished, the room was lit up as though it was Christmas.

I searched my iPod for the Dave Matthews album Matt and I used to listen to in our glory days and put it on low. I didn't need Ray coming round to complain about the noise, but I didn't want to sit there with only my own thoughts for company. I hadn't played those tracks since Matt left and they brought back so many memories of us lying on the sofa with our arms around each other and our faces close, so close I'd feel each breath he'd take.

I shook myself. I'd go crazy if I started to think of him like that. I sat there with the flowers all around me, flickering in the light of the candles, and I drank my tea and thought about what I was going to do. Panic fluttered in my belly. There seemed no way out.

And then in the brief moment of time between one song and another, I heard a sound, a scraping sound. I thought it came from the kitchen.

My heart began to pound so hard my chest wall hurt.

Someone's in my house.

SLOWLY I STOOD UP. I felt dizzy from the adrenaline rush and had to steady myself on the sofa. I strained my ears but couldn't hear anything.

I grabbed my phone and dialed 999, but didn't press Call. I was aware of the irony of calling for help after all that had happened the previous day but knew if I needed backup I wouldn't hesitate to call. Now there was silence and I wondered whether I'd imagined the sound.

I twisted the living room door handle and opened the door

slowly. Tentatively. The hall was dim and nothing stirred. The kitchen door was open but the room was in darkness. I hesitated, then realized who it was. Who it must be.

I stepped forward into the hall. I could feel my head buzzing and at that moment I truly felt I was going out of my mind.

"Matt?" I said. My voice sounded shaky and I swallowed. "Matt, is that you?"

I must be wrong. There's nobody here.

I turned back to the living room and saw my face in the mirror, lit up by the glow of the candles. I was so pale and thin I could hardly recognize myself. My cheeks were flushed with excitement and my eyes were sunken and black.

I looked mad, completely mad.

Then in the mirror I saw someone's face behind mine and my body jolted with shock.

It was James.

Chapter
Sixty-one

"I WAS RIGHT," he said.

I swung round. He stood in the doorway, blocking my path. He looked taller than usual, though that could have been the shadows. His eyes flickered over my bare arms and I crossed them, quickly, but I knew he'd seen the scratches. He seemed pumped up. Furious. He stared at me as though he couldn't believe his eyes.

"What?" I said. "What are you doing here?"

It was as though I hadn't spoken. "Why did you kill her?"

I tried to speak but my mouth was dry as dust.

"No," he said. "No. Don't even think of denying it."

He took a step toward me and I backed away. My heart hammered in my chest.

"Don't worry, I'm not going to hurt you." There was a pause and then he said, "I'm not like you. That's not what I do."

I stood stock-still.

"Did you think I didn't know what you were doing?" he asked.

"What?"

"I've always known, Hannah," he said. "Right from the day Matt left you."

I swallowed. "What do you mean?"

"You were hitting him," he said. "That's why he left."

"What?"

"Just as you hit me," he said, "when we were together. That's why I left you, remember?"

SUDDENLY THE GROUND felt unsteady beneath my feet. I grabbed hold of the side of the sofa and held on to it, using it as a shield between us.

As I looked at James in the flickering candlelight, I remembered him as he was when I was with him that summer. I thought of us lying on his single bed making love for hours, walking arm in arm through the night around our little town, dreaming about the future. We talked nonstop that summer and I told him things I'd never told anyone since.

And then I recalled, too, the nights when I'd just see red. I flinched as I remembered the way I couldn't stop hitting him and thumping him and calling him names. He'd laughed at first and tried to ward me off, but I was stronger than I looked. I always have been. And I'd learned from a master, too. Even as a small child I'd learned how to hurt the ones you love.

"You didn't leave me," I said. "I dumped you."

He raised his eyebrows. "Really? You have a very short memory."

I flushed. I remembered all right. He'd written me a letter and told me exactly why it had to end. We hadn't spoken again until more than ten years later, when he'd started dating Katie. The first time I saw him with her he took me to one side and said, "The past is past, Hannah," and then had acted as though we were friends.

I should have known that we weren't. How could we be?

"And now here we are again," he said. "You and your temper. You're out of control, Hannah."

My face burned and I realized that the embers of the fire that had been in my belly when I'd fought with Katie hadn't died. Not quite.

I tried to stay calm. "I'm not out of control."

"You were there, though, weren't you?"

I was silent, my brain working frantically to see how I could get out of this.

"You were there," he said again, louder now. "Don't pretend you weren't."

"All right," I said, still trying to quell the fire inside me. "I was there. But I didn't kill her."

"Of course you didn't," he said. "You just happened to be chasing down your old boyfriend and you found him with your best friend. And you have a problem with keeping your hands to yourself when you're angry and now she's dead and he's in a coma and, funnily enough, you're covered in scratches."

I looked down at the livid marks on my arms and winced. I knew bruises would soon appear all over my body from the kicks and punches Katie had landed as she tried to fight me off.

"Did she put up a fight?"

I couldn't speak.

"Well, good for her," he said. "I can't say I forgive her for having an affair, particularly with Matt, but I'm glad she gave you a hard time."

I probably shouldn't have said anything after that but I couldn't help it. "I can't forgive her, either. I just can't. She looked me in the eye day after day and lied to me." My voice broke. "She was supposed to be my friend!"

"I know," he said. "She told me you were her best friend. She said it again and again. But she was a bitch to you. And to me, too, it seems. She didn't deserve to die, though."

"I know she didn't! I didn't want her to die!" At first I thought that was all I'd say, but then I found I couldn't stop. "I didn't mean to do it."

He groaned, as though he was winded.

"She just kept on talking. She wouldn't shut up!" My heart raced at the thought of it. "She said they were getting married, that they'd have a baby." I still burned with the injustice of that. "And yes, I hit her. I hit her to shut her up. But she hit me, too. Look at me! Look what she did!" I thrust my arms at James. "It was like being in school, the fights we'd have then. And then she fell against the little railing of the balcony and . . ."

I couldn't go on. The image of her falling, her mouth in an open scream, would always be with me and I was so, so angry about that. What had she done to me, leaving me with that memory of her?

"And what?"

Suddenly my head was full of a red mist and I thumped my fist against it again and again. As if from miles away I could hear James shouting at me to stop but I couldn't. He grabbed hold of me and I twisted away, banging my head against the mantelpiece. I heard him swear and reach up to steady the candlestick, I think, and I leaned back and banged my head a second time. This time I saw stars and for a moment there was relief.

Just like he used to years ago, he grabbed me again and held me to him. "Tell me," he urged. I could feel his breath, jagged against my hair. "Tell me what happened."

"The railing broke away," I whispered. "I reached out to her, to grab her, but she didn't see me. She was looking at Matt." My face was hot and streaming with sweat. "She fell back." I gulped. "We were three stories up and she didn't stand a chance."

He let go of me then and sat heavily on the sofa. "And Matt?"

"After Katie . . . after the balcony broke, Matt started to run. He wanted to go down to her. And," I whispered, filled with shame, "he wanted to run away from me, too. Katie's bag was on the floor. She'd left it there when she came in. He fell over it—his foot caught in the handle—he fell and banged his head on the television table. You know, that black glass table that used to be in the living room here."

There was a silence, then he said, "That's what the police said they thought happened."

I froze. "The police?"

He nodded. "The nurse told me. His ankle's bruised from the strap of the bag and his blood was on the table."

All I felt was relief. They couldn't say I'd done that to him.

My head was throbbing both from banging it and from stress, but I felt better now. I'd needed to tell someone.

Eventually James spoke. "Katie told me she was away with work tonight. She was very convincing."

I nodded. "She convinced me, too. Though I should have known she was involved with Matt as soon as he left home."

"Why?"

"Remember I came round to your house one night, not long after he'd left? She told you that Matt had changed the bed linen back to one of my own sets. I hadn't told her that and she hadn't been up-stairs since he'd gone. The only way she could have known is if he told her. Or if she was there." I shook my head. "There was some-thing niggling, just out of reach all that time. I couldn't think what it was, but I knew it was there. It's only today that I've realized what it was."

We were quiet, then. I think both of us were thinking that if I'd noticed what she'd said then, none of this would have happened.

And then something else dawned on me. I turned to James. "How did you get in?"

Slowly he took a key from his pocket and put it on the coffee table in front of us: a key with a pink plastic hoop through it.

I frowned. "Isn't that the key I gave Katie when I first moved in?"

He nodded.

I'd forgotten all about it but seeing it now I remembered us going to get it cut together. I was so excited about my new home, but this was the first time I'd lived alone and I was worried in case I locked myself out. She'd linked my arm and squeezed me tight, promising to keep it safe. Clearly she hadn't.

I don't know whether the blows to my head were affecting me, but I just didn't understand. "But why didn't you ring the bell?"

He looked at me. I could see bravado on his face. And something else, too.

Shame.

"No," I said. "No." I closed my eyes. I couldn't believe it. "It was you?"

"What?"

But he knew, and he knew I did, too.

"That was you? The flowers? The texts? The note that disappeared?" The fury returned. "You came into my house?"

He just looked at me.

"None of it was Matt? Nothing at all?"

"Why would Matt come to your house? Why would he send you anything?" he said at last. "He was off having his affair with Katie. He'd forgotten all about you."

Now, that made me smart, the thought that Matt hadn't given me a second thought.

"But the texts were from Matt's number," I said. "How did that happen?"

After the longest pause, he said, "You can buy an app."

"What? To make it look like you are phoning from another phone?"

He nodded.

"That should be illegal!"

He looked at me and I flushed. "You're not really in the strongest position to discuss legalities," he said.

"But why, James? All those things. You made me think I was going mad."

"That's how I felt when we were together," he said. "I thought it was about time you knew what it was like."

I stared at him. "What do you mean?"

"As soon as Matt disappeared I guessed you'd hit him. When I came round that night I half thought he'd be there, dead on the floor."

I flinched. "I was never that bad."

My words resounded around the room. *Katie is dead. She's dead because of you.*

"You were, Hannah. You still are! And I was only seventeen when you hit me. Have you any idea what that was like?"

We'd never talked about this. Never.

"Have you any idea what it means to be a young man . . . a boy, even . . . and to have a girl who you love more than anything in the world . . . a girl who says she loves you . . . hit you like that? I couldn't tell anyone! Who could I tell without sounding pathetic? A failure." His voice broke and he sounded like a teenager again. I felt as though my heart was being squeezed. "It was . . . if you hadn't said you loved me, it would have been easier. But you told me you loved me day after day. You bought me presents. We listened to the same music, we liked doing the same things. In bed . . ." He didn't say anything more about that. He didn't need to. "You said we were soul mates. You said . . ." He couldn't go on.

My throat was swollen with tears. I remembered it all. "It was true," I said. "All of it was true."

"It wasn't true!" he yelled. "How could it be? You don't hit someone you love! And you promised, again and again, that you'd stop, that you'd get help."

I closed my eyes, remembering the same conversation with Matt earlier today. They were right. They were both right.

"But then when I was driving here tonight, I realized something. You've been scared for years, long before I met you."

I stared at him, wondering how he knew.

"I used to wonder why you let Katie put you down all the time."

"You knew she was doing that?" For some reason I'd thought it was a private dance between Katie and me, where we'd each vie for prime position.

He nodded. "Of course," he said. "I'd see you sometimes, anticipating it. She was like your dad, wasn't she? You wouldn't stand up to her, just as you wouldn't stand up to him."

I stared at him, horrified. I don't know why I'd never seen that.

"You told me about him, remember?"

And then I did remember, one night early that summer when I was seventeen, when I'd run from my house crying because I could hear my dad hurting my mum. I'd been out with Katie and my parents hadn't heard me return. I heard what he did to her and I didn't stop him. I never did. I ran to James's house. Not to Katie's; I could never have told her what was really going on at home. I talked to James about everything that night, and in the letter he wrote to me when he finished with me, he told me to move away and to get counseling, otherwise I'd end up just like my dad. And I'd done all that, but . . . well, it was harder than I'd thought. Impossible, really. Blood is blood, you know.

I shuddered. It was almost easier to think of what had happened today than what had happened when I was at home, blocking my ears to my mother's cries.

I stared at the candles, flickering wildly in the draft from the open door. "So the phone calls . . . They were you?"

He said nothing but I knew I was right.

"Do you normally phone women up and smash something so they scream?"

He gave an embarrassed laugh. "Sorry," he said. "I broke that Vera Wang glass by mistake. I tried to buy another but it was out of stock."

"So you came and took mine?"

He shrugged. "You know how she liked them."

Even right to the end, Katie had to have what she wanted.

Then another piece of the puzzle fell into place. "You sent me that photo, didn't you?"

"Which photo?"

"The one of me in Sainsbury's buying the candles." I felt like I was going mad. So it wasn't Matt? He hadn't been in the supermarket with me? "I got it on my phone this morning. Was that you?"

It seemed so long ago now and really I hadn't paid it the attention I should.

"Buying wine and candles and flowers," he said. "And brie." He stared at me. "Are pregnant women meant to eat brie and drink wine?"

My face flamed and I said nothing.

"But you're not pregnant, are you? Did you really think you were fooling anyone?"

"I was pregnant," I said but even to my ears it sounded unconvincing. "I was, but I lost it."

"Bollocks!" he shouted. "Stop lying, will you? You weren't pregnant. I knew right from the start."

"How?" I snapped. "How did you know?"

"Because when you were pregnant with my baby, you looked different."

Chapter
Sixty-two

SUDDENLY THE ROOM was quiet. I could hardly breathe. We hadn't spoken of this in more than fifteen years.

"You looked softer then. I think I knew you were pregnant before you even said a word. And now," he said with disgust, "well, look at yourself, Hannah." He jumped up from the sofa and grabbed me by the shoulders, pushing me around to face the mirror.

Tears blurred my vision. His hands gripped me and when I said nothing he shook me. And I thought of that last time I'd seen him, before he met up with Katie again, when he'd gripped me in the same way as I told him I'd been to the clinic and was no longer pregnant.

He'd screamed, "But that was my baby!"

I remember the way my body jerked as though it was yesterday.

I'd tried to tell him that my dad wouldn't let me have the baby, that he'd taken me to the clinic and arranged everything, that he was going to disown me completely if I went ahead with the pregnancy and that he'd almost knocked my mother out he was so angry with her for letting me sleep with James, but he wouldn't listen.

"You said you'd marry me!" he'd shouted. "You said we'd get married and have the baby together!"

And I was still sore from the procedure and my hormones were all over the place. I hadn't slept in a week and my head was pounding. I shouldn't have been at James's house that night; my dad had forbidden it and when he did that you didn't disobey him. He was away for an hour visiting a client and this was my only chance to speak to James. That hour was nearly up and the fear of my dad discovering I'd gone out had nearly tipped me over the edge. So when James screamed and cried and shouted and just wouldn't listen to me, I could feel my blood pressure rising and my head whirling, and I couldn't answer his questions because I just didn't know the answers and then I hit him.

I'd hit him before and he'd always forgiven me, but this time . . . Well, this time I hit him harder than usual and I knew that his eye would be black the next day. It was already swelling and closing and all of a sudden James just stopped dead in his tracks and said, "Get out."

I'd stared at him, still fired up. In a way I wanted him to hit me back so I could hit him again, harder. The disgust on his face, though, stopped me.

"Get out," he said again and my eyes had filled with tears. Even then I was sorry for myself. And I picked up my bag and my coat and I got out. I was home just minutes before my dad, and my mum was nearly beside herself with worry. I told my dad that night that I wanted to go away, to go to Australia, the furthest place I could think of, to work, I said, just for a year. The word "work" mollified him, though he was probably glad to be rid of me, too, and he paid for a ticket there and then. I was gone within a week. I told Katie none of this, only that I was going to take a gap year and go to Australia. She told me I was lucky and I said nothing to make her think otherwise.

I hadn't seen James from that moment until the day I saw him with Katie, though I can't say I'd never thought of him.

"JUST TELL ME the truth," he said. "Why did you tell us you were pregnant?"

I sat down on the sofa, feeling weak with shame and regret. I couldn't look at him. "It just happened," I said. "I was stupid. Sam suggested I might be and I thought for a minute it was possible. When I realized I wasn't, I knew that if I said I was, people would understand why I was trying to find Matt."

"But why did you want to find him?" he said. "I don't understand. Surely you knew why he'd gone?"

"I didn't know," I said. "We'd been okay for the last few months. At Christmas . . . well, we had a fight and I went out and Katie called round and found him hurt."

"Katie? How do you know that?"

"She told me. Today." I shook my head. "Yesterday." I hardly knew what day it was.

He was quiet. "She said nothing to me."

"She wouldn't have told you. That's when things changed between them. And . . . I don't know . . . things were better between Matt and me then for a while. I knew something had changed, but I couldn't put my finger on it. I never thought he was having an affair. But things were easier between us and I just didn't question it."

"Between Katie and me, too," he said. "I noticed that. We were hardly sleeping together but we were getting on well. I knew something was up, but I just couldn't think what it was. It was only today, driving back from the hospital, that I realized that she was happy. Happier than she'd been in a long time."

"So was he."

"And I should have known it was Matt." He sounded so sad. "I'm such an idiot."

"Why should you have guessed?"

"Well, that's how Katie and I got together, isn't it? She tracked me down on Facebook."

"I thought you met in a club?" I could remember that phone conversation, Katie excited and happy, telling me she'd bumped into James in Liverpool the night before and he'd asked her out to dinner.

He shook his head. "No, I joined Facebook and a few days later Katie got in touch with me." He rubbed his eyes and said, "She always wanted what you had. I should have known she'd want Matt."

I should have known, too.

We sat in silence. I was thinking of Matt and Katie and wondering whether their relationship would've lasted, whether it was happiness they had or just the illusion of it.

"She would have left me the same as he left you," James said, almost in a conversational tone. "Once he was safe and you'd gone off the boil, she would have gone, too."

I thought of her then, that day in school, her face scrubbed, her smile eager, as she asked me to be her best friend, and then time and again throughout the years when I had something she wanted and she'd said, "You're really lucky, Hannah!"

"I know," I said. "She would have left both of us."

OF COURSE I knew that this was the end of it. It was the end of everything. Katie was dead, Matt in a coma. The moment he woke up, he'd tell the police what I'd done. But James would tell them first, I knew. And he'd be right, too. This had to end now.

I wanted to ask how her parents were, but I didn't dare. I hoped they would be able to cling to each other for comfort. Everyone needed someone to hold.

"Do you think Matt will be all right?" I asked.

He shook his head. "I've no idea."

We sat in silence for minutes, our arms barely touching. The night James and I got together, we'd spent hours like that, listening to music, neither of us wanting to break the spell. *Crash* was on repeat and it started now for the third time. I used to think I'd never tire of hearing it, but now I knew I wouldn't play it again.

Matt and I used to make love in here, on the floor, listening to that album. He'd never known that I'd heard it first when I was with James, that he and I had played it as we lay together on his single bed when we were seventeen. I wondered whether either of them played it to Katie. If they had, I didn't want to know.

"Why did you play that song on the phone?" I asked. "'You've Lost That Lovin' Feelin'.'"

I'd caught him unawares, I think, and he looked as though he didn't want to answer, but then he said, "Don't you remember?"

And suddenly I did.

James would call me at night when my parents were asleep and we'd talk for hours in our separate beds. When I looked at him now, I knew that he might hate me, but when he played that song to me the other night and we lay in the dark listening to it, it wasn't just hatred he felt. There was that moment as the song ended when I thought he'd speak and I wondered now what he would have said. It might have changed everything.

I felt completely lost.

"Why did you come here tonight, James? If you knew what had happened, why didn't you just call the police?"

He said nothing for a long time, just sat staring at the candles in the fireplace. Then he looked at me. "I wanted to talk to you. Just one last time."

My eyes filled with tears and his did, too.

"Do you wish we'd stayed together?" he asked suddenly.

Slowly I shook my head. "I'm glad we split up," I said. "I would have destroyed you."

We were quiet for a long time, then he said, "I think that's happened anyway."

He stood up and took his phone from his pocket.

My blood ran cold. I'd known this moment was coming; I just hadn't expected it to be so soon. I forced myself to speak. "What are you doing?"

"Hannah, I have to." He moved back to the doorway, one hand on the handle, as though for safety. He was safe, though he might not feel it. I wished I could say the same for myself.

The thought of him turning me in made me feel worse than doing it myself. "I know," I said. "I'll talk to them."

He dialed and asked for the police to come to my address. I couldn't do anything. I didn't know what to do, and besides, I thought I'd done enough lately.

"We'll let them deal with it," he said. "Just tell them everything."

My knees started to shake. I knew what was going to happen now. I knew I'd end up in prison. I think I'd always known my anger would lead to this. How could it not? And it was better to tell them what had happened myself, without them hunting for me. I shuddered at that thought and I saw James close his eyes. I couldn't let him see my fear. He was doing the right thing. The only thing.

I tried to stay cool. "Well, I'm glad you called them," I said. My voice shook but I made myself go on. "I'll be able to have a word with them about all the things you've done to me."

"Like what?" said James.

He went to the candle in the window and blew it out. It spluttered, then died. At the hearth, he knelt and blew on the wicks of the big candles until they shuddered and gave up their flames.

"What will you tell them? That there was warm water in your

kettle? That you thought you could smell your boyfriend's cologne, even when he wasn't there? That your living room light was on?"

He walked around the room, blowing out each candle, and the light grew dimmer with every step he took.

"You beat up your boyfriend and tracked him down when he escaped. You beat up his new girlfriend, your best friend. You pushed her and she fell to her death. He was so scared of you he nearly killed himself trying to get away from you. What will you complain to the police about? That your Vera Wang glass went missing?"

He blew out the last candle and all I could hear was the gasp of the flame as it died.

"It's time to face the music, Hannah," he said.

He stayed by the door, guarding me from myself now, I think, and I sat with my head against the sofa, my face turned toward him, searching him out in the dark. For a while all I could hear was the sound of us breathing and then all I could see was the reflection of the blue light from the police car on the walls of my living room as it raced up the street toward me.

Epilogue

Two and a half years later

"HANNAH MONROE?"

I nodded.

A middle-aged woman stood in front of me, her arm full of files. "I'm Janine Evans and I'm your new offender manager. I was here to see another client, so I thought I'd pop in and introduce myself." She seemed harassed, as though her previous meeting hadn't gone as well as she'd hoped.

"What happened to Vicky?" For the last few months I'd had occasional visits from another probation officer—or offender manager, as they called themselves—who had guided me through the leaving process.

Janine sat down opposite me and nodded at the prison officer. "We'll be okay now, thanks." The officer left the room and then it was just the two of us sitting there.

"She's transferred to another area. So, big day tomorrow?"

I nodded.

"How do you feel about it?"

How did she *think* I'd feel? "Happy," I said. "Excited."

"Are you feeling nervous?"

I thought about it for a second. If by *nervous* she meant was my stomach churning, then yes, of course it was. If she meant was my heart racing, then yes to that, too. And if she was asking whether I felt like I was going crazy with the knowledge that I had to spend one more night in here, then yes, I definitely was.

"I feel a bit scared," I said.

She smiled at me and instinctively I smiled back. "That's only to be expected. Two and a half years is a long time to be inside." She looked at her file again, licking her finger and flicking through papers. "So the charge was manslaughter and you were given five years?"

I shut my eyes for a second, then nodded.

"And tomorrow morning you will have served two years and six months, including time spent on bail, which is half of your five-year sentence. For the rest of the term you will be on license and, as you know, there are conditions you have to stick to." She passed me a document. "You should take this with you and make sure you understand it fully. You know that if you don't abide by these conditions, you could be sent back to prison."

I knew all about this. Each condition had been drummed into me at my meetings with the offender supervisor who worked here.

"I can see you lost some privileges early on." She looked up at me. "Fighting."

I nodded. I'd been such an idiot. I'd been warned that if I was involved in anything more serious, I'd lose days rather than television privileges, and the thought of that had been enough to make me stop. "That was at the beginning. In the first few months. I haven't done anything like that since."

She carried on looking at me, as if she was trying to weigh me up. "And you've attended counseling?"

I nodded. "It was a big help."

"You'd never had any before, to help you cope with your child-hood?"

She'd obviously been doing her homework.

"Only at university. I had some there the first year. I didn't see how it could help me then."

"And now?"

"It has really helped me. It's something I'll carry on with."

"That's good. I think you'll find it useful. Now I notice you haven't had any visitors while you've been here?" She sounded surprised, though I don't know why. There were quite a few women in the same boat.

My smile froze. "No," I said. I could hear that my voice sounded colder now and she looked up. I hadn't been able to stand the thought of anyone seeing me here.

"What about your mum? Are you close to her?"

I avoided her question. "She lives in Scotland. I didn't want her to come here. She . . . she's not been well. She'll be at my new apartment for a few days, though, to help me settle in."

She gave an understanding nod. "What about your dad?"

I tried to hide my shudder. "No, I didn't want him to come."

I'd had a few letters during the time I'd been inside from people asking whether they could visit, though I hadn't heard a word from my father. Sam had been quite persistent. He'd written to tell me that Lucy had been fired for sending the wrong documents out in my name. She'd done it on purpose, he said, as a shortcut to getting my job. "As if she would have got your job!" he'd said, as though he was loyal to the end. He didn't mention their relationship and I assumed she was dumped now. He told me that the emails HR had sent me, which I hadn't opened, were to invite me to a meeting to rescind my suspension. Mind you, his letters had been sent before the trial; I didn't hear from him afterward and I assumed HR had changed their mind.

My mum had wanted to visit but I couldn't bear to put her through that. A mother shouldn't have to see her daughter incarcerated, should she? She was living near her sister now. I had written to her to tell her I didn't want any visitors and I thought she'd probably be relieved about that. That's one good thing about prison; nobody can visit you without your consent. I'd see her the next day, as she was helping me settle into my new home, but I knew the real test would come after she went back home. In prison it was hard to think realistically about what life would be like outside; I was used to hearing the other women talk about leaving as though they'd feel like they'd won the lottery. I knew it wouldn't be like that. Everything I'd had, I'd lost.

"I believe you had a house before you were arrested," said Janine.

I nodded. "My mum sold it for me."

"You couldn't have rented it out while you were in here?"

"I don't want to go back there," I said. "Not now."

"Was there equity in it?"

I nodded. "Yes. I'll put a deposit on another house later."

"What's happened to the equity?"

I was used to having absolutely no privacy by now. "I got a third-party mandate on my bank accounts. My mum's been managing my money for me."

She had been a changed person since she left my dad. She'd seemed to find strength from somewhere, and when I was sentenced, she came down from Scotland and put my house up for sale. When it finally sold, she came down again with her brother-in-law and a couple of his friends. There was no way my dad would confront her if she had backup. She wrote to tell me she'd sat at the end of the road and watched him leave for work, then they'd gone into the house and taken all her things. She'd gone from there to my house and emptied that, too. She told me Ray and Sheila had watched out of their living room window the whole time. Everything I owned was in storage now, though I don't think I want to see any of it again.

"I know Vicky has talked to you about work. Don't forget I can help you look for suitable jobs," Janine said. "Well, I can point you in the right direction. And I'll need to see you every week as a condition of your parole. It'll take you a couple of weeks to settle into your new home, but you should start to look for work as soon as you can."

My stomach clenched. I'd already been told it was very unlikely I'd be employed as an accountant again. Or as anything. I'd have to tell any future employer that I was fresh from prison: a sobering thought in a depressed economy. I'd spent the last couple of years trying to figure out what I could do and I still wasn't sure. Self-employment seemed my only option; I couldn't even think of explaining my prison sentence in a job application.

"There's just one other thing I need to talk to you about," said Janine. She turned to another page in her file and looked up at me. "When you first came in here I can see you blamed other people for the position you were in. For what you did." She glanced at the page. "Matthew Stone in particular. He testified against you at your trial, I believe."

My chest tightened at the memory of Matt, pale and thin, standing up in court telling everyone that I'd hit him. As soon as he said it, every eye in the room turned to look at me. Every eye except his, that is. He didn't look at me at all. It was as though I wasn't there, but I could tell. I could tell he was aware of me. Hyperaware. I knew that feeling.

"So you are saying she would regularly hit you?" asked the prosecuting barrister.

Matt nodded and was prompted to say "yes" for the transcriber. His voice shook as he did.

"And when did this start?"

"I'd known her a couple of years when she first did it." He looked steadfastly away from me. Of course I was staring at him and I think he could tell, the way your face smarts when someone's looking at you. "She'd always had a temper, but she'd never taken it out on me before then."

It was cold in the courtroom and my hands were inside the

sleeves of my sweater, partly to keep them warm but also to stop them shaking. Or to stop people seeing them shake. As he spoke, my fingers found the marks on my arms where I'd taken my anger out on myself, late at night as I lay in my tiny cell, thinking about my home and about Matt and Katie. About what I'd missed.

The prosecutor's voice broke into my thoughts. "And how often would these attacks occur?"

Attacks? I hadn't thought of them like that. I saw the jury staring at me, agog. I knew that, despite the rules, they'd be talking about me that night.

"Whenever we argued," he said. "Perhaps once a month. Sometimes a few months could go by without a row, but I'd always be on edge. It was like walking on eggshells, just waiting for the row to start." He'd hesitated. "I used to think it was an excuse. I think she just wanted to hit me and she'd start the row so that she had a reason for it."

I forced myself to keep a neutral face, knowing that everyone there wanted a response from me. He was such a liar. Yes, we would row. Every couple had rows. He'd do something to annoy me, something he knew would drive me crazy, and then yes, of course I'd respond. Who wouldn't? It smarted to think that everyone believed him and not me.

"Can you give us an example of when these attacks would occur?"

"I never knew when they were coming," he said. "One night I might be a bit late coming home and she'd make me a drink and chat about her day. Another night she might go for me. Hit me. Punch me."

I winced. It did sound bad when I heard it like that, but he just didn't understand how infuriating he was to live with at times.

"And sometimes . . ." he continued, clearly getting into his stride.

That's enough, I thought. *They only wanted one example.*

"Sometimes she thought a woman from work was getting too close for comfort. She was always checking my phone, reading my messages. She used to check the mileometer on my car, too, if she thought I was lying about where I was. And then she'd hit me."

That was a complete exaggeration. Of course I checked his phone every now and then. Everybody does that! Nobody wants their partner to make a fool of them, do they? It didn't mean I was being irrational. After all, if I'd checked his phone in the few months before he left, I would have seen he was having an affair with Katie, wouldn't I? Unless he'd had another phone . . . I'd never found out whether he had or not; it hadn't come up in court and I could hardly ask him myself.

I was thinking all this when the next question was asked and I suddenly became alert.

"Can you tell us why you stayed in the relationship, Mr. Stone? Why didn't you leave earlier if things were so bad?"

There was a long pause. Everyone's eyes swiveled to Matt then, as though he and I were playing in the Wimbledon finals and they wanted to follow each shot. He'd closed his eyes and suddenly my eyes stung with tears.

"I loved her," he said. "She was great fun most of the time. Very loving. And she'd always apologize afterward and we'd make up."

Out of the corner of my eye I could see James sitting on the other side of the court looking at me. I flushed and averted my eyes.

"She always said she'd get help. She knew she was in the wrong. And . . . and I loved her. That's why I stayed."

"But then you decided to leave and this triggered the events which occurred on July 18. Can you tell us why you left?"

"We'd had an argument at New Year and she hit me. It was worse than usual and it frightened me."

"Did you go to hospital?"

He shook his head. "I never went to hospital. No matter what happened."

"Why not?"

"It would have meant telling people my girlfriend was hitting me," he said. His voice broke. "How could I do that?"

There was a bit of a commotion then. His mum started to cry

and then Matt did, too. I was already crying. The judge banged on the table and ordered a recess and within seconds I was taken out of the courtroom.

Now I TURNED to look at Janine, careful not to let her see how much that memory had affected me.

"I don't blame him," I said. "He was right. I did need help."

"And you've been taking anger management classes here? Have they helped?"

"Very much. I've learned how to control my temper and how to walk away rather than confront someone if I'm angry."

"Have you tried to have any contact with Mr. Stone?"

"No," I said quietly. "I haven't."

She looked through the file again and I wondered whether there was a list of letters I'd written, phone calls I'd made, and whether she was checking to see if his name was there. She needn't have worried, though. My mum had written to me to say she'd heard from James that Matt had moved yet again. I hadn't made any response to that. I didn't know what I was expected to say.

"And tomorrow," Janine continued, "you'll be going to temporary accommodation? I can see you've discussed this at length with Vicky." She read out the address.

She said "temporary accommodation" as though it was a night shelter. My mum had rented an apartment for me in another part of the Wirral, a place where I knew nobody. Somewhere I could go out without being recognized. I longed to go for walks, for a run or a swim. I'd felt as confined as if I was in a coffin while I was in prison. The yard where we exercised was too small to do much in and it was always crowded with groups of women hanging around chatting, so I'd end up pacing the cell, trying to burn off energy. It hadn't worked. Each night I'd be restless, unable to sleep.

"How will you get there?"

"I'm getting a taxi," I said. "My mum will be there."

"You didn't want her to pick you up?"

I shook my head. "I don't want her anywhere near this place."

She went through everything then, all the dos and don'ts and the rules and regulations. I tuned out. All I could think about was the next day. Of freedom.

I TOOK A bus instead of a taxi. My first rebellion. There was a taxi rank near the prison and I knew it would be obvious I'd just been released. I couldn't stand the thought of sitting in a taxi, watching the driver's furtive glances in the rearview mirror.

I left the prison at ten that morning. There were only a couple of other women being released that day and each of them had someone waiting for her. I kept my head down as I walked away but nobody seemed to be paying me any attention. It was a bright, cold January morning and I wore jeans and a leather jacket. Apart from my holdall, I didn't look different to anyone else I saw that morning. I definitely had a prison pallor, though. The sun was shining as if in celebration; I'd woken before dawn and stood for hours at my window, staring through the filthy Plexiglas. The bus stopped in the center of town and the driver didn't even glance at me as I got off. I'd clearly reached that age where I was invisible, despite the efforts I'd made that morning. Well, that wasn't always a disadvantage.

I thought of my mum, waiting for me in my new home. I hadn't given her a time when I'd be back; I'd told her I didn't want a deadline that first day. I knew she would have cooked something for me, probably something I used to love when I was young. I knew my bed would be made, the lights on low, just how I liked them. And I knew she'd try to hug me. I shuddered at the thought of that. My skin was raw from constant scratching—another reason I didn't let her visit me—and I was so on edge that if she touched me, I think I would have collapsed.

The station wasn't too busy at that time of day. In one of the meetings I'd had with the staff before I left prison, I'd been asked if I wanted a rail pass. I quickly declined, picturing the ticket clerk glancing up at me as I passed it over the desk, wondering who I was and what I'd done. I couldn't have that. I'd said I would pay for my own ticket, thank you, and the officer had looked at me as though I was mad, but I didn't care. My mum had kept hold of my purse while I was away and sent it to the prison ready for my release. It seemed so odd now to see something from my old life. It was as though it belonged to someone else.

At the station I took out my bank card; it seemed so long since I'd used it and I panicked for a moment in case I didn't remember the PIN. Luckily it was still valid for another year or so. Once I'd bought my ticket I went to the ATM and took out the first money I'd seen in two and a half years. Just the sensation of the notes in my hands was strange to me now. I bought myself a sandwich and a couple of magazines for the journey, then made my way to the platform, making sure I stood apart from the other passengers. The last thing I wanted was to talk to anyone.

On the train, too, I sat away from other people and put my holdall on the seat beside me so that nobody would ask to sit there. It was so quiet on that journey, away from the noise of the women in prison. It was hard to find a moment's peace inside and you can imagine how stressful that was for me. There were only a few people in the carriage and most of them were plugged into their phones, ignoring everyone around them. That suited me fine. Of course I didn't have a phone anymore. That had been taken away by the detectives on the first night and by the time I remembered it I was in custody so it was never given back to me. I assumed my mum had it, but to be honest I've forgotten a lot about those early days and what happened when. If you block things out for long enough, you soon forget, though as I found out the hard way, your memories do come back at times, sometimes when you're least expecting them.

I dropped off my bag at the left luggage counter at Lime Street station. There wasn't anything I would need from it tonight. I knew my mum would drive me there to pick it up tomorrow; today I wanted to be free, to have nothing with me to remind me of prison.

I took the train out to West Kirby, where I was going to live. The carriage was full and I panicked, thinking there might be someone I knew from before I went inside, but it was the middle of the day by then and virtually everyone I knew would be at work. I sat at the end of the carriage, though, and watched carefully as people got on and off. I couldn't afford to relax yet.

That afternoon I walked along the coastline feeling the winter sun's rays on my face. I looked out to the horizon, at North Wales just visible in the distance. It had been years since I could see so far. I thought I would run down here at night, when nobody was around. I knew I'd struggle at first after being cooped up for so long, but that soon I'd break through the pain barrier and feel free again. I couldn't wait.

My body was chilled and my hands were in my pockets in an effort to keep warm, but there wasn't anywhere I'd rather be right then. Or hardly anywhere. In prison I'd borrowed books on yoga and meditation from the library and spent hours trying to empty my mind. That afternoon, for the first time, I managed to do that, just for a while.

I turned back toward the town as the light faded and found a café that was still open. I sat at a little table in the corner and looked around me. The pretty china and the tiny glass vases of fresh flowers looked as though they came from another world than the one I'd become used to. I wanted so badly to be part of their world again.

"What would you like?" asked the waitress.

For a moment I couldn't decide. It's strange how quickly you become accustomed to having no choice. Panicking in case she became impatient with me, I asked for hot chocolate. She smiled and brought it to me. The cup was laden with whipped cream, and a little chocolate Flake bar lay on the saucer. It seemed such a treat, such a nice thing to do for me, that I was overwhelmed for a second and I had to drink a glass of water to compose myself.

I sat in the café until I was the last customer left. It was so peaceful, such a lovely, unexpectedly lovely afternoon.

As I started to make my way to my new home, I stopped at an off-license and stood for ages at the displays, unable to choose. Even though I used to drink quite a bit, I've never been fussy about wine, but now, for my first alcoholic drink in more than two years, I just couldn't decide. I left the shop without buying anything. Just knowing I could was enough.

As the evening closed in, lights popped up in houses nearby and the streetlights glowed. I started to make my way to my apartment. At the bottom of the hill I stopped still. There was a library there. I'd forgotten that. The lights were on and I could see people working, others borrowing books, a few children playing. I looked at my watch. It was 6:30 p.m. As if a magnet was drawing me in, I walked to the entrance of the library. A noticeboard displayed the opening times: tonight it was open until 7:30.

I stood still. My mouth was suddenly dry and I could feel my face tightening with stress. I closed my eyes.

What should I do?

The door to the library suddenly swung open toward me and my body jolted. I could hear the low hum of chatter within the building and then my ears started to buzz. They hadn't done that for a couple of years, not since the day I found Matt with Katie. Suddenly I was light-headed and as I swayed I grabbed the door handle to steady myself. I looked around. There was nobody else there. I tried to tell myself that the doors contained a motion sensor and opened automatically when someone came near them, but I knew it wasn't just that. The door had opened for me.

It's a sign.

I went into the library and spoke to the woman working at the desk. I couldn't show proof of my address, though I had my driving license in my purse to prove my identity. She looked at the photo on the card and then back up at me. "It was taken a long time ago," I explained and she laughed, telling me it was okay, I was still recognizable.

Oh, but I'm not, I thought. *I'm not the same person at all.*

She told me I could have a free half hour, logged me on to the computer as a guest, then left me alone. My hands trembled and my breath caught in my throat. Despite the fact I'd been away from computers for two and a half years, the opening screen still looked exactly the same. I opened Internet Explorer and it opened at Google's home page.

I rubbed my arms to get rid of the goose bumps that had appeared when I'd first realized what I was going to do and pulled my hair back into a ponytail, the way I always did when I wanted to concentrate. I felt like an alcoholic must, faced with the chance of a drink she has no intention of refusing.

You see, the thing I'd learned in prison is this. Matt could take away the photos, he could take away the messages. He could take away every physical reminder of himself—and God knows he had. He couldn't take away the memories, though. Nobody could do that. And it worked both ways. He'd always be in my mind and I'd always be in his. That much was true.

I flexed my fingers. Into the search engine I typed "Matthew Stone Architect."

Within a second the results were on the screen. I sat back and relaxed. I felt like I was home.

The search was on.

Gone Without a Trace

Mary Torjussen

Discussion Questions

1. What did you think of the relationship between Hannah and Katie prior to the beginning of the novel? Do you think they were good friends, or do you think their relationship was always toxic?

2. How reliable a narrator is Hannah? Do you think she doesn't know why Matt has gone? She remembers all the good times; do you think it's possible to block out the bad times when you're in crisis?

3. Mothers play a significant role in this novel. To what extent do you think Hannah's mother presented a poor role model for her? It seems Katie's mother was aware of the violence within Hannah's childhood home; do you think she could have done more to help Hannah then?

4. Hannah seems reluctant to spend time with her mother. She rejects her calls and avoids visiting her. Why do you think this is?

5. Do you believe that when Hannah and Katie were fighting in Matt's apartment, Hannah wanted Katie to die? Do you think she should have been charged with murder rather than manslaughter?

6. How much do you think Katie was responsible for the events that led to her death? Do you think her love for Matt was sincere, or do you think she simply wanted what Hannah had?

7. Do you think Hannah was betrayed by Matt and Katie? If so, whose betrayal do you think was greater?

8. To what extent do you think domestic violence is learned? Hannah knows she has her father's blood running through her; do you believe this is a reason for her behavior or merely an excuse?

9. One of the themes of this novel is secrets. It is common for victims and witnesses of domestic violence to keep this secret from others, thus protecting the violator. Do you feel that if Hannah had been able to talk about the violence she witnessed in her home at a young age, she might not have become violent herself?

10. Did you feel Hannah and James's relationship could have been reignited when he called her at night and played "You've

Lost That Lovin' Feelin'" if he'd spoken to her when the song ended? Did you think at any time that James was still in love with Hannah?

11. How much do you think James's activities were responsible for everything that happens in the book?

12. What impact do you think Hannah's abortion as a teenager had on both her life and James's life?

13. Do you think prison was the right punishment for Hannah? Were you expecting her to be rehabilitated there?

14. What do you think will happen if Hannah finds Matt again?

Photo by Jennie Miles Photography, 2016

Mary Torjussen has an MA in creative writing from Liverpool John Moores University. She worked for several years as a teacher.